SPAWN OF THE SERPENT GOD

A Scourge of the Serpent Novel

ALSO AVAILABLE
FROM TITAN BOOKS

Conan: Blood of the Serpent

Conan the Barbarian: The Official Motion Picture Adaptation

Conan: City of the Dead

Conan: Cult of the Obsidian Moon

Conan: Songs of the Slain

SPAWN OF THE SERPENT GOD

A Scourge of the Serpent Novel

TIM WAGGONER

TITAN BOOKS

Conan: Spawn of the Serpent God
Print edition ISBN: 9781835411834
E-book edition ISBN: 9781835411841

Published by Titan Books
A division of Titan Publishing Group Ltd
144 Southwark Street, London SE1 0UP
www.titanbooks.com

First edition: October 2025
10 9 8 7 6 5 4 3 2 1

A CIP catalogue record for this title is available from the British Library.

EU RP (for authorities only)
eucomply OÜ, Pärnu mnt. 139b-14, 11317 Tallinn, Estonia
hello@eucompliancepartner.com, +3375690241

Printed and bound by CPI Group (UK) Ltd, Croydon CR0 4YY.

THE
HYBORIAN
AGE
WHEN CONAN
- WALKED THE EARTH -
NORDHEIM
VANAHEIM
ASGARD
HYPERB
CIMMERIA
BORDER KINGDOM
BRYTHUNIA
PICTISH WILDERNESS
BOSSONIAN MARCHES
NEMEDIA
AQUILONIA
CORINTHIA
ZAMORA
OPHIR
ZINGARA
KOTH
KHORAJA
ARGOS
SHEM
WESTERN SEA
STYGIA
KUSH
DARFAR
PUNT
KESHAN
BLACK KINGDOMS
ZEMBABWEI
BLACK COAST

HYRKANIA
KHITAI
VILAYET SEA
GHULISTAN
KOSALA
VENDHYA
EASTERN SEA
SEA
N
0 50 100 200 500
MILES
0 100 200 500 1000
KM

PART ONE

Near midnight in Arenjun, a gibbous moon floating in a sea of glittering stars, light breeze stirring cool air. Conan, near the end of his eighteenth year, crouched behind an acacia tree, senses alert. A Zamorian woman a couple years older crouched next to him, and she leaned close to whisper in his ear.

"I have never stolen a god before."

Conan grunted but otherwise did not reply.

They had come this night to the Temple District, the section of the city reserved for houses of worship. All gods were welcome in the City of Thieves, provided their priests regularly shared a portion of their tithes with the crown. There were no temples or shrines in Conan's homeland of Cimmeria. His people's god was Crom, a grim and distant deity who gave mortals their first breath of life and had nothing to do with them after that. Crom demanded no prayers, accepted no sacrifices. He wanted his people to leave him alone to brood in peace, and the Cimmerians were only too happy to do so. As did many in Zamora, Valja honored Bel, the god of thieves, and gave a portion of whatever she stole to his temple. A *small* portion.

The two thieves—one experienced, one still learning—

crouched near the Temple of Ishtar. Acacia trees marked the borders of the temple grounds, while rows of date, pomegranate, and olive trees grew closer to the building. The temple was a large, three-story stone structure, with crenellated towers flanking a pair of high doors fashioned from ironwood. Above the doors was a tile mosaic depicting the goddess, naked and smiling, a variety of fruits and vegetables piled at her feet. In her right hand she held stalks of wheat; in her left, a severed ram's head.

A paved walkway lit by rows of burning torches led to the temple entrance, and a steady progression of late-arriving worshippers filed into the building. A pair of guards—one Argossean, one Kothian—garbed in tunics and metal breastplates stood outside the entrance, sheathed longswords hanging from their belts. Their hands rested on the pommels of their weapons as they scrutinized the new arrivals with suspicious eyes. Midnight marked the beginning of the spring solstice, Ishtar's high holy day, and the faithful had gathered to celebrate. Ishtar was a fertility goddess of the Shemites, although her worshippers could be found throughout the known world—no surprise, given the orgiastic rites that took place in her temples. Conan wondered how many of her followers were true believers and how many merely pretended to believe so they could enjoy the pleasures of the temple prostitutes. So long as her worshippers made the proper sacrifices, perhaps Ishtar did not care how sincere their devotion was.

"Ready?" Valja whispered.

Conan was not certain this was a good idea—Ishtar might not take kindly to a pair of thieves invading her temple on her most holy day—but he had promised Valja he would aid her in this foolishness, and so what if he had done so after drinking too much wine? To a Cimmerian, a vow was a vow, never to be broken.

He nodded, rose to his feet, and began running toward the

temple, Valja close behind him, their booted feet nearly silent on the hard ground. Conan wore a tunic and breeks, his sole weapon a broadsword sheathed in a leather scabbard strapped to his back. A coil of rope around his left shoulder while an empty leather satchel was slung over his right. He opted for speed and maneuverability when thieving, and armor such as chainmail would only slow him down.

Valja wore a thin tunic, along with a hooded black cloak, and carried an empty satchel. She appeared to have no weapons, but a half-dozen throwing knives were concealed on her person, along with a pair of daggers, the blades' edges all sharply honed. She was short, broad-shouldered, with light brown skin and steel-blue hair in the manner of her people. Conan seemed like a giant next to her, and she often teased him about his height. *It is better to be small when you're a thief. Easier to hide.* She kept her hair cut short, not only so it would not get in her eyes while she worked but also so opponents had one less thing to grab on to.

Conan did not bother cutting his long black hair, other than keeping his bangs trimmed so they would not interfere with his vision. As far as he was concerned, if he allowed a combatant to get close enough to take hold of his hair, he deserved to die.

The temple's only windows were on the third floor, to prevent thieves from gaining entrance as well as to keep voyeurs from gawking at the activities within. Conan and Valja had discussed posing as worshippers and walking in through the main entrance with everyone else, but they had ultimately decided against it. The guards would not have allowed Conan inside with his sword, and they would pat down Valja if for no other reason than to have an excuse to run their hands over her body. They would find her hidden knives, and a fight would likely break out. While Conan was confident that he and Valja could handle the guards, they would be forced to flee afterward, without acquiring what they had come for.

So the windows it was.

The temple was constructed from large blocks of gray stone, cut so precisely and fitted so perfectly that the seams were all but invisible. As a boy, Conan had climbed the sheer faces of rocky cliffs in Cimmeria with naught but his hands and feet. This wall posed no challenge to him. He moved upward swiftly, finding purchase where another would feel only smooth stone, and within moments he had reached one of the third-floor windows. Its wooden shutters were open, and Conan crouched on the sill and peered inside. Moonlight shone past him to reveal a large room with a dozen beds, wooden wardrobes, and dressing tables. Quarters for the temple prostitutes, he guessed. A lingering scent of perfume told him this was the females' room. He assumed the males' quarters were located elsewhere in the building. As he and Valja had hoped, everyone was busy celebrating the solstice, and with luck they would have the top floor to themselves.

Conan climbed into the room, removed the rope coil from his shoulder, tied one end around his waist, then tossed the other end through the window and down to Valja. He gripped the rope with both hands, it went taut, and he leaned back to brace himself as Valja climbed. A moment later, she joined him in the room, and he pulled the rope inside, untied it from his waist, and started to coil it around his shoulder once more. Valja stopped him. She took the rope, tied it to the wooden frame of the bed closest to the window, then dropped the rest of it onto the floor.

"In case we need to make a hasty departure," she said.

Conan saw the wisdom of this and nodded. He had been thieving for only a few months, and he still tended to fight his way out of situations rather than use his wits, but he was learning, and he had Valja to thank for that. They had met two months ago, outside the shop of Hutai the Nemedian, a merchant who sold knives and daggers, from simple, sturdy blades good for slipping between someone's ribs in a dark alley to more ornate weapons primarily used as fashion accessories by the wealthy. Hutai was also a fence, one of the most well regarded in the city, for he never divulged a secret and cheated his clients far less often than others.

Conan had been leaving Hutai's shop, his purse heavier by a dozen pieces of silver, just as Valja had been entering. They had nearly bumped into one another, but Valja stepped aside at the last instant with a fluid grace that impressed the young barbarian. On impulse, he invited her to have a drink with him once her business with Hutai was finished, and to his surprise she agreed. One drink had become two, then three, and after that they stopped counting. They ended up sharing a bed in a room above the tavern that night and had been together ever since, spending their nights thieving when they were not making love.

Valja walked to the closed door, and Conan followed, taking note of the wooden crossbar propped against the wall. It was thin and did not look particularly strong, but he supposed it served well enough.

Valja leaned forward, cocked her head, listened.

"I hear music," she said softly. "People talking, laughing..."

"Drinking too, I hope," Conan said. The more drunk the revelers were, the less likely they would notice a pair of thieves in their midst.

"I have heard the priests burn incense derived from the black lotus during celebrations. If the worshippers breathe in enough of it, we could step on them and they would never notice." Valja looked Conan up and down, then grinned. "Well, they would not notice if *I* stepped on them. You, I am not so sure about."

She reached into a tunic pocket and withdrew a small clay jar, then removed the wax stopper and dipped an index finger into the tallow inside. She then smeared the thick, viscous substance on the door hinges, replaced the stopper, slipped the jar back into her pocket, and used the edge of her cloak to wipe the excess from her finger. The tallow was a precaution to prevent the hinges from creaking when the door was opened. It was doubtful that anyone but themselves was on this floor at the moment, but there was no sense taking unnecessary chances.

Valja listened at the door one more time, and then, satisfied, she turned the knob and opened it slowly. The hinges remained silent, and when the door was fully open Conan drew his sword and stepped into the hallway. He looked in both directions, saw no one, and motioned with a jerk of his head for Valja to follow him. A knife appeared in her hand as if by magic, and not for the first time Conan marveled at his lover's unearthly speed with a blade. She closed the door behind them and the two thieves began making their way down the hall. It was wide enough for them to walk side by side. They moved silent as shadows, keeping close watch on doors as they passed rooms in case someone should suddenly step into the hall. No one did.

When Conan had first come to Arenjun, he had resorted to thievery in order to survive. Cimmerians bartered for goods or services, and they farmed and hunted for their food. But in the civilized world, people required copper, silver, and gold to purchase the things they needed. It did not take Conan long to realize that thieving was a different kind of hunting. You identified your prey, entered its domain, employed patience and stealth as you stalked it, and struck when the time was right.

The hall terminated in an open doorway, and the sounds of celebration grew louder as they approached. Conan could see the orange glow of firelight, and the air was heavy with the sickeningly sweet scent of the black lotus. Without saying anything, Valja reached into a pocket and removed a pair of scarves. Conan laid his sword quietly on the stone floor, accepted a scarf from Valja, and tied it tight around his nose and mouth while Valja tied a scarf around her own face. Then he retrieved his sword and they continued to the doorway. The young barbarian had no idea how much protection the scarves would provide against the intoxicating fumes of the black lotus, but they were better than nothing.

The hallway opened onto a mezzanine level above the temple's sanctuary. Conan and Valja lowered their weapons, stepped to the iron railing at the edge of the mezzanine, and gazed down at the revelers. Burning braziers and torches in wall sconces lit the sanctuary, casting dancing, writhing shadows on smooth stone walls. A thirty-foot-tall marble statue of Ishtar stood in the center of the sanctuary. Like the mosaic on the outside of the temple, the statue depicted the goddess as naked, but this version had huge swollen breasts, a round protruding belly, and a sex organ as large as the statue's head. She stood with her hands on either side of her stomach, head bowed, looking upon her worshippers with a beatific expression. The goddess' symbol—an eight-pointed star—had been carved into her forehead. *A goddess of fertility, indeed*, Conan thought.

But that was only one side of the statue. The other side depicted Ishtar in her male aspect, as a slender man with a goat-like beard, short, curly hair, and a huge erection—also with an eight-pointed star on his forehead. Conan had known little of Ishtar or her worshippers before coming to Arenjun, but Valja had told him that the goddess could manifest as either male or female, and that among her various titles was the Black Goat of the Woods with a Thousand Young, which Conan supposed explained her male half's beard as well as why the ram's head was her symbol. Valja had also told him that, to the faithful, images of Ishtar were not mere representations of their goddess; they believed she literally inhabited all objects—statues, paintings, carvings, woodcuts—that depicted her. Some said she even dwelled within her written name, though Conan had difficulty understanding this concept. And while he could see how a god might live inside a single statue, Ishtar's worshippers believed she inhabited *every* image of herself, no matter how large or small, grand or humble, at the same time, and that seemed to him to be a feat beyond even a god's capabilities.

The worship chamber was filled with men and women from across the known world, although Shemites predominated. The vast majority of celebrants were naked, and many were engaged in exploring carnal pleasures, sometimes in pairs, more often in groups, their sweaty bodies writhing on the numerous couches and pallets spread throughout the chamber. Not everyone indulged in sex, though; wooden tables laden with meat, cheese, fruit, and wine were positioned at regular intervals throughout the temple, and men and women—most of them naked, too—talked and laughed as they sated appetites of a different sort than those of their fellow worshippers. Some of the congregants wore scarves over their noses and mouths, and Conan was glad to see this as it meant that he and Valja would not stand out as much. Priests both male and female, garbed in white robes, stood in a circle around the statue, arms raised, singing praises to their deity accompanied by a small group of flute players and drummers. Firepits had been built into the floor on both sides of the statue, and curls of dark smoke rose from the flames—fumes of the black lotus. Those closest to the fires reclined upon pallets, eyes half closed, expressions of dazed bliss on their faces. The priests seemed unaffected by the lotus fumes, perhaps having grown used to the drug's effect in the performance of their duties.

Guards were stationed throughout the chamber, hard-looking men and women in leather armor, sheathed swords and daggers hanging from their belts. They looked like professionals, and Conan assumed they were mercenaries hired by the priests to watch over the night's proceedings and ensure none of the revelry got out of hand—and to protect against thieves, of course. He counted fourteen guards, and while he was certain Valja and he could best any of them one on one, they would have more difficulty if all fourteen came at them at once. Best to make sure that did not happen.

Scattered around the chamber, resting atop stone pedestals, were smaller statuettes of Ishtar, each a foot tall and fashioned from gold. Conan was a blacksmith's son, and he thought the gold was likely alloyed with silver to make it stronger, as the precious metal alone was too malleable for sculpting. The statuettes depicted various aspects of the goddess—Sower, Reaper, Lover, Life-Giver, Warrior—sometimes female, sometimes male, sometimes a combination of both. Conan did not know what purpose these statuettes served, and neither did Valja. Perhaps they were merely decorative, or perhaps they were designed to make celebrants feel that the goddess had joined them in their revels. Whatever their purpose, it was these statuettes that had brought Conan and Valja to the temple this night: they had indeed come to steal a god—more than one, if they could manage it.

He had been doubtful at first. *Steal the statuettes while worshippers celebrate all around us? Are you mad?*

Think about it, she had said. *It will be easier to move unnoticed among so many people, especially when they are distracted by food and drink and sex. And the spring solstice is the only time the statuettes are brought into the main temple. The rest of the year, they are kept locked away in an underground vault.*

They will be difficult to sell, he had pointed out. *Even Hutai will be reluctant to buy objects stolen from one of the city's temples.*

Then we will take them to Shadizar, or go somewhere else, even if we must leave Zamora altogether.

Your mind is set on this course, is it not?

Valja had only grinned in reply.

Conan's lover tended to choose jobs that carried what he viewed as unnecessary risks. But he admired her wild, impulsive spirit, and he always ended up going along with her schemes. After all, as she was fond of saying, a life without risk was not worth living.

Conan could not carry his sword on the main floor—the guards would never permit it—so he unbuckled the scabbard and removed it from his back. He would have to hide the weapon somewhere downstairs and retrieve it later. Valja's throwing knives were concealed, so she should have no trouble with the guards, at least not on that score. Conan would have felt perfectly comfortable walking among the worshippers unclothed, but without a weapon he would feel truly naked.

Two stairwells led from the mezzanine down to the bottom floor, one on their left, the other to their right.

Valja's eyes crinkled as she smiled. "Time to join the party."

He smiled back. "May your Bel favor us."

Valja went left, Conan went right, and they began their descent.

A pair of ferns in large clay pots stood on either side of the stairwell's bottom entrance, and Conan quickly stashed his sword behind one and then walked away without a backward glance. He waited for someone to raise an alarm, but when that didn't happen he knew no one had seen him hide his weapon—or if anyone had, they didn't care. It would have been safer to leave his sword on the mezzanine, but he wanted it nearby in case he needed it.

He looked across the chamber and saw Valja walking away from the other stairwell entrance. She noticed him looking at her, winked, then moved on, striding with easy, relaxed confidence. The more dangerous a situation, the more she enjoyed herself. Such an attitude might well result in her early death, but he knew she cared not. *I intend to get the most out of life while I am alive, however long that may be*, she had once told him.

He admired that philosophy, for it was one he shared.

It was uncomfortably warm in the sanctuary, the air thick with the mingled odors of sweat, sex, and black lotus. The temple's entrance remained open, presumably to let fresh air in, but it helped little; there were definite disadvantages to not having any windows on the first two floors. Conan began making his way through the sanctuary, weaving among the celebrants, keeping clear of both guards and priests, as well as the fires where black lotus burned. He knew his scarf could do only so much to protect him from the drug's fumes, and he wished to remain as far from their source as possible. He already felt a little lightheaded, so he began taking short, shallow breaths, hoping to lessen the effects of the lotus.

He tried to stay focused on their mission, but it was difficult with so many naked people rutting like animals all around him. He did not find the sight of their bodies distracting—he was not attracted to men, and while many of the women were comely, just as many were plain. What *did* distract him was the variety of sexual positions on display. He had learned much of lovemaking during his short time with Valja, but Ishtar's worshippers were doing things that he had never conceived of, let alone done himself. He wondered if he could convince Valja to forget about stealing the statuettes and try out some of the techniques he had witnessed. He was about to head off in search of her when an older Shemite woman wearing a sheer gown and nothing else stepped in front of him.

"My, you're a *big* one, aren't you?"

The woman was in her forties, Conan judged—nearly

ancient to a young man like him—with the dark brown eyes and curly black hair of her people. Like most in Arenjun, she spoke Zamorian, but in her case with a thick Shemitish accent. Despite having been in the city for only a few months, Conan had discovered he had a talent for languages, and he had picked up Zamorian quickly.

The woman was of medium height, but next to Conan's six and a half feet she looked as small as a child. She was not unattractive, but he already had a lover and few women could compare to Valja. He gave the Shemite woman a nod of acknowledgment and moved to walk past her, but she stepped into his path to block him.

"Don't be in such a hurry," she chided. "On this most sacred of nights, Ishtar demands we enjoy ourselves in her name—and I would most *definitely* like to enjoy you."

One of Ishtar's golden statuettes stood on a pedestal ten feet away. It depicted the goddess in the process of slipping out of a long, flowing dress, one shoulder and breast exposed. Conan had the feeling the statuette was watching the two of them closely, as if curious to see what would happen next. It was a foolish fancy, no doubt brought on by what Valja had told him of the statuettes, but it was one he could not escape.

The Shemite woman wore no facial covering to protect against the black lotus fumes and her eyes were half lidded, her speech slightly slurred. Conan was surprised she was conscious enough to remain standing, and he assumed she was a regular user of the drug and used to its effects. That meant she had money, for black lotus was not cheap. A merchant's wife, perhaps, likely used to getting her way. Not tonight, though.

"I am pledged to another," Conan said.

The woman looked at him blankly for a moment, then laughed. "What does *that* have to do with anything? That's my husband over there."

She pointed to a pallet where a portly, gray-haired Zingaran man was being vigorously ministered to by a pair of well-endowed Vendhyan women half his age.

"It's only fair that I get to have some fun too, don't you think?" She reached out and trailed her fingers down Conan's left arm, her eyes widening in delight. "Big *and* strong! Praise Ishtar for bringing you to me this night!" She frowned. "But how can you kiss me properly with that cloth covering your face?"

She moved her hand toward Conan's scarf, but he caught her wrist before she could take hold of it. Her eyes widened in surprise at first, but then her mouth stretched into a slow smile. If she had been a cat, she would have purred.

"My, you have a masterful grip for one so young! I simply *must* feel those big, strong hands on my body!"

She attempted to pull free from his grip, but Conan held her fast. He tightened his grip slightly, not enough to hurt her but enough so she felt it. He had little patience for the games so-called civilized people played, and none for those with money and power who felt they could do whatever they pleased with him. He was no one's toy.

He leaned his face close to the woman's and spoke in a low, dangerous voice, cold fire burning in his ice-blue eyes. "Listen closely, for I will not say this again. I am not interested in lying with you. There are many others here tonight. Choose one of them and leave me alone."

He tightened his grip on her wrist a little more, and she gasped in pain. He held her like that for a moment more before releasing her. She took a step back, massaged her wrist with her other hand, and looked at him in fear. Behind his scarf, Conan smiled grimly. The woman had gotten off lightly. In Cimmeria, if you touched someone you did not know without permission, man or woman, you would be lucky to lose only a hand.

He walked on, glancing at the statuette of the disrobing

Ishtar. It looked the same as the last time he had seen it, but now he heard a faint echo of laughter in his mind. He took his gaze off the statuette and continued moving. He did not truly believe Ishtar was present in the small gold figures, but he would avoid eye contact with them from now on even so.

Just in case.

He met Valja at one of the food tables, the satchel on the floor next to her feet. She had removed her scarf and was eating a pear, unconcerned about the juice running down her chin. The table was located near the open entrance, and the scent of black lotus was almost nonexistent. It was a little cooler here, too. Conan had done no more than walk through the sanctuary, but he was dripping with sweat. As big as he was, the Cimmerian still had not attained his full growth, and he examined the spread on the table with an eager eye. There were platters filled with roast beef, mutton, goat, pork, and poultry; bowls overflowing with dates, figs, plums, pomegranates, olives, and of course pears; a variety of nuts and cheeses for dessert; and pitchers full of wine and ale to wash it all down. Worshippers could serve themselves, and Conan lowered his scarf, filled a clay plate with meat, and began feasting.

"Any luck?" Valja asked.

Conan answered through a mouthful of mutton. "If you call almost getting groped by a Shemite matron luck, then yes."

Valja laughed. "I had to fend off a few lustful hands myself, men *and* women. Have you filled your satchel yet?"

Conan swallowed the mutton and wiped his mouth with the back of his hand. "None of the statuettes appealed to me, but I do not have an eye for art. The guards may not be drinking, but they *have* been breathing in lotus fumes all night and are not as alert as they should be. Some are even asleep on their feet, or near enough to it. If we take a pair of statuettes near the entrances to the mezzanine, I believe we can leave the way we came without being seen."

Valja nodded approvingly. "It is a good plan. There's only one problem."

Conan was about to toss a slice of beef into his mouth, but he returned the meat to his plate. "What is it?" he said.

Valja knelt, took hold of the satchel's strap, then straightened. Conan saw that the leather pouch hung heavy as it came off the floor, and when Valja cradled it in her arms she opened the flap and he leaned forward to look. He already knew what he would find, and he was proved right when he saw a glimmer of gold. It was a statuette of Ishtar in her warrior aspect, dressed in a breastplate, leather skirt, and boots, holding two swords crossed over her chest. Valja quickly closed the flap, tied its leather thongs to hold it secure, and grinned. "We need only one more now."

Conan returned her grin. Their job was half done. All they needed to do now was—

His thoughts were interrupted by a woman shouting.

"There he is! That's the young brute who accosted me without my permission!"

Conan turned to see the Shemite matron he had spurned standing close by and pointing at him. A pair of guards stood on either side of her—a turbaned Vendhyan and a short, stocky Argossean—and neither looked drugged in the slightest. What's more, both had drawn longswords, and they looked ready to use them.

Without a weapon, Conan was forced to improvise. He gripped the edge of the table, intending to flip it at the guards with all his strength—it would be a shame to waste so much good food, but he could see no other recourse. Before he could follow through with his plan, however, Valja put her hands on her hips and glared at the Shemite matron.

"Mother! You promised you'd leave him alone!"

The matron's mouth dropped open in astonishment, and the guards exchanged puzzled looks.

Conan did not throw the table, but neither did he release his grip on it.

"I know you think the solstice gives you the right to ___ him..." Valja had spoken a Shemite word that was not familiar to Conan, but from the way the matron's eyes widened, he guessed it was a less-than-polite term for what most of Ishtar's worshippers were engaged in at that moment. Valja moved next to Conan and laid a hand on his forearm possessively.

Conan continued gripping the table, waiting to see how this was going to play out.

"But he's mine," Valja continued, "and I do *not* intend to

share him. Besides, you couldn't handle him. One good thrust and you'd break apart like dried clay."

The matron's face contorted with fury, and she tried to speak, but all she managed was incoherent sputtering. The look the guards shared this time was a knowing one and they smirked as they sheathed their swords, turned, and walked off.

Only when Conan was certain the men were not going to change their minds and return did he let go of the table.

Valja fixed the matron with a sharp look.

"You should leave the lying to those who are better at it." She gave the matron a mocking smile, then added, "*Mother*."

The Shemite woman's eyes burned with hatred. Her body tensed, she balled her hands into fists, and for a moment Conan thought she would launch herself across the table at Valja. He hoped she would. Valja had already taught the woman one lesson, and he would enjoy watching her teach her another. But after a moment, the matron let out a growl of frustration, turned, and walked away, head high, back straight, pretending she had not just been humiliated by a girl half her age—at least—whom she doubtless considered a piece of Maul trash.

Valja grinned at him. "There are many ways to fight a battle," she said.

"Perhaps," he admitted. "But my way would have been more satisfying."

They ate and drank their fill, pulled their scarves over their noses and mouths once more, and then left the table. Conan gave his empty satchel to Valja and took the one containing the gold statuette of Ishtar. The statuette was heavier than it looked—gold always was—but he carried it easily. He was the stronger of the two, but Valja was by far the better thief, and it made sense for her hands to remain free so she could steal the next statuette.

They wandered through the sanctuary, Valja occasionally stopping to admire a gold statuette for a few moments before moving on. Conan followed close behind, keeping an eye on the hired guards lined up against the walls. Any man carrying a heavily laden satchel would certainly have drawn Conan's notice if he were tasked with guarding the sanctuary, yet no one paid him any attention. All the guards were drowsing now, thanks to the black lotus, and several sat cross-legged on the floor, heads bowed, deep in slumber. Many of the celebrants had abandoned their revelry by this point and slept blissfully in tangled clusters of naked bodies. The priests continued their chanting, although their voices were quiet, their words slurred, and the musicians accompanying them played so softly now they could barely be heard. It would not be long before everyone in the temple succumbed to lotus fumes, Conan thought, including him and Valja.

He placed a hand on Valja's shoulder to stop her, and she turned to look at him with bleary eyes. Barely able to stand upright, he feared she would soon pass out if they remained in the temple much longer. They were near the entrance to the mezzanine where he had stashed his sword and he steered her toward it.

"We must go," he said.

His vision grew slightly hazy, his tongue lay thick in his mouth, and he began to sway. They needed to move swiftly. The goddess might not require human sacrifices as a rule, but her worshippers might decide to make an exception in the case of two thieves who had attempted to steal a fragment of their deity.

They were less than three yards from the stairwell entrance when Valja said, "Oh, how beautiful!" She slipped out from under Conan's hand and ran toward one of the golden statuettes of Ishtar which was located near the giant marble sculpture of the goddess and the priests who surrounded it.

"Ymir's beard!" he swore and ran after her.

The statuette depicted Ishtar, grape vines encircling her body in place of clothes, right hand stretched outward, offering a bunch of plump grapes to the observer. This was the Reaper aspect of the goddess, sharing part of a bountiful harvest with her devoted worshippers. Conan had to admit it *was* beautiful, but not enough to be worth risking their lives for.

Valja's gait was unsteady as she drew near the pedestal upon which the statuette rested, and Conan thought she might trip and fall before she could reach it. His own body felt sluggish, hands and feet numb. But Cimmeria lay in the far north, and its people endured harsh winters that would slay weaker folk. As a child, Conan had learned how to function with extremities deadened by cold, and he called upon those memories now. He did not try to feel his feet falling but instead went by the sound of his boots hitting the floor. He flexed his fingers rapidly to work some life into them, and when he had closed the distance between himself and Valja, he reached for her...

He could not compensate for his increasingly blurry eyesight, however, and he misjudged the distance between them. The tips of his fingers jammed into her back, and the impact caused her to stumble forward, palms outward, and collide with the pedestal. The pedestal was carved from stone, and Valja hitting it did nothing more than make it shake a little, but that was enough—the statuette of Ishtar wobbled and fell forward. Valja attempted to catch it, but her reflexes were dulled by black lotus, and the statuette slipped through her fingers and struck the floor with a high-pitched ringing sound. Gold normally resisted breaking, and this gold was alloyed with silver to strengthen it further, but even so the bunch of grapes in Ishtar's hand broke off when the statuette hit the floor, skittering across it for a few yards before coming to a stop. Everyone in the sanctuary fell silent, and all heads turned in their direction. In the quiet, the pinging of the statuette's impact lingered in the air for a moment before finally fading.

Valja looked at Conan, horrified by what had just happened, but his attention was focused on the worshippers surrounding them. His survival instincts were strong after growing to young manhood in Cimmeria, and they had been further honed in the sack of Venarium as well as in his time raiding with a band of Aesir. He knew the onlookers' shock would not last long. Soon it would give way to outrage, which would quickly lead to demands to seize the blasphemers who had dared to insult their beloved goddess. He had no intention of waiting for that to happen.

Fighting back the lethargy caused by the black lotus, he darted forward, snatched the (slightly) broken statuette off the floor, turned, and hurled it toward the nearby firepit. The replica of Ishtar tumbled through the air, and the worshippers cried out in alarm as it plunged into the flames. Both gold and silver had high melting points, and Conan knew a simple fire would not be hot enough to damage the statuette, but he had counted on the worshippers not knowing this, and indeed, judging by their reaction they believed the object that served as host for at least part of their goddess' essence was melting. A priestess impulsively leaped into the firepit to save the statuette and shrieked in agony as she was instantly wreathed in flame. Distraction achieved, Conan grabbed Valja, threw her over his shoulder, and sprinted for the mezzanine's entrance.

"Put me down!" she shouted.

"Not until you can walk in a straight line," he replied.

The mercenaries hired by the priesthood to guard the celebration were *not* worshippers, and they cared nothing about the statuette. They had been forced to watch people indulging in all manner of pleasures while being forbidden to join in, and those whose minds had not been completely deadened by black lotus were excited by the prospect of finally getting to do something.

A half dozen of the warriors for hire came at them from different directions, including the Vendhyan and Argossean who had accompanied the angry matron. Conan's system had fought off the worst effects of the lotus, and while he moved fast for a normal person, he ran more slowly than usual. He knew he would not be able to reach the mezzanine entrance—and his sword—before at least some of the guards got to them, so there was no point in trying. He stopped running and set Valja down on her feet.

"I hope you can still throw a knife straight," he said.

She ignored the jibe and stepped behind him to cover his back, then drew one of her daggers from its sheath and offered it to Conan over her shoulder, hilt first. "Take it!" she shouted.

Conan gave the blade a quick glance, then laughed. "No need. I already have a weapon."

Before either of them could say anything more, the first of the guards was upon them. As the Vendhyan came at Conan, shortsword in hand, eyes gleaming with bloodlust, the Cimmerian slipped the satchel off his shoulder, grabbed the strap in one huge hand, and swung it like a war hammer at the mercenary's head. The satchel—and, more importantly, the heavy gold statuette of Ishtar it held—slammed into the Vendhyan with devastating force. There was a sickeningly loud *crack* as the left side of man's skull, from crown to chin, shattered. Blood spurted from his nose and mouth, along with several teeth, and he fell to the floor limp, like a giant rag doll, and did not move. Conan didn't know if the man still lived, and he didn't care. All that mattered was that the Vendhyan was no longer a threat.

The Argossean roared a furious challenge as he came at Conan, sword raised to deliver a chopping strike to the side of the young barbarian's neck. Conan stood his ground, and when he judged the Argossean was close enough, he swung the satchel upward as hard as he could. The bag smashed into the man's testicles, instantly crushing them. Air gusted from the man's lungs as he toppled sideways and crashed to the floor only a few feet from his Vendhyan comrade. The mercenary still lived, although given the amount of pain he must be in, Conan thought he likely regretted this, and he decided to come to the man's aid. The Argossean still gripped his sword, so Conan stepped forward and pressed his foot down on the man's wrist so he was unable to wield the weapon. Then he raised his other foot and brought it down hard on the man's throat. There was a loud *snap* as the man's neck broke, then his eyes went wide and he stopped moving. Conan switched the satchel to his left hand, then bent and grabbed the mercenary's shortsword. It wasn't as if the man was ever going to use it again.

He spun around to see how Valja was faring. Two guards lay dead on the floor, one with the hilt of a throwing knife protruding from her right eye socket, the other with a blade embedded in his heart. It seemed even breathing in black lotus could not hinder Valja's skills, or perhaps being under attack gave her body the jolt it had needed to throw off the worst of the drug's effects. Conan understood. He never felt so alive as when he was facing death.

Evidently, the next pair of guards to attack had gotten a stronger dose of lotus, for they moved more slowly than their companions, their gaits and footfalls clumsy and heavy. Conan started forward, intending to cut down the easy prey with his newly acquired sword, but Valja laid a hand on his arm to stop him and shook her head. He got the message. As much as his warrior's spirit longed to destroy all his enemies, Valja and he could not afford to remain in the sanctuary any longer.

With no one left to toss more lotus into the fires, the air in the sanctuary was beginning to clear. The guards who had been too drugged to attack right away were rising unsteadily to their feet, regaining enough control over their bodies to become a threat. And the City Watch would soon be upon them. Conan slipped the satchel over his shoulder, grabbed Valja's hand, and together they ran toward the stairwell to the mezzanine along with the fleeing worshippers and priests shouting for the City Watch.

A lone guard whose head had not yet fully cleared staggered into their path. Conan laid open the man's throat with a single stroke of the shortsword as they ran past. Blood fountained from the wound and Conan heard a dull thud behind them as the man's body hit the floor.

When they reached the mezzanine entrance, Conan released Valja's hand. "Go first," he said. "I will follow."

Valja scowled but acquiesced, running up the stairs. Conan put the shortsword on the floor, retrieved his broadsword from behind the clay pot where he had hidden it, and swiftly donned and buckled the scabbard. He then drew the broadsword and picked up the shortsword—and then a thought occurred to him: With everyone evacuating the temple, the golden statuettes of Ishtar were unguarded and ripe for the taking. For an instant, he considered attempting to obtain a second statuette before heading up the stairs, but while the prospect was tempting, he decided against it. He was not sure there was enough room in the satchel for a pair of statuettes, and he did not want to be slowed down by the additional weight.

He sighed and bolted up the stairs, a sword in each hand, satchel bouncing against his hip.

Valja was waiting for him at the top of the stairs, daggers in hand. Now that there was no chance of their obtaining a second statuette, she had tossed her empty satchel to the floor, along with her scarf. Her eyes were clear and sharp, and Conan knew the black lotus was fully out of her system now, or near enough to it. When she saw him, she smiled with relief, but her gaze flicked to the satchel and her smile became a grin.

His hands were full, so Valja removed his scarf for him and let it drop to the floor.

"Did you think I would leave our prize behind?" he asked.

"Leave, no. Lose, maybe."

Anger darkened Conan's face. She should have more faith in him than that! But before he could say anything, they heard boots pounding on the steps, accompanied by the shouts of men and women calling for their heads. The rest of the guards were coming, and they were coming fast.

In a single, smooth motion, Conan whirled around to face the stairwell and extended his broadsword in a one-handed lunge. The first of the guards—an Afghuli male, tall and powerfully built, with brown skin, curly hair, and a long beard—ran straight onto the blade. His torso was protected by studded leather armor, but Conan was strong and his blade too sharp, and the sword sank into the man's gut and burst out of his back in a gout of blood. The warrior behind him—a Brythunian female with pale skin and long, blonde hair—had been following too close, and she was unable to stop in time to keep from being impaled on Conan's sword too. The Afghuli still lived, and his eyes focused on Conan as the Cimmerian youth planted a booted foot on his chest and shoved at the same instant he withdrew his sword. The Afghuli and Brythunian flew backward, colliding with the other guards on the staircase and knocking them down. Conan heard some cry out in pain while others shouted profane curses as they tumbled down the stone steps in a tangled mass of arms and legs.

He wagered the fools still had some black lotus in them, else the short fight would have gone very differently. Whether wounded or dead, the Afghuli and Brythunian guards would not be coming after them anymore, and with luck some of the others had broken enough bones to cause them to abandon their pursuit as well. But some was not all.

He turned and gave Valja a shove. "Go!" he shouted.

The two of them ran down the hallway toward the room they had used to gain entrance to the temple, but they were still ten feet away from the door when the first of the uninjured guards emerged from the stairwell, howling for the thieves' blood. The guards began running, weapons in hand, faces twisted into expressions of pure rage. Conan and Valja raced the rest of the way to the temple prostitutes' room, threw open the door, dashed inside, then slammed the door behind them. Conan dropped his two swords to the floor, grabbed the crossbar, and slipped it into the iron brackets attached to the door.

"That flimsy thing will not last long," he said.

He picked up his broadsword and sheathed it, but he left the shortsword where it lay, for he had no more use for it. He and Valja ran to the bed that she had tied the rope to, and Conan shoved the bed to the window. Valja gave him a questioning look.

"The wall will brace the bedframe and better support our weight on the way down," he explained.

The guards reached the barred door and the metal knob rattled as they attempted to open it. When that failed, they began striking the door's surface with sword pommels, axe handles, and fists, trying to knock it down. Conan knew that, once the guards realized they should work together to hurl the combined mass of their bodies at the door in unison, the crossbar would break and they would rush inside.

He grabbed the coil of rope, threw it through the open window, then faced Valja. "Get on my back and lock your arms around my neck," he told her.

"Why?"

"Because we must reach the ground as fast as we can."

For an instant she looked horrified, but then she sheathed her daggers and grinned. "Sounds like fun," she said, then eyed the satchel still hanging from his shoulder. "Leave the statuette here. We do not need its extra weight."

"After everything we've gone through this night? I would sooner die."

Her eyes narrowed. "You are jesting… are you not?"

Conan did not answer. He bent over and Valja climbed onto his back, wrapped her arms around his thick neck, and grabbed hold of each wrist with her opposite hand to secure herself. Conan reached down, took hold of the rope, then straightened. At that moment there was a loud crash, the crossbar broke in two, and the door was flung inward so hard it tore partway off its hinges.

Their time was up.

Conan bent his powerful legs and launched himself through the window, while Valja let out a scream that was as much from joy as fear and held on for her life. Conan relaxed his grip as they fell, and his palm began to heat up quickly as it slid over the rope, but he wasn't concerned about friction burns. His hands were calloused from a lifetime of hard work and swordplay and would take little damage. But even if the flesh of his hand was stripped to the bone, it would be worth it to escape with their lives—and their loot.

When they were a third of the way down, Conan tightened his grip, and they jerked to a stop. He closed his other hand around the rope for a better grip, then angled his body to face the temple wall. As they swung toward it, he bent his knees, and when the soles of his boots hit stone, he allowed his legs to bend the rest of the way and then shoved, sending them flying out into the air once more. He loosened his grip with both hands this time and they slid down another third of the way. Again, he tightened his grip, swung toward the wall, kicked off, and then they slid down the rest of the way. When they landed, he bent his knees to absorb the impact, but a painful jolt still lanced up his legs and into his lower back, likely due to the extra weight he carried. The pain began to lessen almost immediately, and he thought no more of it.

Valja still held onto him, and she leaned her head forward and kissed him on the side of his face. "You have to teach me how to do that," she said.

Conan still held the rope, and he felt it jerk. He looked up and saw that one of the guards had crawled through the window and was in the process of climbing down. He leaned to the side, a signal for Valja to get down, and she did. He straightened and then yanked the rope downward with both hands as hard as he could, which was very hard indeed. The other end tore through the section of bedframe it was attached to, and the rope and the guard holding on to it plummeted downward. Conan and Valja quickly moved back, and the guard hit the ground where they had been standing. Upon impact, the man's back snapped like kindling. He coughed an impressive amount of blood and then lay still.

Conan looked up and saw a pair of guards standing at the window, gazing down at him and Valja. One of them, a red-bearded Vanir man, held the shortsword Conan had discarded, and with a snarl he hurled it at them like a spear. Conan drew his broadsword and casually batted the blade away as if it were a bothersome insect. The sword tumbled through the air and *thunked* into the ground a dozen feet away. The guards cursed and quickly withdrew into the room. Conan knew they would head back to the stairs, return to the sanctuary, and then rush outside to pursue them.

Worshippers covered the temple grounds, most of them naked, standing in groups, shivering in the night air, and talking loudly about the two thieves who had ruined the solstice celebration. Priests stood among them, but instead of talking they were looking around, trying to spot the pair of rogues who had blasphemed against their god. Normally, Conan would have taken advantage of the confusion to slip away, but by now the City Watch had arrived—only a handful of officers so far, but more would come, and those present had drawn their swords and begun to patrol the temple grounds, already on the hunt. The joke in Arenjun was that if you needed the City Watch's aid, it was best to summon them two weeks in advance, but either the priests of Ishtar paid regular graft for them to respond so swiftly or officers had been amongst the celebrants tonight. Likely both, Conan thought.

He and Valja had a choice to make: run and risk drawing the Watch's attention, or calmly walk away and hope no one noticed their departure. Conan would have chosen the latter tactic if he had not been carrying the statuette of Ishtar, but any Watcher coming upon them would demand to look in the satchel, and while Conan was confident he and Valja could escape if that occurred, he doubted they could do so without slaying one or more officers. Slay a random citizen, especially a Maul denizen, in Arenjun and the City Watch would not blink an eye, but slay one of their own and the Watch would never stop looking for you. Worse, they would offer a reward for your capture, dead or alive, and every criminal, mercenary, and assassin in Arenjun would seek to collect it. If that happened, Conan and Valja would have to flee the city, assuming they could manage to get out of it alive in the first place.

Neither choice appealed, but the longer they stood there, the greater the chance they would be discovered, either by the Watch or by the surviving guards who would emerge from the temple at any moment.

To the nine hells with it, Conan decided. The thought of running galled him. Better to stay where they were, make a stand, and take as many of the bastards with them to the afterworld as they could.

"We can offer you a third choice."

The voice—a woman's—came from directly behind them. Valja drew her daggers and she and Conan spun around, ready to attack. But just as Conan was about to swing his broadsword at this unknown enemy, he stopped himself. There were two women, both older than Valja and him by ten years, perhaps a bit less, though their sex had nothing to do with why Conan restrained himself. Cimmerian women could fight as well as their men, but they were also far more important to a clan's survival than men. When clan feuds erupted, which was a regular occurrence in Conan's homeland, the men were careful to avoid slaying women if they could. The survival of the entire Cimmerian people depended on it. Conan had inherited this cultural reluctance to harm women, but what stayed his hand in this case was that one of the women appeared to be a priestess of Mitra.

She wore leather armor over a tunic and a metal helmet with a phoenix—the symbol of Mitra—engraved into its surface. She carried dagger and flail, both hanging from her belt, and wore a pair of well-worn leather boots, which told Conan that she was a priestess who walked among the people rather than remaining secluded in a safe, comfortable temple. Her tan skin, dark hair, and lean body marked her as Ophirian.

The other woman was a Kushite, tall and lean, with dark skin and close-cropped black hair. She wore a long-sleeved green shirt, brown pants, boots, and a hooded green cloak. Her clothes were well worn, and from the faded colors Conan assumed that she spent a great deal of time outside. He had met only a few Kushites before, but like his own people, they were fierce warriors with a strong connection to the land, and he thus felt a kinship with them.

"I am Naerys, priestess of Mitra," the Ophirian woman said,

then gestured to her companion. "And this is Anot, shaman of the Wild."

The Kushite bowed her head. "Well met," she said.

It had been her voice that Conan had heard a moment ago. *Almost as if she had read my thoughts...*

He scowled. Shamans were not sorcerers, but many of them could work some measure of magic, such as the bear shamans of his own people. All magic was unnatural as far as he was concerned, and it was the only thing he feared in this world. He considered burying his broadsword in the shaman's chest, just to be on the safe side, but he restrained himself. The shaman was with a priestess of Mitra, and Conan did not need another god angry with him after the way things had gone in Ishtar's temple. He would listen to what the priestess had to say; if he did not like it, he could always slay the shaman afterward.

"I am Conan, a Cimmerian," he said. "This is Valja of Zamora."

Valja nodded a curt greeting.

"I can hide you both from the eyes of those who would do you harm," Anot said. "Just as I hid Naerys and myself from your sight."

"But there is a price," Naerys cautioned.

Valja smiled wryly. "Of course there is."

"A small one," Naerys said. "You need only have a drink with us and listen to a proposition."

Valja looked at Conan and shrugged. "I could use a drink. How about you?"

Conan did not look at Valja. Instead, he glowered at the other two women. "If we accept your aid, how do we know you will not enslave us with a spell?"

"You have my word," Naerys said.

That was not good enough for Conan, even if the woman *was* a priest. "And how is it that the two of you happened to appear at the exact moment we could use your help?"

"We can explain everything," Naerys said, a note of impatience creeping into her voice. "But later. Make your choice. The searchers draw closer."

Conan did not trust this priestess, and he wanted nothing to do with whatever sorcery the shaman possessed. He was about to tell the two women to go to hell when Valja said, "We accept your terms."

Anot nodded, then began whispering in soft, breathy voice. The words she spoke, if indeed they were words at all, did not sound like any language Conan recognized. They sounded more like the blowing of a gentle breeze. The hair on the back of his neck stood up as air began to swirl around them, caressing their bodies with a smooth touch. Goose flesh rose on his skin and fear gripped his mind, threatening to overwhelm him. But whatever was happening to him and Valja, he sensed no ill intent in it, and while it felt decidedly strange, it did not feel wrong. He had trusted his instincts all his life, and they had never failed him. He decided to trust them again now, and his fear subsided, although it did not leave him completely.

When Anot finished her spell, she said, "Make no sound. The magic deceives the eye, not the ear."

The two guards who had pursued them into the prostitutes' room came running out of the temple entrance then, weapons in hand. The Vanir gripped a broadaxe, and his companion—a tawny-haired Corinthian woman—wielded a longsword, and together they ran across the temple grounds, heading straight for where Conan and Valja stood with Naerys and Anot. As the mercenaries drew near, Conan took a reflexive step forward to meet their charge, but Valja put a hand on his arm to stop him. He ground his teeth in frustration, but he stayed put.

"There is the sword I threw," the Vanir said.

The pair stopped when they reached the shortsword.

"Some throw," the Corinthian said. "The big fellow knocked

it aside easily with his broadsword. And one-handed at that."

The Vanir ignored his companion's assessment of his sword-throwing skills and swept his gaze across the grounds. He looked right at Conan and the others at one point, but he gave no sign that he saw them.

"I don't see them," the man said. "Do you?"

"No, but are you surprised? Did you think they would stand around chatting and give us a chance to reach them? They're probably halfway to the Maul by now, if the City Watch hasn't captured them yet."

The Vanir snorted in frustration. "We should search the district before we give up. If we bring their corpses back to the temple, the Ishtar-lovers may reward us." He grinned. "One way or another."

"I don't think much of our chances," the Corinthian said, "but we might as well." And with that, the pair jogged off into the night.

Despite himself, Conan was impressed by Anot's spell, not that he would ever admit it to her.

The shaman spoke then. "If we walk slowly and quietly, the winds of the Wild will continue shielding us as we leave the Temple District without being detected."

"Then we can have that drink," Naerys said, smiling. "I know a place where the ale is so thick and rich, you can practically chew it."

Valja gave Conan a look. "Sound good?"

He sighed, wondering what he was about to get into.

"Lead on."

3

Conan had never been to the One-Eyed Owl before, but in many ways it was like any other tavern in the Maul: small, crowded, and foul smelling, with too many rats of both the four-legged and two-legged variety. The majority of customers were Zamorian, but other races were represented as well, and their professions ranged from pickpockets and cutpurses to kidnappers and killers, young toughs out to make a reputation for themselves, and hard-bitten mercenaries who would take on any job if it paid well enough. Some spoke in loud voices, boasting of their exploits, while others laughed like braying donkeys. Others spoke softly, casting furtive glances around the tavern as they made deals that they wished no one to overhear. The room was lit by guttering torches slid into iron sconces, and their feeble flames filled the air with a thin, gray haze that made breathing uncomfortable. The dirt floor was covered with straw to soak up spilled ale, blood, vomit, and urine, and the place smelled like a combination of horse stall and slaughterhouse.

The first time Conan had set foot inside a tavern like this, the din and stench had been too much for his wilderness-bred senses and he had immediately turned around and walked out.

He had since gotten used to the environment and had come to like it. The people here might care only about themselves and whatever sordid pleasures they could take from the world, but they did not pretend to be anything other than what they were, unlike many so-called civilized men and women he had met since leaving Cimmeria. The denizens of the Maul might cut your throat as soon as look at you, but at least you knew where you stood with them.

The One-Eyed Owl differed from other Maul taverns in one important respect: its ale did not taste like rancid horse piss. In fact, it was fairly decent. Naerys had not misled them about that, and while this didn't make Conan more inclined to trust her, he was more amenable to listening to what she had to say.

The four of them had taken a table near the back of the room, and Conan had chosen a seat that allowed him to keep his back to the stone wall. Valja sat next to him, while Naerys and Anot sat on the other side of the table. Everyone had stared when they entered—priests of Mitra were not known for patronizing Maul taverns—but they soon looked away, minding one's business was a vital survival skill in the Maul. Four tankards of ale sat on the table before them, and while the others drank deeply, Naerys —who had removed her helmet when she'd sat, revealing her dark hair—only sipped hers. Conan knew little about the woman's religion, he didn't know whether her restraint was expected in her order or because, despite recommending the ale, she did not care for the taste. She had paid for their drinks, so she obviously had not taken a vow of poverty, and that was all that mattered to him.

The leather satchel containing the gold statuette of Ishtar sat on the floor next to Conan's left leg. Valja had wanted to stop at the inn where they were staying and leave the satchel in their room, but Conan refused to let the hard-won prize out of his sight. He did not trust the innkeeper not to check their room once they departed, and he was confident in his ability to prevent anyone from taking the treasure from them.

Two Zamorian men, scrawny and dressed in threadbare tunics held together with numerous patches, sat at a nearby table, arguing over near-empty mugs of ale.

"The town is called *Arenjun!*"

"Its name is *Zamora!*"

"That is the name of the *country!*"

"So? Who says it can't be the name of the city, too?"

"Because it's too confusing!"

Conan had heard variations on this argument in taverns and on the streets ever since coming to the city. Zamora, Arenjun... Who cared what the place's true name was? Besides, a thing could have more than one name. His own father was sometimes called Steelhand because of his skill at the forge. Conan thought *City of Thieves* fit the place best, but some Zamorians considered Shadizar to be the City of Thieves. The issue was tiresome to Conan, and he thought it another example of civilized folk's lunacy. In Cimmeria, a thing's essential nature never changed, regardless of what it was called. Why argue with someone about the name of a mountain when the damned thing was right in front of you both?

Naerys took another sip of ale and then looked at Valja. "Before we discuss my proposition, tell me—how did you decide to visit the Temple of Ishtar this night?"

Valja looked puzzled, but she answered the question. "I went to the shop of Hutai the Nemedian yesterday. I had an item I'd recently come into possession of that I wished to sell."

The item had been an opal ring she'd taken off the finger of a drunk noble she'd found passed out in an alley. The upper classes of Arenjun sometimes got the itch to avail themselves of the base pleasures the Maul had to offer, especially when they were young, curious, and stupid. They tried to dress as they imagined Maul denizens might, but despite their efforts, they never blended in—clothes too new, bodies too clean, hair cut too neatly. And while they left the most expensive jewelry they normally wore at home, they often forgot to remove it all, especially pieces they considered of little value. But even a noble's cheapest jewelry fetched a good price in the Maul. Conan thought the man Valja had encountered had been fortunate. Most of the Maul's citizens would have slit his throat before taking the ring. Valja had at least left the idiot with a chance at survival, although Conan doubted the man had lived to see the sun rise.

"While I was there," Valja went on, "Hutai asked if Conan and I planned to attend the solstice celebration at the Temple of Ishtar. I told him I knew nothing about it. He said he had often gone as a youth and had enjoyed himself immensely. He described the festivities and spoke of the temple itself, its grandeur and its riches, particularly the statuettes."

Naerys smiled. "I paid him to tell you those things."

Sudden rage flared hot in Conan. Moving lightning fast, he stood, drew his sword, and pressed the point to the base of Naerys' throat. Everyone in the tavern stopped talking and turned to watch the drama playing out in their midst, eager to see blood spilled, as long as it wasn't theirs.

Anot gasped in alarm. She raised a hand, fingers curled into a mystic gesture, but Conan fixed the shaman with a deadly glare. "*Don't*," he growled.

Anot looked deep into the young barbarian's eyes, and what she saw there caused her to slowly lower her hand. Conan returned his attention to Naerys.

"Do you think us fools?" he demanded.

Despite having a sword point pressing into the tender flesh of her neck, the priestess appeared calm. "On the contrary. I think the two of you are exactly what I have sought," she said.

Conan held his sword in place a moment longer, then Valja laid a gentle hand on his forearm. "Let's hear what she has to say. What can it hurt?"

"Perhaps many things," he said sullenly, but he sheathed his sword and sat. Disappointed the entertainment had ended so soon, the other customers returned to their drinks and conversation.

"What game are you playing, priestess?" Conan said.

"A very serious one. May I continue?"

Conan made a sour face, but he nodded. Why could civilized people not just say what was on their minds? They used so many words to say so little.

"Anot and I have a task to perform," Naerys said, "but it is one we cannot do alone. I visited Hutai because of his reputation as a dealer in items obtained by… *creative* means. I told him I needed people highly skilled in the art of acquisition, but I did not simply want him to give me names. I wanted to observe the candidates in action, to see for myself what they were capable of. Anot had helped me devise a test—"

The shaman smiled. "The spring solstice is a time of great power, not just for the Wild but for all the world. I knew Naerys would find what she needed on this day."

"And during my education as a priestess, I was taught about the world's other religions," Naerys said. "Thus I knew how Ishtar's followers celebrate the solstice, and that they display the gold statuettes of their goddess only at this time of year. I asked Hutai to tell the most highly skilled *acquirers* he knew about the celebration, with special emphasis on the statuettes. Hutai agreed to help—for a substantial fee, of course. My hope was that only the most talented and daring of his clientele would take the challenge."

"Take the bait, you mean," Conan muttered.

Naerys went on as if he had not spoken. "Anot and I went to

the Temple District not long after sunset. She used her power to hide us from all eyes, and we watched and waited."

"And then you two came," Anot said. "You were not the only ones. Just the only ones to make it inside the temple alive."

"And make it out again," Naerys said. "With a handsome reward for your efforts. By the way, Hutai said that if anyone actually succeeded in obtaining such a prize, they could sell it to him, and he would in turn sell it to the temple priests, who would be only too happy to take it back with no questions asked."

So far, this was the only part of Naerys' tale that pleased Conan, although he was irritated with the merchant for helping the priestess manipulate Valja and him.

"So, we passed your test," Valja said. "What would you have us do? More importantly, how much will you pay?"

Naerys' expression became grim. "What do you know of the Cult of Set?"

A young Stygian man moved through the moonlit streets of the Merchants' Quarter, his stride purposeful and confident. He did not *feel* confident, but in Arenjun you needed to avoid showing the slightest weakness unless you wanted to end up as someone's prey, especially at night. Shengis served Uzzeran, a powerful Stygian sorcerer, and this should have afforded him a certain measure of respect and even protection on the street, but his master practiced his dark arts in secret, thus Shengis' need for the camouflage of feigned confidence.

Shengis was a rail-thin man of twenty-four years, garbed in a simple brown tunic and sandals, his only weapon a poison-coated dagger sheathed on his belt. At his master's insistence, he also wore a leather armor vest when he went out into the streets. *I don't need you to get stabbed in the back one night when you're not paying attention to your surroundings*, Uzzeran had said. *I have put too much work into training you.* He knew his master had not said this out of any real concern for his safety, but it had made him feel valued nonetheless.

Shengis had been born into Stygia's lowest class, which made him a slave in all but name. He did not resent his station, for Mother Set—praise the Great Serpent's dread name—had chosen it for him and he was proud to serve Uzzeran. But one of the things Shengis liked about Arenjun was that most of its citizens couldn't tell his class simply by looking at him. To them, a Stygian was a Stygian. The only thing they cared about was how much money you had and how swiftly they could divest you of it. Because of this, he was treated better in the City of Thieves than back in his homeland, and he wouldn't mind spending the rest of his life here. But Uzzeran had come to Arenjun only to complete his work away from the covetous eyes of other sorcerers, especially those of the Black Ring. Uzzeran hated the city. He considered its inhabitants little better than vermin and refused to walk its streets unless absolutely necessary. He preferred to send Shengis out to conduct whatever business he needed done.

Uzzeran had been the first person Shengis had heard refer to their god as Mother Set. In the streets, the poor and lame prayed aloud to Father Set, and Shengis had therefore assumed the god was male. He'd asked Uzzeran about this one day.

At their core, the gods are raw power, Shengis, and that power can present itself however it wishes at any given moment. Male, female, both, neither, human, animal, beautiful, monstrous... The gods wear many masks, Shengis. To me, Set has always been female, so I call her Mother, but regardless of which words we use, Set is always the same—eternal darkness, never-ending hunger, and the death of all that is.

Shengis didn't fully grasp Uzzeran's explanation, but in

deference to his master, he began calling Set Mother as well, and it wasn't long before it felt natural to him.

Aside from his dagger, Shengis carried one more thing, worn on a thong around his neck and hidden beneath his tunic: a silver amulet his master had created, the image of a coiling snake, tail in its mouth, engraved upon its surface. The charm felt cold against his bare skin, so much so that it hurt. He never complained about this discomfort. Uzzeran had entrusted him with it—a great responsibility!—and it was imbued with a portion of the sorcerer's power, which alone made it special to Shengis, regardless of what it could do. His master had not named the amulet, but Shengis called it the Snare. When he told Uzzeran this, the sorcerer had shrugged and said, *As good a name as any, I suppose.* It was the highest praise Shengis had ever received from his master, and whenever he recalled this moment, which was often, it always made him feel warm inside.

The spring solstice was a time when great feats of sorcery could be performed, and Uzzeran had attempted such a feat this night. It had taken him hours to prepare, but when he had finally begun the ritual, it did not go as planned, to say the least. His test subject had died horribly, screaming in agony as her blood welled forth from the pores of her skin until none remained in her body. Uzzeran had been furious with himself—and with Shengis, who had assisted in the preparations—but he had forced his anger aside. *The mystic power of the solstice will remain strong until midnight tomorrow*, he'd said. *Success is still possible, provided I begin new preparations and finish them in time,* and *if you procure me a new test subject.*

This was why Shengis now roamed the streets of the Merchants' Quarter, desperately hoping to find what his master needed, for if not—

A white spider the size of a man's hand emerged from a wide crack in the ground in front of Shengis, and the servant stopped, a cold sensation rippling down his spine that had nothing to do with the amulet around his neck. The spider crouched motionless before him, its eight black eyes reflecting moonlight like pieces of polished obsidian. It was the largest spider Shengis had ever seen, and he liked not the way it was watching him—no, *observing* him, as if an inhuman intelligence lay behind those black eyes. He knew little about spiders, certainly not enough to identify what kind this was, and he had never seen a white one before. Was it venomous? He feared it might be, and he began to slowly take a step backward. The instant he began moving, the huge spider reared up on its back four legs and raised the other four into the air as if in warning: *Move any further and I will attack.*

Shengis froze, heart pounding in his chest, sweat beading on his forehead. He had no love of spiders, but he generally suffered no fear of the creatures. But this one was different.

Rumor had it that the Cult of Zath, the spider god, had established a presence in Arenjun over the last several years. The cult was based in the Zamorian city of Yezud and was strongest there, but like so many gods—Set included—Zath desired to spread its influence across the world. The cult had even managed to gain a foothold in Shadizar, from what Shengis understood. This spider before him now had to be one of the Brood of Zath, or perhaps even an avatar of the god itself. What else could account for its strange behavior, not to mention its unearthly size and strange color? Shengis could guess why the creature had come to confront him. Zath must have become aware of the great feat of magic Uzzeran was attempting to perform at the behest of Set herself, and the spider god, curious, wished to know more. His suspicion was confirmed when the spider made clicking sounds with its mouth parts and Shengis heard a single word in his mind.

Speak.

Twin pearls of venom welled forth from the spider's fangs, and the second part of Zath's message needed no further translation: *or die.*

Shengis would never betray his master or their god, so die it was. He prayed to Set that the spider's venom did its work swiftly, then took a step forward. The spider tensed, preparing to leap...

A shadowy form darted out of the night like ebon lightning and streaked across the ground toward the spider. It was a snake, black as pitch, thin and built for speed, but long as a man's body. The white spider must have sensed the serpent's attack, for it leaped straight up a split second before the reptile's curved fangs could plunge into its body. Hissing with anger, the snake whipped around to attack again, but it was too late. The spider landed, raced toward the fissure it had emerged from, and disappeared into it.

For an instant, Shengis thought the dark snake would give immediate pursuit, but instead it looked up at him. The serpent's eyes were filled with disquieting intelligence, just as the spider's had been.

Shengis bowed his head and made a quick sign of obeisance. "Thank you."

The serpent regarded him an instant longer, then slithered quickly toward the fissure and followed its foe down into the earth.

Shengis stood for several moments as his pulse and breathing slowly returned to normal. He stared at the crack and wondered where it led—beneath the ground or to a shadowy realm outside this world? He decided he was better off not knowing. Mother Set had saved his life so he could aid his master in his holy work, not stand in the moonlight wasting precious time. The solstice would not last forever.

He continued walking down the street, and soon he felt the amulet begin to grow warmer against his chest. Not much, but enough to be noticeable.

Shengis' heart raced with excitement. He had found one! "Glory unto Set," he cried, not caring who heard him.

He walked faster until soon he was running, and with every step he took, the amulet grew warmer.

Naerys continued speaking, but before she got too far, Conan stopped her and signaled for the serving girl to bring another round of ale for the table. If Naerys was anything like the priests he had come to know since leaving Cimmeria, she would have much to say and take her time saying it. He might have to listen to her, but that did not mean he had to do it sober.

Once their ale had arrived and Conan had taken a large gulp, Naerys resumed where she had left off.

"My parents were priests of Mitra, and I their only child. They raised me in the faith, of course, and they taught me it does no good for priests to remain shut behind temple walls, saying prayers and conducting rites, separated from the people they were pledged to serve. They traveled throughout the world, spreading the teachings of Mitra and doing whatever they could to help others—setting a hunter's broken leg, assisting a sheep herder round up a wayward flock, bringing in the harvest for a farmer who had fallen ill. Almost from the moment of my birth, my parents took me with them on their journeys, and as soon as I could walk I joined them in their holy work. It was the only life I had ever known, but I came to love it as much as my parents did. Sometimes we would stay in villages for several days so I could play with children my own age, and I enjoyed those times very much, even if they never lasted long."

She sighed wistfully and took an actual drink of ale this time instead of a mere sip. Then she continued.

"In my twelfth year, we were in one of the city states of Koth—I do not recall which—when one morning my mother told my father and me of a dream she'd had the night before. In the dream, she had stood on a rocky plain beneath a night sky filled with stars whose constellations she did not recognize. The ground began to shake beneath her feet, the tremors so strong that she could not maintain her balance and fell. In the distance, she saw two gigantic figures locked in battle. She pushed herself into a sitting position and put both hands on the ground to brace herself during the tremors. 'I am not sure how it happened,' she told us, 'but somehow the space between the figures and me shrank. Or perhaps I was magically transported to them. However it occurred, I found myself much closer to the titanic beings, and I could see who they were. One was Mitra—long black hair, thick beard, heavily muscled, wearing only a breechcloth. The other was an unimaginably huge serpent, an evil thing with burning red eyes, gigantic fangs, and black coils that stretched past the horizon. It was Set, of course, and the two gods were locked in a battle to the death. Set had wrapped around Mitra's torso and was squeezing him, while Mitra had his mighty hands locked on the foul serpent's throat. Their struggles became more vigorous, and the ground began to shake constantly. Chunks of rock sheared off the mountains and fell to the plain, and one of them—so large it blotted out the stars—descended toward me. I knew I could not hope to escape, so I closed my eyes and prayed to Mitra for a quick death. But when I opened them, I was lying in my bedroll, safe, the morning sun shining down on me.' "

Naerys took another drink of ale.

"Not long after this, we stopped at a desert village to help them dig a well. The job took several days, and each night we would sit with the village folk and talk. My parents spoke little Kothian, but I had been learning languages all my young life and had picked up enough to serve as translator. The villagers like to tell stories to frighten one another. For some reason I did not understand, they found this amusing. They spoke of ghosts and devils, undead sorcerers and murderous shapeshifters. But one story they told had a profound effect on my mother. They spoke of how, in the great cities of Stygia, large serpents—some big enough to swallow a human whole—dwelled within the temples of Set and were worshipped as avatars of the foul demon. At night, priests would leave the temple doors open, allowing the serpents to go out into the city streets. The devout would go outside and lie in the streets, hoping to be found worthy of the serpents' attention, whether that meant getting bitten, crushed, or eaten. It was considered a huge honor to be slain by one of the serpents, and harming them—harming any snake—was an unforgivable sin.

"To the Kothites it was simply another grisly story meant to entertain, but to my mother it was a revelation from Mitra himself. She told us later that she now understood her dream and knew what our god wished us to do. We were to go to Stygia and cast the great serpents out of the cities so no one would ever be harmed by the monsters again."

Conan had heard stories of the serpents of Set before. He did not know if the creatures were real or merely legend, and he had little interest in discovering the truth. Still, giant snakes *would* be something to see, would they not? And they'd prove a unique challenge for a fighting man to test his strength and skill against. How would he have fared against one of the scaled monsters? Put a freshly sharpened sword in his hand, and by Crom, he would find out!

Naerys finished her ale. Conan had long since emptied his second tankard, as had Valja. Anot was still working on hers, but Conan nevertheless ordered a third round. Why not? He wasn't the one paying. As they waited for the drinks to arrive, Valja said, "I doubt the people of Stygia greeted you and your parents with open arms."

Naerys smiled wryly. "Hardly."

A couple of serving girls came to the table, delivered full tankards, removed the empties, then hurried off to take care of other customers. Conan gulped down a good portion and smacked his lips. "By Ymir, I swear that this ale tastes better with every drink!" He lowered his mug to the table and looked at Naerys. "I have no wish to speak ill of your mother, but her plan sounds foolish to me."

"Not to mention highly dangerous," Valja added.

"You are both right, of course," Naerys said. "Father believed Mother's dream was a true vision sent by Mitra, and I naturally believed whatever my parents did. They decided to start with the city of Khemi, for it had the greatest concentration of temples dedicated to Set in the entire kingdom. We left Koth and traveled through Shem, not stopping to help a single person, and eventually we arrived in Khemi. My parents dressed much as I do now, and they walked the streets openly. The citizens were cold to us, shouting curses in Stygian or ignoring us altogether. I feared they would try to hurt us, but Mother said Mitra would protect us. Perhaps he did, for no one attempted to harm us."

"Khemi is located on the southern shore of the River Styx," Conan said. "It is Stygia's greatest port. Much trading happens there, and the people, while still not fond of outsiders, are more tolerant of them." He had never been to Khemi, but during his time in Arenjun he'd spoken with many different people and listened to conversations in taverns and on the streets, learning as much as he could. He was a Cimmerian, born and bred, but he was unlike his people in one respect: from the time he was a child, he wondered what lay behind the next tree, the next hill, the next forest, the next mountain. How far away was the horizon? How long would it take to reach it, and what, if anything, lay beyond? And, most important of all, what new challenges might await him? His father often teased him about his "searching eyes and itchy feet," and he had not been surprised when Conan had eventually left their village.

"Perhaps that is why the priests did not have us imprisoned or executed," Naerys allowed. "For our first week in Khemi, we explored the city, noting the location of each temple of Set. Then, one afternoon, Mother said the time had come, so the three of us left the shabby inn near the river—the only place in the city that would give us lodging—and we headed for the largest temple in Khemi. We took a position in a nearby alley and waited for sunset."

Conan didn't like where this story was headed.

"When night fell, we left the alley and stood in the street in front of the temple entrance, Mother on my right, Father on my left, me in the middle. I was scared—so scared—but my parents held my hands, and that gave me strength. I felt as if the power of Mitra was flowing through them and into me." She smiled sadly. "That was what I believed, anyway. I don't know how long we stood there. It seemed like hours. But eventually we heard the horrible sound of something large and heavy slithering down the stone steps of the temple toward us. There was only a crescent moon that night, but the sky was overcast, and the great serpent was visible only as a shadow against the darkness. It was as if Set herself had manifested before us, and despite my determination to be as brave as my parents, tears began to run down my face.

"My mother began speaking in a loud, clear voice, her words echoing as if she were shouting from atop a high mountain.

'Mighty Mitra, who is adored by all worlds, give us your great protection! Lead the children of Stygia from the darkness of Set to your holy light! Turn away this abominable creature and cast it into the abyss of eternal nothingness!'

"For a long moment, there was only silence, and I imagined the serpent had vanished from our world, never to return. Then I felt a rush of air, and Mother's hand was torn away from mine. I was shocked. Had Mitra taken Mother as well as the giant snake? I had no idea what was happening, but my father did. He released my hand, shoved me backward, and shouted for me to run. I couldn't see him in the darkness, but I believe he turned back to the serpent, raised his arms and began to repeat my mother's words. He got as far as 'Mighty Mitra' before the serpent took him as well.

"I ran through the streets, silently crying, terrified of making too much noise and drawing the serpent's attention—or the attention of the other serpents roaming the city. Eventually, I collapsed from exhaustion near a stable. I could tell what it was by the smell, although I found out later it held camels, not horses. I reasoned that if any giant snake came this way, it would eat the larger animals instead of a small child. I huddled against the side of the building and cried until dawn."

Naerys broke off and gazed down at the table, a haunted look in her eyes.

"Your parents were fools," Conan said, "but they showed great courage in confronting the monstrous serpent. And knowing his wife was gone, your father's first thought was not for his own loss but rather to ensure your survival. That action brought much honor to his name."

Naerys raised her head and gave Conan a wan smile. "I ran. What does that say of me?"

"That you were a child," Valja said. "An obedient one, for you did as your father told you."

"And a *smart* one," Conan added. "I have seen soldiers freeze from fear when they could have run."

Naerys' smile widened a bit. "Thank you, my friends. Your words help ease my pain."

"I still do not understand what you want from us," Valja said.

"After that night, I wandered the streets of Khemi as another orphaned child, forced to beg and steal to survive. Eventually, I was found by a man named Uzzeran. He was a powerful sorcerer, and while I feared him, I went with him willingly. I was starving and desperate. At first, I thought he wanted to force me to worship Set and teach me her dark arts. I vowed to take my own life before I allowed that to happen."

Conan grunted in approval.

"But he had other plans for me." Naerys turned her head to the side and brushed hair away from her ear, revealing a patch of green-scaled skin that until now had been hidden. She allowed her hair to fall back into place and faced the others once more. The sight of that reptilian skin repulsed Conan, and the Cimmerian's instinctive dread of the unnatural made him want to reach for his sword. He resisted the impulse. There was no need to slay her—yet. He wondered if she had patches of scales on other parts of her body. The thought turned his ale-filled stomach, and he decided he'd only have a few more tankards.

"After a year of being Uzzeran's plaything, I escaped. I stowed away on a Shemite ship and left Khemi behind forever. My parents were both Ophirian, but since I was born during their travels, I had never set foot in my ancestral land. So I went there and, having no idea if I had any relatives in the kingdom, I went to a temple of Mitra and begged the priests to take me in. They did, and formally trained me in their ways. When I became an adult and it was time for me to go out into the world and find my place as a servant of Mitra, I decided I would follow my parents' path—or at least, my own version of it. I dedicated my life to opposing Set and all her servants so that I might rid the world of their evil and avenge the deaths of my parents."

"When you say 'rid the world'..." Valja began.

"I mean permanently," Naerys said, her voice cold.

Valja frowned. "I thought priests of Mitra swore an oath not to kill."

"We vow not to take *innocent* lives," Naerys said. "Those who sacrifice others in Set's name are anything but."

Conan again grunted approval.

Valja looked doubtful, but she said no more, and Naerys continued her tale.

"I eventually encountered Anot, and we discovered we both had reasons to hate Set and her worshippers. We joined forces, and we've worked together ever since. Over the years, we've developed a network of men and women throughout the known world, primarily Stygians, who have no love of sorcerers. They search for signs of any in their lands and relay word to me when they find one. Recently, we learned that Uzzeran himself had left Khemi and come to Arenjun to practice his foul necromancy. *This* is why I have sought you out, Conan and Valja.

"I want you to help me slay the bastard."

The amulet was searing hot by the time it led Shengis to a modest home in the Merchants' Quarter. From what he understood, the wealthiest merchants in the city lived in mansions located near the palace. They owned a number of shops in the quarter staffed by paid employees, and the only work they did was counting their profits. However, less successful merchants also lived in the district, usually in rooms in the same building that housed their business, and they either hired guards to watch over their wares during the night, or kept their shops open throughout the night or were open only after the sun set. These merchants specialized in items of dubious legality, even more dubious than usual for Arenjun.

The Snare had led Shengis to one such merchant, for there was a lone candle burning in the front window—a sign that this purveyor was open and ready to deal. He walked to the front door, found it unlocked, and entered.

He had been walking through the city for hours, his eyesight was well adjusted to the dark, and the lone candle provided more than enough light for him to see. The interior of the shop was small and contained a wooden counter with an array of knives and daggers spread upon it and, behind the counter, a sturdy-looking door, undoubtedly locked. The room was unoccupied, but the mystic amulet burned like molten iron against his chest, and he knew that what he was searching for was near, most likely behind that door. Heart pounding, he walked toward the counter, intending to step behind it and knock on the door to let the merchant know he had a visitor, but before he could reach it a shadow emerged from the corner of the room and flowed silently toward Shengis. A cold twist of nausea in his gut warned the Stygian that the thing coming at him was not human, and he swiftly grabbed the leather thong holding the Snare and lifted the amulet free from his tunic, thrusting it toward the shadow-thing just as it was reaching for him with long, claw-tipped fingers. The shadow-thing recoiled, and Shengis heard a shrill scream in his mind as the creature turned and fled back into the darkness whence it had come.

Shengis stood for a moment, breath held and heart pounding, waiting to see if some other creature would emerge from the shadows to attack him. None did, and Shengis slowly released the breath he'd been holding. Uzzeran had told him the Snare would turn aside any ghost, demon, or devil that attempted to harm him, but until this moment Shengis had not known if it would work. He should never have doubted his master. He tucked the amulet into his tunic and grimaced as the white-hot metal came into contact with his chest once more.

He then heard the *snick* of a lock being undone. The door behind the counter flew open and a man rushed into the room. He was tall, fair-skinned, blond-haired, bearded, and wore a maroon tunic over a long-sleeved white shirt with brown breeks and black boots. He gripped a shortsword in his left hand, and judging by his furious expression he was more than ready to use it. He stepped out from behind the counter and leveled his sword at Shengis.

"How did you turn aside my guardian?" the man demanded. "You do not look like a sorcerer. Who are you?"

Shengis smiled and hoped he projected more confidence than he felt. "The question, good sir, is who are *you*? I wager few merchants in Arenjun employ a shadow spirit for a guard."

"I am Hutai the Nemedian, and while my shop might appear to be that of a humble merchant, I am a most dangerous man. If you wish to live to see another sunrise, I suggest you leave. Immediately."

"I have heard of you," Shengis said. "You are a buyer and seller of extremely questionable goods. But that is not all you are, is it?"

Shengis raised the Snare once again and held it out toward Hutai. The merchant stared at the amulet for several seconds, and then his eyes glazed over and his features went slack. His grip on the sword loosened and the weapon thumped to the wooden floor. An instant later, his features blurred and reformed into a face that was no longer human. It was green-scaled, with serpent eyes, a flat nose with two slits for nostrils, a pair of long, curving fangs, and a forked tongue. Its hands were scaled as well, with fingers ending in sharp claws, but despite its reptilian appearance, the creature had no tail.

Hutai was a Serpent Man, a child of Set, whose people had ruled Earth long ago, during an epoch when humans were small apelike creatures hiding in trees. The Snare had nullified the Serpent Man's human disguise and pacified him in the process, otherwise, Shengis knew he would've had his head torn off by now.

The Stygian smiled with grim satisfaction, basking in the power he had over Hutai. "Tell me who you are," he said.

The Snare's magic made it impossible for the Serpent Man to resist Shengis' command. "I am Kekk."

"What is your real purpose in Arenjun?"

Serpent Men considered humans a plague upon the world, a foul pestilence to be eradicated in Set's name. To further this end, they used magic to masquerade as humans, then sought positions of power and influence to advance their goal of destroying humanity. Shengis thought their quest a fool's game—there were simply too many humans and too few Serpent Men for them to ever succeed—but they were single-minded creatures—immortal, too—and they would never stop trying to reclaim what they viewed as their rightful place as the lords of creation. *Deluded idiots.* As far as Shengis was concerned, Serpent Men were subhuman abominations, unworthy of serving the great, dread glory that was Set.

"As a fence, I am privy to a great deal of valuable information, and I pass it on to others of my kind in the city so that they might use it to our advantage."

There was a saying in Arenjun: If you want to know something, ask a thief.

Or a fence, Shengis thought.

"Assume your human guise," he said.

Kekk's features blurred, and when they came into focus he again appeared as Hutai the Nemedian.

"You are to accompany me," Shengis instructed. "You will

not attempt to escape my control or harm me physically, and you will speak only when I speak to you first. Do you understand?"

Kekk nodded.

"And whatever sorcerous skill you possess, you will employ it only at my direction and never against me. Nod again if you understand and will obey."

Kekk did so. All Serpent Men could work magic to a degree, even if they weren't full-fledged sorcerers. It was how they disguised themselves as human, and in Kekk's case was most likely how he'd been able to conjure and control his shadow guardian.

"Good. Let's go."

Shengis slipped the amulet, which was now cool to the touch, back into his tunic. He then turned and walked out of the shop, not bothering to look back to see if Kekk followed. The Snare's enchantment ensured he would.

Shengis hoped this new test subject would prove more successful than the last. If not, the solstice would end before he could obtain another and Uzzeran would have to wait an entire year before attempting the ritual again. The master would no doubt blame Shengis for the failure and this time would surely punish him. If that happened, Shengis thought Kekk wouldn't be the only one who found his body turning inside out.

Kekk followed Shengis like a faithful dog through the Maul. Few people were foolish enough to be out on the streets this late at night, for shadowy figures lurked in doorways and alleys, intently watching any pedestrians who passed, debating whether to attack. In the night streets of the Maul, attacking the wrong person could result in a swift, painful death. This gave Shengis and Kekk a certain amount of protection, and as they kept up a good pace and walked with the appearance of confidence, the predators let them be.

Shengis began to relax as they neared the Temple District. The churches hired guards and paid substantial bribes to the City Watch to patrol the area, and because of this it was one of the safest places in Arenjun, day or night. But as they entered the district there were far more Watch officers on the streets than usual, and Shengis knew something significant must have happened to draw their attention. Temple guards were out, too—rough-looking men and women armed with a variety of weapons, all of them sharp and deadly. Those Watchers who saw Shengis and Kekk eyed them with suspicion but said nothing. Whoever they were looking for, Shengis and Kekk evidently did not fit their descriptions and they were allowed to go about their business. This came as a considerable relief to Shengis; if the Watchers looked at Kekk closely, they might have noticed his dull-eyed gaze and expressionless face and decided the two of them were worth questioning after all.

"You there!" came a man's voice, deep and commanding.

Shengis froze, then slowly turned in the direction the voice had come from, while Kekk, who had stopped with him, remained immobile, staring mutely at nothing. Shengis expected to see a Watch officer approaching, but instead he saw a red-bearded Vanir man and a Corinthian woman walking toward them with determined strides. The man held a broadaxe at his side while the woman gripped a longsword, and from their angry expressions they were eager for their weapons to taste blood.

The two figures stopped when they reached Shengis and Kekk, eyeing them suspiciously. Shengis' hand itched to reach for his poison-coated dagger, but he resisted. He was no warrior, and he knew either of these two would cut him down before he could draw the blade from its sheath.

"Have you seen a tall, muscular youth with long black hair?"

the Vanir asked. "He's a northerner, like me. A Cimmerian."

Shengis knew little about Cimmeria, other than it was a cold, harsh land inhabited by people who were colder and harsher. But before he could respond, the Corinthian spoke.

"He was with a woman. A Shemite or perhaps a Stygian."

The Vanir gave his partner an irritated look. "I told you, she's Zamorian."

The woman scowled. "And I told *you* that you didn't get a good enough look at her to tell her race for certain."

"My vision is sharper than yours," the Vanir said.

"The only thing sharp about you is your axe-head," she snapped.

Shengis couldn't afford to linger here. He needed to get Kekk to his master before the City Watch became aware of them. Best to hurry this along.

"What did they do, this youth and his companion?" he asked.

"They broke into the Temple of Ishtar during the solstice celebration," the Corinthian said, "and stole one of the sacred gold statuettes."

"At least one," the Vanir said. "They may have gotten away with more."

From the eagerness in the man's voice, Shengis guessed these two were less interested in bringing the pair of thieves to justice than they were in acquiring the statuette for themselves. "I'm sorry, but we've seen no one like that," he said. "My friend and I spent the evening in the Maul gambling, but the dice were no friends to us this night and we lost what little coin we had."

The Vanir opened his mouth to say something, but he was interrupted by Kekk. The man was still gazing off into the distance, but he spoke a one-word question.

"Gold?"

Shengis groaned inwardly as Kekk turned toward the two mercenaries. The Snare dulled the will of Serpent Men, making them compliant and obedient, but it did not entirely rob them of intelligence. How could they follow commands if their minds were empty? This meant that they sometimes reacted to outside stimuli, especially when it related to something important to them. Kekk, in his guise as Hutai, was a fence, and news that a rare gold object had been stolen had cut through the fog enshrouding his mind and caused him to react.

The mercenaries got their first good look at Kekk, and the Corinthian frowned.

"Say, aren't you Hutai the Nemedian?"

Kekk did not respond to her question. "Gold?" he said again, his tone hopeful this time.

The Vanir spoke to his companion without taking his gaze off Kekk. "Who is Hutai?"

"He plays at being a merchant who deals in knives, but in reality he's a fence, one of the best connected in the city. It's said that there are those in the palace who make use of his services from time to time, perhaps even the king himself. I have had occasion to visit his shop, and..." She trailed off, eyes widening in realization. A slow, sly smile spread across her face as she turned her attention to Kekk. "What would you be doing in the Temple District this time of night, Hutai?" she asked. "I did not see you among the celebrants at Ishtar's temple earlier, and none of the other faiths were holding solstice rites this evening."

The Vanir frowned. "What are you getting at, Rosilia?"

"I can think of only one reason why a fence would be in the district this night," she said.

It was the Vanir's turn to smile now. "To accept delivery of a stolen item. A special item."

"A *gold* item," the Corinthian added.

Hutai grinned. "Gold!" he shouted happily.

Shengis sighed. The mercenaries raised their weapons and stepped closer to Kekk. The Serpent Man continued grinning, unconcerned that he was now within weapon's range of the two warriors. Both the Vanir and the Corinthian seemed to have forgotten that Shengis existed.

"I don't suppose you'd be willing to tell us where the statuette is?" the Corinthian said. She looked him up and down. "Clearly it's not on your person, and you carry no satchel or bag."

"Does the big youth still have it?" the Vanir asked. "Tell me where he is and I shall consider letting you keep your head attached to your body."

This had gone on long enough. Shengis drew his dagger and said, "Kekk, reveal your true self and slay the Vanir."

The Vanir shot a glance at Shengis. "What in Ymir's frozen jewels are you—"

That was all the man got out before Kekk's human guise gave way to his reptilian aspect. He bared his fangs, hissed, and plunged a clawed hand into the Vanir's chest. Ribs splintered, blood sprayed, and the mercenary's eyes went wide with shock as he watched Kekk tear his heart from his body. He turned his head to face the Corinthian, and his mouth moved as if he was trying to speak, but all that came out was a gush of crimson that splattered onto his companion's face. She cried out in disgust and took several quick steps back, desperately trying to wipe away the blood with her free hand. The axe slipped from the Vanir's fingers and thudded to the ground. An instant later, his corpse joined it there.

Kekk gazed at the warm, wet treat in his clawed hand with undisguised hunger. Then he opened his mouth far wider than a human could and jammed the entire heart inside. He closed his mouth, swallowed, and his throat bulged hideously as the organ slowly began to make its way down.

The Corinthian stared in horror as the Serpent Man swallowed her friend's heart, but then a combination of fear and rage gripped her and she raised her sword and stepped forward to end the life of the monstrosity that had slain the Vanir.

That was when Shengis rammed his poison dagger into her lower back, sinking the blade into her right kidney. The woman gasped, and then her jaw clenched tight as the deadly poison swiftly began its work. Every muscle in her body became rigid, and she toppled over and fell to the ground next to the Vanir. Foam bubbled from her nostrils and her eyes rolled white, but otherwise she lay statue-still, her right hand still clasping her sword handle, yet Shengis knew she was not yet dead. The venom caused total muscular paralysis, so she was unable to breathe, but it would take several long, agonizing moments for her to suffocate.

He bent down to wipe his dagger clean on the Corinthian's tunic, then straightened, returned the dagger to its sheath, and regarded Kekk. The bulge in the Serpent Man's throat was almost gone now, and soon the heart would slide down far enough that there would be no outward sign of it. The lower half of the Serpent Man's face was slick with blood, as was his right hand, and blood had dribbled onto the front of his tunic. Shengis sighed. Good thing they were close to his master's workshop. With Set's blessing, they might make it before they ran into anyone else.

"Resume your human guise," Shengis commanded.

Kekk did so.

"And if anyone mentions the word *gold* again, ignore it."

Shengis knew it would be better if they concealed the mercenaries' bodies before leaving, but he couldn't afford to take the time. The City Watch would be even more up in arms than they already were once they discovered the corpses, but there was no help for it. He had to get Kekk to Uzzeran as soon as possible. There was nothing more important to his master than achieving success in his experiments. Nothing more important for the entire world.

He started walking, and Kekk automatically followed. They

saw figures moving through the district, some in shadow, some carrying lit torches or lanterns, but no one saw them, and before long they came to a huge mass of broken stone and splintered timber that had once been an impressive structure known as the Elephant Tower. Shengis breathed a sigh of relief.

They had made it home.

"I do not see how you managed to sleep after everything that happened last night," Valja said. "All I did was toss and turn."

She and Conan were walking down a street in the Maul in the early-morning light. The Maul never looked good, but it looked, and smelled, even worse in full daylight. The alleys stank of urine and feces, and men and women sat with their backs against walls, heads lowered to their chests, or lay in the mud, on their backs or facedown. Some of them were passed out, the result of too much strong drink or black lotus, while others were dead, slain by human predators in the night. It was impossible to tell which was which without closer inspection, and no one in the Maul was foolish enough to approach one of the bodies lest they discover that the "corpse" was actually a thief lying in wait to slice the throat of a foolish do-gooder.

Conan shrugged. "I was tired, so I slept. My people believe that whatever troubles lie ahead of us, they are best faced when both our minds and bodies are well rested."

"I have known you to go without sleep for several days in a row," she pointed out.

"Yes, when I have no other choice. Last night I had a choice, so I chose sleep."

They had returned to their room with only a few hours remaining until dawn, so he had not slept for long before Valja woke him, but he was used to functioning on minimal rest and felt as refreshed as if he'd had a full night's sleep.

Valja grinned and shook her head. "Sometimes I cannot decide if you are the most simple-minded man I have ever met or the wisest."

Conan shrugged. The leather satchel containing the statuette of Ishtar hung from his shoulder, his left hand resting on the bag. They had wrapped the statue in cloth before leaving their room and had put some fruit on top to further conceal it. It was an old trick, and not one that would fool any Maul denizen past infancy, but it might slow a thief down for a moment or two, and that would be all the time Conan would need to draw his sword and end their life.

"It's early," Valja said. "Do you think Hutai's shop will be open?"

"If it isn't, I'll pound on the door until the man answers," Conan said. "If necessary, I'll knock it down so we can enter, and I'll grab the old goat's beard and pull him out of bed."

Valja chuckled. "I doubt we'd get the best price out of him if we did that."

Conan doubted they would get a good price for the statuette this day regardless of whether he tugged on Hutai's beard or not. A nervous thief who wanted to be rid of the evidence of their crime as soon as possible had to settle for whatever price a fence was willing to pay, and it was usually the merest fraction of what the item was truly worth. Fences argued that they took on a higher level of risk buying an item that the City Watch was actively searching for and thus were reluctant to enter into a deal, but if you were willing to part with the item for a pittance then they might see their way clear to taking on that risk. And the statuette of Ishtar was more than a mere diamond or ruby, it was a unique item, and as the goddess' worshippers believed she—or at least a part of her—inhabited her likeness, the church was no doubt searching for it vigorously, with every intention of making the thieves who took it pay dearly for their blasphemy. The previous night, Conan had proposed hiding the statuette somewhere safe and waiting for several weeks to pass before attempting to sell it, but Naerys had convinced him it was too dangerous to hang on to. Still, it galled him that they would be forced to take whatever price the Nemedian set.

"What do you think of Naerys' offer?" Valja asked.

"She may have paid for the ale last night, but priests of Mitra are not known for their wealth. I would like to see if she actually has the gold she offered us before we accept the job. But even if she were a rich as a Turanian silk merchant, I do not like the idea of confronting a sorcerer."

"Ah, but think of the challenge," Valja said.

Her reckless nature had come to the fore once again, but Conan didn't find it charming this time. Attempting to rob Ishtar's Temple while the solstice celebration was in progress had been one thing, but bearding a sorcerer in his own lair, where the man would have ready access to all the tools of his dark craft? That struck him as madness. And yet he was not without sympathy for Naerys. Uzzeran had used her as a subject for his foul experiments, and she still bore the mark of his magic. Not long ago, he had been captured by Hyperborean slavers, and he knew what it was like to be the plaything of others who had control over you. Like him, Naerys had escaped her captivity and made a life for herself, and he admired her for that. He also understood her need for revenge. If he were in her position, he would hunt the sorcerer down and slay the bastard or die in the attempt. But he was not in her position, and neither was Valja.

Why should they risk their lives for someone they had just met?

But Naerys, along with Anot, had helped them escape the notice of the City Watch and the Ishtarians' hired guards last night. Conan was confident that he and Valja would have been able to escape on their own, but not without leaving a trail of dead bodies in their wake. The City Watch would never stop searching for them after that, and the king might even task his soldiers to aid them. He and Valja would be forced to flee Arenjun then, and he was not done with this city yet. He was learning much here—of thievery, yes, but also of the peoples of the known world, their customs and languages, strengths and weaknesses. In Cimmeria, survival depended on one's knowledge of the land, its plants and animals, terrain and weather. He needed to learn all that he could about civilized folk if he intended to thrive among them.

It wasn't as if he hadn't defeated a sorcerer before. No one in Arenjun knew it, not even Valja, but it had been he who had brought about the downfall of the sorcerer-priest Yara, who had been the true ruler of the city. Conan had sought to steal a fabled mystic jewel called the Heart of the Elephant, which Yara had had in his possession, and had entered Yara's stronghold in the Tower of the Elephant. Ultimately, the sorcerer had become imprisoned within the jewel and the tower had collapsed. Of course, Conan had not confronted Yara directly; the alien god Yag-Kosha, who had been Yara's prisoner and the source of the man's power, had told the barbarian what to do. Conan had helped free Yag-Kosha from Yara's control and gain revenge upon the sorcerer.

But he hadn't had time to thoroughly search the tower before it had collapsed, and who knew what treasures might still be found in its ruins? Plus Valja was right: it would be a challenge...

"There were many statuettes at the temple," Conan said. "Why did you choose one of Ishtar as a warrior?"

She shrugged. "I know not. Perhaps it just called to me."

When they reached Hutai's home, Valja knocked on the door. When there was no response, she knocked harder, but still the merchant did not answer.

"Step aside," Conan said.

Valja remained where she was and tried the door latch, finding it unlocked. She pushed the door open, then turned and grinned at Conan.

The young Cimmerian pursed his lips in irritation. It would have been more fun to break the door down.

"Hutai?" Valja called. "Are you awake? It's Valja and Conan. We have come to inspect your new wares."

This last phrase was a code Hutai had thieves say to indicate the true reason for their visit. If the merchant was at home and awake, it should bring him to the door. Conan and Valja waited for several moments, but there was still no sign of Hutai.

"He must be out," Valja said.

"No merchant would leave their home without locking the door."

Conan stepped past Valja and entered the outer room of Hutai's home, which served as his shop. At first glance, nothing seemed amiss inside: knives and daggers were displayed on the front counter—all serviceable weapons, but Hutai kept his best merchandise locked in a back room to which only customers who could afford his finest blades were permitted entrance. Conan inhaled deeply, scenting the air. He did not detect the odor of blood, so if Hutai had been attacked and injured, it had not happened here. He did, however, smell the unmistakable odor he associated with Hutai's shop, a rank fustiness that he associated with a reptile's den. Since coming to Arenjun, he'd learned that some people kept lizards and snakes as pets, which made no sense to him. Reptiles were good for food, but only if you were starving and had nothing else to eat. Dogs and wolves made better pets, as did birds of prey, for you could go hunting with them. All you could do with reptiles was look at the damn things.

Normally, the smell was faint, but it was stronger than usual, and it held a harsh tang that stirred his wilderness-bred instincts. It made him think of an animal, tense and alert, prepared to attack and slay if it had to.

"Conan?" Valja said. "What's wrong?"

He didn't have the words to explain what he sensed, so all he said was, "Something is amiss. Let us search the rest of this place."

They did so, but they found no sign of Hutai, save for a bed that had not been made. This meant nothing to Conan, though. Why make a bed if you were just going to sleep in it again? Several rooms were closed and locked, and their doors were much sturdier than the front one. Valja attempted to pick one of the locks, but the instant she inserted her tools, there was a flash of sparks accompanied by a sizzling sound. She cried out, more in surprise than pain, and dropped her picks to the floor. They were now fused into a single lump of metal, and when Conan bent down to inspect it, he found it hot to the touch. He sensed magic at work here and he wanted nothing to do with it.

"He's had a protective spell placed on this lock," Valja said. She sounded puzzled.

"This is not a common precaution?" Conan asked.

She shook her head. "It's expensive, and whoever cast the spell can undo it, meaning they can return any time, go inside, and steal whatever it is you're trying to protect."

Conan thought for a moment. "Hutai cast the spell himself."

"Yes. He is the only one he can trust, after all. But what I don't understand is why he didn't place a similar ward on the front door."

"Maybe he does not wish to advertise that he possesses command of magic," Conan said. "All it would take is one person attempting to pick the lock on the front door and then word would spread quickly that Hutai is a sorcerer."

"If he were a true sorcerer, he wouldn't need to deal in stolen merchandise," Valja said. "He could use his powers to gain wealth. More likely a client sold him a mystic artifact that allows him to lay an enchantment on the locks."

That made sense to Conan, but who could understand the mind of a sorcerer? As far as he was concerned, they were all mad.

Conan and Valja left, closing the front door behind them but leaving it unlocked lest they advertise to Hutai that someone had been there. As they walked away from the merchant's home, they discussed what to do with the statuette.

"We could return it," Valja said. "It would be fun to try to sneak it back into the temple without anyone knowing."

The idea offended Conan. They had worked too hard to steal the statuette to simply give it back. "We can hide it within the pallet in our room," he said. "If we survive helping Naerys tonight, we can worry about what to do with it tomorrow."

"Very well. Perhaps Hutai will be at home then."

"Perhaps," Conan said. But he had a feeling no one would ever see Hutai again—not alive, anyway. "But let us forget about the man for now. We have hours ahead of us before we must meet Naerys and Anot. How would you like to spend them? Drinking? Gambling? Fighting?"

Valja laughed. "Yes to all three! But first, I think we should take advantage of the fact that our pallet does not yet have a lumpy gold statue inside it."

Conan grinned and slipped an arm around her narrow waist. "I like the way you think, Valja of Zamora!"

Later that day, as Conan and Valja, relaxed and happy, placed wagers on an arm-wrestling competition in the One-Eyed Owl, Anot sat cross-legged on the sward outside the Temple of Mitra, eyes closed and meditating, while Naerys prayed to her god for strength and guidance inside. Naerys had invited Anot to accompany her into the temple, but the shaman had politely declined. While Naerys had never shown any sign of intolerance toward religions that were not hers, some followers of Mitra persecuted those who adhered to other faiths and Anot did not feel welcome in their place of worship. Many religions were practiced in the southern kingdom of Kush, where her people lived, with the worship of one's ancestors being most common. Unfortunately, Set—known as Damballah in the southern lands—was revered by many in Kush, including her own tribe, known as the People of the Red Harvest.

She had been raised to worship the Old Serpent, and as a child regularly witnessed the sacrifice of outsiders to the dread demon-god. She had cheered and clapped along with the others as priests plunged sharp stone blades into the chests of nonbelievers and tore their still-beating hearts from their bodies and held them up for all to see. She had marveled at the great black snakes that slithered forth from the jungle to devour those hearts and then sway hypnotically, as if dancing to silent, dark music. At times, parents overcome with religious fervor would snatch up one of their children and rush forward to offer it to the serpents, who swallowed the little ones with ease, especially the infants. Anot had lived in fear that her parents would offer her to the giant snakes one night, but they never did. Instead, they had sacrificed her older brother, Onor, to Damballah's avatars, and she had watched in horror as Onor slid down one of the great serpents' throats, his muffled screams still audible from inside the monster for several moments before finally dying away.

She would never forget the look of adoration on her parents' faces. Anot's mother had placed a hand on her shoulder and smiled down at her. *Now your brother will be one with Damballah for all time. Is it not wonderful?*

Then her father smiled. *Perhaps it shall be your turn soon*, he said. *I wish my parents had loved me enough to give me such a great gift.*

I feel this way, too, Mother said. *And one day, if you are fortunate, you may be able to grant this blessing to a child of your own.*

Why they could not have offered themselves to the serpents instead of Onor, she did not know. She hated her parents that night, almost as much as she hated Damballah, and when the first rays of dawn touched the eastern sky, she stole out of their hut and ran from her village as fast as her small legs could carry her. Two days later, thirsty, hungry, and exhausted, she stumbled into the village of a neighboring tribe who called themselves the Landkeepers. She was taken in by a couple who had recently lost their only child to a deadly fever. It did not take her long to regard them as her new mother and father.

Her adoptive tribe lived in harmony with the natural world. Wind, rain, earth, plants, animals, insects, birds—the Landkeepers revered them all, cared for them all, loved them all, and in return the natural world spoke to Anot's new people, revealing secrets, giving warnings, telling fortunes, and granting boons. The tribe despised Damballah and her worshippers, for the false god was an ancient creature from the Outer Reaches, a foul, unnatural thing whose sole desire was the eradication of all life on the planet. No matter what name humans called it—Damballah, Yig, Jörmungandr, Set—it was the same vile pestilence, an evil to be fought wherever it reared its dark, scaly head. But no one in Anot's new tribe hated Damballah as much as she did, for she had seen what sacrifices the monster demanded from her worshippers.

When she reached her fourteenth year, she led a party of Landkeeper warriors against the People of the Red Harvest. They executed every adult who would not renounce the worship of Damballah, including Anot's parents, whom she beheaded herself. All children were spared, as were the men and women who turned away from the Old Serpent, and they were taken to the Landkeepers to be taught their ways. Some adults had lied, of course, and they fled in the night or attempted to assassinate Anot for her betrayal. All failed. All paid the ultimate price. The remaining survivors of the People of the Red Harvest were successfully assimilated into the Landkeepers and were happier than they ever had been with their original tribe.

One night, when Anot lay in her hut, drifting off to sleep, the wind spoke to her.

The Serpent's shadow lies heavily across much of the world. You can help change this.

Half believing she was dreaming, she fell asleep. But when she woke in the morning, she knew the wind had truly spoken to her. It had not demanded she leave her tribe to fight the power of Set wherever it might manifest itself; it had only pointed out that she was capable of helping. But once she knew this, she could not in good conscience stay with the Landkeepers any longer. She said goodbye to her adoptive parents with many a tear shed on all their parts, and then set off.

For nearly ten years, she walked across the face of the world alone, combating the forces of Set wherever she found them. Then, one day, on the northern border between Shem and Koth, the wind had spoken to her again.

Go to Eruk and seek out a woman who is a priest of Mitra. You have much in common.

Anot did as the wind bade, and she was not surprised when she found Naerys drinking alone in a tavern. She sat down at the woman's table, and the two talked. Anot soon discovered the wind had been right. She and Naerys shared an all-consuming hatred of Set rooted in very similar childhood traumas. Before the sun set that day, they had decided to become partners in the crusade against Set, and they had been together ever since.

It had been a satisfying partnership, in all ways, and in their time they had slain many minions of Set—cultists, slavers, priests, sorcerers, bandits, murderers—and never once had Anot been afraid. But she was scared now. Tonight, they were going to face Uzzeran, the sorcerer that Naerys had spent half her lifetime seeking. By all accounts, the Stygian was more skilled at magic than any other sorcerer they had ever fought, and the wind had told Anot that the two of them stood no chance against him alone. They needed help, and thus Naerys had come up with her scheme to find allies and put them to the test. Anot had been skeptical of her plan, but she had to admit that Conan and Valja seemed well suited for the task, despite their youth—not that she and Naerys were that much older—and she felt good about their chances for success tonight. While the thought of battling Uzzeran frightened her, she was more scared that, once Naerys had achieved her long-sought goal of slaying the sorcerer, she would feel her quest for vengeance was fulfilled and decide her time as a hunter of Setites had come to an end. Anot did not know if she could ever abandon the fight against the Old Serpent and her servants, but she also did not know how she could live without Naerys.

She was wasting her time with all this woolgathering. She needed to calm herself so she could prepare her mind and spirit for whatever was to come this night. She breathed in for a ten count, held it the same length of time, then let it out slowly. She did this ten times, and she began to feel the grass beneath her stir gently, felt the wind caress the skin of her face and hands.

Better, she thought.

She continued breathing deeply and listened to the wind.

Beneath the ruins of the Elephant Tower, in a chamber below ground that had mostly escaped destruction when the edifice collapsed, Shengis watched as his master worked.

The floor, walls, and ceiling were fashioned from hewn stone and the chamber was furnished with tables, shelves, and cabinets that Shengis had salvaged from the ruins and, when necessary, repaired. He had been surprised how many items remained amidst the tower's mass of shattered stone and splintered beams here in the vaunted City of Thieves. Arenjun's larceny-minded citizenry wanted nothing to do with the ruins. Given the reputation of the sorcerer-priest who had supposedly raised the tower in a single night, Shengis understood why ordinary men and women avoided the area, but even the city's other sorcerers behaved as if the ruins were under a curse so powerful they would not risk coming close. Uzzeran had experienced no such reluctance, but then Set herself had directed him to come here to complete his work, and why would their god lead them astray?

The shelves held books bound in human skin still soft and warm to the touch after centuries, scrolls that made your eyes bleed if you looked upon their contents too long, and stone tablets upon which were engraved words in languages that predated life on Earth. The tables were covered with clay bowls and jars filled with foul-smelling powders and chemicals along with scattered bones—some human, some from things that were almost human—and piles of dry, shed snakeskin. Braziers in which green fire burned lit the chamber, the flames smokeless and cold as ice, illuminating a pair of tables arranged near each other in the middle of the chamber.

Upon one of the tables lay a naked man, a slave Shengis had purchased for his master. He was a Pict—short, stocky, dark-skinned, with a tangle of wild black hair—and his hands and feet were bound tight with leather thongs while his mouth was gagged with a cloth tied around the back of his head. His eyes were wide with terror, yet he did not move, nor did he make a sound. Uzzeran had given him a potion derived from the same venom that coated Shengis' dagger, diluted enough so it would not stop his heart but still strong enough to paralyze him and keep him docile.

Kekk lay on the table next to the Pict, in his natural form. Like his companion, the Serpent Man was naked, but his hands and feet were unbound and no gag silenced him. Snake venom of any sort had no effect on his kind, but none was needed to keep the creature silent and compliant.

Between the two tables sat a four-foot-tall stone column atop which lay a black jewel the size of a man's fist. A layer of shadow periodically rippled across its surface like waves of ebon water, and when this happened sudden nausea gripped Shengis and he quickly looked away until his discomfort subsided. Ordinary mortals such as himself were not meant to gaze upon the Eye of Set for long.

He had done his best to clean the room after the last Serpent Man Uzzeran had used in his experiment had burst apart like a rotten melon, but he still saw a few bloodstains here and there, along with the occasional bit of green-scaled flesh. Uzzeran had not complained about his servant's work, though Shengis didn't know if that was because his master thought he had done a creditable enough job or if Uzzeran had simply been too preoccupied with his preparations for the rite that he hadn't noticed. Most likely the latter, Shengis thought.

Uzzeran leaned over the Pict, chanting in low tones as he carved runes into the man's flesh with a thin, sharp dagger. Tears of agony streamed from the man's eyes, but no sound emerged from his throat. Rivulets of blood trickled from his wounds, pooled on the table around him, and joined the numerous dark stains already there. Shengis loved watching his master work. Uzzeran's slender hand was as deft as it was steady, and he formed the runes with the ease and confidence of long practice.

Uzzeran was a member of Stygia's ruling class, and his appearance was common to those of his station—tall, thin, black-haired, with sharp, bronze-skinned features. He was in his early forties and wore a simple dark gray robe and sandals. *Considering the sort of messes a sorcerer makes, there is no point in donning finery,* he'd once told Shengis.

The Pict's eyes bulged suddenly, and the cords of his neck drew tight. Despite the venom-induced paralysis, his back arched, then his body went limp and he fell back onto the table, eyes wide and unblinking.

"Set's sacred coils!" Uzzeran's features twisted with anger and he hurled the blood-slick blade to the ground. He slammed a fist onto the dead man's chest, then turned away from the corpse in disgust. "The weakling's pain and fear exacerbated the effects of the venom, and his heart gave out." He turned to Shengis and spoke bitterly. "Why did you bring me such a useless specimen?"

"Master, I did the best I—"

Uzzeran cut him off with a sharp gesture. "Take him away and bring me another. Time is against us, Shengis, and we must make haste if we are to have any hope of success."

"Of course, master."

There was a small four-wheeled cart in the corridor just outside the room, and Shengis went to it, gripped the rope attached to its front, and pulled it inside. He took it to the table where the dead Pict lay and, grunting from the effort, maneuvered the man onto its flat surface, then took hold of the rope once more and pulled the cart into the corridor. As he stepped out of the room, he glanced back over his shoulder and saw Uzzeran pull one of his thick books from a shelf, place it on a table, open it, and start reading, murmuring softly to himself in a language so ancient only the most educated sorcerers knew of its existence.

Feeling bad for his master, Shengis faced forward and continued down the corridor.

Coldfire braziers had been placed at thirty-foot intervals, providing more than enough light for Shengis to see as he made his way down the long hall. The stone was cracked in numerous places, and chunks—some as small as pebbles, others as large as a man's head—had broken free from the walls and ceiling and lay on the floor. Shengis had moved most of them aside to clear a path for the cart, but there were always new ones. The structural instability was a result of the tower's collapse, and while Uzzeran assured him that the rooms they used were absolutely safe, Shengis was never comfortable down here. He feared the ceiling would break apart and slabs of rock would fall and crush him. This, of course, had never happened, at least not yet—but it would only need to happen once.

But there was more to his uneasiness than the ruins' instability. The atmosphere within the tower's intact chambers felt charged, like the air before a violent lightning storm, and at times his skin tingled, almost to the point of pain. Now and again he heard voices, too, whispering in strange, sinister tongues, each syllable stabbing into his ears like cold, sharp steel. Fearing he was going mad, he had told Uzzeran about these sensations. His master, as usual, was not sympathetic. *Has nothing I have tried to teach you over the years stayed with you? We came to these ruins because the Tower of the Elephant was a powerful magical construct. A residue of that power still exists in its stone, and I draw upon it to strengthen my own spells. Hopefully, this power will give us the edge we need for success.*

When Shengis had asked his master how he had learned of the tower ruins' existence, he had said, *Mother Set told me.* He had explained no further.

Shengis knew not how much mystic power remained in the

tower ruins, but it had been little help to Uzzeran so far. Perhaps tonight would be different.

He stopped the cart before an open doorway through which a scent like old leather emanated from the room beyond, mingled with the rank odor of meat on the verge of spoiling. He had still not grown used to the smell, and Set willing, he never would.

He lifted the Pict's body off the cart, slung it over his shoulder—marveling at how such a short man could be so heavy—and carried the corpse into the room, grateful that Uzzeran had not placed one of his braziers in here. As it was, green light from the hallway filtered in, and while it was dim inside the room, Shengis could still see more than he would have liked. The shadowy forms of dead bodies lay on the floor—eleven of them at last count, which meant the Pict would make an even dozen. All of the corpses—six humans and five Serpent Men, all in various states of decomposition—were naked with runes carved into their flesh: the results of Uzzeran's failed experiments. They had died just as the Pict had, their hearts unable to withstand the strain of the mystic power that flooded their systems. Some of the bodies had been here for weeks, but Uzzeran had cast a spell to slow their rotting, and thus all remained more or less intact.

Corpses were not the only things the chamber contained, though. Long, thick, sinuous shapes were draped over the bodies, dozens of them, and while Shengis was unable to make out the details of their bodies, he felt their inhuman eyes watching him with cold indifference. He shuddered, and his face immediately burned with shame. He was a follower of Set. Snakes were sacred in his religion. They were to be admired, respected, revered, loved—and yet he felt uneasy around the creatures and had done so his entire life. While he had always managed to hide it well—even Uzzeran was unaware of his secret—he feared that Set's children knew the truth and, through them, so did their mother.

"I have brought another for you," he said, fighting to keep

his voice steady. He leaned forward and allowed the Pict's corpse to slide off his shoulder and fall to the stone floor with a dull, meaty thud. An instant later, the shadowy forms of serpents began undulating toward the body, and Shengis turned and hurried out of the room. He knew what would come next and he did not want to watch the serpents remove the Pict's eyes.

He shuddered a second time, bent to pick up the rope, and continued pulling the cart down the corridor, walking significantly faster than he had before. He came to a branching point and went right. The left corridor led to nothing but a mass of rubble deposited when the tower collapsed, but the right led to a second chamber, a brazier burning green next to the open doorway. Shengis left the cart in the hall and stepped inside. The proximity of the coldfire brazier meant that he could see quite well in here, but there was nothing to fear in the room—no corpses, no serpents. The smell was even worse, though for a different reason.

There were four metal cages in the room, each large enough to hold a human being, assuming they sat and hugged their knees to their chest. Two of the cages were empty, one having previously contained the Pict and the other the Hyrkanian woman who had been part of the previous night's experiment. Her bloodless corpse now lay in the chamber with the other bodies… and the serpents.

The other two cages were still occupied, one by a boy from Keshan and the other by an older Vendhyan woman. Both were naked, unwashed, and caked with their own filth, hence the smell. Whichever one he chose, Shengis would have to clean him or her before taking them to Uzzeran's work chamber. Neither said anything to him. The woman sat with her head down, chin to her chest, and Shengis was not certain she was aware of his presence. The boy was livelier, though, and now gripped the bars of his cage, staring at Shengis with hate blazing in his eyes.

Which one, which one...? The woman would be easier to manage, but while both were thin and weak from malnourishment, the boy remained the stronger of the two. Perhaps strong enough to put up a fight. But he had a better chance of surviving the preparations for tonight than the woman did.

His choice made, from his tunic pocket Shengis removed a small wooden tube containing a dart whose tip was coated with Uzzeran's snake-venom sedative—not too much, just enough to make the recipient drowsy for the trip to see the master. He stepped forward until he stood less than a foot away from the boy, then raised the tube to his mouth and blew a hard puff of air. The dart flew between two bars and lodged in the boy's left shoulder. He hissed with pain, yanked out the dart, and threw it back at Shengis, cursing loudly in his native tongue. The dart missed Shengis—not that it would have penetrated his skin at such low speed—and landed on the floor.

Despite the boy's show of defiance, he quickly succumbed to the drug. His eyes closed and he slumped against the side of his cage, breathing slowly but steadily. Shengis felt no pity as he unlocked the cage, carried the unconscious boy into the hall, and placed him on the cart. Yes, it was regrettable that so many had to die in order for his master to achieve his ultimate goal, but if Uzzeran did not succeed, the entire world would be in peril. What were a few lives when compared with all those who had lived throughout the known world and beyond?

So long as it is not my life that is sacrificed, what do I care?

He chuckled as he turned the cart around and began pulling it back the way he had come.

Conan and Valja met Naerys and Anot after sunset in front of the One-Eyed Owl. It had not been dark for long, and the night denizens of the Maul had yet to emerge from wherever they holed up during the daylight hours. Conan was disappointed. He could have used a good fight or two to limber up before they reached Uzzeran's lair. Maybe he could start one along the way.

Valja wore her thief's cloak and leather armor vest and had brought a new rope to replace the one they had lost the previous night. She had also brought a half dozen new throwing knives, and a set of new lockpicks hung from her belt in a small leather bag. The blades were not from Hutai, who still had not returned to his home, and Conan was beginning to think that the fence had been slain by an unsatisfied customer, or perhaps taken by one of the many two-legged predators that stalked the night streets of the Maul.

Conan had his broadsword and a dagger, as well as his own leather armor vest, breeks, and boots. He needed nothing else, and he could have done without the vest; the damn thing itched. Plus, it was too hot. Every place he had visited since leaving Cimmeria felt too warm to his northern-bred body, and he would have been most comfortable walking around in nothing but a loincloth much of the time. Valja wouldn't allow it, though. *You draw enough attention clothed. You would draw a great deal more if you went about nearly naked.*

Thieves, of course, were not supposed to draw attention to themselves. He thought it a foolish rule, if a necessary one, and he complied with it mostly to please Valja. Speed was one of a Cimmerians' greatest weapons, and every ounce of unneeded clothing or equipment only slowed you down and put your life—and, more importantly, your victory—at risk.

Anot carried no weapons, at least none Conan could see, but she had her enchantments as well as her own leather bag dangling from her belt. He assumed it held items to aid in her spellcasting, but he was not about to ask her. In general, it was useful to know what weapons your allies carried before heading into a battle, especially if they died and you needed a replacement weapon. But Conan wanted nothing to do with Anot's spell bag, and it was hardly as if he could—or would—use the components himself.

Naerys wore the same outfit and carried the same weapons as she had last evening: leather armor, metal helmet, dagger, and flail.

Conan would have been more comfortable if they'd had another strong fighter or two among them, but there was no use wishing for what you did not have. Given the harsh environment of their homeland, Cimmerians learned early on to work with what they could get.

"Are we all ready?" Naerys asked. The Ophirian sounded calm, but Conan detected an undercurrent of excitement in her voice. She was going after the sorcerer who had used her like an animal in his foul experiments. If Conan had been in her place, he would have been excited, too. Vengeance was sweet, but vengeance delayed was even sweeter.

He held out a hand that was already well calloused despite his youth. "Our payment?"

Naerys had promised to give them half their fee up front and the other half after Uzzeran was dead. It was a standard arrangement, but Conan would not take a single step from this place until he had the coins in hand.

"Of course," Naerys said, then untied a leather purse from her belt and tossed it to Conan. There was no clinking of metal when the bag hit his hand and, fearing Naerys might be playing some kind of trick, he opened the purse and rooted around inside. The coins were there but were wrapped in layers of cloth, so many that the entire purse was stuffed full. He looked at Naerys, puzzled.

"It is so the coins do not make noise and alert Uzzeran as we attempt to take him by surprise," the priestess of Mitra said.

That was a good idea. He would have to remember that.

He closed the purse and tossed it to Valja, who made it disappear somewhere on her person as swiftly as she could make her knives appear in her hands. Conan grinned at the surprise on Naerys' and Anot's faces. Valja wielded her own sort of magic, a kind Conan could admire.

"Satisfied?" Naerys asked.

Conan and Valja nodded.

"Excellent!" The priestess turned to Anot. "What do the elements say about our fortunes this night?"

Anot cocked her head as if listening closely to a sound only she could hear, then crouched down and stuck the tips of her fingers in the muddy ground. Again she listened, then straightened and shook her hand vigorously to get the muck off of it. "They... predict success."

Conan detected uncertainty in the shaman's tone, as if the elemental spirits had told her more but she did not wish to speak of it.

Naerys did not seem to notice. "A good omen," she said. "I spent the day praying to Mitra, and I believe he has blessed our endeavor."

Conan had only a simple prayer for his god, one of the few he ever said. It was likely Crom would ignore it, but he spoke it in his mind anyway.

Crom, let my steel taste hot blood this night.

They had discussed strategy in the One-Eyed Owl the previous evening. Conan had been surprised to learn Uzzeran's lair was located beneath the ruins of the Tower of the Elephant, and Anot had looked amused at his reaction. *I do believe our young warrior is familiar with the site*, she had said.

Conan had kept his expression carefully neutral at that, which seemed to further amuse the shaman. When he asked her how she and Naerys knew for certain that Uzzeran laired in the ruins, Anot said, *A rat told me.* At first, Conan thought she was jesting, but after a moment passed, he realized she was being serious. *He also told me of a way we can enter that part of the ruins—a passage that he believes neither Uzzeran nor his servant are aware of.*

Believes? Valja said.

Anot shrugged. *The rat does not watch the sorcerer all the time. He has a mate and little ones to feed.*

When they reached this entrance, Anot would check for magical defenses and attempt to counter any she found. After this, Conan and Valja would examine the entrance for defenses of a physical nature. Well, Valja would. Conan had little experience at that task, and even less patience for it. If Valja found traps, she would disarm them. The four of them would then enter the ruins and make their way carefully to the heart of Uzzeran's lair, alert for whatever threats they might encounter.

It is still the solstice, Naerys had said. *A time when great feats of sorcery are possible. If we are fortunate, Uzzeran will be too caught up in spellcasting to be aware of our arrival. When we find him, do not hesitate to attack. Although I admit I am looking forward to his death with great anticipation, my hand does not need to be the one that ends his life. He is an extremely dangerous opponent and must be slain as swiftly as possible by whatever means necessary.*

Conan had smiled grimly at that. It was a strategy of which he strongly approved.

Uzzeran gazed upon the boy lying on the table, carefully examining the runes he'd carved into the youth's naked flesh by the green light of coldfire. This was the third time the sorcerer had gone over his work, searching for the slightest flaw. He could sense the power of the solstice already beginning to wane, and if this attempt failed there could not be another for an entire year.

The boy was much stronger than his last subject, and he had endured the agony Uzzeran had inflicted upon him and survived. More than that, his body, while somewhat weakened, remained strong. He would need that strength for what was to come.

The sorcerer felt no pity for the boy. The peoples of the far south, like those of the far north, were barely human savages, little more than animals—but then, that was true of all who were not Stygian. *Higher-caste* Stygian, that is. Shengis was of the lowest caste, and thus only slightly more human than this boy.

Uzzeran had been working toward this moment for decades. He'd long ago lost count of how many people he had experimented on, how many had died, and how many had been... changed.

And after years of slow, incremental progress with little to show for it, Uzzeran had begun to lose faith in his ability to carry out the dread mother's plan.

Six months earlier, he had decided to slay himself and offer his life as a sacrifice to Set in the hope that the Great Dark Serpent would forgive him for his failures. So, one night in his home in Khemi, he prepared a potion for himself, waited for Shengis to go to sleep in the servants' quarters so he could not interfere, then drank the potion, lay down on his fine, soft bed, closed his eyes, and waited for death to take him.

But Death did not come.

Set did.

As if in a dream, Uzzeran found himself floating in a starless black void. Although there was no obvious source of light in this place, when he waved his hands in front of his eyes, he could still see them. He seemed to be able to breathe, too, but he had no idea where the air had come from—an illusion, perhaps? Was this a realm of the spirit, a place where he only seemed to have substance and solidity? He had read of such dimensions while studying with the sorcerers of the Black Ring in his youth, but he had never imagined he would ever actually experience one. Were there other beings here, ones he could not see, and which in turn could not see him?

He called out into the darkness: "Hello! Can anyone hear me?"

He waited, listened, heart pounding with equal amounts of excitement and fear. And just when he thought he would not receive a reply, he heard a voice, one so loud it filled the entire shadow realm, so sibilant that its words sounded more like the hissing of a thousand snakes—a thousand times a thousand.

I gave you a task. Why do you seek to abandon it?

He instantly recognized the voice, for he had heard it once before. It was the voice of his god. It was Set.

Twin red suns flared to life an unknowable distance away

but which Uzzeran sensed was farther than any human could ever hope to calculate. The suns remained motionless for several moments, but then they began to sway slowly back and forth in unison, and with each swing, they appeared to grow a little larger. He realized then that they were not suns at all but rather the eyes of his god, and the darkness all around him was the coils of Set. This place, this entire universe, *was* Set, and Uzzeran had never felt so small, so insignificant, so unworthy of existing. But even then, in the midst of terror greater than any emotion he had ever known, he also experienced a deep sense of wonder and joy. He was a sorcerer, and while sorcerers sought power, as much as they could possibly obtain in one lifetime, the pathway to that power was through learning, and thus a sorcerer's thirst for knowledge was unquenchable.

Uzzeran wanted to answer his god's question, but he could not make himself speak. In that moment, he was not certain he could even recall how to form words.

Do you remember when I first came to you?

How could Uzzeran ever forget? He had been studying in one of the Black Ring's libraries late one night, and when he had opened an ancient volume on transformation magic, a tiny black snake had slithered out from between the pages. It had raised its small head to look at him, its red eyes miniature versions of the two suns now blazing against the vast darkness.

What did I show you?

The small serpent had not spoken with words. Instead, it had reached out to Uzzeran's mind and directly implanted images there.

"You showed me a realm beyond space and time, where the laws of nature as humans know them do not exist. Unimaginably powerful entities dwell there, beings as far beyond humans as humans are beyond the simple life forms that dwell within a single drop of water. These beings are ancient, predating the dimension where humans dwell, predating all existence of any kind anywhere, even the so-called gods that humanity so foolishly reveres. You are one of these Great Old Ones—the greatest of them all."

I do not need your flattery, worm!

Despite Set's apparent anger at his words, Uzzeran could sense that he was nevertheless pleased.

Continue.

"Some of the Great Old Ones are indifferent to the presence of others, some build alliances—if only temporary ones—while others seek to dominate and destroy the rest until only they remain. One such Ancient is called The Woeful Eye, and his gaze has settled upon your world."

Exactly why such a being would care about what to him surely must be nothing more than a meaningless speck in the cosmos, Uzzeran wasn't entirely clear on. Set had attempted to show him, but the concepts were beyond his limited human understanding, even with all the sorcerous knowledge he had acquired. But he understood one thing quite well: The Woeful Eye could not have Earth. Earth belonged to Set.

And what did I tell you of your destiny?

"You said that The Woeful Eye will one day succeed in returning to Earth, and that the only way he will be stopped is by a superior race created from the fusion of humans and Serpent Men—a race created by me." What this race of Serpent Lords, as Uzzeran thought of them, could do against an entity as powerful as The Woeful Eye, Uzzeran did not know. He was also unaware why Set had chosen him for this great honor.

If you understand the importance of all these things, why do you seek death?

Uzzeran felt a deep sense of shame upon hearing this question. "Because I have spent years trying to do your will, Great Mother, but all I have done is fail you."

Do you question my wisdom in choosing you?

"I would never question you!" Uzzeran said, horrified. "But… it is taking so *long*."

You are mortal. The entire length of your species' existence is less than the blink of an eye to my kind. But take heart. You shall soon receive assistance.

Set went on to detail what that assistance would be. First, she told Uzzeran that a tower infused with great magic would soon fall in the Zamorian city of Arenjun. The sorcerer could tap into that power to help him accomplish his task. Then Set said another of her worshippers—a woman who lived in a stronghold located in the mountains to the east of Arenjun—had come into possession of an ancient mystic artifact that would further help Uzzeran draw upon the power held within the tower ruins, and that she would deliver this artifact to him once he was in Arenjun.

Uzzeran turned his attention away from the paralyzed boy—the runes cut into his flesh were, of course, perfect—and looked upon the ebon majesty of the Eye of Set. He smiled.

The Great Serpent provides.

The City Watch maintained a strong presence in the Temple District following the previous night's events, and Anot had to use her magic to cloak their party. The officers stayed well away from the tower ruins, however, for rumor had it that the spirit of Yara lingered there and would slay anyone who came near. Conan wasn't concerned; he had witnessed Yara being drawn into the fabled gem known as the Heart of the Elephant, where he was trapped with the spirit of a vengeful Yag-Kosha. Conan doubted the alien entity would allow Yara to die for some time, if ever. More likely the elephant-headed god would punish the priest until the end of eternity, and perhaps beyond.

This was Conan's first time back since the night when the tower fell, and his hackles rose when he saw the massive mound of stone and timber glowing eerily in the moonlight. Anot had said the rubble still contained a measure of magic, *like a sound that echoes for a time before finally fading away.* Conan wondered how long this sound would echo. Years? Decades? Centuries? Would magic remain in the ruins even after the rest of Arenjun had long fallen away to dust around them? He thought it possible.

He did not relish the idea of entering the ruins, and if he had been on his own, he might have turned around, headed for the nearest tavern, and drank until he forgot about this place. But he had made a bargain with Naerys, and Cimmerians always honored their word—which was why they were so cautious about giving it. Nothing would make him back out now. Besides, he did not want to lose face in front of Valja, who not only showed no sign of fear, but, from the wide grin on her face, was excited by the adventure that lay ahead.

Anot led the way, and they walked around the ruins until she signaled them to halt. She then pointed to an opening between two large chunks of stone and said, "Here."

Conan examined the narrow space with a critical eye. He thought he would be able to squeeze through, but not without losing some skin in the process.

"Is it spell-warded?" Naerys asked in a whisper.

Anot placed her hand on the stone and held it there for several moments. Finally, she whispered back, "It is not," then lowered her hand.

"Valja?" Naerys said.

Valja turned to Conan and also spoke in a whisper. "Your night vision is like a panther's. Come help me."

They stepped toward the entrance. Valja ran the tips of her fingers lightly across the stone, sometimes pausing at a section for a few seconds before moving on. Conan gazed intently at the stone, eyes sweeping back and forth, searching for anything that looked amiss.

When Valja had finished, she looked at Conan. "See anything?"

The barbarian shook his head.

"And I felt nothing," Valja said, then looked at Anot and grinned. "It appears your rat friend was right."

"Animals rarely lie," the shaman said. "It is not in their nature. It is humans who bend and twist truth for their own advantage."

Conan had been around animals both wild and domesticated during his entire childhood in Cimmeria, and he could attest to Anot's words. Animals were what they were and did what they did, without hesitation or guilt. He was the same way.

"Did you bring torches?" Valja asked. "We shall need them once inside."

Anot's only response was to smile. She made an intricate series of gestures with her fingers and a swarm of small insects descended from the sky. Conan raised a hand to swat at them, but Anot caught his wrist and held it in a surprisingly firm grip. He could break free easily, of course, but he was impressed by the woman's strength.

"Watch," Anot said softly.

Conan did so. The insects spread out to form a cloud around the four of them, and then their abdomens began to blink with greenish-yellow light.

"Fireflies," he said in a rough whisper. "But even a group of them cannot make enough light to guide us through the ruins."

Anot spoke a word in a language unfamiliar to Conan, and the insects' abdomens began to glow steadily and with greater intensity. After a few seconds, they glowed so strongly that it hurt his eyes to look directly at them for too long. He still did not trust magic, but at least this spell was a useful one.

"We must enter quickly," Naerys said, "before the light draws the City Watch's attention."

"I will go first," Conan said. He removed his broadsword and scabbard from his back and handed them to Valja. "Hand me my weapon once I am inside. I will not fit through the opening while wearing it."

"But what if there is something on the other side that immediately attacks you?" she asked.

Conan shrugged. "If I cannot slay it with my bare hands, I shall use my dagger."

He stepped toward the narrow entrance and began wriggling his way through.

The three women watched Conan crawl into the ruins of a structure that had been created by a being from another world. None of them noticed the small black snake coiled in the grass ten feet away, observing them with cold, inhuman eyes—

—and the snake was so intent upon watching the women that it did not see the overlarge white spider crouched atop a stone slab high on the tower's debris pile, watching *it*.

Shengis stood in the doorway of Uzzeran's work chamber, praying as his master began the spell: *Please, Set, most powerful and feared of all gods, let it work this time…*

The sorcerer stood between the two tables, hands pressed against the Eye of Set, rapidly speaking words in a soft, sibilant language that sounded like a snake hissing. Beads of sweat dotted his brow and his muscles trembled, testifying to the great effort required to cast the spell. Both the Keshan youth and the Serpent Man were awake and aware, the boy paralyzed thanks to the diluted snake venom Uzzeran had given him. The Serpent Man was immune to all snake venom, but the power of the Snare prevented him from moving. Deep runes like the ones covering the boy's flesh had been carved into Kekk's scaly hide, and dark blood flowed from the marks.

Uzzeran's voice grew louder as he continued to chant, and Shengis felt the hair on the back of his neck stand up. A low humming came from the walls and ceiling, and he could feel the floor vibrate beneath his feet. Uzzeran was tapping into the power contained within the tower ruins and using it to further fuel his spell. Two tendrils of what looked like solidified shadow emerged from the Eye, writhing and coiling as if alive, one arcing toward the boy and the other toward Kekk. They plunged through their foreheads and into their brains, merging with them on levels both physical and metaphysical.

Shengis held his breath. This had been the moment the previous night when the Serpent Man had burst open like a scale-covered cyst. Uzzeran's chanting grew even louder, the words flowing even faster from his mouth, as if he were pouring extra effort into the spell to prevent that outcome from repeating—and he succeeded! Kekk's body remained intact, and Uzzeran, looking visibly relieved, continued, his voice becoming steadier and more confident. Shengis fell to his knees, leaned forward, extended his arms, and touched his forehead to the floor's cold stone, prostrating himself before his god. *Thank you, Set! Thank you!*

After a moment, he got back on his feet and watched with mounting excitement as Kekk and the boy began to change. The spell was designed to create a hybrid of human and Serpent Man—a Serpent Lord—but instead of the two bodies combining, there was to be an exchange. The boy would receive reptilian qualities from Kekk while the Serpent Man would receive human qualities from the boy. If all went well, Uzzeran would succeed in creating two Serpent Lords, and from there he would go on to make many more, until there was an army of the creatures, and then… Well, Shengis wasn't clear on exactly what the Serpent Lords were supposed to do to stop The Woeful Eye's conquest of the planet, but he had faith that Set would make her plan clear in time.

Patches of scales began to appear on the boy's flesh, while swathes of human skin emerged on Kekk's body. Kekk's serpentine facial features softened while the boy's took on a reptilian aspect. The vibrations in the stone structure of the chamber became more pronounced as Uzzeran drew on more of the tower's mystic energy, and the floor began to shake violently as if the ruins were caught in an earthquake. Jars on the worktables fell over and spilled their contents, books tumbled off their shelves and thudded to the floor, and the humming sound became louder, to the point where it hurt Shengis' ears. He prayed that the spell would be completed before the vibrations caused the ceiling to collapse and brought the broken stone and timber above crashing down upon them.

Then Uzzeran's eyes flew wide open. "Intruders!" he shouted. "Deal with them, Shengis! I cannot afford to be distracted at this juncture!"

Shengis asked no questions. He turned and ran out of the chamber, determined to do whatever it took to safeguard his master and ensure the ritual's success.

Once Conan had made it through the opening, with only minor cuts and scrapes, he immediately drew his dagger, prepared to meet any threat that might confront him. Anot's fireflies followed, and by their light he saw that they stood within a short section of corridor that ended in stone steps leading down to a lower level. The corridor was empty, and he sensed no danger, but when Valja passed his broadsword through the opening to him, he quickly sheathed his dagger, took the scabbard, strapped it to his back, and drew the weapon. Now that he held strong steel in his hand, he moved away from the opening to make room for the others to enter and turned to face the steps, standing guard in case anyone or anything—human, animal, or unnatural creature—should come up from the lower level to attack.

Valja entered next, followed by Anot and then Naerys. With a gesture from Anot, the fireflies rose to the ceiling and spread out, providing illumination without getting in the humans' way.

Valja drew a pair of throwing knives and Naerys gripped her flail. Anot possessed no weapons—at least, no physical ones. She pointed at the stairs and several fireflies streaked toward them, their light dimming and fading away as they flew down to the lower level.

"I sent them forward as scouts," Anot whispered. "They shall remain dark as they search through the ruins, and they shall return to tell us what they found."

Conan nodded his approval. It was an effective strategy, but he did not intend to wait around for the insects to come back.

"We should follow them," he said. "Can you make the others dim their light? The brighter they are, the more likely someone will see us coming."

Anot glanced at the fireflies and their light dimmed to half its original intensity. Conan thought it was still too bright, but his night vision was stronger than most, so he decided this level of illumination would do well enough.

He looked at Valja. "Ready?"

She grinned and gave him a quick kiss. "Always."

He returned her smile, and they started toward the stairs, Naerys and Anot following behind.

Shengis stood in the doorway of the chamber where the corpses of Uzzeran's test subjects were gathered, the large black serpents lying coiled around and on top of the bodies. The snakes had not stirred when he'd arrived, but he could feel their attention focused on him.

"There are intruders. The master commands you to deal with them."

The serpents moved rapidly for creatures of their size, slithering into the corpses' open mouths and squeezing through empty eye sockets. When the last serpent's tail-tip had disappeared, all of the corpses abruptly sat up and rose to their feet. Shengis knew he was witnessing a miracle of Set, channeled through the arcane arts of his master, but he felt a wave of intense revulsion as the dead things shuffled toward him. He quickly stepped back as the eyeless corpses of five Serpent Men and six humans came out into the hall and stood motionless, awaiting further orders. Uzzeran had not said where the intruders had gained access to the undamaged section of the ruins, so he did not know precisely where to send the revenants.

"Six of you go this way," Shengis said, pointing to the left, then gestured to the right. "Five of you go that way. Slay the intruders on sight."

The creatures regarded him with their eyeless, expressionless faces.

"Er, I mean, slay them the instant you encounter them. Now go!"

As he had directed, six went left and five went right, their ranks a mix of human and Serpent Man. The six on his left continued on, moving more swiftly than should have been possible for dead things, but the five on his right stopped after taking only a few steps. Shengis scowled.

"What are you doing? Did you not hear—"

Something small flew by his face—some kind of insect, he thought, but he did not immediately recognize the type.

The revenant closest to him—a human one—spun around. A serpent lunged from the corpse's mouth, snatched the insect out of the air, and then retreated as swiftly as it had emerged. A Serpent Man revenant turned its head, and a pair of snakes extended from its empty eye sockets. Each grabbed what Shengis presumed were more insects before returning to their host's hollowed-out skull. None of the serpents inside the other revenants emerged, and a moment later the five headed off, moving as swiftly as the others had.

Shengis was uncertain what had just transpired. He supposed it was possible the snakes had simply been hungry, but as he understood it the ebon serpents were no more natural creatures than the ambulatory corpses that housed them. Did such things even need to eat? He thrust the trivial thought aside. His master needed protection while he completed the creation of the Serpent Lords.

He drew his poison dagger and began running back toward Uzzeran's work chamber.

Conan examined the stone that surrounded them as he led the group through the ruins' lower level. The walls, floor, and ceiling were riven with cracks, some shallow and some deep, and chunks had broken loose in places and fallen to the ground. When he reached out and brushed his fingers against the wall, the stone was soft, and bits crumbled into dust at his touch.

"What do you think?" Valja asked him in a whisper.

"That if we are fortunate, we will be crushed to death swiftly when the ceiling falls on us." Hardly the death he had always envisioned for himself—that would be dying from a dozen mortal wounds on a blood-soaked battlefield after slaying several hundred well-armed and highly skilled opponents—but still preferrable to dying of old age.

"The stone will hold," Anot said.

"How do you know?" Naerys asked.

"It told me."

They fell silent after that, and as Conan's wilderness-bred senses remained alert for any danger, he thought how strange it felt to return to the tower—or at least its ruins—following his previous visit here. That occasion had been his first time meeting a god, as well as his first time slaying one. Yag-Kosha had claimed not to be divine, just a highly evolved being from another world. Rumor had it that he had used his vast powers to raise the tower in a single night, and if such a feat was not sufficient to make one worthy of the title *god*, Conan didn't know what was.

They reached a corner, turned, and Conan saw an unnatural green light glowing in the distance. He didn't like the color—it indicated the presence of dark magic—but it was nevertheless a sight most welcome to him, for it meant Uzzeran was likely nearby.

"Something is wrong," Anot said. "The firefly scouts I sent ahead should have returned to us by now, and the air feels charged with energy. The sensation grows stronger with each step we take."

"Uzzeran?" Naerys asked.

"Yes. I believe he is in the process of casting a spell. An extremely tricky one, given the amount of power he is using."

"Then we must make haste while he is distracted," the priestess said. "Will you be able to lead us to him without the fireflies' help?"

"The energy released by the sorcerer's spell will continue to build, like a sound that increases in strength until it becomes deafening," said Anot. "I should have no trouble following it to our quarry. For now, we should keep going straight."

Valja snorted. "As if there is any other way to—"

She broke off as the fireflies above them began swirling around in a frenzy, as if something had greatly disturbed them. An instant later, Conan felt a tingling on the back of his neck and knew the four of them were no longer alone in the corridor. He fell into a fighting stance.

"Make ready. Something is coming."

Anot knelt and pressed her right hand to the floor. "There are four—no, five of them." She frowned. "I am not sure what they are, but they possess auras of the darkest magic."

"Foul creations of Uzzeran," Naerys said. "May Mitra stand with us as we battle these unholy foes!"

Conan thought it could not hurt for Naerys to call on Mitra, but like all Cimmerians he was raised to rely on his own strength and instincts instead of any deity. Gods might help you or not—or even harm you—depending on their whims, but he would rather put his faith in himself and strong, sharp steel.

They heard the pounding of bare feet some distance ahead of them, and Anot sent half of the glowing fireflies ahead so the four companions could get a look at the approaching threat. The insects' light revealed creatures dredged up from the deepest, darkest pit in Hell. Naked men and women, their bodies covered with strange cuts, their eyes missing. There were inhuman creatures with them, unlike anything that Conan had ever seen—hideous two-legged reptilian things who were also covered with wounds and missing their eyes. A stench of putrefaction preceded the nightmarish quintet. Conan had smelled death many times in his short life, and with a stab of horror he realized that the creatures running toward them possessed no life.

Conan feared no human or animal, but these creatures aroused a primal fear deep within him. But he was Cimmerian, and he would stand his ground no matter what.

Stand? Like hell!

He bellowed a battle cry that was as much beast as man, then sprang forward like an enraged lion and ran toward the undead monsters, his blue eyes blazing with a lust to slay. Valja followed an instant later.

The fireflies Anot had sent to illuminate the creatures provided more than enough light for Conan to see, and as he drew near the undead things, one—a Pict—put on a burst of speed and outpaced the others. As the Pict came toward the young barbarian, he opened his mouth wide and thrust his head forward. Conan's sword arm moved before he was aware of it, and he swept the blade in front of the Pict's face just as something thick and dark emerged from the dead man's mouth. Conan registered a momentary impression of a black-scaled serpent's head, fangs bared and dripping poison, and then his blade decapitated the snake as easily as slicing through water. There was no blood, but as the snake-head fell, it evaporated like black smoke, and its headless body did the same.

"Crom!" Conan swore, half in amazement, half in disgust.

Distracted, he did not see at first the two serpents lance forward from the Pict's eye sockets, and by the time he had started to swing his sword at them, he knew he would not be quick enough to keep from being bitten.

Thuk! Thuk!

A throwing knife slammed into each serpent, penetrating its flesh and sinking into its host's eye socket, pinning it there. The ebon snakes thrashed and hissed for a couple seconds before turning into smoke and evaporating just as the first had. Conan thrust his sword into the Pict's naked chest, but while the wounds covering the man's body were crusted with dried blood—wounds that Conan could now see were in the shape of runes he did not recognize—no blood issued from where his sword struck. The Pict suddenly became dead weight, and as the man collapsed to the floor Conan pulled his sword free, the blade dry and unmarked by blood. It appeared he had slain the Pictish fiend after all.

There was no time to revel in his victory, though, for the other four creatures drew near. Their bodies were less fresh than the Pict's, and Conan assumed that was why they were slower. Valja moved past him, bent over, yanked her knives free from the Pict's empty eye sockets, and stepped to Conan's side.

"My thanks," he said.

She let out a bark of a laugh. "Thank me if we live through this."

Together, they moved forward to attack the remaining creatures.

Anot intended to join Conan and Valja, but Naerys clapped a hand on her shoulder to stop her. "Behind us!" the priestess shouted.

Anot turned back and saw a number of shadowy forms running toward them from the other direction—more of Uzzeran's undead monstrosities, some human, some reptilian, just like the ones Conan and Valja fought. The revenants did not seem intelligent enough to plan both a frontal and rear assault at the same time, and she thought it likely a matter of simple misfortune that the four of them found themselves beset on both sides.

She needed to do something to even the odds.

She crouched and slapped her palms over a pair of shallow fissures in the stone floor, then reached out with her mind, her awareness spreading rapidly through the floor, walls, and ceiling, exploring every flaw and imperfection with the speed of thought. When she had found what she sought—a crack in the ceiling two inches long and half an inch wide—she focused all her concentration on it, pictured reaching into the crack with phantom hands and pushing the sides apart with all her might. Pain exploded in her skull from the effort, but she refused to let up, pushing harder, *harder...*

There was a rumbling sound, followed by the grating rasp of stone against stone. Then, all at once, the ceiling above the attacking revenants collapsed, depositing several tons of rock and dust into the corridor. Both Anot and Naerys coughed as the dust cloud rolled over them, and the shaman rose shakily to her feet, wincing at the pounding in her head, and tried to catch her breath. Had she gotten all of the revenants? It had happened so fast, and she had been unable to—

A scaled, clawed hand thrust out of the dust cloud and grabbed her by the throat, cutting off her air. She took hold of the reptilian hand and frantically tried to pull it off her, but the creature it belonged to was unbelievably strong and she could not budge it. The inhuman thing took a step closer, and even though its eyes were missing and its hide was covered with blood-encrusted wounds, she recognized it as a Serpent Man. There had been rumors in Kush that her original tribe had dealt with such creatures from time to time, but until now she had never seen one herself. She found the creature beautiful in the way one might admire a well-adapted, highly efficient predator—as long as it wasn't stalking you for its dinner.

"Release her!"

Naerys swung her flail and lashed the Serpent Man's snake-like face. The leather thongs tore lines of flesh from his forehead and cheek, but the injuries did not bleed, nor did they seem to cause the creature any pain. Its grip on Anot's throat did not slacken, but Naerys *had* managed to get its attention. The revenant's other hand streaked toward the priestess, swift as a striking cobra, and fastened on her throat. Naerys dropped her flail and, like Anot before her, tried to break the Serpent Man's grip by clawing at his hand with both of her own, but in this she had no more success than Anot had. Darkness began to creep in from the edges of her vision, and the shaman feared she was going to suffocate, but just as she was about to lose consciousness, a pair of shadow snakes emerged from the Serpent Man's eye sockets. One flew toward Naerys and fastened its fangs into the tender flesh of her cheek while the other came at Anot and sank its teeth into the soft skin beneath her chin. Both women tried to scream, but all that came out were strangled wheezes.

Then the shadow snakes' venom began to do its work.

Anot stood alone on a vast, barren plain beneath a sullen gray sky. She could breathe again, but the air was thick and humid, like the jungles of her homeland after a heavy summer rain, although the ground was dry and rocky without the slightest hint of moisture. A huge black orb hung in the sky, and she sensed that in this strange place it served as a sun. The obscene thing was an unspeakable violation of the natural order, and she looked away, unable to bear the sight of it.

Where *was* this place? How had she gotten here? She tried to remember, but her thoughts were slow and sluggish, as if she had been…

Drugged!

She recalled the sharp pain of fangs penetrating her flesh, the burning sensation of venom as it had spread through her body. Everything came back to her in a rush—the tower ruins, the attack of the revenants, Conan and Valja running to meet them, another group coming at Naerys and her from behind, her causing the corridor's ceiling to fall upon the revenants, crushing them. But one must have escaped harm, for it had attacked both her and Naerys, shadow serpents emerging from its eyes sockets to bite them, injecting venom that caused hallucinations.

What you are seeing is very real, shaman.

She heard the voice inside her mind, but she sensed it came from somewhere near her feet. She looked down and saw a small black snake on the ground, looking up at her with crimson eyes.

This is what your world will become after I claim it for my own. You and your companions attempted to interfere with my plans, but you failed. Everything you see is a result of that failure. But you bear the lion's share of the blame, woman, for you were the champion of the natural world yet you failed in your duty to protect it.

"No!" Anot shouted. "This place, your words… they are lies!"

But even as she said this, she knew the serpent spoke true. She could feel it, deep in her soul. What was more, she *was* responsible for the blasphemous landscape that surrounded her.

More snakes, identical to the first, began to slither forth from the ground, just a few at first but then these were joined by more, and then more after that, until the entire plain was a writhing mass of black-scaled bodies from horizon to horizon. And when next the serpent spoke, its voice was echoed by all the thousands of others that had emerged, and its words roared like thunder in her mind.

I am Set, Damballah, Jörmungandr, and Yig. I am darkness without beginning or end, and I hold dominion over all… thanks to you.

She sensed movement above, and although she did not want to see what it was, she was unable stop herself from looking skyward.

The black sun slowly uncoiled, revealing itself to be a gigantic serpent that filled the entire sky. It gazed down upon her with burning red eyes the size of planets, and she felt small, insignificant, meaningless…

You can perform one last service for me, shaman. You can feed my children.

The small serpents covering the plain surged toward her in ebon waves. They washed over her, and their combined weight forced her to the ground. She tried to scream, but when she opened her mouth, serpents flooded into her body and began tearing her apart from within.

Naerys' first thought was, *I am in my mother's dream.*

She gazed upon a mountain rage beneath a night sky filled with unfamiliar stars, and atop the tallest peak, Mitra—the god to whom she had devoted her life—grappled with the great darkness that was Set. The ancient serpent had wrapped her coils around Mitra's chest and abdomen, while the god attempted to strangle the monster. Set's eyes blazed a baleful red and her head kept lunging forward, jaws snapping, hoping to sink her huge fangs into Mitra's holy flesh. The deities appeared to be locked in a stalemate, neither able to gain an advantage over the other no matter how hard they strained, muscles bulging and bodies shaking from the tremendous effort.

"I am so sorry, my child."

The voice—a woman's—came from Naerys' right, and she turned to see her mother standing next to her, Angerida's gaze focused on the titanic struggle occurring on the mountain before them.

"It was this dream that caused me to believe we should help the worshippers of Set to leave their dark god and walk in Mitra's divine light." Angerida shook her head in disgust. "If I had not heeded the dream, your father and I would likely still be alive and you would not have wasted your life in an empty pursuit of vengeance."

Naerys was so surprised to see her mother after all this time that her words did not register for several seconds. But once they did, they were like a slap in the face.

"My life has not been a waste!" she exclaimed. "I have done my best to honor your memory and do what I can to rid the world of Set's evil—all in Mitra's name!"

Angerida sighed and turned to look at Naerys for the first time since the dream began. "Set cannot be defeated, my child," she said sadly. "Certainly not by a false god such as Mitra."

She turned back and pointed, indicating that Naerys should

look as well, and mother and daughter watched as, atop the mountain, Set's coils tightened even further around Mitra's midsection. The terrible sound of snapping bones echoed throughout the world, and the god's face became a mask of agony. He coughed a gout of dark blood and his hands slipped away from the Great Serpent's throat. Set struck then, burying her fangs into the side of Mitra's neck. The god stiffened as venom flooded his system, and then he fell limp. Set still held Mitra in her coils, and she withdrew her fangs from the god's flesh, positioned her mouth over Mitra's head, stretched her jaws wide, and then lowered her mouth and began the slow process of swallowing the dead deity.

Naerys refused to believe what she was witnessing. Nothing could defeat Mitra, strongest of all gods! She looked to her mother, hoping Angerida would tell her that this was a false vision that Set was using to torment them. But when her mother turned to her this time, Naerys saw that her eyes were now those of a snake. Angerida's mouth stretched into a wide grin.

"Set is the one true god, my daughter, and you must fall to your knees and worship her."

Angerida gripped Naerys' shoulders with surprising strength, turned her around to face the mountain once more, and shoved her into a kneeling position. She fought to rise, but her mother was too strong, and there was nothing she could do but remain on her knees and watch the corpse of her god be devoured by his ancient enemy.

And Angerida laughed.

Conan decapitated a revenant with his sword while slamming the head of another against the corridor wall with his free hand, its skull bursting like a boil filled with black ichor. He spun around, chest heaving, blood singing in his veins, searching for another foe to slay, but all he saw was Valja bending over the last dead revenant, withdrawing a pair of her throwing knives from its eye sockets. She looked at him and grinned, and the fierce joy of victory burned hot and bright within him. He wanted to bellow a roar of triumph, but at that instant a section of ceiling a dozen yards behind them collapsed.

Conan and Valja whirled around to see if Naerys and Anot had been caught in the collapse, but that part of the corridor was now choked with dust, making it impossible to see. He and Valja started running back that way, shouting the women's names, but Conan heard no replies.

The dust remained thick as Conan and Valja reached the collapse, and all the young barbarian could see were faint suggestions of forms—three of them, two kneeling and one standing. He had known Naerys and Anot for less than a full day, but an existence lived on the razor edge between life and death had taught him to be a quick judge of character, and he was certain both women would willingly die before kneeling to anyone.

Conan did not slow. He angled past Naerys and Anot, then thrust his broadsword at the upright figure's chest, using his momentum to add to the strike's impact. Within the span of an eyeblink, the blade penetrated flesh, muscle, and bone, skewered the heart, and burst out of the figure's back in a spray of blood. He held tight to the sword's handle and let his weight bear the figure to the floor.

He sensed movement in front of his face and reared back just in time to avoid being bitten by a pair of lunging shadow snakes. He yanked his sword free from the revenant's body and was about to use it to decapitate the shadow snakes, but Valja beat him to it, sliding onto her knees next to the revenant's head and swinging her knives so fast the blades seemed to hum in the air. She sliced through the necks of the ebon snakes and the creatures' remains drifted away like smoke and vanished.

Much of the dust caused by the collapse had settled by now, and the light of Anot's fireflies showed Conan that the revenant he had just defeated had been another loathsome snake person. He waited to check if it truly *had* been defeated—you could never tell for certain with undead things—but when several seconds had passed without the thing moving, he was satisfied and turned his attention to Naerys and Anot. Valja knelt in front of the women, a hand on each of their shoulders, and Conan was startled by the expressions of agonized despair on the older women's faces. Tears streamed from their eyes, and their bodies shook like leaves in a windstorm. Both were speaking, but so softly he was unable to make out their words. They each had snakebites on their flesh, Naerys on her cheek, Anot beneath her chin.

Valja spoke their names, giving their shoulders a small shake. "Anot? Naerys? Can you hear me?"

Neither woman registered her presence. Their eyes were wide open, but they stared off into the distance, focused on something only they could see. Valja said their names once more, and this time gave their shoulders a harder shake. Still no response.

"Those foul serpents struck them," Conan said. "They have been poisoned."

"I think it is more than that," Valja said. "It is like they have experienced a shock so deep they have retreated deep inside themselves. Anot, Naerys, please hear me! We need you! We cannot stop Uzzeran on our own."

At first, these words seemed to have no more effect than her previous ones, but Conan saw Anot's eyes flick toward the ceiling, and a second later her fireflies descended from the ceiling to hover around them.

Anot, like Naerys, had continued to mumble this whole

time, but now her voice grew louder as she struggled to clearly enunciate a single word. "Fffffffollllllooooow..." Her brow knitted in fierce concentration and she tried again. "Fol-low. *Follow!*"

A firefly darted in front of Conan's face, and the Cimmerian understood. Whatever had happened to the shaman and the priestess, they would not recover in time to help them against Uzzeran. But he and Valja were not entirely on their own; Anot's fireflies would lead them to the sorcerer. Valja understood the message as well, for she jumped to her feet at the same instant Conan did.

The cloud of fireflies streaked down the corridor, and the two young thieves followed at a run, both determined to make Uzzeran pay for what he had done to their companions.

Conan and Valja soon reached a section of corridor lit by braziers containing the strange green fire that provided illumination but no heat. The fireflies continued to lead them onward, and after a time Conan became aware of a voice—a man's—chanting in a language that he did not recognize, though the sound of it made him deeply uneasy. It had to be Uzzeran in the process of casting a spell. Given that they had encountered the sorcerer's undead minions, Conan thought it likely that Uzzeran was fully aware of them, so stealth was no longer needed. Speed was. Whatever dark enchantment the sorcerer was working on, he might abandon it to deal with them—or, if he chose to complete it, he might do so before the fireflies could lead Conan and Valja to his lair, and then Uzzeran would be free to attack when they arrived. And all of this was assuming the sorcerer had no more of those thrice-damned revenants or, perhaps, something even worse guarding him.

Conan knew the odds of Valja and him defeating Uzzeran without the aid of Naerys and Anot were not favorable, and for an instant he considered abandoning this fool's mission, leaving the tower ruins with Valja and heading off to the One-Eyed Owl to drink the rest of the night away. But while that might be the smart move, it was one he could not make. As self-reliant as Cimmerians were, they also knew that survival in harsh climes sometimes depended on the alliances they made with others. And in Conan's homeland, once an alliance was made, it remained in force until both sides agreed to end it. Conan would have no problem forgoing the rest of the fee for slaying Uzzeran—although he would not return the half he and Valja had already been paid, of course—but he would not abandon two comrades while they were unable to defend themselves. The best way to protect them was to finish the job and slay the sorcerer, so that was what he would do.

That decided, all doubt left his mind and he ran on alongside Valja, grinning wolfishly in anticipation of the battle to come.

None of Naerys' party had witnessed a large white spider the size of a man's hand enter the ruins after them, nor had any of them—Conan included—seen it climb up the wall to the ceiling and begin quickly scuttling toward Uzzeran's work chamber.

The air thickened as Conan and Valja approached Uzzeran's chamber, and the Cimmerian felt as if he were running through water. Sharp pains pinpricked his skin, but he ignored them and pressed onward. He knew nothing about magic, but he believed the sensations they were experiencing were the result of the power Uzzeran had gathered for his spell, like a fierce wind that accompanied a strong storm. He and Valja needed to keep moving forward and try not to think about what effect these unnatural energies might be having upon their minds and bodies.

The sorcerer's chanting grew louder as they neared his chamber, and his voice echoed as if he were shouting into a deep canyon. Each alien syllable of the rite struck Conan's ears like a hammer blow, and the sounds made him wince. Warm blood began to trickle from his nose, as if something had broken inside him, but this only further fueled his desire to slice Uzzeran open from chin to crotch, and watch as the sorcerer's steaming guts spilled onto the floor. But at the last instant before Conan and Valja reached the chamber, a thin Stygian man dressed in a brown tunic and leather-armor vest stepped into the hall to confront them. He gripped a dagger in his right hand and brandished it before him as if to cow the two would-be assassins. Conan saw the blade was slick with a clear, viscous substance that he assumed was venom.

Damned snake-lover!

"Halt!" the Stygian said, his voice tremulous with fear. "I cannot allow you to disturb my master while he—"

Conan did not allow the Stygian—a servant of Uzzeran's, he assumed—to finish his threat. The young barbarian backhanded the man, the powerful blow sending his opponent flying toward the corridor's opposite wall. His right shoulder struck the stone first, his hand sprang open, and the dagger went flying. The man slid to the floor and Valja kicked him in the side of the head before he could recover, and he fell limp.

Good kick, Conan thought, although if he'd done it, the man's neck would have broken like a twig.

The sorcerer's chamber was lit by that strange green flame, and Anot's fireflies remained in the corridor while Conan entered, Valja close on his heels. The instant they set foot inside, they both came to an immediate halt, shocked by the horror of the scene before them.

A slender, middle-aged Stygian with the patrician features of the ruling class garbed in a dark gray robe, whom Conan knew at once was the sorcerer Uzzeran, stood with his hands pressed to the sides of a large ebon orb atop a stone column positioned between two wooden tables. Upon one table lay another of the snake-headed, rune-covered creatures Conan had fought in the corridor. But unlike the revenants, its chest rose and fell, so he assumed this one was alive.

On the other table lay an unconscious boy from the jungle kingdoms south of Stygia, mouth gagged, hands and feet bound. The boy's naked flesh was also covered in runes, and the thought of the pain he must have endured at Uzzeran's hands made the young barbarian even more determined to slay the sorcerer.

Uzzeran continued chanting, his voice nearly deafening at this close distance. Loathsome tendrils of dark energy stretched from the ebon gem to penetrate the foreheads of both the boy and the creature. But as horrifying as all this was, the worst part was the transformations that were occurring to each of Uzzeran's test subjects. Patches of scales would arise on the boy's flesh, only to fade, and the snake-head's scales would be replaced with smooth, human skin in places, only to revert to their original shape and texture. In addition, each subject's face took on aspects of the other's, the boy's features became more reptilian, the snake-head's more human. The changes to their bodies appeared and disappeared every few seconds, and watching the cycle repeat revolted Conan on a primal level.

"May Bel take the memory of this awful sight from me!" Valja exclaimed.

Uzzeran had been so consumed with his spellcasting that he had been completely unaware of them until that point, but Valja's plea to her god caught his attention and he stopped chanting and fixed his gaze upon them. He looked confused at first, but then understanding came into his eyes.

An additional pair of black tendrils lanced forth from the mystic orb and came at Conan and Valja so fast that neither of them had time to react. The tendrils struck their chests and entered their bodies with ease, as if flesh and bone were no more substantial than air to them. Pain greater than anything Conan had ever known flooded his body, and though he fought to endure it, it was too much and drove him to one knee. The hand gripping his broadsword fell numb, and he managed to maintain his grip on it only by a supreme act of will.

Valja fared worse. She lay on the floor, writhing in agony, blood streaming from her nose and ears, screaming like a woman plunged into the hottest fires of Hell.

Conan gritted his teeth, pressed the point of his sword to the floor, and used the weapon to steady himself as he stood. His heart was racing, and he felt as if he was unable to draw in enough air to breathe. Uzzeran smiled in smug satisfaction before returning to his chanting, and the cycles of transformation that affected the boy and the reptilian creature became even faster. Conan tried to raise his sword and attack, but the pain was so intense that it took all his strength to hold on to consciousness. But in times of great distress, people often notice the most trivial and unimportant details around them, and so it was with Conan now. His attention was snared by a large white shape clinging to the ceiling above Uzzeran's head. Seeing it sparked a single thought that managed to cut through the pain and rise to the forefront of his consciousness:

Where, by all the demons in all the hells, had that spider come from?

Shengis' eyes fluttered open.

At first, he did not know where he was or what was happening. His right shoulder felt like it was aflame, and he was unable to move the arm on that side. To make matters worse, he had a headache as if he had spent a week guzzling cheap Maul wine, and the side of his head felt like it had been kicked by a horse.

He was sitting on a stone floor, leaning against a wall for support, and strange insects were swirling in the air near the ceiling, their abdomens glowing with yellow light. He had never seen their like before, or at least not that he could recall. They were quite beautiful.

A woman's agonized scream cut through the air, startling him, and this was followed by the sonorous chanting of a male voice, one he thought was familiar, but—

His memories flooded back then and he recalled the two intruders, a woman and a man, attempting to enter the master's chamber. The man, a big, northern savage, had struck him with a backhanded blow, sending him crashing into the wall. The woman had kicked him in the head after that, and he must have lost consciousness for a short time. But he was awake and aware now, and his master needed him.

His poison-coated dagger lay on the floor several feet away. He attempted to stretch out his right arm—the one that had struck the wall—but when it refused to obey him, he reached out with his left and grabbed the hilt. Thank Set he hadn't accidentally cut himself when he had collided with the wall! Uzzeran had insisted he build up a tolerance to the venom so it would not harm him, but while he had tried to do so, he hadn't had much success. Maybe if—

Focus! he chided himself.

Since he only had one working arm, he sheathed his dagger and put his left hand on the wall for support as he rose to his feet. This action heightened the pain in his skull, and for a second he thought he might pass out. But then the master's chanting broke off and Shengis heard him shriek in agony. His own pain forgotten, Shengis drew his dagger with his left hand and staggered toward the work chamber's entrance.

Conan took a two-handed grip on his sword handle and fought to lift the weapon, but the pain from the ebon energy Uzzeran had struck him with was so intense that all he could manage was to raise the blade a few inches off the floor. He was starting to feel cold inside, and his vision narrowed to pinpoints. He knew he was dying, but that meant nothing to him. When you lived by the sword, Death was your constant companion and, in many ways, your only true friend. But if he was fated to die this night, he intended to take that bastard sorcerer with him.

Clenching his jaw and straining every muscle to breaking point, he slowly began to raise the broadsword. Six inches... twelve... eighteen...

And as if the white spider clinging to the ceiling above Uzzeran had been waiting for that exact moment, it released its grip and dropped onto the chanting sorcerer's head, then quickly crawled down onto his face and sank its fangs into his left eye. The orb popped like a rotting grape and the sorcerer screamed as viscous fluid mixed with blood ran down his cheek. The black tendrils affixed to Conan and Valja winked out of existence. The barbarian's pain vanished in an instant, and he was able to move normally once more.

Several things happened within the next five seconds.

Conan bellowed a cry of primal exultation as he raised his broadsword above his head in a two-handed grip and swung it downward at the black orb on the pedestal.

Shengis stumbled into the room, poison dagger in hand. His gaze fixed on Conan. He raised his blade and headed straight for the young Cimmerian.

Valja's pain had ended at the same instant Conan's did, and when she saw the younger Stygian shuffling forward, clearly intending to stab her lover, she drew one of her own blades from a cloak pocket and hurled it at the man. But she was still weak, and while she had intended for the knife to embed itself in the Stygian's throat, her aim was off and the blade flew toward his left shoulder.

Still shrieking, Uzzeran clawed at his face and dislodged the white spider, which tumbled to the ground. The sorcerer attempted to crush the foul thing beneath a sandaled foot, but the spider managed to skitter out of the chamber a split second before Conan's sword blade struck the Eye of Set with the full force of his combined might and fury. The orb shattered and black energy exploded outward in all directions. Conan was lifted off his feet and thrown against a wall. He fell to the floor and lay there, stunned and semiconscious.

The dagger Valja had thrown sank into Shengis' left shoulder, and the impact caused the servant to spin around and stumble forward. At the same instant, a small fragment of the Eye shaped like a miniature spear flew toward Kekk, far faster than the human eye could detect. It struck the right side of the Serpent Man's head, drilled through his brain, broke through the other side, and continued on. Its momentum had been severely curtailed by its trip through Kekk's gray matter, so when it struck Shengis on the forehead and penetrated into his brain, it remained lodged there.

Shengis felt a sharp pain in his head and was hit by a wave of dizziness. He instinctively extended his right hand to prevent himself from falling. That arm should not have worked, let alone the hand, but they did, and he managed to slap his palm against the wall and remain on his feet. Then he registered the pain in his shoulder and realized that the woman's throwing knife had struck him. Without thinking, he reached up, yanked the blade from his shoulder, and dropped it to the floor. The pain of the wound was already fading, and Shengis put it down to shock. Only later would he discover that the injury, like his broken arm, had healed itself.

Other fragments of the Eye—dozens of them—had cut into Shengis' skin, but none seemed to have any effect on him other than stinging like hell. Hundreds, perhaps thousands of fragments were stuck in the walls, floor, and ceiling, and several dozen jutted from the skin of the two intruders. The idiot savage who had destroyed the Eye appeared dazed by the explosion, and he had a deep cut on the left side of his head where he had been grazed by a shard of the Eye, but otherwise he seemed relatively unharmed. His companion lay on the floor, staring up at the ceiling, not blinking, a shard now jutting from the center of her chest through a tear in her tunic. She appeared to be dead, and Shengis thought it a shame, for a swift death was better than scum like her deserved.

He then looked at his master, and to his horror, he saw that a similar shard protruded from his left eye socket, as if it had purposefully flown there to fill the void created when the white spider had destroyed the eye. Like the barbarian, Uzzeran appeared stunned. He kept turning his head slowly back and forth, taking in the damage to his chamber, struggling to process it all.

Like the woman, the Keshan boy wasn't breathing. Evidently the shock of being connected to the Eye when it was destroyed had been too much for his system to withstand. Kekk no longer breathed either, but the reason for the Serpent Man's death was less apparent to Shengis—not that it mattered. What was one more dead Serpent Man in the scheme of things?

Think any more thoughts like that and I shall see to it you have a stroke.

The voice—Kekk's voice—came from within Shengis' mind.

I am delirious from my injuries, Shengis thought. *That's all.*

Wrong, Kekk said, *but we do not have time to sort out our situation now. You need to get your master out of here while you can.*

Shengis glanced at the barbarian. "The northerner is no threat," he told Kekk. "I shall stab him with my dagger and he will be dead within seconds." Then he realized he no longer held his dagger and glanced around the room for it.

Forget the Cimmerian! You have a much greater threat to contend with. Did you not see the spider that attacked Uzzeran?

The image of the white spider clinging to his master's face flashed through Shengis' mind, making his stomach cramp with nausea.

So you did, Kekk said, as if reading Shengis' thoughts. *It was no ordinary spider but a child of Zath. The spider god is an ancient enemy of Set, and he sent one of his children to stop Uzzeran's spell. Arenjun is infested with Zath's brood, and since you and your master yet live, the spider god may well send more of his children to finish both of you off. If you want to save your master's life, not to mention yours and mine, you need to get moving!*

Shengis feared he was going mad, but whatever the origin of the voice inside his head, its counsel was wise. Uzzeran was in no shape to use his magic to protect them, whether from Zath or the City Watch. They needed to leave this place.

He walked toward Uzzeran, his stride surprisingly strong and steady now, and held out his right hand to his master. He had already forgotten that the arm had ever been injured.

Conan, still not fully conscious, watched the sorcerer's servant take his master's hand and guide him toward the chamber door. Uzzeran's left eye was gone and in its place an ebon shard, and the servant's eyes… For an instant, Conan thought they resembled those of a reptile, cold and inhuman, but he blinked and the man's eyes appeared normal once more.

He decided he must have struck his head against the wall a little too hard when the ebon orb had exploded. Cimmerians possessed remarkable recuperative abilities—a vital adaptation for survival in the harsh, bleak environment of their homeland—and Conan's were stronger than most of his people's. Indeed, his strength was already returning, and he rose to his feet, determined to slay the bastard sorcerer and his servant before they could escape the chamber. He gripped his sword tight and started toward the Stygians, but he managed only two steps before remembering Valja. Cursing himself for letting his anger get the better of him, he turned to look for his lover and found her lying on the floor several feet away, eyes wide and staring, body motionless, an ebon shard jutting from her chest. He knew death when he saw it, but he still went over, knelt at her side, put down his sword, and took her small right hand in his large callused ones. He knew he would not feel a pulse, but he still pressed his fingers against the soft flesh of her wrist and hoped. Nothing. He spoke then, in a voice tight with sorrow and rage.

"I will not rest until I lay Uzzeran's severed head upon your grave."

He gazed upon her face for several more seconds, then gently placed her hand on the floor, retrieved his broadsword, and stood. Uzzeran had been injured and moving slowly when his servant had escorted him from the chamber, so unless they knew a secret way out of the ruins, he should be able to catch up to them and—

"That is sweet of you to say, but I am not dead yet."

Conan had already started toward the entrance, but he froze when he heard Valja speak. He slowly turned around and saw her sitting up and looking at him with her familiar wry smile… and her unblinking eyes.

Valja was alarmed when she saw the shard embedded in her chest, and she immediately tried to pull it out. It hurt like blazes, but she ignored the pain and kept trying. But no matter how hard she tugged, the thing refused to budge, as if it had fused with her skeletal structure. Conan was glad for this, for it seemed the shard was what kept her in this state of non-life.

"We must find Anot," Conan said. "Perhaps she can help."

But as powerful as the shaman was, Conan feared there was nothing she would be able to do to cure Valja's bizarre condition—one Valja herself did not yet seem to be fully aware of. And that was assuming Anot and Naerys had recovered from whatever the revenant's shadow serpents had done to them. The shaman might not be capable of working magic right now, and perhaps would not be for some time.

Valja's body seemed to function normally enough. She could move and speak as normal, and her mind remained sharp as ever, but it seemed she needed to breathe only when she wished to speak. As they walked down the corridor, the four of them removed the tiny ebon shards embedded in their skin and let them drop to the floor. Valja had no more difficulty pulling these shards from her body than Conan did, but unlike him her skin did not bleed when they were removed. She occasionally touched the shard protruding from her chest, running her fingers over its glossy black surface. Conan found her exploration, understandable as it was, deeply disturbing, but it seemed to cause her no discomfort, and for this he was glad.

Anot's fireflies accompanied them along the way, providing light for them to see by. They did not encounter Uzzeran or his servant, and Conan assumed the two had gone to a different section of the ruins or, more likely, fled them. He burned to face the sorcerer again, but first he needed to tend to Valja. Uzzeran would have to wait for another day.

Conan had no way of knowing just how long it would be before that day finally came.

When the last of the humans had departed the ruins, the snakes drawn there by Uzzeran's magic abandoned the place as well. With the sorcerer gone, they had no one to serve, and the hunting was poor within the ruins, so the serpents had to go elsewhere for food. But there was one type of creature that loved dark, enclosed spaces, especially in these ruins, now that Uzzeran had awakened the magic that suffused the stone.

Just before dawn, the Brood of Zath—hundreds of them, led by a white spider—entered their new home, found places for themselves, and settled in. The spiders would feast on the power loose within the ruins, and they would grow strong—and large. And when the day came for them to move against Set in the name of their father, they would be ready.

PART TWO

Conan had walked through corpse-strewn battlefields that smelled better than this.

The wagons in the trading caravan, twenty in number, were each pulled by a pair of sturdy oxen. Nine of the caravan's mounted guards rode *haraghi*, Turanian horses bred for endurance and speed, but Conan, the largest of the guards, rode a *lakan*, a heavy-framed Hyrkanian horse bred for strength and a mount better suited to carry his weight. Both breeds were good horses, although Conan thought the Hyrkanians bred better.

The caravan traveled west on the hard-packed ground of the Road of Kings, the trading route that stretched from Turan to Messentia. Conan was posted near the rear of the caravan, on its left, next to a wagon carrying a cage holding a dozen small, long-tailed monkeys from Vendhya. The damn things chattered incessantly, and they exuded an odor that was at once sweet and rank, like Shemitish perfume mixed with donkey piss.

The Cimmerian was now in his thirty-third year, and he carried himself with a confidence born of vast, hard-won experience, as the numerous scars across his body attested. He wore a mail shirt over a blue tunic, along with black leather boots and a scarlet cape that stirred in the cool breeze. He carried a broadsword in a scabbard attached to his belt, as well as a dagger, but so far during this trip he had needed to draw neither. He had signed on as a caravan guard in Turan because it was an easy way to make some coin, but they had traveled for nearly two weeks without incident and the tedium was beginning to wear on him.

A month ago, he had been the captain of a raiding vessel that sailed the vast inland sea of the Vilayet, commanding a crew of Red Brotherhood pirates. During their last voyage, they had gone ashore and he had become separated from his crew in the Colchian Mountains. Before he could rejoin them, they returned to the ship and sailed off, doubtless with a new captain at the helm. He had felt no anger toward them, for he would have done the same thing in their position. On his own once more, he'd decided to head west, with no goal in mind other than to see what life had to offer him this time.

The caravan belonged to the Sülale, a Turanian word that meant *extended family*. The caravan master was a middle-aged and well-fed Turanian named Delger, and his wife, children, siblings, and assorted cousins all rode along, working in one capacity or another, young ones included. The guards, however, were hired men—some Sülale, some not—including Delger's brother-in-law, Kuta, who rode on the right-hand side of the lead wagon and was in charge of overseeing the guards. Kuta had been against Conan being hired, but Delger ignored his reservations. *See how big he is*, Delger had said, *and how fiercely he scowls? Bandits will take one look at him and be afraid to approach us!* Kuta had glowered at Conan but had made no further protest.

Conan had encountered men like Kuta before, those who were used to intimidating others with their size and strength but felt threatened when they met anyone bigger and stronger than themselves. Kuta had wanted to assert dominance over him, which was why Conan was stuck riding next to a cage full of foul-smelling monkeys. Ordinarily, the Cimmerian would have challenged the Turanian to fight one on one, and once he had slain the bastard he would have taken his position as overseer of the guards, but since the man was Delger's kin Conan doubted the caravan master would look kindly upon such a move.

At least he wasn't the only one forced to ride next to the malodorous monkeys. On the right of the wagon rode a Khitan a few years younger than Conan. His name was Qiang, but that was all Conan knew about the man, for he spoke little and revealed nothing about himself. Conan appreciated that. Why speak unless you had something worth saying?

Conan had no idea what Qiang had done to get on Kuta's bad side. Perhaps his being Khitan had been enough. Qiang's people lived far to the east, beyond Hyrkania and the Wuhuan Desert, and while the Turanians did a good deal of trade with the Khitans—for the Silken Road began where the Road of Kings ended—Khitai was a land of dark and powerful sorceries and its denizens were viewed with suspicion, if not outright hatred.

Conan had traveled in Khitai before, and he had nothing against its people. He judged individuals by their actions, not their race. Most viewed him as barely human because he was a barbarian, so he knew what it was like to be judged solely on one's place of birth. Even Stygians, whose upper classes could be haughty, cold, callous, and cruel, were not all of a kind. The average citizen of Stygia was no different than the average denizen of any other land. They were just trying to survive from one day to the next, like anyone else not born to royalty and wealth.

Qiang had a thin mustache and a neatly trimmed goatee, and his black hair was tied back in a short ponytail. He wore a red silk robe belted with a sash and sandals, and he carried an eastern sword called a katana sheathed on his back. Conan had never handled one of the thin blades himself, but in the past he had seen Khitan warriors wield them with deadly precision.

Conan could tell Qiang was the only caravan member aside from himself who was a true warrior. To anyone else, the man might have seemed relaxed, even drowsy in the saddle, but Conan saw how closely he watched their surroundings and noted the subtle tenseness in his manner. This was a man ready to spring into action in an instant.

Qiang must have sensed Conan's scrutiny, for he turned to look at the Cimmerian, gave a slight nod, then faced forward once more. They were like a pair of male lions in their prime, each acknowledging the other as a worthy opponent.

Delger rode in the lead wagon, his niece Aigia sitting by his side, garbed in a silken dress, the lower half of her face veiled, as was the custom for Turanian women. She was Kuta's eldest daughter, and she paid far too much attention to Conan whenever he was nearby, which no doubt was another reason Kuta had positioned him next to the monkeys.

The two wagons after Delger's had small cabins built onto them, and these were where his family members rode during the day and slept during the night—especially the women, since Turanian females were not permitted to be outside after dark.

The guards slept on the ground in bedrolls, but Conan preferred sleeping atop a thin blanket. Given the harsh environment in Cimmeria, and all the places he'd visited in his wanderings since leaving his homeland, he'd learned to sleep in nearly any condition and circumstance. To him, a blanket was as good as a rich man's feather bed.

The fourth wagon contained supplies—barrels of drinking water, along with stores of dried meat, hard cheese, and tasteless flatbread—while the fifth carried tools and extra parts for maintaining the wagons. The rest of the wagons contained goods for trade, such as Turanian silk and Vendhyan spices. All of these wagons were covered with leather tarpaulins, tied down tight to protect the goods within from the elements.

In addition to the monkeys, other animals included a pair of restless tigers that paced constantly in their cage, pawing the thick bars, testing for any weakness; a quartet of colorful peacocks; and huge cobras coiled inside woven baskets bound for Stygia.

The last wagon in the caravan held a large cage containing a dozen human prisoners destined for the slave markets in Arenjun and Shadizar, mostly Brythunians and Ophirians. Cimmerians did not keep slaves, but that was primarily because when Cimmerians went to war, they left no survivors to be enslaved.

Tethered behind the slave wagon were nine additional haraghi and one lakan, fresh animals that could take over should any of the guards' mounts become ill or fall lame.

The most lucrative—and illicit—item Delger transported, however, was a wagonload of black lotus from Khitai, highly prized by many in the Western lands. Before the caravan had set out from the Turanian city of Secundarem, Conan had overheard Delger and Kuta discussing the lotus. They spoke in their native language, unaware that the Cimmerian knew the tongue, having served in the Turanian army when he was younger.

"Are you certain the lotus is well concealed?" Kuta had asked.

"In the wagon carrying the tigers is a false bottom, and the lotus is beneath. So not only is it well hidden, it is well protected, too," replied Delger.

Conan preferred wine and ale to black lotus. He did not begrudge other people their pleasures, but black lotus was illegal in many kingdoms for good reason. It was too easy to over-indulge in the drug and lose control of your mind and senses, becoming a danger to yourself as well as others.

The winter rains had passed, but the air was still cool and damp. Western Turan was mountainous, which made this section of the Road of Kings one of the more arduous to travel. The plateaus and valleys had been formed from soft volcanic rock shaped by wind and rain over thousands of years, resulting in bizarre formations resembling large pyramids and cones. Little grew here save shrubs and juniper trees, and the animals were sparse, mostly lizards, steppe mice, and mountain hares—all prey for hawks and falcons. It was a desolate landscape, but one not without its own strange beauty, though the rock formations concerned Conan. They were numerous and large enough to conceal men on horseback.

"Be wary," he called out. "Those big rocks make good hiding places, and bandits may be lurking close."

His fellow guards turned to looked at him, some nodding in agreement, others regarding him quizzically as if to say, *Who are you to give us orders?* Qiang was the only one who did not look at him. The Khitan was too busy scanning the terrain around them, alert for any sign of threat.

Up by the lead wagon, Kuta let out a loud curse in Turanian—"By Erlik's hidden face!"—then turned his mount around, rode back along the caravan until he reached Conan, and turned his mount again to ride parallel to the barbarian.

Kuta was a lean man with a hawkish face and a neatly trimmed mustache and goatee. Silk was common in Turan, and nearly everyone in the country, men and women alike, wore clothing made from it. Kuta was no exception. He wore a turban—common for males in his land—along with a cape, a loose silk robe with flaring sleeves, billowing pants, and boots, all light blue in color except for his black footwear. He wore no armor, not even leather, but carried the curved scimitar favored by his people tucked beneath his belt—a good weapon, Conan thought, though he preferred his broadsword.

Kuta's eyes blazed with anger. He spoke Zamorian, unaware that Conan was fluent in Turanian. "Are you in command of the guards?" he demanded.

I should be, Conan thought. Aloud, he said, "No." The Cimmerian was aware of Qiang watching them closely.

"That is correct. *I* am. Perhaps you have forgotten this? You *are* but a savage. It must be difficult for you to keep more than one thought at a time in that ugly head of yours."

Conan's eyes narrowed but otherwise he did not react.

Kuta's lips drew back from his teeth in a half smile, half snarl. In Turanian, he said, "Afraid to face me, coward?"

Conan's hands tightened on his horse's reins. Kuta noted this, and his smile widened. In Zamorian, he said, "Do not forget your place again, barbarian, or I will gut you like an animal and piss on your bleeding corpse."

Conan knew Kuta was attempting to goad him into attacking, but he would not give the bastard the satisfaction. He continued sitting in his saddle, still as death.

Kuta looked at him a moment longer before letting out a derisive snort. Then he tapped his heels to his horse's flanks and the beast broke into a gallop, bearing him back to the front of the caravan. Conan watched him go, picturing a hundred different ways he could slay the man, each one slower and more painful than the last.

Qiang had been silent during Conan's exchange with Kuta, but now he spoke in Zamorian. "That man is so small these monkeys are giants compared to him."

Conan smiled. "They smell better, too."

Both men laughed. Conan decided he liked Qiang, and he was about to ask the man for his thoughts on the katana as a weapon, but before he could speak, his vision blurred. When his eyesight cleared, he no longer saw the Khitan warrior, the caravan, or the Road of Kings, and no longer did he sit upon his horse. Instead, he stood in a place he had not seen in fifteen years—the Temple of Ishtar in Zamora, braziers aflame, firepit burning, but no worshippers or priests present.

He was alone. In the center of the temple was a large statue of Ishtar—not the one he remembered but a thirty-foot marble sculpture of a mother heavy with child. This one was as tall as the other had been, but it was fashioned from gold and depicted the goddess in her warrior aspect, dressed for battle, holding two longswords crossed over her chest, a six-pointed star carved into her forehead. It was the statuette that he and Valja had stolen from the temple during the solstice celebration so many years ago, only greatly increased in size.

Was he going mad? Had Kuta somehow snuck black lotus into his waterskin? No. Whatever was happening here had the stink of magic to it.

The fierce expression on the statue's face did not change, but the voice Conan heard in his mind was soft and gentle when it spoke a single, unfamiliar word.

Charhelm.

"Who or what is that?" he demanded.

But the goddess deigned not to answer, and his vision blurred, then cleared, and he found himself sitting upon his horse's back once more, if indeed he had ever left.

"Cimmerian!" Qiang shouted.

Conan heard the whisper of an arrow in flight and immediately reached for his broadsword, but even as he did so he knew the weapon would not clear its scabbard in time. A glint of sunlight on steel caught his eye, and he saw the Khitan warrior swipe his katana through the air with a speed Conan wasn't certain even he could match. The razor-sharp blade struck the arrow in midflight and sliced its wooden shaft neatly in two. As the pieces fell to the ground, Qiang whipped his head around, searching for another threat. Conan knew that, had the Khitan not intervened, the arrow would have slain him. But there was no time to thank the warrior, for the caravan was under attack.

Four Turanian archers had climbed to the top of conical and pyramidal rock structures on both sides of the wagons and now loosed arrows at will. They wielded powerful Hyrkanian bows, designed to be used on horseback, and their arrows struck their targets with deadly force. Three of the caravan's ten guards were hit in the first volley, and had it not been for Qiang then Conan would have been the fourth. All three guards fell off their mounts—injured or dead, Conan could not tell, but either way they would be no further use in this battle.

In the lead wagon, Aigia screamed in alarm and Delger called for all the drivers to go faster, evidently hoping to put distance between the caravan and the archers. But the heavily laden wagons could not move swiftly, and oxen could go only so fast. But even if the big animals could have flown like the wind, Conan suspected the archers were not the only threat facing the caravan.

His suspicion was proven correct a few seconds later when eight Turanian raiders came riding out from behind the rock formations, four on the caravan's right, four on its left, waving scimitars and shouting war cries as they galloped toward the wagons. Meanwhile, the archers continued firing and one more guard went down, leaving only six to defend the caravan.

The raiders rode swift haraghi horses, wore helmets beneath their turbans, and sported studded leather armor over their silken robes. The lower halves of their faces were covered by silk scarves to conceal their identities. Conan had no intention of waiting for the raiders to reach the caravan, and since Kuta had yet to give any orders, he shouted, "Attack, you dogs!" then drew his broadsword and, wielding the huge weapon one-handed, rode forth to meet the raiders' charge, a savage grin on his face.

Arrows streaked past him as his mount's hooves thundered

across the rocky terrain, but none struck him. He angled the horse toward the biggest raider on this side of the caravan, and as they closed upon each other, the raider swung his scimitar at Conan's neck. But the Cimmerian moved faster, and with a single swing of his blade he struck the man's sword hand at the wrist, severing it. Hand and scimitar fell to the ground, blood jetted from the wrist, and as the raider howled in pain Conan used the backstroke to hit the side of the raider's head. The blade struck the helmet beneath the man's turban, but the metal was little protection against a blow from a warrior as strong as Conan and the raider's skull shattered. Blood gushed from his eyes, nose, and ears, and the man fell out of his saddle, dead.

An arrow flew by Conan's head, hit the flank of the raider's now riderless mount, and sank deep. Blood gushed from the wound and the horse screamed, reared back, and then galloped off, most likely to die in the next few minutes. The archers would remain a threat as long as their supply of arrows held out, and Conan knew something needed to be done about that, so he cracked the reins and his mount galloped toward the rock formations where the two archers were perched. The fools had chosen to climb formations next to each other, and Conan decided to find out just how soft this volcanic rock truly was. He urged his horse to greater speed and crouched down in the saddle to make himself a smaller target, although at his size this maneuver was only partially effective.

The closest formation was cone-shaped, and as his mount drew near Conan jumped out of the saddle and ran toward it, angling his right shoulder and then slamming into it, hard. He ignored the pain—it would soon pass—and watched.

At first nothing happened, but then the base of the conical structure began to crack, and then it began to topple slowly toward the pyramidal formation next to it. There was a loud crash of rock striking rock, and then the two formations collapsed underneath the archers, leaving the bowmen to plunge twenty feet to the ground. Conan heard the satisfying sounds of their bones breaking as the raiders hit, and an instant later he was on his feet and running toward them. As he reached the rubble, he saw that both men, while battered and broken, still lived, though two quick sword thrusts remedied that situation.

He examined the stony debris, searching for the Hyrkanian bows. One had snapped in two during the formations' collapse, but the other remained intact, lying next to a quiver with three unbroken arrows inside. Conan laid down his blood-slick sword and drew the bow from the rubble. It was still strung, so he nocked an arrow, drew back, aimed, and loosed the shaft. Hyrkanian bows were made to shoot over long distances, and Conan watched as the arrow arced up, then down, and pierced the throat of another archer. The man's eyes flew wide with shock and he lost his balance, falling from the formation he had been standing on.

Before the raider could hit the ground, Conan nocked a second arrow, drew back, aimed, and let fly. This shaft struck its target in the left eye and passed through his brain until the steel point broke through the back of the Turanian's skull. The impact knocked that raider off his perch as well, but Conan did not need to hear any bones breaking to know the man was dead before he hit the ground.

He had slain five of the twelve raiders so far.

His bloodlust now up, he nocked the last arrow and scanned the caravan, searching for a third target. Only five raiders still remained. Two of the others had been cleanly decapitated, and Conan attributed those kills to Qiang and his katana. Kuta had been slain while Conan had dealt with the archers and now lay facedown on the ground near the slave wagon, still clutching his scimitar—too bad; Conan would have enjoyed slaying the man himself. Four guards still lived, including him, which made the odds nearly even. The other three fought four of the raiders, all the men on horseback, swords clashing, steel ringing against steel.

The fifth surviving raider had reached the lead wagon, and Conan realized what the man intended. While the others kept the guards busy, this raider would force Delger to surrender and order what guards remained to stand down. It was a smart enough plan, but it would not work. Conan would die before surrendering, and he thought Qiang would do the same. He barely knew the other two guards, a Turanian and a Kothian, and therefore could not predict what they might do if Delger ordered them to stop fighting. They might ignore his command and continue battling the raiders or they might cut and run.

Delger evidently did not intend to give in without a fight, though, for the portly caravan master had climbed down from his wagon and now crossed scimitars with the raider, who had dismounted. Delger was clearly no warrior, but he fought hard to defend his family and their livelihood. Conan admired the man's courage. Unfortunately, he could tell that the raider was toying with Delger, like a cat tormenting a mouse, and that he could finish off the man whenever he wished.

Conan had his final target.

He raised the Hyrkanian bow, drew back, aimed, and released.

The arrow struck the back of the raider's head, broke through the skull, and continued until the point jutted out of his mouth. He stiffened in shock and coughed a gout of blood, but he did not immediately fall. Delger had been surprised to see the man suddenly pierced by an arrow, but he quickly recovered and thrust his scimitar into the raider's gut, then withdrew it with a violent twist, disemboweling him. He toppled and Delger looked in Conan's direction, then gave him a nod of thanks. Conan nodded back, his estimation of the caravan master rising a few notches.

There was still work to be done, though. Conan's mount had run off, so the barbarian retrieved his sword, then ran toward the caravan to join Qiang and the other guards in their fight.

It did not take long to finish off the four remaining raiders. The Kothian guard died in the fighting, but the Turanian survived, as did Qiang and Conan. Now the bodies lay on the ground near each other, their blood soaking into the porous volcanic earth.

Delger ordered several of his younger male relatives—sons, nephews, or cousins, Conan did not know which—to gather the raiders' horses and tether them with the rest, and then remove any items of value from the corpses and store them in one of the wagons. *Men like Delger would try to sell the stars in the night sky if they could*, Conan thought.

The Turanian guard was helping several of Delger's older male relatives drag the bodies of the dead raiders and guards off the Road of Kings. Conan and Qiang stood with the caravan master next to Kuta's body, which still lay where the man had fallen.

"We shall bury the guards here where they fought so valiantly," Delger said. "The ground is soft enough to make digging graves light work. As for the raiders…" He spit on the ground. "They can rot where they lay."

He then looked down at his brother-in-law and sighed. "Kuta and I fought like rabid wolves much of the time, but I know my wife will miss the old bastard, as will his own wife and child. I suppose we shall have to bury him here too, but I think we should take him farther down the road and find a better place for him. Perhaps somewhere with a nice view."

Aigia came toward them then, still wearing her veil and

holding up the hem of her silken dress with her left hand so it would not get dirt or blood on it. Her long black hair seemed to gleam in the sunlight as she drew near.

When Delger saw his niece approaching, he frowned in disapproval and said to her in Turanian, “You should not be here. This is no place for a girl. Where is my sister?”

“Mother is too distraught to say prayers over Father, so the duty falls to me.”

Delger’s frown remained for several more seconds, then his expression softened. “You are a fine young woman, Aigia, and you bring much honor to the Sülale. Kuta would be proud.” He spread his arms and stepped forward to embrace her.

But before he could reach her, her right hand swept up and Delger staggered back, clutching his throat, crimson streaming between his fingers. Aigia glared at him with hate-filled eyes, her uncle’s blood dripping from the small dagger clutched in her hand.

Delger fell to his knees, his hand dropped away from his throat, and blood streamed like a red waterfall. A few seconds later, he slumped onto his side and lay motionless, blood continuing to trickle from his wound.

Both Conan and Qiang drew their swords and leveled them at the girl.

“What treachery is this?” the Cimmerian demanded in Turanian, no longer caring to pretend he did not know the tongue.

“No treachery at all.”

Conan and Qiang turned to see a grinning Kuta rise to his feet, scimitar held tight in his hand, the front of his robe unstained.

Conan and Qiang trained their swords on the seemingly resurrected man, but Kuta raised one hand in a placating gesture, bent down, lay his scimitar on the ground, then straightened.

He nodded at Aigia and she discarded her dagger, although she did not look happy about it. Kuta then walked over to his daughter and slipped an arm around her shoulders.

"Good work," he said.

Her mouth was not visible behind her veil, but Conan could see the smile in her eyes. "Thank you, Father."

Kuta then faced the two warriors. Since he was now unarmed, they lowered their swords partway.

"You were behind the raid," Conan said.

"Were those Turanians more of your relatives?" Qiang asked in Kuta's language. "Is that why they hid their identities?"

Kuta smiled. "You are both smarter than I thought. I tried to convince Delger not to hire you, Cimmerian. I could tell you were an experienced warrior, and I did not want you interfering with our plan." He looked at Qiang. "You, however, I underestimated. I did not believe a thin sword such as you wield would prove effective against men armed with scimitars. I was wrong."

An older woman approached now, her long black hair threaded with gray. She was veiled and wearing a dress similar to Aigia's, but she also had gold rings set with jewels on each of her fingers.

"You are Delger's wife," Conan said, "and Kuta's sister."

"Yes. My name is Erya."

"You do not appear to be upset by your husband's death at the hand of your niece," Qiang observed.

"I am quite happy my husband is dead." Erya's voice was filled with cold satisfaction. "This caravan once belonged to my father. In certain parts of Turan, the firstborn male inherits their father's wealth when he dies. But if the firstborn is a woman, her *husband* inherits that wealth. So when my father died, Delger became caravan master. That inheritance was mine by right, tradition be damned! So I decided to do something about it." She smiled at Kuta. "With my brother's help."

"By the customs of your people, you are still unable to inherit the caravan," Conan said.

"True. But my firstborn son is still a child, which means *I* hold the caravan in custody until he is old enough to assume control."

"And when he becomes old enough?" Qiang asked.

Erya shrugged. "Accidents happen."

Conan scowled at the woman before turning his attention to Kuta. "Delger was supposed to die in the raid, as were the guards and any of your relatives in the caravan who you knew would not go along with your scheme," he said.

"Precisely," Kuta said. "I do not want to do battle with you both."

"You would lose," said Conan.

"Yes," Kuta said with gritted teeth. "Instead, I have a proposition. We will offer you gold to leave us in peace and remain silent about what happened here this day. We will give you the pay for all the guards to divide between you both."

"And if we do not agree?" Conan asked.

"Gold can be used to hire assassins," Erya said.

The three of them—mother, brother, and niece—stood silent after that, waiting to see which path the Cimmerian and Khitan would make.

Conan and Qiang looked at each other and a silent understanding passed between them.

The two warriors stepped forward.

An hour later, Conan and Qiang rode away from the caravan on the backs of two horses, one lakan, one haraghi. Each carried a pouch fat with gold Kuranian coins, a full waterskin, a full wineskin, and enough food to last several days. The cage on the slave wagon now held those Turanians who were loyal to Kuta and Erya. The brother and sister were naked, the former slaves now wearing their fine silk clothes. The Turanians loyal to Delger were in charge of the caravan, at least for now, and had agreed to allow the freed slaves to ride along with them, though Conan made sure each slave received a scimitar in case any of the Turanians were tempted to go back on the deal.

The tiger and monkey cages were empty, and the peacocks were gone. Conan did not know how the animals would fare in this land, but he figured their lot would be better here than in a cage in some royal's palace.

The cobras he slew.

As for Kuta, Erya, and Aigia, Conan and Qiang bound their hands and wrists and then turned them over to the loyal Turanians.

By the time the pair departed, the Turanians and the freed slaves were still digging. It was a good thing the ground was soft in this place, for they had many graves to dig.

The two warriors traveled the Road of Kings in companionable silence for a time, but after a while the Cimmerian asked the Khitan a question.

"Do you know what *Charhelm* is?"

After Delger was buried and his grave prayed over, the Turanians loyal to him acknowledged his eldest son, Cemil, as caravan master. There was some discussion about whether an attempt should be made to recapture the animals the Cimmerian had freed, but Cemil decided against it. He thought it highly unlikely they would ever catch the monkeys, and the tigers were too dangerous to pursue. They had a pair of empty cages now, but no one suggested trying to force the former slaves into them.

The Turanians had given their word to Conan that the slaves would remain free—and the fact those slaves were now armed with scimitars would ensure that word was kept.

As Cemil oversaw preparations to get the caravan moving again, his younger brother, Hakan, tended to the messenger pigeons kept in a wooden cage in one of the cabins. Their extended family had members spread throughout Turan, Hyrkania, Shem, Iranistan, Koth, and Zamora, and all were connected to the trading profession in one form or another, whether as buyers, sellers, or thieves. The Sülale used the pigeons to communicate with each other over great distances, and Cemil had tasked Hakan with writing messages to inform everyone of Delger's death and his own ascension to caravan master.

Hakan had been part of the conspiracy against their father, however, and if events had proceeded according to plan, Cemil would have been slain in the "bandit attack" as well, clearing the way for Hakan to become caravan master when their mother eventually decided she'd had enough of the road and wished to retire.

Hakan wrote the messages Cemil requested on tiny bits of parchment, tied them to the pigeons' legs, and released the birds to the sky. But he wrote a different message for the pigeon bound for Arenjun to carry, and he wrote it in the special code the Sülale used only in the direst of circumstances. He told of how a Cimmerian and a Khitan warrior had slain his parents, uncle, and cousin, along with all the guards—not *quite* the truth, but near enough for his purposes. He gave a brief description of the two men, along with their names, and ended his message with these words:

If you see these men, slay them. Make it painful and make it last.

He attached the message to the pigeon, stepped outside the cabin, released the bird, and watched with grim satisfaction as it took wing and headed west.

10

Shengis sat on the hard wooden seat of a four-wheeled wagon, holding the reins of an old brown mare. He had no need to guide the nameless animal as she trudged along the well-worn dirt path that cut through a verdant sward, for the horse had made the trip home numerous times and could probably travel it in her sleep. It was nearly spring in southern Zamora, the air pleasantly cool, but Shengis was wrapped in a heavy robe with the hood pulled up.

The sun is out and there are no clouds in the sky, so why is it so damned cold?

"You know why. Stop complaining."

For fifteen years he had shared his body with Kekk, and yet the Serpent Man was always surprised when he felt chilled. His kind had existed for untold millennia, and their bodies had long ago adjusted to the varying temperatures in the different regions of the known world. They had no need to sun themselves the way ordinary reptiles did. But Kekk no longer had his own body, and unfortunately for Shengis what one of them felt, so did the other. Thus if Kekk was cold, so was he.

He shivered and drew the robe tighter around him.

Years ago, Uzzeran had explained to Shengis how he had come to host Kekk's mind within his.

I believe one of the Eye's shards passed through Kekk's brain without slowing and continued on to enter yours. The shard captured the Serpent Man's spirit as it passed through him, and when the shard lodged in your brain, Kekk took up residence inside you. I could attempt to remove the shard by cutting into your head, but the procedure would most likely slay you. And I know of no spell that could separate the two of you.

Shengis had no choice but to learn to live with Kekk's presence inside his mind, and for the last decade and a half he had done his best, although it had not been easy. There were some benefits, however. His body healed rapidly now and his senses were heightened, especially at night. Also, Kekk possessed knowledge accumulated over the course of untold millennia and would sometimes share some of that knowledge with Shengis—but only when it benefited the Serpent Man. Shengis told himself his joining with Kekk had been Set's will, but deep down he believed it was merely the result of an unfortunate accident and that the Serpent Man was a burden he would be forced to carry until the end of his days.

The cart creaked and wobbled as the mare slowly clopped along, and Shengis thought it would need repairs soon. There was a small village five miles to the north called Whitehaven, where Shengis went whenever he and the master needed basic supplies—they were returning from there now, in fact, as the full cloth bags in the bed of the cart testified—and there was a blacksmith there who could restore the cart. He'd have to remember to ask Uzzeran to create more "silver" coins so he could pay for the repairs during his next trip. Working magic took a great deal out of Uzzeran these days, and transforming a handful of stones into false silver—a feat which once would have been simple for the sorcerer—wearied him to the point where he would take to his bed for an entire day, maybe two.

After another hour of travel, a simple stone farmhouse with a thatched roof came into view. When Shengis and Uzzeran had fled Arenjun after the Eye of Set's destruction, they had traveled on foot for a number of days before stumbling across this house. The farmer and his wife who had lived here along with their two young children had been kind enough to take in a pair of weary travelers. Uzzeran repaid that kindness by slaying them and turning all four into revenants. That feat had nearly slain him, which was how he and Shengis had first learned of his new limitations.

They had taken up residence in the house and eventually discovered a cave half a mile away, which Uzzeran claimed as his new workspace in which to continue his magical experimentation. The revenants—the farmer and his family, as well as those unfortunate souls the sorcerer had experimented on over the years—dwelled there, still as statues as they waited for their creator's command, along with the many shadow snakes that Uzzeran had summoned. The sorcerer's progress was slow, and the work was made even more difficult since Set had chosen not to bless them with another mystic artifact to replace the Eye.

Uzzeran will never succeed, Kekk said. *Leave the useless old fool.*

This was not the first time Kekk had urged Shengis to abandon Uzzeran, and each time it seemed a little more attractive. He would never desert the master, though. Set had tasked Uzzeran with a mission, and Shengis would not turn his back on the Great Serpent.

What your master seeks to do is an abomination! Set created my kind while yours were still apes. We are her true heirs! Uzzeran is mad, or else he was tricked by some being masquerading as Set. It matters not which. The two of you are not following Set's wishes. You are blaspheming against the Dread One!

Shengis felt a headache coming on. This happened whenever

Kekk became angry and did the mental equivalent of shouting in Shengis' ear. Unfortunately, the Serpent Man was angry most of the time. "I liked you better when you were posing as Hutai," he growled.

Kekk had no response to this, and Shengis allowed himself a small smile. It was rare that he got the last word with the Serpent Man.

Shengis parked the cart close to the house, unhitched the mare, and led her to her paddock, where she drank deeply from the trough and then began placidly grazing on grass. Then he returned to the cart, picked up one of the cloth bags filled with supplies—dried meat, vegetables, and candles—and carried it to the front door. As he reached for the metal handle, he paused and scented the air.

Someone was here. A woman, perhaps.

He became instantly alert, and a cold calmness settled on him. He put the bag on the ground, drew his poisoned dagger, quietly opened the door, then stepped inside, moving slowly and silently as a snake. His muscles were tensed, ready to strike at the intruder, whoever it might be. He knew Kekk would help him, for if he died then so would the Serpent Man.

Uzzeran sat at the simple wooden table. Across from him sat a woman Shengis recognized but had not seen for fifteen years.

"Rynthia?" he said.

She smiled. "Hello, Shengis."

She was a Zamorian woman in her late thirties with black hair, dark eyes, and deeply tanned skin. She was dressed for travel—tunic, breeches, boots, hooded cloak—and her clothes were worn and dusty. She carried a dagger tucked beneath her belt, and her pack and waterskin lay on the floor behind her, propped against the wall. Her gaze moved to the dagger in his hand, then she looked up at him, still smiling.

He reluctantly sheathed the blade and closed the door behind him, then looked to his master for a cue on how he should react. Uzzeran motioned for him to come and sit with them.

The sorcerer wore his usual gray robe and sandals, but the last fifteen years had not been kind to him. He was skeletally thin now, and while he was only in his late fifties, he looked thirty years older. His parchment-thin skin was drawn tight to his bones and his hands had a constant tremor. Worst of all was his left eye, or rather the socket where it had been. The ebon shard of the Eye of Set still protruded from it and the wound there remained as fresh as the night it was made. On the rare occasions when Uzzeran left the farmhouse, he donned a black cloak with a large hood that hung down and concealed the upper half of his face. He did not appear self-conscious in front of Rynthia, though, and if Uzzeran's appearance bothered her, she gave no sign.

Shengis hesitated for a second but then went over and took a seat between Uzzeran and Rynthia.

If you know this woman, why are you suspicious of her? Kekk asked.

It had been Rynthia who had given the Eye of Set to Uzzeran, with no explanation other than Mother Set had bade her do so. Uzzeran had been so excited to have the mystic artifact that he had not questioned Rynthia further. Shengis had sensed there was more to the woman than her being a follower of Set, but at the time he had been unable to put his finger on what exactly this might be. Now he burned to question her himself. Where had the Eye been? How had she managed to obtain it? How had she known where Uzzeran's lair was? Where had she gone after delivering the Eye to them, and why had they not seen or heard from her over the last fifteen years?

"How did you find us?" he asked instead.

"When you go to Whitehaven, you use your real name," she said. "Once I discovered you went there for supplies, it was easy enough to find this house. It's not much, but I suppose it's a step up from that subterranean chamber you used to dwell in."

Shengis felt like a fool. It had never occurred to him to conceal his identity.

"I have a horse," Rynthia continued, "but I left him tethered to a tree half a mile or so from here. No one lives near this place, but I did not want to leave him outside where someone passing by might see him."

Uzzeran spoke with the enthusiasm of a much younger man. "Rynthia has brought wonderful news! She knows the location of the second Eye of Set!"

Shengis frowned. "There is another?"

"Well, of course, you idiot!" Uzzeran snapped. "Set is..." The sorcerer trailed off and a blank expression came onto his face. He sat motionless, his one good eye staring at something only he could see.

Rynthia gave Shengis a questioning look, but the servant was uncertain how to respond, or even if he should. Ever since the shard had become lodged in Uzzeran's eye socket, his master had periodically experienced episodes like this, when his mind seemed to go elsewhere for a time. He always returned to full awareness eventually, but it was impossible to tell how long an episode would last. Some took only a few seconds, while the longest Shengis had witnessed lasted more than hour. Uzzeran was never aware of the episodes, and when Shengis had once attempted to explain them to his master, the sorcerer had threatened to flay him alive if he ever spoke of anything so ludicrous again. Shengis prayed to Set that this episode would be a short one, for if it continued too long then Rynthia would begin to wonder if something was wrong with Uzzeran's mind, and Shengis wished to preserve his master's reputation as a great sorcerer.

Then Uzzeran's good eye blinked and he began speaking again exactly where he had left off.

"...a serpent, and serpents have two eyes, do they not? Do you not see what this means?"

Shengis was too relieved his master's episode was over to care about the answer to his question, so he shook his head instead of attempting to answer.

"The spring solstice approaches! Set has given us an opportunity to atone for our failure fifteen years ago!" Uzzeran turned to Rynthia. "I have had many years to ponder what went wrong, and I have conducted numerous experiments to discover what I might do differently if I ever had another chance. Of course, without the Eye my successes were minimal at best, but now..."

An Eye of Set fused us, Kekk said. *Perhaps an Eye of Set can separate us as well.*

For the first time in many years, Shengis felt hope. To be his own person again, to have thoughts that were private, to have *quiet* inside his head... It would be glorious.

"Where is the second Eye?" Shengis asked. "Surely you did not leave it with your horse."

"I discovered the first Eye myself," Rynthia said, "and Set spoke to me through it and commanded that I take it directly to you, which I did. Someone else discovered the second Eye, and it is currently sealed within a vault inside a castle hidden within the Kezankian Mountains. I can take you there and help you obtain it. Then you can use the castle, and its inhabitants, to complete the holy task Set has charged you with."

Shengis frowned. "How can you help us gain entrance? Is this castle not guarded?"

"It is," Rynthia admitted. "But I know a way we can bypass the guards."

She smiled.

"I do live there, after all."

Valja sat at wooden desk, reading an ancient scroll, or at least trying to. Normally, scholars wore black gloves when handling materials this old to prevent the oils of their skin from damaging the parchment. Valja did not need to take that precaution, however, for her too-pale skin was always dry as bone. More scrolls, as well as a stack of books, lay atop the desk, and when other scholars passed by, they gave her disapproving looks. In the library, it was considered rude to take more than one piece of reading material at a time, for doing so meant someone else who might need one of the volumes you had would be forced to wait until you were finished with it. Valja had not been big on rules before coming to Ravenhold, and that had not changed much in the intervening years.

The library was one of the largest areas in the castle, second only to the repository itself. The room was lit by numerous chandeliers holding beeswax candles hanging from the high ceiling, and scholars were not permitted to have candles or oil lamps at their desks due to the risk of reading materials catching fire. The walls were lined with shelves twenty feet tall, all of them filled to bursting with books, scrolls, stacks of loose parchment, and tablets of wood or stone. Ladders were placed throughout the room so the library attendants could reach tomes stored on the higher shelves.

There were fifty-seven reading tables—Valja had counted them soon after she had arrived here—each large enough for two scholars to use, either sitting side by side or across from each other. In the center of the room was a round table containing maps of the known world and its kingdoms from various periods in history, of lands long since vanished such as ancient Atlantis, and of strange, incomprehensible realms far beyond Earth. At times Valja could feel the weight of all the years the works stored here represented, and it was like being in the midst of Time itself.

But her favorite part of the library was the animals.

Positioned at intervals around the room were the bodies of creatures that had roamed the world long ago but were now extinct, or nearly so. The beasts had been preserved by taxidermy to keep them looking as fresh as the day they had died. There were half a dozen, most of which were prehistoric versions of common animals—a giant black bear, a huge gray elk, a tawny cat with gigantic fangs—but there was one she disliked looking at, and whenever she came to the library, she chose a table where it wasn't in her line of sight. It was a massive serpent with verdant scales, amber eyes, and a pair of fangs that rivaled the ancient cat's. The snake was positioned so that its lower half was coiled and its head and neck were raised, as if it was ready to attack any second. After Valja had learned about Naerys' experiences in Khemi—and what had happened with Uzzeran—she wanted nothing to do with serpents ever again.

"Interesting reading?"

She looked up and saw Renwick standing next to her. She had been lost in her thoughts and had not noticed him approach. She smiled sardonically. "How should I know? My command of Valusian is shaky at best."

Renwick was a middle-aged Nemedian man, tall and fair-skinned, with gray eyes, white hair, and a beard to match. He wore the typical male scholar's uniform: black tunic with a sash around the waist—red, a symbol of his station—and sandals. Valja wore the uniform for females: black dress, sash, and sandals, though her sash was white, marking her as still a novice, even after fifteen years.

Renwick spoke in a voice dripping with mock disdain. "My dear, you give yourself *far* too much credit. Your Valusian is *abysmal.*"

The two were silent for a moment and then burst out laughing.

"May I take a look?" Renwick asked, his tone kindly now.

Valja gestured to the chair next to her, and Renwick pulled it out and sat. She slid the scroll over to him and he donned his gloves and spent several minutes perusing it. While he read, Valja pressed her fingers to her chest and absently rubbed the black shard hidden beneath the cloth. It was a habit she had picked up not long after that night in the ruins of the Tower of the Elephant, and was one she found impossible to shake. She remembered to keep breathing while Renwick examined the scroll's contents, even though she had no need to and it took a conscious effort for her to do so, but she found that people who spent any time near her always began to feel uneasy when they did not hear her breathe regularly. She had known Renwick longer than anyone else at Ravenhold, and while he was the most comfortable of all the scholars in her presence, he still grew nervous if she did not breathe when around him. She had tried forcing herself to blink as well, but she could never get the rhythm quite right, and her attempts only disturbed people, so she stopped. At least her not blinking seemed not to bother Renwick. He was one of the few scholars who would look her in the eye for longer than a few seconds when speaking to her.

He was also one of the few who treated her like she was a woman in her thirties, even if she still looked like she was only nineteen. Sorcerers and philosophers had searched for the secret of eternal youth throughout the history of the human race, but she alone had discovered it. It was simple, really. All you had to do was *almost* die and then remain trapped in that state for… well, who knew how long? Maybe until the end of time.

Renwick looked up from the scroll and turned to her. "This is a treatise on healing magic. You are still seeking a spell the magisters can use to cure Taolin."

Only the three magisters in residence at Ravenhold could actually work magic, and the scholars and seekers supported them through research and field expeditions. They understood the basics of magic on a purely academic basis but did not cast any spells themselves.

Rynthia had brought Taolin to Ravenhold nearly six months ago. The seeker had found the young boy living on the streets of Shadizar—no parents, no brothers, no sisters, no home—doing his best to remain hidden and subsisting on what meager scraps of food he could find in refuse piles. The boy's eyes were a bright red, and his skin held a pinkish tinge. If his eyes had been normal, no one would have thought much of his skin color, but *with* the red eyes, his skin looked unnatural. People often accused him of having been cursed by a demon or of actually being one. And to make his situation even worse, he was in constant pain. *My skin feels like someone stuck a thousand needles in me*, he had once told her.

Despite the hardships he had endured, Taolin was a sweet boy, though he was shy and spoke little—understandable behaviors given how difficult his life in Shadizar had been so far. He had no memory of family, and the scholars theorized that his mother may have been exposed to dark magic while he had still been developing in her womb, but none of them knew for certain. If his parents still lived, they had most likely abandoned the child, leaving him to roam the streets like an unwanted pet.

Valja's heart had gone out to Taolin the instant she had met him, for she knew what it was like to be something that frightened people.

"I keep hoping that if I can find a spell that will alleviate his pain and give him a normal appearance, I can petition the council to permit one of the magisters to use it on him," she told Renwick.

The council was formed from the most senior scholars, and

while the magisters were permitted to use magic, they could only do so with the council's approval. If a magister broke this law, they would be cast out, never to return, but only after the other two magisters had wiped their memory so they could never reveal Ravenhold's location to the outer world.

Renwick had been a seeker fifteen years ago when he had found Valja wandering the Zamorian countryside. She thought of how he had described Ravenhold to her when they had met:

A thousand years ago, a powerful Khitan sorcerer named Pingxia came to the Kezankian Mountains on the southeastern border of Zamora. She chose the mountain known as Skycrest and used her magic to shape the substance of the rock into an edifice she named Ravenhold, due to the large population of the night-black birds in the area. Ravenhold was no ordinary castle, for not only had it been born from the mountain but Pingxia had designed it to look like a natural part of Skycrest, thereby hiding it from the rest of humanity. She also placed powerful warding spells on the castle to cloak it from the mystical awareness of other sorcerers.

Once this was done, Pingxia recruited the first generation of scholars, magisters, and seekers and tasked them with two missions. First, they were to collect deadly magical items and tomes of forbidden knowledge from across the known world and lock them away in a special vault she had created called the Repository, where they could never be used for evil again. Second, they were to search for those unfortunate souls who had been the subjects of sorcerers' experiments and then discarded when they no longer were useful. Pingxia commanded the magisters to use their power to cure the afflicted, as she termed them, or, failing that, to give them a home in Ravenhold where they could live out their lives safely, should they wish to.

According to legend, one of the scholars asked Pingxia why she had done all this. The sorcerer thought for some time before answering. "I have lived a long time and done much harm in this world. I wish to make what amends I can before I travel the Shadow Road, although I know that, whatever good may come from my actions, it can never be enough."

That night, Pingxia vanished, never to be seen again. Some of the scholars said she had returned to Khitan while others theorized that she had traveled to far-distant lands to create more refuges like Ravenhold. Still others suggested she had used her magic to destroy herself out of guilt for some unknown sin in her past. A few went so far as to claim she was in truth a goddess, or perhaps a demon, only posing as a human sorcerer, and that she had returned to whatever otherworldly realm she called home. Whatever the truth, Pingxia was never seen by the inhabitants of Ravenhold again, and no word of her did seekers hear during their travels across the known lands.

Sorcerers could not use the afflicted as sacrifices to their dark gods, as they were too flawed for the foul entities most served in exchange for power. Usually, they slew the afflicted outright—or ordered their servants to do it—or kept them imprisoned until they died. In some rare cases, though, they set them free. If an afflicted individual was able to pass as an ordinary human, they could live among others, even have something approaching a normal life—assuming they were both careful and *lucky. But all too often the afflicted displayed physical signs of what had been done to them or manifested dangerous abilities. The ignorant saw the afflicted as witches and demons, and demanded they be burned at the stake. Sometimes they managed to flee in time to avoid this fate. Often, they did not.*

Renwick brought her to Ravenhold, but as she had feared, the magisters were unable to cure her of her condition, so she became a resident. She found life in the castle boring after all the adventure and mischief she had experienced in Arenjun, so she soon requested to be trained as a scholar, and with Renwick's recommendation to the council, her application was approved. Not only had she become a scholar there but she had worked as a seeker as well, and had made a new life for herself at Ravenhold, a life she dearly loved and found deeply satisfying. Whoever would have thought that a Maul street-thief would end up in a place like this, she thought, helping those who had been cursed like her? The old saying was true: *None can divine the path the gods make for us.*

Valja's thoughts returned to the present. "Even though Taolin must stay with us for the rest of his life," she said, "I would like him to feel..."

"Comfortable in his skin?" Renwick ventured.

Valja rolled her eyes at her mentor's bad joke.

Once someone came to Ravenhold, they were never permitted to leave. It had been Pingxia's most important command to the newly gathered scholars: Ravenhold's existence must be kept secret at all costs. Otherwise, sorcerers from across the world—and worlds beyond this one—would seek to claim the power it held for their own use. Only seekers were allowed to come and go from Ravenhold, and only then under very strict conditions.

"I sincerely hope you find some kind of treatment for the boy," Renwick said. "But if you cannot, perhaps he will adjust to his condition in time, as you have."

Adjust? Her? She would give anything to feel her heart beat again, to fill her lungs with air that actually nourished her body, to eat food again, to sleep, to feel any sensation but mild pressure on her flesh. She fought to keep her smile in place, not wishing Renwick to know how much his words had stung.

"Perhaps," she said.

Renwick left her table soon after that to tend to studies of his own. Valja continued struggling to read the Valusian scroll for another two hours, and while she could not understand every word, she understood enough to know the spells detailed in the scroll would not work for Taolin, for they required ingredients that could be obtained only in Atlantis, which had sunk beneath the turbulent waves of the Western Sea millennia ago.

She returned the scroll, along with the other tomes she had consulted, to an attendant, and then departed the library, careful not to look at the preserved body of the dire wyrm on the way out. Then, since Taolin was still on her mind, she decided to go in search of the boy.

Because Ravenhold had been "grown" by magic, it was not constructed with stone blocks laid by masons and held together by mortar but had been carved from the very substance of the mountain. Walking its walls, it was as if you were inside the mountain itself, wandering naturally occurring tunnels and caves that only happened to resemble halls and rooms. Surfaces were a mix of granite and shale displaying visible strata, colors varying from black to white to gray to greenish-gray, with a rough, lumpy texture. Valja had been told the interior of the castle had a pleasant earthy scent, but since she was unable to smell, she could not confirm this. Ravenhold was a place of beauty and wonder, and she considered it a great privilege to live here.

Dinner would not be served for several hours, so she doubted Taolin was in the dining hall. Nor would he be in the baths, the laundry, or the lesser library. She supposed he might be in the boys' bed chamber, but it hurt him to lie down or sit so he spent most of his day on his feet, and she had once found him in a hallway napping while standing. She did not even consider that he might be outside as Ravenhold had no gardens, trees, or walking paths, because Pingxia had created it to look like part of the mountain.

That left only three places she could think of where he might be. He sometimes climbed the stairs to the top of one of the tower rooms to gaze out of a window. The views from the towers were spectacular, and it felt as if you could see all of the world from that vantage point. But walking up that many stairs might be too much for his feet to endure, depending on how bad his pain was today.

Perhaps he was in the gaming hall? Most of Ravenhold's residents were adults of varying ages, but those children who dwelled in the castle spent many happy hours in the hall. Taolin was unable to play the more physical games, but he liked to watch others enjoy themselves.

The last place he could be was the one he visited most frequently.

The infirmary was located on the main floor, on the opposite side of the castle from the dining hall, and Valja decided it was her best bet, so she walked to the end of the hallway and took the stairs down a level. Many of the afflicted visited there regularly as they suffered from serious physical and mental conditions, some so bad that the sufferers spent most of their time there, seeking whatever relief they could get from the healers. When Taolin's skin became especially painful—*Sometimes it feels like I'm burning alive*—that was where he went.

The door to the infirmary was always unlocked, and Valja opened it and walked in.

The room was large enough to fit a dozen beds spaced several feet apart, and on this day eight were occupied. Two healers and five assistants were on duty, the healers dressed in scholars' uniforms with blue sashes, the assistants in the plain brown tunics worn by all general castle staff. The three windows were open to allow as much fresh air and sunlight as possible to enter, but they did little to counter the atmosphere of pain and fear.

Taolin was not among the patients in the room.

Valja was about to turn and leave when one of the healers, an Aquilonian woman in her thirties named Kaniphera, saw her, smiled, and came over. "Hello, Valja. Has there been a change in your condition?"

The woman sounded almost eager. While most people thought Valja was some sort of undead monster, the healers of Ravenhold were fascinated with her, for even in a sanctuary for victims of sorcery, she was unique. The assistants, however, did not feel the same, nor did the patients. Some stared at her with fear in their eyes while others pretended she wasn't there, the staff bustling about their duties in her presence while the patients closed their eyes and feigned sleep.

"Sorry to disappoint you, but I am the same as always." She smiled to take the sting out of her words. "I was just looking for Taolin."

"He's there," Kaniphera said, nodding toward a door at the back of the room, this one closed. The door was the entrance to the second part of the infirmary, the isolation area, where patients with more severe conditions who might in some way prove a threat to others were kept, in small rooms with open doorways. Only healers and magisters were permitted to go through that door, and Valja was immediately concerned. If Taolin was there, that meant something bad must have had happened to him.

"What's wrong with him?" she demanded.

The other healer, an older Argossean man named Erien, joined them, and Valja held back an irritated sigh. She liked Kaniphera, but Erien was both officious *and* humorless. Every time Valja spoke with him, she ended up wanting to stab him in the eye.

"He developed a new symptom overnight," Erien said. "Sound now causes him discomfort. A soft whisper is painful to him, and anything louder makes him scream in agony."

"We are not certain," Kaniphera said, "but we believe the aspect of his affliction that causes his skin to constantly feel pain is starting to move *inside* his body."

Valja stared at her in horror. "So he will hurt outside *and* inside?"

Erien nodded. "It will be as if he becomes pain itself."

"We tried plugging his ears with bits of wool, but it hurt too much and he could not tolerate it," Kaniphera said.

Valja glanced at the door to the isolation area. Somewhere inside the chamber, Taolin stood inside a cell, eyes closed, breathing shallowly and trying not to listen to the sound of his own heartbeat. Too bad he wasn't almost dead like her; then he would feel nothing. But if Taolin's condition worsened to the point where he was in constant agony, the healers would petition the council to allow a magister to cast a death spell on the boy and end his misery.

Valja wanted to cry. Too bad her tear ducts didn't work.

11

Valja would have loved to visit Taolin for a bit, but given his new sensitivity to sound, she knew she would only cause him more pain. Worried and depressed, she returned to her room on the third floor of the castle. The room was small, with a single bed, a chamber pot beneath it, and a tiny desk and chair set against one of the stone walls in case she wished to do some studying in private. She was lucky to have a window—most residents didn't—and she'd opened the shutters soon after waking that morning to let in the cool mountain air. She liked knowing it surrounded her, even if she couldn't smell or feel it. Against the wall opposite the desk, there was a small wardrobe closet where she kept her meager collection of clothes, along with her old throwing knives, which lay at the bottom wrapped in a cloth. She had not touched them since coming here fifteen years ago and wondered if she would ever pick them up again. Most likely not. What need did a Ravenhold scholar have for weapons?

She possessed only one other personal item, and it sat atop the desk.

She pulled out the chair, sat, and gazed upon the golden

statuette of Ishtar the Warrior—wearing a breast plate and leather skirt, holding a pair of swords crossed over her chest, her beautiful features set in a fierce expression.

"Please look after Taolin," she said. She doubted there was much Ishtar's warrior aspect could do for the boy, but it hurt not to ask.

The three magisters had allowed Valja to keep the statuette in her room since their examination of it when she had first arrived revealed it held no magic. They assumed she was a devotee of the goddess—all religions were welcome in Ravenhold, except for Setites and worshippers of similar dark gods—but while Valja acknowledged and respected Ishtar's divinity, she'd held on to the statuette because it reminded her of that night in the temple, the last time she'd truly felt free and alive—and because it reminded her of Conan. She had lost track of the Cimmerian after they had parted ways in Arenjun.

"You mean after you left him," she muttered to herself.

Valja had been born in a small village to the east of Shadizar to a pair of skilled potters. Her parents' plates, bowls, and jars were so well made that traders detoured from the Road of Kings to come buy their wares, which they then resold in Shadizar and Arenjun for much higher prices. Her parents didn't mind, though. *Your mother and I are happy where we're at*, her father had once told her.

They were less happy when one of the traders brought a fever to their village. When the disease had finally run its course, two-thirds of the villagers were dead, her parents included. Valja had been only nine years old. She had been assisting her parents in their work since learning to walk, and they had taught her much about the craft of pottery-making, though sadly not enough for traders to make a special trip to buy her work. None of the surviving villagers would take her in, for they believed witchcraft was the only way she could have avoided catching the fever herself while tending to her parents during their short illness. They set her parents' home aflame—to cleanse the "evil"—then cast her out of the village without food or water.

She found her way to the Road of Kings and walked it alone for several days until a Turanian merchant's caravan found her. The caravan master took her onto his own wagon and his wife gave her food and drink. The couple were kind, and she allowed herself to hope that she could stay with them permanently, but when they reached Arenjun, the man tried to sell her at the slave market. But before the caravan master could put her on the dais for the buyers to get a good look at her, she kicked his left knee so hard his kneecap shattered and fled into the crowd, leaving the Turanian howling in pain.

Thus began her life as a thief on the streets of Arenjun.

That life was good, and it became significantly better after she met Conan. Their time together was brief, only three months, but it had been the best period of her life. Once she had left to live at Ravenhold and begun working as a seeker, she started hearing stories about Conan, and she asked other seekers to listen for word of him, too. Over the years, she had learned that, after his time as a thief, he had served as a soldier, hired himself out as a mercenary, and sailed the sea as a pirate. He had traveled across the known world and back again, in the process becoming something of a legend. He had been a curious, restless young man when she had known him, always ready to test his strength and will against any challenge. It appeared that those qualities had never left him.

"Good for you, my love," she whispered.

She reached out and gently touched the statuette of Ishtar. She knew it was silly, but since Conan had held it all those years ago, touching it now made her feel close to him again, if only for a moment.

Make yourself ready.

She jerked her hand away from the statuette. It had spoken to her! Not aloud, though. She had heard the voice—the *goddess'* voice—in her mind… or had she? Perhaps she had merely imagined it? Or perhaps, like poor Taolin, her condition was worsening, and she was beginning to lose her mind.

Ravenhold had three lower levels. The bottommost contained the repository, while the level above that was the menagerie, where those afflicted who were more beast than human were kept locked away. The level immediately below the castle's main floor was where the afflicted who had been struck with madness were confined. If her mental state continued to worsen, she might well find herself locked away there, and sooner rather than later.

The thought terrified her.

She looked upon the statuette's face once more. She did not hear the goddess' voice again, but she stared at the statuette for several moments. Now it was as if the goddess was speaking directly to her spirit, and she had no conscious awareness of her words.

She walked over to her wardrobe, knelt, and removed the clothes she had been wearing on her arrival at Ravenhold with Renwick: a black tunic (with a hole in the chest), dark brown boots, and hooded gray cloak. She quickly slipped off her robe, let it drop to the floor, and donned her old thieving outfit. Her body hadn't changed at all since she was nineteen, and everything fit perfectly. Lastly, she grabbed the bag with her throwing knives, removed them, and with deft, swift motions concealed them in the pockets sewn to the inside of her cloak.

She was ready, but for what, she didn't know. She supposed she would find out soon enough.

Now to find Renwick.

She opened the door to her room, stepped out, and ghosted down the hall, silent as a midnight shadow.

"—need to be most careful of are the three magisters," Rynthia was saying. "They'll be the ones wearing purple sashes. Individually, none of them are a match for you, Uzzeran, but working together, they could prove most formidable."

Uzzeran nodded absently, and Shengis knew his master was only half listening to the woman. His sole eye had lit up with avarice when Rynthia had told them about Ravenhold and the mystic treasures it held, and it had been all the sorcerer could think about for the four days it had taken them to travel from the farmhouse to Skycrest Mountain.

Can you blame him? Kekk said. *From what the woman told us, their library might even contain some of my people's magical knowledge, information recorded before you humans were a glint in the eyes of the gods. It's possible we might find a spell that will separate us!*

Now *that* got Shengis' attention. For fifteen years the Serpent Man had been living inside his skull. To be free of his unwanted passenger, to have blessed silence inside his mind at last, would be glorious.

The three of them—four, if you counted Kekk—walked up a steep series of stone steps in a narrow tunnel. Uzzeran clutched a cloth in his right hand, and from time to time he used it to dab away the blood slowly oozing from his wounded eye. There was only enough room for them to walk in single file and Rynthia led the way, carrying a burning torch for light. Uzzeran followed her and Shengis came third. Behind him trailed a small army of two dozen revenants, most of them human but with three Serpent Men in the mix. Shengis disliked having the undead things so close and kept imaging a shadow-snake lunging from an eye socket to bury its fangs in his shoulder.

They shall not harm you so long as we are one, Kekk said.

Shengis hoped the Serpent Man was right.

According to Rynthia, this was an escape route for the inhabitants of Ravenhold. A broader, less steep tunnel served as the main entrance, and a third wound around the mountain in a gentle incline, its floor flat so that horses and carts could bring in supplies. The escape tunnel had never been used throughout the long history of Ravenhold, and because of this very few people remembered its existence, which made it the perfect route for them into the castle without alerting anyone. She had learned about it only by chance, on finding mention of it in an ancient tome of history that had been misshelved in the philosophy section of the library.

Shengis wondered how much farther they still had to climb. This damn tunnel seemed to go on forever. He was no longer a young man, and even with the extra stamina he had gained when Kekk's mind had merged with his, his legs were starting to ache.

Humans are so disgustingly weak, Kekk said.

Shengis ignored him and continued trudging upward, one foot after another.

This time Set's plan would work, Rynthia was certain of it, and that success would be in no small part due to her.

She had started life as a slave. Her parents, whom she had never known, had been slaves in the manor home of one of the most powerful merchants in Arenjun, a man who, among other business interests, bred and sold slaves. Some customers liked to buy theirs fully mature, but others preferred to purchase children and train them to work in their household, and the merchant specialized in the latter. Of course, some customers bought children for purposes other than labor, dark purposes, but the merchant cared not how the children he bred were to be used. All he cared about was being paid. Once a slave was sold, they ceased to exist for him.

When she was three, Rynthia was bought by a trader who took her to the slaver city of Sukhet in Stygia, bordering the cannibal country of Darfar. There, she was purchased by a servant of the sorceress Nabishut and taken to the woman's estate in the capital city of Luxur. Rynthia could speak only Zamorian, but she learned Stygian quickly, and when she was older she was taught to read and write by one of the tutors the sorceress employed. Her duties consisted primarily of light housework, and as far as the life of a slave went, hers wasn't all that bad. Of course, she had never known freedom, so she had no real basis for comparison.

Nabishut used her magic to create art, and her chosen medium was human flesh. She *sculpted* people; at her touch, skin, muscle, and bone became as malleable as wet clay.

Rynthia did not feel the sorceress' touch until she was nine. She had been working in the kitchen then, and one of the older slaves gave her a cup of tea to take to Nabishut in her study. Rynthia had never interacted with their mistress before and she was afraid, but she did as she was told. Nabishut's study had shelves filled with books, and when Rynthia saw them, she stared in wonder. She had not known there were so many books in the entire world. How could one person possibly read them all within a single lifetime?

Nabishut stood at a table, looking over a piece of parchment upon which several constellations had been drawn in black ink. She kept her gaze lowered as she approached the sorceress as she'd been taught, and when she reached the table she stood and waited for her mistress to notice her. After a time, Nabishut took the tea and said, "You may go." But as Rynthia began to turn away, the sorceress said, "Hold a moment. Look at me, child."

She was afraid, but she had no choice but to do as Nabishut commanded and looked up at the tall, thin Stygian woman wearing a diaphanous blue dress that seemed no more substantial than mist.

"You are comely, girl," the sorceress said. "But your eyes are too far apart."

Nabishut took hold of her face, placed her thumbs over her eyes, and pushed.

Rynthia screamed.

As the years passed, Nabishut adjusted Rynthia's face and body whenever it suited her. By the time she was fourteen, she was the most beautiful slave in the sorceress' household. Nabishut had a standing mirror in her study, and after each adjustment she allowed Rynthia to examine her reflection. Each time Rynthia marveled at her mistress' skill, and despite the pain that came with each adjustment, she felt great pride to be Nabishut's canvas.

Then one day, another slave discovered Nabishut lying on the floor in her study, dead, her body wrapped in thorny vines. No one knew if she had cast a spell that went wrong or had been attacked by a rival sorcerer, but the specifics of her death did not matter. Her slaves were free. Some of them left the estate, but many stayed, unable to muster the will to go, and waited for someone to come find them and take them to a new master. Rynthia left with the others, terrified but excited, and began to explore Luxur. She quickly discovered she could use her beauty to get men to do whatever she wanted, if she was willing to share her body with them, and eventually found a man willing to take her back to Arenjun. She knew it was likely hopeless, but she wanted to try to find her parents, and perhaps discover if she had any siblings.

But once they were in Arenjun, the skin on Rynthia's face began to sag, and she realized with horror that the effects of

Nabishut's magic were not permanent. Soon her face looked as if she wore a mask fashioned from melted wax, and the man who had brought her to Arenjun, disgusted with her appearance, abandoned her. She lived on the street after that, begging passersby for coins. People avoided looking at her, or they stared in sickened fascination as they walked by, but few dropped coins into the bowl she held.

But then one day Renwick, who had been not much older than she was at the time, found her. He was a seeker then, and he recognized her condition as being an effect of magic, so he took her to Ravenhold, where the magisters were able to restore her face to the way it would have looked naturally had Nabishut never touched her. She was no longer a great beauty, but she cared not. She was just happy not to be a monster anymore. At Ravenhold, she found the home and family she had never known, and eventually she became a seeker, determined to help victims of magic just as Renwick had helped her.

Several years later, she returned to Stygia. A scholar examining a newly found ancient scroll discovered a reference to a mystic artifact called the Eye of Set, which supposedly was hidden somewhere in the city of Pteion in eastern Stygia. Pteion was rumored to have been built by the Serpent Men thousands of years ago, but it had been abandoned for centuries and people shunned it for it was said to be cursed. Since Rynthia had grown up in Stygia and was fluent in both the language and the customs of the land, the council chose her to go in search of the Eye.

It was a long and difficult journey, and Pteion was not without its hazards, but after an exhaustive search of the city Rynthia discovered a series of underground catacombs containing the skeletal remains of hundreds of Serpent Men, and within a hidden chamber she found the Eye of Set. Elated, she began preparing the artifact for transport to Ravenhold when a voice spoke inside her mind.

My daughter, I welcome you back to your true homeland. I have a task for you.

Deep in her soul, she knew she was hearing the voice of Set, and without thinking she fell to her knees. Nabishut had worshipped the Great Serpent and had insisted her slaves do the same. The sorceress had performed dark rites to honor the god and had required her slaves to participate.

And by doing so, the voice went on, hearing her thoughts, *your immortal soul was bound to me for all eternity. That makes you my servant, and you shall do as I command.*

She felt a darkness rising within her and knew she had been a fool to think she could ever truly escape slavery.

She bowed her head. "I am yours, Dread Mistress."

As instructed, she took the Eye of Set to Uzzeran in Arenjun, then went back to Ravenhold, reported to the council that she had been unable to find the artifact, and then returned to her normal duties as a seeker and waited for Uzzeran to use the Eye to fulfill Set's plan.

And waited.

And waited.

Until one day, she realized that Uzzeran had failed somehow. *All that work for nothing.*

That night, she dreamed she was back in the catacombs of Pteion, holding a torch, surrounded by the bones of thousands of Serpent Men. Set's voice echoed from the mouths of the creatures' skulls, the force of her words shaking the catacombs like an earthquake.

Be patient, my daughter. Another opportunity shall come.

It took fifteen years, but eventually a different seeker brought an artifact to Ravenhold, a twin to the Eye of Set. He had discovered the second Eye in a Nemedian museum, had stolen it after hours, and hurried to bring it to the council. The council members were sorely tempted to allow the magisters to examine the Eye and explore its capabilities, but in the end they decided the artifact was simply too dangerous and locked it away in the repository, where it remained.

But not for much longer, Rynthia thought with a smile.

Shengis was gasping for breath by the time they all reached the top of the stairs. Before them was a smooth iron door with neither handle nor lock. Behind them were the revenants, as silent and patient as only the dead could be.

"The magisters have laid a spell on the door so that only a Ravenhold resident may open it," Rynthia said. She pressed her hand to the iron surface and after several seconds the door swung slowly open with the grating sound of metal against stone. But the seeker did not step inside immediately.

"This is the level where the menagerie is kept," she said. "Magical creatures from across the known world and beyond, some small as insects, others large as mammoths, still others that appear almost human. None are caged, for iron bars could not hold most of them. The magisters have placed stasis spells upon them, rendering them immobile and unaware of their surroundings. Only a magister"—she looked at Uzzeran—"or another powerful sorcerer can lift the enchantments and restore them to full life." Now she turned to Shengis. "We will be perfectly safe inside."

Shengis tried to look offended at the woman's assumption that he would be frightened within the menagerie, but in truth he *was* nervous.

Pathetic, Kekk said.

Rynthia entered first, lighting the chamber with her torch. Uzzeran followed, Shengis came after, and what both sorcerer and servant saw took their breath away.

They stood in a cavern so vast that the torchlight could illuminate only a small part of it, and what it revealed in that flickering glow was a group of beasts straight from the most feverish of nightmares. Some resembled animals Shengis was familiar with, such as a huge shaggy black wolf the size of a horse, or a falcon twice as large as it should be, with a long lizardish tail and human-like eyes, but other creatures were like nothing he'd ever seen or imagined. Things with long teeth and even longer talons, with too many eyes and mouths, segmented insect legs or smooth, boneless tentacles jutting from their misshapen bodies. Still others were hideous combinations of flesh-and-blood beasts merged with plants, stone, wood, and iron.

Combinations like us, Kekk said.

Shengis was too revolted by the sight of these abominations to respond to the Serpent Man. Rynthia had said these things were not dead, just frozen, and while she had also said they had no awareness in this state, he imagined he could feel their eyes on him, watching him, resenting his freedom to move, hating him for being able to come and go as he pleased, wishing they could be released from stasis just long enough so they could use their teeth and claws to tear him to bloody ribbons…

When Rynthia spoke again, he nearly jumped.

"Many of these creatures were the result of sorcerous experimentation," she said. "As you can see, some were more successful than others."

"This is fascinating," Uzzeran said. He looked at Rynthia and didn't try to conceal the raw, undisguised greed in his voice. "But what I *really* want to see is the repository. Where is it?"

She glanced at Shengis before replying to the sorcerer. "It lies one level below us. The only access is through a hidden passage in this chamber."

"Show me. *Now*."

"I… don't think that would be wise," Rynthia said.

Uzzeran clenched his jaw, balled his hands into fists, and black energy crackled around the shard lodged in his wounded eye. "*Why not?*" the sorcerer growled.

Shengis quickly stepped between the two of them and raised his palms in a placating gesture. "Because you do not have time to properly examine the objects in the repository, master," he said. "We have to deal with the magisters before they become aware of our presence and move against us."

"The guards, too," Rynthia put in.

Uzzeran flicked his angry gaze from Shengis to Rynthia and back again. His white-knuckled fists trembled and dark energy continued to coruscate around the shard. Shengis thought Uzzeran would slay both him and Rynthia right there and leave their bodies where they fell, but after several nerve-wracking seconds the tension drained out of Uzzeran's body. He relaxed his hands and the dark energy around the shard disappeared. He forced a smile.

"You are right, of course. Shall we continue?"

Rynthia looked at Shengis once more, and the Stygian servant gave a slight shrug in return. He was unsure what had caused Uzzeran to become so furious, but the mood had passed as quickly as it had come.

It's the shard, Kekk said. *It's responding to the strong presence of other magic in this place. The stronger its response, the more unstable the sorcerer's mind becomes—and it wasn't all that stable to begin with.*

Shengis felt a cold sinking sensation in his gut. That was a complication they did *not* need.

Rynthia nodded to Uzzeran. "The entrance to the next level up is on the other side of the cavern."

"Lead on," the sorcerer said with a smile.

Rynthia turned and started walking, as did Uzzeran. Shengis hesitated for a moment before heading after them, and the revenants, who had remained in the stairwell the entire time the humans had been speaking, took that as their cue to file out into the cavern and follow.

Valja was unsurprised to find Renwick in the library. If the council allowed him to move a bed in there and have his food delivered from the kitchen, he would never leave.

Most of the tables were occupied by scholars, and attendants circulated among them, collecting books and scrolls to return to the shelves. Most ignored her, but some noticed she wasn't dressed in her scholar's uniform and looked up from their reading, puzzled. Scholars and seekers *always* wore their uniforms while in Ravenhold. She found it a refreshing change of pace to have people stare at her because of what she was wearing rather than because of her condition.

Renwick had chosen a table in the middle of the library and now ran a magnifying crystal over the pages of a huge open book with a black-gloved hand, so he could read the small, cramped writing. He did not look up as Valja approached.

"Why in the name of Mitra do people write so damnably small when they keep a journal?" he grumbled.

"Because parchment doesn't grow on trees," she answered, then leaned over his shoulder to see what he was reading. "Is that Maklass' collection of counterspells? It is, isn't it?" She grinned as she realized what Renwick was doing. "You're searching for a spell to help Taolin, aren't you?"

He placed the magnifying crystal on the table, sat back in the chair, massaged his temples, and released a weary sigh. "And having absolutely no luck, I'm afraid. I—" He broke off, frowning, then turned his head to look at her, taking in her outfit briefly. "Have you decided to start seeking again?"

She ignored the question. "I need you to come with me. Right *now*."

His frown deepened. "Why? Is something wrong?"

"Yes, but I don't know what it is yet. I just know that it's important you accompany me."

Renwick looked at her quizzically for several seconds, then stood.

"Let's go," he said.

"And that was all she said? Make yourself ready?"

"Yes, and the words were accompanied by a strong feeling that I needed to get you, after which we must depart Ravenhold immediately."

After leaving the library, they had gone to Renwick's room so he could change into traveling clothes. He now he wore a brown leather vest over a long-sleeved white shirt, brown pants, and black boots. He had also donned a black travel cloak.

The two walked briskly down the first-floor hallway, heading in the direction of the infirmary.

"And you do not intend to seek the council's permission?" Renwick asked.

"No time," Valja said. "You know it takes them at least a week to make even the smallest decision."

"And right now we are going to…?"

"The infirmary. I want to check on Taolin and see if his condition has improved."

"You mean to take the boy with us? Is that Ishtar's will, too?"

Valja didn't answer.

"Valja, I know you believe the goddess spoke directly to

you, and many such events *have* been recorded throughout history, but not every voice someone hears in their mind is a divine message. We know so little about your condition, and it is possible—"

Sudden anger flared bright and hot within her. "What? That after fifteen years, my dead brain has finally started to rot?"

The truth was, she had no idea why she felt such a strong compulsion to check on Taolin. Ishtar had said nothing about Ravenhold being in danger, yet she could not escape the feeling that it was. Once she knew Taolin was safe—if still in isolation—she would be able to calm down and—

There was a stairwell at the end of the hall, leading down to the castle's lower levels. The entrance lay fifteen paces past the infirmary, and as Valja and Renwick drew near, a Zamorian man dressed in the simple tunic of a farmer emerged from the stairwell and started walking toward them with an awkward, stiff-legged gait.

A man with no eyes.

Valja's blood turned to ice water. She halted and grabbed Renwick's arm to stop him. "Ishtar, save us!" she whispered.

A Corinthian woman in a dress made from coarse brown fabric followed the man, and she also had no eyes.

A human-like creature with the head of a snake—eyeless, like the man and woman—followed, and Valja could see more coming up the stairs behind that one. She realized then that she had seen creatures like this before, fifteen years ago in the ruins of the Tower of the Elephant. How many of the damn things were there?

"Mitra!" Renwick said. "Is that... a Serpent Man? No, it can't be—their race died out thousands of years ago! And what happened to its eyes?"

Valja wanted nothing more than to turn and run back the way they had come, but she knew she couldn't do that. She had no idea where these revenants had come from or why they were here, but she would not allow them to hurt her family.

"Find the magisters and tell them what's happening," Valja said. "I shall do my best to hold them off as long as I can."

"But you cannot—"

"Worry not about me. I am already dead, remember?"

She reached back into her cloak, drew a pair of throwing knives, and ran toward the revenants.

Renwick watched Valja race to confront the eyeless creatures, moving with a speed he hadn't imagined her capable of. He had known about her previous life as a thief on the streets of Arenjun, of course, but given her unique affliction she should not have been able to move like this, lithe and strong as a jungle cat. Then he realized that she wasn't a walking corpse like the revenants, that the mystic shard embedded in her chest had frozen her at the *moment* of death, which was why she did not age. The shard's magic had preserved her exactly as she was then, with all her skills and physical abilities intact and undiminished. His reasoning was confirmed an instant later as Valja engaged the undead farmer who had been the first to emerge from the stairwell.

The revenant stretched out his arms to grab her, but she stepped to the side and easily evaded his grasp. The farmer turned his head toward her and a long black thing—a *snake*?—extended from his mouth and lunged toward her. Valja swept one of her blades upward and the steel edge passed through the reptile's substance as if the thing were no more solid than a shadow. The snake jerked back as if wounded by the blow, then dissipated into the air like black smoke. Two more ebon snakes started to slither forth from the farmer's eyes, but Valja rammed both of her knives into the revenant's sockets, then jerked the blades free. There was no blood, only black wisps that curled upward into the air, and the farmer's body went limp and collapsed to the floor.

The snakes were what animated the bodies of the revenants, Renwick realized. Destroy the snakes and the host body became nothing more than harmless dead meat.

Valja saw him then and shouted, "Get the magisters!"

Renwick had been in a state of shock up to this point, but Valja's whipcrack voice brought him out of it. He didn't want to abandon her, but right now the best thing he could do for Valja—for all Ravenhold—was to bring help. But before he could start moving, the Serpent Man revenant took advantage of Valja's momentary distraction to step forward and swing a vicious backhand strike at her head. She must have seen the movement from the corner of her eye, for she tried to throw herself aside to escape the blow, but she wasn't fast enough and the Serpent Man's fist grazed her right shoulder. The revenant was so strong that even such a glancing blow was enough to knock Valja off her feet and send her crashing into a wall. She fell to the floor, landing hard on her back, and the impact caused her right hand to spring open. The blade she had been holding flew away from her and skittered across stone for several feet before coming to a stop.

Valja had managed to maintain her grip on her other knife, however, and when the Serpent Man leaned over her, she sat up and thrust the blade toward his right eye socket before the shadow snake laired within could attack. But before her knife could strike home, the Serpent Man raised a clawed foot, planted it on Valja's chest, and shoved her back onto the floor. She squirmed, trying to wriggle out from under the Serpent Man's foot, but it was no use. Even dead, the creature was too strong. She began stabbing the leg furiously, but he felt no more pain than she did, nor did the wounds she inflicted bleed. All three of the Serpent Man's shadow snakes emerged from his head, and they moved toward Valja with slow, swaying motions as if toying with her before they struck.

Revenants had continued to emerge from the stairwell while Valja and the Serpent Man had been fighting, and they now filled the hall behind them. Several, including the Corinthian woman in the brown dress, had moved past them and were making their way slowly toward Renwick, but as she drew near the infirmary door, it opened and Kaniphera stuck out her head.

"What in Mitra's name is—"

Shadow snakes streaked from the Corinthian woman's head and sank their fangs into the healer's neck and shoulders. Kaniphera's eyes went wide, her body stiffened, and she collapsed in the open doorway. She did not appear to be dead, though; she appeared to Renwick to be... crying?

The Corinthian woman, ebon serpents still out and writhing in the air, stepped over the healer and entered the infirmary. Screams came from inside as patients and staff beheld the nightmarish thing that had suddenly appeared in their midst. Then other revenants walked into the infirmary and the screams of the humans inside grew louder.

Renwick was paralyzed with indecision. If he left now to summon the magisters, the Serpent Man revenant would destroy Valja and the other creatures would advance farther into the castle, attacking everyone they encountered.

His gaze fell upon the knife that Valja had lost. He had been a seeker before settling into the life of a scholar, and there had been more than a few times during his travels when he'd been forced to defend himself. He knew how to wield a blade. Now if only he could muster the courage...

Valja had continued to stab the Serpent Man's leg, and although bone was now visible through gaps in the ragged flesh, the creature showed no indication it was aware of the damage she was inflicting. The swaying shadow snakes were mere inches from Valja's face now, and when they advanced one more fraction of an inch closer, she tore her knife blade from the Serpent Man's leg and swung it toward them. But as if the serpents had anticipated her attack, they swiftly withdrew into the Serpent Man's head and her knife sliced through empty air.

The snakes remained inside their host's skull after that, and the Serpent Man leaned forward and pushed its foot harder against Valja's chest. Renwick was confident she experienced no pain from the pressure, but if it kept up much longer her ribcage would splinter like kindling and her spine would snap in two. He could not let that happen.

He ran toward the dagger.

Valja heard Renwick's boots pound stone as he came toward her, and she turned her head in time to see him lean down, snatch up the dagger she'd lost, and hurl himself at the Serpent Man. He thrust the blade into the revenant's right eye socket, destroying the shadow snake within. The momentum of Renwick's strike caused the Serpent Man to lose balance, and the creature tilted backward, raising its foot just enough for Valja to quickly slide out from under it.

She sprang to her feet, ready to help Renwick finish off the Serpent Man, but before she could attack the revenant lashed out with a clawed hand and in a single, swift motion tore out her mentor's throat. Blood sprayed the air, splattered onto the floor, stippled her face and hands. She had just enough time to lock her eyes with Renwick's before the life drained out of them and he fell to the floor, where he lay in a widening pool of his own blood.

Rage and sorrow filled Valja, merged into a single incandescent fire, and she gripped her knife so hard that her hand trembled from the strain. But before she could attack the foul abomination that had slain the kindest, gentlest man she had ever known, a sudden image flashed through her mind: Taolin naked, chained hand and foot to a wooden table. Tears streamed from the boy's eyes, whether from fear or from the pain of his skin touching the table's wooden surface, she didn't know. There were ten other tables, and upon each was a naked man or woman, all of them chained, runes carved into their bleeding flesh. The tables were arranged in a circle around a stone column atop which rested the Eye of Set, and behind the glossy black orb stood the sorcerer Uzzeran. Ebon energy crackled around the shard embedded in his left eye socket while his right eye blazed with wild madness. He placed his hands on the Eye and ten shadowy tendrils extended from the surface of the unholy artifact, wavering in the air for a moment as if unsure what to do, and then lancing forward to plunge into the foreheads of the ten prisoners, including Taolin. The boy screamed in agony, his back arching as his body strained against his chains.

And Uzzeran laughed in mad delight.

The vision faded as quickly as it had come, and Valja understood that Ishtar had shown her what would happen to Taolin if she didn't leave this very instant and find help.

Please watch over the boy, she prayed to the goddess. But before she departed, she had one last thing to take care of.

She hurled her knife at the Serpent Man's left eye, and while the blade was still in the air, she drew another from her cloak and threw it at the revenant's mouth. Both blades struck their targets, and she whirled around and ran down the hallway as the Serpent Man's heavy body crashed to the floor.

Uzzeran had sent forth his small army of revenants to deal with the castle's residents while he, Shengis, and Rynthia waited one level down, outside the confinement area. Rynthia explained that the most dangerous residents were kept here in magically warded cells so that they could not escape and wreak havoc throughout the castle. Uzzeran amused himself by wandering among the prisoners' cells, trying to determine what magical conditions their insane occupants suffered from as they ranted and raved, screamed and sobbed. When he sensed the revenants had accomplished their task, he informed Rynthia it was safe for them to emerge from hiding and the trio began climbing up the steps toward the first floor.

The surviving revenants were waiting for them there when they stepped out of the stairwell. Shengis did a quick count.

"I estimate we lost roughly half," he said.

"Yes, and most of those were slain by the so-called magisters. But the third-rate sorcerers fell in the end, just as all will before my might."

Then Shengis heard sobbing and moaning coming from the room on the right. The venom of the shadow serpents did not slay the physical body; it infected the mind and spirit, causing victims to be gripped by deep despair and self-loathing, the feelings so intense they were incapacitating. No doubt many in the castle had died at the hands of the revenants, but others still lived, minds trapped in a prison of dark emotion. The dead would become new revenants, replacing those that had been lost, and the survivors would serve as test subjects for Uzzeran's experiments. Their takeover of Ravenhold was complete.

Uzzeran dabbed the cloth to his bloody eye and smiled with cold satisfaction. "We had best get to work," the sorcerer said. "The solstice will be here before we know it."

Rynthia felt a pang of regret upon seeing Renwick's corpse lying on the floor, surrounded by revenants who stood waiting with inhuman patience for their master's next command. Renwick had been a kind soul who had gone out of his way to give his help to anyone who had needed it, and his accomplishments as both seeker and scholar had been stellar. What a waste. Still, he was a nonbeliever and would have had no place in Set's new world. It was a mercy that he had died now.

And his corpse would make a fine revenant.

In the mountains near Ravenhold, the Brood of Zath crawled forth from the darkness of the caves and crevasses where they laired, abandoned great webs stretched between peaks, and emerged from deep pits in the earth. Some were the size of large dogs, others as big as horses, and still others would dwarf mammoths. They had traveled from Arenjun fifteen years ago, after bathing in the mystic energies contained in the ruins of the Elephant Tower, and here they had grown large and strong. They had waited with inhuman patience throughout the years, knowing that one day they would fulfill the purpose for which their god and father had created them. And that day was fast approaching.

Moving slowly on thin, segmented legs, and led by a white spider the size of a wolf, the giant creatures began making their way toward Ravenhold.

The agony Taolin experienced was so far beyond pain there was not a word for it in any of the thousand languages and dialects spoken in the known world and beyond. This was because it wasn't just his pain; it was the pain of his ancestors going back three hundred generations and more, all of them feeling each other's agony, the pain multiplied exponentially to a degree that would make even the gods weep and beg to be put out of their misery.

The ancestor responsible was a sorceress named Irass who had lived on a small island off the coast of Argos. Nothing had mattered to her more than the acquisition of power, and she had spent her days summoning the spirits of long-dead thaumaturges in order to learn the secrets of their magic. But even in death, those who mastered the dark arts guard their secrets jealously, and Irass learned little from them. Frustrated by her lack of progress, the sorceress began summoning demons from the lower dimensions, minor ones at first, then more powerful beings. She made deals, paid prices too terrible to name, until one day she dared to summon one of the most powerful and feared infernal entities of them all, an archdemon.

She offered the demon anything it wanted, including her soul, but the foul thing merely laughed, its voice like the screaming of a thousand damned souls.

You have already sold your soul many times over to those less powerful than I. What could you possibly have left to offer me?

Then an idea came to Irass, one so awful that it made even her reluctant to consider it. But her lust for power was too strong.

"I shall pledge to you the lives of my descendants, from now until the end of time, to torment as you will."

The demon agreed, and the bargain was struck. In exchange for all the power she desired and more, one member of Irass' family line in each generation would became the plaything of the archdemon. The foul thing visited unspeakable agonies on them and its awful laughter echoed throughout all the hells that ever were or ever would be.

Taolin was the latest in Irass' line to inherit this curse. Like all those who had come before him, he knew not the origin of his pain, though even if he had, the knowledge would not have brought him comfort. And so the boy suffered in ignorance, as so many of his ancestors had, until the day a sorcerer named Uzzeran had come to him. Uzzeran understood the nature of Taolin's terrible affliction, and what's more, he knew how to make good use of it for his own ends.

Several days had passed since Uzzeran and his accomplices had taken control of Ravenhold, and while they had made progress toward their ultimate goal, Shengis feared it wasn't enough.

The magisters had workrooms near their quarters on the third floor, and Uzzeran had selected one for his own use and equipped it to his liking. After that, Rynthia unlocked the repository, removed the second Eye of Set, and carried it up to Uzzeran's new workroom. All of Ravenhold's dead had been transformed into revenants, a feat that did not tax Uzzeran overmuch; the shadow snakes required came directly from Set, each the tiniest fraction of the dread god's substance, and all the sorcerer needed to do was open a pinpoint passage between dimensions for the creatures to enter this world. After that, the shadow snakes slithered through the castle and selected hosts on their own. The revenants now numbered nearly two hundred and Shengis had led them one by one to the dining hall, where they lay in rows, bodies motionless and silent. Shadow snakes coiled close by, waiting to be summoned.

Uzzeran had spent some time examining the surviving afflicted, both those held in isolation and those locked in confinement, selecting the ones he deemed to hold the highest degree of mystic energy in their bodies, which he could drain to power the second Eye of Set. One boy in particular, Taolin, contained more magic in his body than all the others combined due to the powerful family curse he'd inherited. Uzzeran would use him well.

Other men and women locked away in confinement, those whose minds had been warped by their magical afflictions, would form the human part of the Serpent Lord hybrids Uzzeran wished to create. Shengis thought it unwise to use insane men and women in the spell, and he voiced this concern to his master, risking the sorcerer's wrath, but Uzzeran merely said that their mental problems were a direct result of both the amount and type of magical energy in their systems, making them perfect. Since the sorcerer didn't have access to any Serpent Men here, he intended to use small amounts of Shengis' blood to help create the Serpent Lords. Shengis shared his body with a Serpent Man's essence, and that made him more than human, if not quite the hybrid creature Set wished Uzzeran to bring into existence.

Shengis did not think much of this plan, as the sorcerer had tried this technique numerous times without any measurable success since the night of the attack in the tower ruins. But Uzzeran had access to the second Eye now, as well as test subjects infused with magic power, and these two things might well make a difference. Still, Shengis would have felt more confident had they actual Serpent Men to work with.

And Uzzeran had one more factor in his favor: the artifacts in the repository.

"You see, the problem is one of power," Uzzeran said. "I am trying to do the work of a god, and for that I need godlike power. The energy suffusing the ruins of the Tower of the Elephant might have been sufficient for the task, if the spell had not been interrupted by those two young thieves and the first Eye of Set destroyed. But now I have the second Eye, as well as the afflicted, and I can also draw on the mystic energy held within the artifacts stored in the repository. All these things combined should give me all the power I require, and perhaps more!"

It was the word *should* in this last sentence that bothered Shengis, but he knew that saying so would make his master furious and so he held his tongue.

After Uzzeran had finished making his initial preparations, he asked Rynthia to give him tours of the repository and the library. He spent an entire day wandering through the repository, marveling at all the mystic artifacts Ravenhold's seekers had collected over the centuries. When Rynthia saw Shengis later, she told him of Uzzeran's reaction to some of the artifacts he had found in the repository.

"He was especially fascinated by an artifact called the Hand of Hanuman," she said. "He stared at it for close to two hours, silent and motionless. I wonder what a sorcerer like him sees when he gazes upon such a thing?"

Shengis feared his master hadn't been truly interested in the artifact but had, rather, experienced another of his episodes. They came more often now that he was in Ravenhold, and they lasted longer. Shengis didn't know what this meant, only that it wasn't good.

The next day, when Uzzeran visited the library, was when he became truly excited. At first, he was overwhelmed by the vast amount of written material the library contained, but he quickly adjusted and asked Rynthia to help him locate information on transformation magic—but he forgot all about this when he saw the preserved bodies of ancient beasts on display. All were impressive, Shengis thought, but only one captured his master's full attention.

Uzzeran hurried over to the giant serpent and gazed upon it in astonishment. "Do you have any idea what this is?" he asked as Shengis and Rynthia joined him.

I do, Kekk said. *And your fool of a master isn't worthy to eat the excrement of such a divine being, let alone stand in its majestic presence.*

"This magnificent creature is a dire wyrm, a member of the first species Set brought into existence on this planet, predating the creation of the Serpent Men by eons. They were, in fact, progenitors of that race."

True, Kekk said. *And they disappeared from this world long before humanity could stand upright. I've only ever seen one myself, and that was an immeasurably long time ago, when I was still very young.* There was a wistfulness to his mental voice that Shengis had never heard before. He hadn't imagined a Serpent Man could be sentimental about the past.

Uzzeran continued, his excitement growing as he spoke.

"I can use the creature's scales in the spell! They will work far better than your blood, Shengis, even better than a Serpent Man itself would! At last, success is within our reach!"

Black energy crackled around the ebon shard jutting from

Uzzeran's eye, as if the mystic fragment was responding to the intensity of his emotions.

He cannot do that, Kekk said, his thought-voice now cold as Nordheim ice. *The dire wyrm has already been desecrated by whichever sorcerer slayed it, then stuffed and mounted it for humans to gawk at. I cannot allow further insult to be visited upon my ancestor!*

Shengis felt a surge of willpower come from Kekk, and his right hand moved of its own volition toward his poisoned dagger. Shengis was astonished. In the fifteen years since he'd become host for Kekk's spirit, never once had the Serpent Man tried to assume control of his body, but that was exactly what was happening now.

Shengis fought to regain control of his hand, but Kekk fought equally hard to keep it. The hand hovered mere inches from the dagger's pommel, trembling from the effort of two separate beings—one inhuman and immortal, one human and short-lived—battling to use it. Images flashed through Shengis' mind: his hand closing around the dagger's handle, yanking it free from its sheath, gripping it tight, then him rushing forward and swiftly jamming the blade into the base of Uzzeran's skull, slaying him instantly.

His hand, palm damp with nervous sweat, gripped the dagger's pommel and slowly drew it from its sheath, and he then took a shaky step forward. Rynthia noted the action and turned toward him, put a hand on his shoulder to get his attention, and mouthed a single word:

Don't.

Kekk fought harder, but Shengis resisted, fighting with his entire soul as he attempted to reassert control over his own body. He shook from the effort, and fiery pain burned in his skull, the agony so intense it took everything he had not to scream.

And then, just like that, it was over. Kekk's control broke, and

Shengis would have fallen forward and collided with Uzzeran if Rynthia hadn't grabbed his arm to steady him. Breathing hard, sweat running down the sides of his face, Shengis looked at Rynthia and gave her a grateful smile.

Uzzeran hadn't taken his gaze off the dire wyrm the entire time Shengis had fought Kekk. Shengis feared Rynthia would say something to his master, warning him that his servant had nearly tried to slay him, but she put a finger to her lips, indicating that she intended to remain silent, and Shengis was relieved. He knew his master had no personal feelings toward him. If Uzzeran thought Shengis was a threat, he would slay him without hesitation.

I wish he would slay you, Kekk said. *At least then I would be free.*

Shengis did not respond, but he understood the Serpent Man's desire for freedom, for he shared it.

Uzzeran ordered Shengis to go to the infirmary, fetch Taolin, and bring him upstairs to the sorcerer's workroom. The master told Shengis to be careful when handling the boy because anything touching his skin caused him a great deal of pain. "Sound hurts him as well, so try to be as quiet as possible."

Shengis was bemused by Uzzeran's instructions. He had never known the sorcerer to care about anyone's welfare but his own. Why did this boy matter to him? Even if Taolin had been Stygian, Uzzeran would not have cared about him. Unwanted children were plentiful in Stygia, at least among the lower classes, which was why sorcerers so often used them in their rituals. If one died, you could easily find ten more to replace them.

It is not the boy, Kekk said. *It is the magic his body contains. Your master doesn't want you to damage what could prove to be a vital component in his work.*

Shengis had no trouble believing that, but he refrained from responding directly to Kekk. After what the Serpent Man had attempted in the library, Shengis wanted as little to do with him as possible, even less than he usually did.

He entered the infirmary. The chamber was in disarray after the initial attack by the revenants—tables overturned, pallets strewn about, clay jars broken, their contents scattered. There were bloodstains on the floor and walls, although not as many as Shengis would have expected. The room was lit by one of Uzzeran's coldfire braziers, which the sorcerer had placed throughout the castle, even in the library since the mystic green flames produced light but no heat.

Shengis went over to the door to the isolation chamber at the rear of the infirmary. He had been here several times before, bringing cheese, bread, and water to the patients. He had emptied their chamber pots as well, and cleaned the messes made by those whose physical conditions prevented them from using one. The door wasn't locked and he opened it easily. The smell coming from within was not too foul, and he decided the chamber pots could wait another day. He heard patients moaning and sobbing, muttering and whispering, and some made noises that did not sound human at all and chilled him to his core. He left the door open so green light from the brazier would provide some illumination within the chamber, and then he stepped inside.

There were several small cells, each containing someone who had been experimented on by a sorcerer, with a resulting condition that made it necessary to separate them from the rest of the castle residents, often for their own safety and comfort. Those whose conditions made them dangerous to others were locked away several levels down in confinement. Shengis sincerely hoped his master would not send him down *there* to get anyone. It was bad enough having to take food and water to those...

creatures in their cells. Getting any closer to them was too risky, and if that meant they had to stew in their own filth, so be it.

Taolin was in the third cell on the left, and Shengis walked slowly toward it, careful to tread as lightly as he could. He had been unaware of Taolin's condition during his other visits, and he felt guilty about the pain he must have caused the boy by stomping around like a clumsy hippo.

He passed the first cell, which contained a woman whose internal organs were now external ones. Shengis had no idea how she was still alive.

She probably wishes she wasn't, Kekk said.

She sat cross-legged on the floor, her beating heart and expanding lungs visible. Shengis' stomach always did a flip when he saw her, so he averted his gaze and continued on, forcing himself not to hurry.

The second cell held a naked Aquilonian man—or was that men?—with two heads, three arms, four legs, and two sets of genitals. Both heads stared vacantly at nothing and steady streams of drool dripped from their mouths. One of the heads had tried to speak to him once, but what had come out of its mouth was the chittering of a small furry animal. The sound echoed through Shengis' dreams at night.

When he reached the third cell, he found Taolin. Like the first two patients, the boy was naked. Shengis had originally thought this was to prevent him from soiling his clothes—and that likely *had* been a consideration—but now that he knew the truth about Taolin's condition, he thought it more likely that wearing clothing would cause unbearable agony for him. He stood on one leg with the other tucked against his body, the way an ibis sometimes did. Shengis had seen him do this before, but he was not sure what good it did for him. Yes, it decreased the amount of his flesh in contact with anything other than air, but it also concentrated his entire weight on that foot. Should that not hurt as much, if not more than both feet being on the ground?

Tears flowed down the reddish skin of Taolin's cheeks, and tremors wracked his body as he fought to endure the pain. Whatever Uzzeran intended to do with Taolin, Shengis hoped it would give the boy release from his agony, one way or another.

Shengis mouthed words, putting the barest amount of breath behind them. Despite this precaution, Taolin winced as he spoke. "My master requests"—he almost said *requires*—"you come with me to his workroom, two levels above. I know walking pains you, but I am afraid it might hurt worse if I carry you. Do you have a preference?"

Shengis couldn't tell whether Taolin understood. The boy did not look at him, nor did he speak. He continued weeping and shuddering for several moments, but then he slowly lowered his other leg until both feet touched the floor. Taolin took in a sharp hiss of air at the fresh pain this caused, but after another moment he took a hesitant step forward. And that was when Shengis' hands, acting without his volition, shot out, fastened around the boy's neck, and began squeezing.

Shengis was so shocked that for several seconds he could do nothing but gape at Taolin.

The boy's eyes went wide with terror, and his mouth fell open in a silent cry of pain. Shengis knew his touch alone made Taolin's flesh burn like fire, but the increasing pressure as his hands squeezed harder and harder would have intensified the boy's agony a thousandfold. Taolin clawed at Shengis' hands in a desperate attempt to dislodge them, but the bloody furrows the boy's fingernails dug in the Stygian's skin healed almost instantly thanks to Kekk's presence in his body.

"Stop it!" Shengis cried.

Taolin winced at the fresh pain Shengis' voice caused him.

I cannot allow your master to succeed in his mad plan! Kekk said. *What he is attempting to do is blasphemy of the highest order! It is an affront to my kind and to Set herself!*

"Set tasked my master with this goal! Your people may have been her favored children at some point in the dim, forgotten past, but we Stygians are her people now! We are her *true* children!"

Kekk exploded in an inferno of rage at Shengis' words, and the intensity of the Serpent Man's emotion was so overwhelming that it caused his control of Shengis' body to slip. Shengis took advantage of the opportunity and bent all his will toward making his hands release their hold on Taolin's neck. *Let go!* he commanded. *Let… go!*

His hands relaxed and dropped away from the boy's throat. Taolin drew in a shuddering breath, then began coughing. The sound caused the boy additional agony, and the accumulated pain finally became too much for him to bear and he collapsed to the floor, unconscious.

Pick him up and carry him to your master. He can feel no pain in his current state.

Shengis did not know if this was his thought or Kekk's, but either way he could not risk laying hands on Taolin again. Kekk might reassume control of his body, and this time he might not be able to prevent the Serpent Man from slaying the boy. Taolin's life meant nothing to him, but the child could be the key to Uzzeran fulfilling Set's plan to save the world from The Woeful Eye, and helping his master accomplish that great work meant everything to Shengis. But he was a threat to the plan as long as the spirit of Kekk dwelled within him. Next time, the Serpent Man might attempt to slay Uzzeran, and that was something Shengis could not allow.

He turned away from the unconscious boy and fled the isolation chamber.

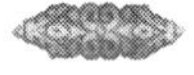

Shengis stood before an open window, gazing upon the magnificent vista spread out before him. He had climbed to Ravenhold's highest tower, and from here he could see the smaller mountains surrounding Skycrest and, beyond them, the hilly plains that stretched away from the Kezankian Mountains toward Arenjun so many miles away. It had been fifteen years since he had set foot in the city, and he was surprised to find himself thinking fondly of it. Arenjun was a pit where the dregs of humanity preyed upon each other, but it had an energy to it that he missed, a feeling that life was sweeter when your next day, or even your next moment, was not guaranteed.

That his mind had taken a turn toward the sentimental and morbid came as no surprise, for he had come here to slay himself—or, more accurately, to slay Kekk. He wished he could explain to Uzzeran why he was doing this, but the master was not safe around him as long as Kekk was able to assume control of his body. Uzzeran would never know what had happened to his servant, only that he had disappeared, but the sorcerer had Rynthia to assist him now, and Shengis was confident she would serve his master well.

He expected no paradisiacal afterlife. If Set found him worthy, the god would devour his soul and he would become one with the Great Serpent. If Set did not find him worthy, his spirit would be cast into an endless void, where it would drift for eternity, lost and alone.

He took a deep breath. No sense in putting it off any longer.

He sat on the stone window ledge and swung his legs over. All he had to do now was push off—

His body froze.

Do not do this.

"Why not? You will finally be free of me. Isn't that what you want?"

I was captured by you, forced to participate in your master's insane experiment, and I have been trapped in your body ever since. I… do not think Set will find me worthy.

Shengis could feel the Serpent Man's fear, and he smiled. For the first time in fifteen years, he had the upper hand over Kekk. "You might be able to stop me today, but you cannot take permanent control of my body," he said. "If you could, you would have done so long before now. Sooner or later, I will succeed in slaying myself, and you will die with me. There is nothing you can do to prevent this."

Perhaps we could… agree to a truce.

Shengis could feel how difficult it was for the Serpent Man to speak these words. To Kekk, they were an admission of defeat. He was about to ask him how he could trust him to abide by whatever terms they set for the truce, but before he could speak he heard footsteps as someone came up the stairs to the tower room. He knew his master's tread, so he was not surprised when Rynthia stepped into the room, a green coldfire torch in her hand. His body was still immobile for the most part, but he was able to turn his head to look at her.

"I was searching for you," she said, "but when I finally found you in the hall on the main level, you hurried up a set of stairs before I could call out. You seemed to be in some distress, so I followed you. It appears to be a good thing that I did. Why don't you get down from the window so we can talk?"

Shengis could sense that Kekk's control over his body wasn't as strong as it had been when the Serpent Man had attempted to slay Taolin. He thought he could regain command if he tried hard enough, and then all he would have to do was lean forward and let himself fall…

"I know not what is going on between you and Kekk, Shengis—especially after witnessing you draw your dagger on Uzzeran—but there is a problem with the master, one that I think I cannot fix on my own. I need your help."

Shengis felt Kekk surrender control of his body—of *their* body—to him. He pulled his legs back in and hopped down from the ledge.

"What kind of a problem?" he asked.

14

Conan and Qiang rode their horses at a walk along the Road of Kings during a sunny if slightly cool afternoon. They had left the mountainous region of southwestern Turan a while ago and now traveled across hilly green terrain as they approached the border with Zamora. Here, both sides of the road were lined with low stone walls. To their left was a small forest of evergreen and oak, to their right a grove of chestnut trees. An hour ago, they had passed an old farmer clearing stones from a field, and Conan had hailed the man in Turanian and asked him what the stone walls were for, as they were not high enough to repel invaders.

They keep the boars from getting to the chestnut trees, the farmer had answered. *And from messing with our pigs.* He had followed this with a wink, one man of the world to another. Conan and Qiang laughed at that and continued on.

Conan had been traveling with Qiang for two days now, and while the Khitan made a pleasant enough companion for the road, the Cimmerian had learned next to nothing about him so far. Qiang was perfectly willing to talk about other subjects, such as the art of wielding the katana, the best techniques for hunting elk, and what life in general was like in Khitai, and while Conan found all of this interesting, he still knew no more of who Qiang was than he had when they had ridden together with Delger's caravan. He understood and respected someone's desire to keep certain aspects of their life private, but the fact that Qiang shared absolutely nothing made him wonder if the man was hiding something from him. A companion with secrets was a companion who could not be fully trusted. Perhaps it would be best if they parted ways.

As if sensing Conan's thoughts, Qiang said, "You must wonder why I wish to travel with you."

This was true. Qiang had told him that Charhelm was a small city in Zamora that lay to the north of Arenjun, and the Cimmerian had decided to go and see what, if anything, awaited him there. But Qiang had expressed no desire to travel anywhere specifically and seemed content to ride wherever Conan did.

"Yes," Conan said.

Qiang nodded. "Then I shall tell you. But my tale is a strange one, and there are parts of it you may find difficult to believe."

Conan smiled. "I have a strange tale or two of my own that I could tell. I will listen to yours without judgment."

Qiang nodded, and the two men continued riding as the warrior told his story.

"I grew up in the city of Rou-Gen in Khitai. For generations, members of my family had the honor of serving in the overlord's royal guard. One male child from each generation is taken to the palace as an infant, and there he is raised to be a warrior from the day he takes his first steps. When he reaches manhood, if his teachers believe he is ready, he joins the royal guard."

"And if he is judged as not ready?"

"He takes his own life rather than bring shame upon his family."

Conan nodded. As a Cimmerian, he understood strict codes of honor, although he did not share that one.

"I was trained in both the art of war and the art of courtly manners," Qiang continued, then gave a small smile. "The two are more similar than most people think. When I was deemed worthy to join the guard, it was the proudest day of my life. The guard's mandate to protect the overlord extends to protecting his territory and his people, and we fought many battles in his name against foes natural as well as unnatural. And while individual members might fall, the royal guard itself has never been defeated since its inception. Years passed, during which I served with distinction, and my superiors told me that if I continued as I was going, I might well get to join the command ranks one day. And then I met a girl."

Conan fought to keep the smirk off his face, for he had no wish to offend Qiang, but this was a part of the Khitan's story that he'd had some experience with himself.

"It was not forbidden for members of the guard to enjoy the company of women, or other men for that matter, but we were not allowed to marry or have children. Our first and only allegiance was to the overlord. No one could come before him."

"Who was she?" Conan asked.

Qiang's tone softened. "Her name was Jingshu. She was one of the workers who tended the overlord's flower gardens, and she had a kind and gentle soul. We saw each other in secret as often as we could, and while I am certain other members of the guard knew, as did Jingshu's fellow gardeners, none gave us away. It was not an ideal situation, but it was the best we could manage given our separate responsibilities, and we considered ourselves fortunate.

"Then one day Jingshu became ill. She went to see one of the palace healers and was told she suffered from the wasting disease."

Conan grunted. It was said that even sorcerers had a difficult time curing this condition, and those who came down with it usually were destined to experience a slow and painful death. In Cimmeria, someone with wasting sickness could request family or friends to spare them such an agonizing end, and they would do so gladly, slaying them as swiftly and painlessly as possible.

"When our overlord, Guangzhi, was informed of Jingshu's illness, he gave her one of the best suites in his palace and commanded his servants to make her as comfortable as possible and tend to her every need. I was very grateful for this, and I was given the opportunity to express my thanks to Guangzhi. 'Her efforts in my gardens brought much beauty and joy into my life,' he told me. 'It is my honor to ensure her final days pass as easily as they can.'"

Qiang's eyes shimmered with tears, but he drew in a deep breath and got control of himself before they could fall.

"My superiors permitted me to visit Jingshu for an hour once a week. It was a great kindness. I watched her decline as the weeks passed, and my sorrow grew with each visit. But that sorrow eventually turned to anger. It was not fair that such a beautiful spirit should depart this world before her time! I was a member of the royal guard, was I not? It was my sworn duty to protect the overlord and his subjects—all his subjects, including Jingshu. If there was any way in this world to save her, I vowed to find it, and I promised myself that I would pay any price, even surrender my own soul, to see my love whole and healthy again. That night, I left Rou-Gen without seeking the approval of my superiors and set out to find a way to save her.

"I traveled throughout Khitai, listening to the counsel of learned men and women, consulting witches and sorcerers, but none could help me. I began to fear my love would die before I could discover a way to save her, but then one day I chanced upon a well in a forest. There were no villages nearby, no sign of any people at all, but the well looked as if it had been dug and its stones laid only recently. I thanked the great god Yun for my good fortune. I watered my horse, and then I drank my fill. I immediately became so weary that I could not keep my eyes open, and I lay down next to the well and slept.

"I dreamed, and in my dream green tendrils rose from within the well and grew into a large, blossoming plum tree. I woke then, but was I in the real world or still in my dream? For to my amazement, the tree was still there. Plum trees blossom just as the world starts to warm from its winter chill, to my people they symbolize hope and resilience. My heart soared to see them, and I considered the tree a sign from Yun that I should not lose faith and continue my search to find a cure for Jingshu. And then the tree spoke to me in a kind voice that was at once male and female, but at the same time neither. I did not hear its words with my ears, but rather with my mind.

"I have heard your prayer, my son, and I will give you what you seek. But you must first perform a task for me.

"I dropped to my knees and lowered myself to the ground in supplication. 'I will do anything you ask if you can save my Jingshu!'

"This pleases me to hear. Your overlord, Guangzhi, is good to his people, but to anyone outside of Rou-Gen he is a monstrous tyrant who wishes to dominate all of Khitai, and indeed the entire world. Thousands pray each moment of the day for deliverance from his cruelty and greed. As I have heard you, I have heard them. I shall heal Jingshu, and in return you shall slay Guangzhi and alleviate your people's misery.

"I was shocked by the god's words, but I could not argue with them, for had I not seen evidence of Guangzhi's evil during my travels through Khitai? Villages that had been burned to the ground for refusing to accept his rule, farmers enslaved and working their own lands to feed Guangzhi's people while their own families starved, women and girls stolen from their homes and forced to work in Rou-Gen's brothels? And had I not participated in all of these actions, and more, as a member of Guangzhi's royal guard? But before I could say anything, the blossoms began dropping from the tree, vanishing before they could touch the ground. When the last blossom was gone, the tree shrank back into the green tendrils from which it had sprung, retreated into the well, and was gone.

"I was so upset that I could not sleep, so I remained awake the rest of the night and prayed to Yun not to make me slay the man I had sworn an oath to protect. But Yun did not respond, and when the sun rose I readied my mount and set out for Rou-Gen as swiftly as the animal could bear me. It took me two weeks to return to my city, and when I arrived the royal guard immediately arrested me for desertion. I did not care, though. All that mattered was Jingshu. My friends in the guard took pity on me, and they came to my cell in the garrison to tell me of my love's miraculous healing. The palace healers were at a loss to explain it, but all signs of wasting sickness were gone. Jingshu had made a full recovery and had returned to working in the flower gardens.

"Eventually, a tribunal was convened and it was determined I had acted out of love, so rather than execute me, the guard cast me out. It was a great disgrace for my family, but so long as Jingshu was healthy again, I was willing to bear that shame. Since Jingshu remained well even though I had not slain Guangzhi, I told myself that Yun had experienced a change of heart and no longer wished me to slay my overlord.

"Because I was a deserter, Jingshu would not see me anymore. She would never know I had left the guard to save her. Yet she was alive, and that was all that was important to me.

"I left the city and began making a living as a woodcutter. It was honest work, if tedious, and it helped the days pass. But one day, a familiar weariness came over me and I collapsed to the ground and slept. Once more, Yun came to me in a dream, only this time not in the guise of a blossoming plum tree but as a huge owl perched in a gigantic black thorn tree that blotted out the sky. In Khitai, the owl is considered a bird of ill omen, and this one glared at me with eyes that blazed like fire. The voice I heard in my mind roared like thunder.

"You failed to do as I commanded, Qiang! For this, you shall be punished!

"As before, I prostrated myself before the god. 'I will accept whatever punishment you deem fitting, but I beg you not to return Jingshu's illness!'

"Fear not. She is an innocent in all this, and so she shall not be harmed. And since you asked my aid out of love, I shall give you an opportunity to atone for your disobedience. Since you have allowed a great evil to continue inflicting harm upon the world, you shall not know rest until you have fought and vanquished an even greater darkness than your overlord. This is the last time I will speak to you, Qiang, and I shall not hear your prayers again until you have redeemed yourself.

"This time I woke sitting with my back against a fir tree that I had intended to chop down. The owl and the great thorn tree were gone, and I could see the sky again. I wanted to believe that Yun had not really visited me either time, that they really had been mere dreams, but I knew in my heart that they had happened and decided I would do everything I could to redeem myself, for my family, and for Jingshu, even if they would never know what I had done. So I laid down my woodcutter's axe, picked up my sword, and began my journey."

Conan and Qiang were both silent for a time after that, but eventually the Cimmerian said, "You spoke true—that is quite a tale. But I have met gods before—slain some of them, too—and I believe it. My people's god, Crom, might be a miserable bastard, but at least he doesn't interfere with our lives. How long have you been on your journey?"

"I have lost track of the years, but I believe it has been no longer than a century, perhaps two."

Conan stared at the man in astonishment, and Qiang smiled sadly.

"Yun said I would not know rest until I until I defeated an evil greater than Guangzhi. So far, I have not found one."

Rynthia led Shengis to the library.

When she had learned that Shengis had become host to a Serpent Man's spirit, she had looked upon him with awe. The Serpent Men were Set's first children to grace this world, and to join with one was akin to joining with the Great Darkness herself. Being near Shengis had made her feel the same way she had on touching the first Eye of Set, as if she was in the presence of a holy thing.

But the longer Shengis was in Ravenhold, the more control Kekk seemed to assume over their shared body, and it was clear the human and the serpent aspects did not share the same goals. Because Shengis had been touched by Set, she wanted to help him, but she could not allow him—or Kekk—to interfere with Uzzeran's plan. There were but a handful of days before the solstice arrived, and if the preparations for the spell had not been completed by then, all would be lost for another year. If this meant she had to slay Shengis herself, then so be it. But right now, she had a bigger problem to deal with.

Uzzeran stood motionless before the preserved body of the dire wyrm. In his left hand was a clay jar and in his right, a sharp knife. He had been in the process of scraping scales from the wyrm and collecting them for use in his spell when another of his episodes had occurred. Dark energy danced around the ebon shard jutting from his left eye socket, as if the artifact was excited to be near the wyrm.

Shengis' features twisted into a mask of absolute rage, and Rynthia knew she was seeing Kekk's reaction to the sorcerer attempting to harvest part of the wyrm for his own use. It must seem like a blasphemous defilement to the Serpent Man. She feared Kekk would make another attempt on Uzzeran's life, and Shengis' hand did grasp the pommel of his poisoned dagger, but he did not draw it and slowly his features eased and his expression returned to normal. He removed his hand from his dagger and looked at Rynthia.

"How long has the master been like this?" he asked.

"It's difficult to say, as I haven't been in here with him the entire time. An hour, perhaps two." She looked at Uzzeran. The sorcerer's face held a beatific expression, as if he gazed upon a thing of unimaginable beauty that only he could see. She wondered what it could be, then decided she was likely better off not knowing.

Uzzeran floated in vast nothingness, just as he had during his first vision of Set fifteen years ago, but this time he did not see two crimson suns approaching from the darkness. He saw nothing. Nevertheless, he knew he was not alone here, for he could sense the presence of others, things so huge they dwarfed galaxies, so incredibly long-lived they had no concept of birth or death. The thoughts that flashed like cosmic lightning through their planet-sized brains were utterly alien and so very, very cold…

He was one of them.

Not the largest, nor the strongest—not even close. There were entities here so powerful that to them he was little more than a gnat is to a human, if they were aware of him at all. Most of them were not, for which he was profoundly, pathetically grateful. His greatest fear was that he might do something to draw their attention, because if that happened and they turned the malignancy of their attention on him, they might remember how unrelentingly *hungry* they were, decide he would make a tasty snack, and start moving toward him, mouths opening wide...

His name was Uzzeran, and he was a man. But in this place, he had another name, too.

He was Set, the greatest of all gods on Earth.

But here in the endless emptiness, he was a very small fish in a very large pond.

Like the others, he was hungry, and with each new world he devoured, he grew a little more. He would keep eating, one world after another, one universe after another, and he would grow strong and huge until he was the biggest of all! Then *he* would dwarf the others, *he* would stretch his mouth wide, and *he* would devour *them*. And when he was all that existed, he would insert the tip of his tail in his mouth and start eating until he too was gone.

Uzzeran let out a wild, unhinged laugh, and Rynthia and Shengis drew back from the sorcerer in alarm. He fixed his right eye on them, madness gleaming on its surface, like sunlight glittering atop poisoned water. He pointed to the shard jutting from his left eye socket.

"I just learned why it's called the *Eye* of Set! It shows me things—wondrous, horrible things..." He cackled, and Rynthia and Shengis paled. "If you'll both excuse me, I must finish collecting scales."

Uzzeran rolled up the left sleeve of his robe, placed the knife against the skin of his forearm, and began scraping.

Hard.

There were benefits to Valja's condition. She did not need to breathe, eat, drink, or sleep, and she did not tire. She had no fear of attack by mountain cats, wolves, or bears, for she had no scent to attract predators. Because of these things, when she fled Ravenhold, she started running and did not stop until she reached Charhelm some days later.

She had last been here fifteen years ago, when she and Renwick had stopped on their way to Ravenhold, and the town looked much the same as it had then—a collection of one- and two-story stone buildings surrounded by tents and stalls where traders loudly hawked their wares. Both Arenjun and Shadizar lay on the Road of Kings, but Charhelm lay on a smaller trading route, one running north from Arenjun and then spreading outward in yet smaller routes through central and northern Zamora—including the Zath-worshipping city of Yezud—then on to Corinthia, Brythunia, and Hyperborea. Charhelm was mostly inhabited by Zamorians, but there were always travelers from other kingdoms who stopped there to rest and resupply before continuing on their way, their purses considerably lighter than when they arrived.

Valja entered the town—the residents called it a city, but it was far too small to deserve the name—at midday. The unpaved streets were crowded with pedestrians going about their business and traders called out to passersby, doing their best to catch their attention and usually being ignored. Wagons laden with goods arrived and departed regularly, as did lone riders on horseback. Despite how busy it was, she knew her ivory skin would not go unnoticed, so she had raised the hood of her cloak and donned black gloves. She could hear a light breeze blowing and wished she could feel it.

She wandered the streets for a time, head lowered, avoiding eye contact with anyone, feeling lost. She had been so focused on getting here that she had given little thought to what she would do once she reached her destination. She had been in such a state of shock when she'd fled Ravenhold that she hadn't been able to think straight. Renwick's death kept playing over and over in her mind, and she would have sobbed like a child all the way to Charhelm had her body been capable of producing tears.

As devastating as the loss of her friend and mentor was, she also mourned for all Ravenhold. She had witnessed the revenants' indiscriminate slaughter, and she knew that everyone there was dead, their corpses likely used to create more unholy servants for Uzzeran. And if the sorcerer had spared anyone, it was so they could serve as fodder for his grotesque experiments.

She thought of poor Taolin and wondered if he was alive or dead. She felt a kinship with the boy, for their conditions were the mirror opposite of each other's—she could not physically feel while he felt with overwhelming and agonizing intensity. And she kept thinking of the vision Ishtar had shown her of Taolin laid out on a wooden table, hands and feet shackled, as Uzzeran activated the second Eye of Set and a tendril of dark power stretched toward him.

Now that Uzzeran had access to the combined knowledge and power of Ravenhold, she felt certain he would succeed in his mad plan to create a half-human, half-Serpent Man hybrid race. At the time she and Conan had gone with Naerys and Anot to the ruins of the Elephant Tower, neither of them had known precisely what the sorcerer's goal had been, and afterward neither Naerys nor Anot had been in a condition to explain it to them. But during her years at Ravenhold, Valja had learned a great deal about magic. She had also learned what the Eyes of Set could do, and this knowledge, combined with what she had witnessed in Uzzeran's lair that night so many years ago, had allowed her to divine the sorcerer's purpose.

Or Set's purpose, rather.

Why the Dread Serpent wanted to create a hybrid race was unclear to her, but she assumed it was because she sought to regain dominion over the planet. Her Serpent Men had dominated the world a million years ago, until humankind rose up to defeat them, rendering them virtually extinct. Ever since, Set had striven to reclaim the power she believed to be rightfully hers, and this time the evil god's conquest would succeed, unless Valja could find a way to stop it.

If only she knew how to get in touch with Conan! But he was likely thousands of miles from here right now, and even if he *was* close by, she was probably the last person on Earth he wanted to hear from.

She had come to Charhelm primarily because it was the nearest inhabited place to Ravenhold and she had hoped to find help here. There were mercenaries for hire in the town, for there were always traders who needed guards to accompany them and the merchants' circle who ruled Charhelm did not provide a watch for the town, so individuals were responsible for hiring their own security. Otherwise, they had to take their chances with thieves, and there were plenty of those here as well. But she had no gold to pay sellswords, and even if she had, how many would be foolish enough to go up against a sorcerer and his undead servants in a castle filled with ancient magical artifacts?

But now that she was here, she realized she'd chosen to come to Charhelm for a secondary reason. When she and Renwick were here, they had taken rooms at one of the two inns in town, and when they had gone into the common room for a meal, Valja had been shocked to see Naerys sitting alone at a corner table, drinking ale. When she had pointed out the priestess to Renwick, her mentor had urged her to go over and talk to her friend. Valja had been unsure that the word *friend* applied, but nevertheless she had gone over. The priestess had been deep in her cups, and when she saw Valja standing next to her table, she peered at her with bleary eyes. But then she brightened a bit, stood, gave Valja a half-hearted hug, and asked her to sit. Valja sensed the woman was ambivalent about seeing her, but she accepted the invitation. A server brought Valja ale without being asked, and since she could not drink the liquid without having to throw it up later, she let it sit while they talked.

Naerys told her what she and Anot had done after leaving the ruins of the Elephant Tower that night.

Both Anot and I were bitten by a revenant's shadow snakes. The foul creatures' venom harms not the body but attacks the spirit instead. We were both shown terrible visions, and while I do not wish to speak of exactly what we saw, those sights... broke us. A great despair settled in our hearts, and we left Arenjun that very night ashamed of our failure and unable to face you and Conan.

We wandered through Zamora for a time and eventually found ourselves here in Charhelm. We did not know what to do. I no longer had faith in Mitra, for I did not believe he existed. If he did, how could he allow an evil such as Set to continue plaguing the world? And Anot's bond with the Wild had been severed; the elements and the animals no longer spoke to her, and she could no longer speak to them. It was as if she had lost her very soul. One morning, I woke to find her gone. She had left a letter telling me she was leaving Charhelm, and would return once she had reestablished her connection with nature. That was months ago and she still has not returned. I do not know if she ever will.

Valja told the priestess of the shard embedded in her chest and what it had done to her, including how it had ultimately ended her relationship with Conan. Naerys offered her condolences, excused herself so she could use the privy, and never came back. Valja had searched for her over the next few days but with no luck, and eventually Renwick gently told her it was time they continued on to Ravenhold.

She had not consciously come to Charhelm hoping to find Naerys still living here after all this time, but that had been exactly what she had done. It had been a ridiculous, desperate notion, and she dismissed it now.

The only aid she had received so far had come from Ishtar, and that had been nothing more than a warning of Uzzeran's assault on Ravenhold. She had left the golden statuette in her room when she'd fled, but she wished she had brought it with her, for maybe the goddess would guide her further if she asked. But she didn't need the statuette, did she? Ishtar inhabited all representations of her, no matter how grand or humble. She knew from her previous time in Charhelm that there were a number of temples in town, small ones that catered to travelers who wished to offer a quick prayer or sacrifice to their chosen deity before heading out again. She could not remember whether she had seen a temple to Ishtar back then, but surely the town had one.

In Arenjun, the Temple District was located in the center of the city, and it was the same in many other places, Charhelm included. Common wisdom was that this arrangement reflected the central importance of religion in people's lives, though Valja believed it was so that people had to travel through other parts of a city to reach the temples, hopefully spending some coin along the way before priests could take it all.

The "temples" in Charhelm were even smaller than Valja remembered. Most were simple square structures of stone, although a few had been fashioned from marble, a single symbol carved above the entrance of each the only way to tell one from another. A spider symbol indicated a temple to Zath while a coiled serpent with its tail in its mouth marked the Temple of Set. Valja was surprised to see the merchants' circle permitted a temple to the Dread Serpent to exist here, but then she remembered that these were businesses more than holy places and the merchants were likely wary of alienating any potential customers.

She continued on, passing temples dedicated to Bel, Erlik, Anu, Nergal, Bori, Asura, Kali… and finally she reached one fashioned from marble with an eight-sided star above the entrance—the Temple of Ishtar. Relieved, she started toward the door, and then saw a woman step out of a neighboring temple, this one also made of marble but with a sun symbol carved above the entrance. The woman wore the blue robe of a priest of Mitra, the neck, sleeves, and hem trimmed with gold. She saw Valja, smiled kindly, and held up a tarnished copper medallion that was a miniature version of Mitra's symbol.

"A good day to you, daughter," the priestess said. "Might I interest you in this medallion in exchange for a small donation to the most holy Mitra?"

Valja gasped.

The woman was Naerys.

When Conan and Qiang were still an hour's ride from Charhelm, the Cimmerian told his companion about his vision of Ishtar, which in turn necessitated him relating the tale of how he and Valja had stolen the golden statuette in the first place, and this in turn led to the story of their meeting Naerys and Anot and joining them in their fight against the sorcerer Uzzeran.

When he was done, Qiang smiled. "That is quite a story. But as you paid me the respect of believing my tale, so too shall I believe yours."

Conan scowled. He couldn't tell if the Khitan warrior was being polite or making fun of him, but as the man had shown no malice toward him during their time together, the Cimmerian decided to give him the benefit of the doubt.

"What do you think awaits you in Charhelm?" Qiang asked.

"Trouble," Conan grumbled. "What else?"

"You never saw Naerys and Anot again?"

Conan shook his head. "Never heard word of them, either."

"And Uzzeran?"

"The bastard went to ground, along with that servant of his. I sought them out from time to time, but I never found them." The Cimmerian's expression darkened. "Every sorcerer I have slain since that night, I slew in Valja's name."

"And where is she now?" Qiang asked.

Conan considered. Qiang had shared what had happened between him and Jingshu, and while he felt he owed the man no further explanation, he thought the warrior would understand the final part of his tale.

"From what I learned of Khitai during my time there, magic is more common there than here, and while your people respect its power, you do not necessarily fear it."

"This is so," agreed Qiang.

"My people are what civilized folk call barbarians. We live with nature, respect it, and do not try to tame it or shape it to suit us. The cold north winds howl in our lungs, the icy waters of the rivers flow in our veins, and the blood of beasts burns like fire in our hearts. To us, magic is an unnatural thing, a violation, an abomination. My people do not hate magic out of superstition or ignorance; we hate it because we can *feel* the damage its very presence does to the world around us. I was young when I knew Valja, and my mind and heart were closer to Cimmeria and its ways back then than they are now."

"It is said that with age comes wisdom."

"I make no claim to wisdom," said Conan. "But I have seen and done much since that night in Arenjun, and while in many ways I am as unchanging as the mountains I used to scale as a boy, in other ways I am a very different man than I was then.

"Valja and I attempted to remove the shard from her body, but each time it caused her agonizing pain—the only physical sensation she could experience—and eventually we stopped trying. We attempted to go on as before, and Valja's condition held many advantages for a thief—she could be silent as a shadow, and guard animals shied away from her rather than attacking—but no matter how hard I tried to accept her as she was, I could not. Touching her filled with me with loathing, and before long I found it difficult to be in her presence. I began spending more time away from her than with her, and one morning when I returned to our room after a night of drinking, she was gone. She left no note, but she did not need to. She took the statuette of Ishtar with her, not so she could profit from it—I knew that—but so she could have something to remember us by."

Conan fell silent for a time after that, and Qiang asked no more questions and rendered no judgment. The Cimmerian appreciated this. Eventually, Conan went on.

"I stayed in Arenjun for a while, but the city held too many memories, so I traveled to Shadizar. I have been traveling ever since."

Charhelm came into view then, a mere dot on the horizon, but Conan was glad to see it. He did not know what Ishtar wanted from him, but he was tired of riding and ready to do something. And if it involved the clash of steel and the shedding of blood, so much the better.

Urak the Hyrkanian was known in Charhelm as the Birdman.

The Hyrkanians were famed throughout the known world—and rightly so—as the greatest horse riders the world had ever seen, but they also produced the best falconers. Urak grew up to be an excellent rider, but he was a genius when it came to working with birds of prey. He had a special bond with the creatures that seemed almost supernatural at times, as if he could read their minds and they could read his. He lived on the Turanian border, and he eventually met and fell in love with a girl from that land whose extended family, the Sülale, were caravan traders. He married the girl and joined the caravan, capturing and selling hawks, falcons, and owls for his new family. As they traveled, he expanded his knowledge along with his wares, and he began selling all types of birds. But his favorites were pigeons, especially the ones which, when released, always returned home eventually.

His wife died of lung sickness before they had any children, and when the caravan stopped at Arenjun he found he no longer had the heart for traveling and remained in the city when the caravan moved on. He began selling birds in the Merchants' Quarter, but his fascination with pigeons only increased with time, and he continued working with them and exploring their capabilities. Then one day it came to him: the pigeons could be trained to carry messages back and forth between two different "homes."

Whenever the Sülale's caravan stopped at Arenjun, he would visit with them, and when he told them about his idea for using messenger pigeons, they thought it inspired. There were five separate caravans within the Sülale, as well as members spread throughout various cities, towns, and villages across the known world. Urak's pigeons would allow them all to communicate more easily across vast distances, and the messages they exchanged would maximize the Sülale's profits to a degree previously unimagined.

Some of the Sülale's young men remained in Arenjun with Urak to become his apprentices, and when they had learned all he had to teach, they moved to other cities and took apprentices of their own. In a remarkably short time, the Sülale had a growing communications network.

Eventually, Urak, who was by now getting on in years, grew tired of city life and his latest apprentice took over his business in Arenjun. He moved to Charhelm, which was smaller and where the pace of life, while still sometimes hectic, was nothing like that in the City of Thieves and suited him well. He still sold birds, of course—mostly songbirds these days—but few people knew that his true profession was sending and receiving messages for the Sülale… and for the occasional client willing to pay enough gold for his services.

This day, a messenger pigeon arrived at Urak's home with a bit of parchment attached to its leg. Nothing special about that, of course, but when he removed the message and read it, he saw it was written in the code the Sülale used only in special circumstances. The message was one that had been originally received in Arenjun and then relayed to him, and it told of two men, a Cimmerian and a Khitan, who had committed an unforgivable offense against the Sülale and were to be slain on sight. Urak did not see why these murderers would come to Charhelm, but his duty was to pass on the message, regardless of what he thought of it.

It was a good thing that the Sülale counted a number of mercenaries in its ranks, and it was an even better thing that several of those sellswords happened to be in Charhelm at that very moment.

"Hello, Naerys," Valja said.

The priestess narrowed her eyes as she examined Valja's face, as if she almost remembered her but could not quite recall when and where they had met before. Then her eyes widened in recognition and she grinned.

"Surely you can't be Valja! You look as if you haven't aged a day in fifteen years!" Naerys' smile quickly fell away as the import of her words hit her. "But then you haven't aged, have you?"

There was so much Valja wanted to say, but now that she was face to face with Naerys, the words wouldn't come.

Naerys' smile returned, smaller and sadder now. "I don't suppose you drink, do you?" the priestess said. "Well, *I* certainly can. Come."

The woman slipped the cheap sun-symbol medallion into a pocket of her robe, turned, and entered the marble temple, but Valja hesitated to follow. Would an unnatural thing such as she be welcome in the house of a god? And not only was she undead but she also carried a piece of Set's Eye within her. *Ishtar, forgive me*, she thought, and entered the temple. She would have held her breath had she needed to breathe, but she crossed the threshold without incident, whereupon she relaxed somewhat.

The inside of the temple was as humble as its outer appearance. It consisted of a single room with marble walls and floor, ceiling beams, two rows of wooden benches for the faithful to sit upon, a block of carved stone for an altar, and, behind it, a ten-foot statue so crudely rendered that, had Valja not known the deity to which the temple was dedicated, she would never have recognized it as representing Mitra.

Naerys gestured for Valja to sit on one of the front benches, then walked behind the altar, knelt, and removed something from a compartment carved into the back of the stone block. When the priestess straightened, Valja saw she held an open bottle of wine, and that it was half empty. Naerys took a long drink straight from the bottle, then came over and sat next to Valja.

Now that she was past her initial surprise at seeing the priestess, Valja was able to assess the changes the years had wrought upon her friend. She judged Naerys to be in her forties now, although her too-thin face and haggard features made her seem ten years older. Her dark hair was longer than Valja remembered and was now streaked with gray. It was greasy, too, as if it had been unwashed for some time, and Valja wondered when Naerys had last bathed. A long while ago, she decided, and was glad she didn't possess a sense of smell.

Naerys noted her scrutiny and laughed. "The years have been less kind to me than to you, eh?" She took another long drink from the bottle and her expression became serious. "I apologize for leaving so abruptly when last we met. When you told me what had happened to you when Conan destroyed the Eye of Set, I was horrified. *I* was the one who involved the two of you in my fanatic quest to stop Uzzeran, and of the four of us, you paid the highest price for my obsession."

"But we did stop him," Valja said. She wanted to add that it had been worth the price she had paid but could not bring herself to speak the words, for they would have been a lie.

Naerys shrugged. "Perhaps. But there's no stopping Set, is there? Despite what *he* would have you believe." She hooked a thumb toward the statue of Mitra.

Valja knew not what to say to this, so she said nothing. After a moment—and another drink—Naerys continued speaking.

"I did not tell you what vision I saw under the influence of the shadow-snake venom, for the experience was still too fresh back then, but enough years have passed that I can speak of it now."

Then Naerys told Valja of her witnessing a titanic struggle between Mitra and Set—a struggle Mitra ultimately lost.

"I knew the vision had been a dark one because it had originated from Set, and thus was not a true foretelling, but I nevertheless experienced a revelation from it. Mitra was *not* all powerful—assuming he existed at all—and it was possible for him to lose the battle with Set. More than possible, it was likely. For the gods of good are bound by rules, and whether these rules are of their own making or are imposed upon them by some greater force, they determine what these gods can do or not do. But the gods of evil have no such limitations on them. They are free to act however they will, and they can use any weapon, employ any strategy, no matter how devious or unfair, to achieve their aims. Because of this, they shall always triumph in the end, and there is nothing the gods of good—or their servants—can do about this."

Naerys took a longer drink this time, draining the bottle. She peered inside to make sure no more wine was left, sighed, and then slid the empty bottle beneath the bench.

"I wanted to return to the inn and apologize to you, but I was too ashamed of what I had done. I knew not where else to go, so I came here. The priest was a kindly old man named

Searle, and he welcomed me. There is a small shack behind the temple with a couple of rooms for priests to live in, and he told me I could stay there for as long as I liked. I thought Searle might demand, well, *payment* for the room later, but he was a good man and made no advances toward me.

"I felt as if I needed to do something to earn my keep, so I started helping him out at the temple—not that there was a great deal of work that needed to be done. I swept and dusted, collected offerings from the travelers who came in to pray, sold worthless trinkets like the medallion I tried to sell you, and bought food and drink for the worshippers—but mostly for us—with what little money we took in. Searle eventually told me that he was in truth not a real priest, that in fact he had been a gambler down on his luck who had come in to beg Mitra to help him win for a change, just a few times until he got on his feet again, and then he would return to gambling on his own, without divine intervention. But when he got here, the temple was empty, and when he checked the shack, he found it deserted as well. He spoke to a priest of Nergal, and the man told him the previous priest who oversaw Mitra's temple had died eight months earlier and no one had come to take his place. Searle had sought a change of luck and had found it. He donned the previous priest's robe and assumed stewardship of the temple, a position he held for the remainder of his life."

"Was his belief in Mitra strengthened by his time here?" Valja asked.

Naerys burst out laughing, startling her. "Searle played the role of a priest beautifully, but he did not revere Mitra, nor any god for that matter. He thought doing your best to help others was what mattered, not which deity you prayed to. I adopted his philosophy, which is how I have been able to do this job despite my own lack of faith. Searle died a year ago, and I have been the sole priest here ever since."

“Searle sounds like he was a truly good man,” Valja said.

“One of the best. I would drink a toast to his memory had I any wine left. So, what have you done with yourself since last we spoke?”

“That is a *very* long story,” Valja said, “and ultimately, it is the reason why I am here.”

After stabling their horses, Conan and Qiang walked the streets of Charhelm to get a feel for the town. There did not appear to be anything special about it, as far as Conan could see. It was a small settlement that existed only to cater to the needs of travelers, not much different than a thousand others he had been to before.

People stared at the two warriors as they explored the town. With his height and powerful build, Conan cut an impressive figure wherever he went, while Khitans were rarely seen in this part of the world and thus were a mystery to most people. But the attention they were paid was due more to the fact that both men moved with the strength and grace of large predators, seemingly relaxed but with a coiled alertness about them, as if they were ready to burst into violent action in an instant. Conan was used to people nervously watching him as if he were a highly dangerous animal, and he ignored it.

“When were you here last?” Conan asked Qiang.

“Many years ago. I stopped briefly for supplies and to have my mount reshod. It appears that little has changed since then. You still have no any idea why Ishtar wanted you to come here?”

Conan shook his head. “Assuming it *was* Ishtar and not some damn sorcerer or spirit playing a trick on me.”

Qiang frowned. “You think you were lured here as some kind of trap?”

The Cimmerian smiled sardonically. "My life has taught me to always suspect a trap. But right now, I would like to wash the dust of travel from my throat."

A bearded man in late middle age was walking toward them, clearly Hyrkanian but wearing a Turanian's turban and silk robe —not a common sight, but not especially surprising as the two peoples were related and their kingdoms shared a border.

Conan stepped in front of the man, and he halted abruptly. He took in Conan's features, then Qiang's, and while he seemed astonished at first, that quickly gave way to what appeared to be thinly veiled amusement.

"How may I help you two fine gentlemen?" the man asked in Hyrkanian-accented Zamorian.

"My friend and I wish to slake our thirst," Conan said. "Can you direct us to a tavern?"

The man's face broke into a broad smile. "I can indeed! I highly recommend the Worthless Dog. They serve the best wine in Charhelm! Just keep following this street and take the first right turn you come to. If you find yourself among the temples, you've gone too far. I just came from the Dog, as a matter of fact. Several of my kinsmen are still there, three fine young men named Aytek, Munir, and Nejit. Tell them Urak sent you and they will be sure to take good care of you!"

"We shall do that," Conan said. "You have our thanks."

The Cimmerian and the Khitan continued on their way. A moment later, Conan heard laughter behind them, but when he glanced back over his shoulder, Urak had gone.

They found the Worthless Dog easily enough. It was a stone building with a slanted wooden roof and a crudely rendered image of a dead dog painted on the door. The dog's throat had been cut and streaks of red paint ran from the wound to simulate dripping blood.

"Subtle," Qiang said.

Conan laughed, pushed open the door, and the two men entered.

They heard a melange of voices—people talking, arguing, singing, laughing—but the instant the pair were noticed, all sound stopped and the patrons stared at them in much the same way Urak initially had. Then their mouths stretched into cold, cruel smiles and they all rose from their chairs, hands drawing weapons. He understood at once that Urak had directed them to a tavern where mercenaries gathered to drink and swap lies between jobs. He had been in many such places during his own mercenary days.

Qiang looked at Conan. "I see what you mean about traps," he said.

Conan ignored the comment as he swiftly assessed what they were up against.

Three Turanian men—Urak's relatives, no doubt—all armed with scimitars, turbans wrapped around metal helmets, chainmail vests over silk shirts.

A blonde-haired Aesir woman in a chain hauberk, wolf-fur cape hanging from her shoulders, with a shortsword in her left hand and a hatchet in her right.

A male Hyperborean, tall, thin, skin nearly snow white, long straight hair of the same hue, garbed in black and armed with a narrow-bladed longsword.

A huge Shemite man, taller and more muscular than Conan, his size likely due to his Stygian blood, bearded, blue-black hair, wearing padded leather armor and gripping a broadsword in his right hand.

A Kothian male, dark-haired, bearded, thick-limbed, leather armor, battle axe.

Three Zamorians—two men armed with tulwars, one woman armed with a saber.

"The best strategy would be to step back outside and let them come at us through the doorway one at a time," Qiang said.

"Yes," Conan agreed. "But where would be the fun in that?"

Qiang grinned, and the two men drew their swords and rushed forward.

When Valja finished her tale, Naerys said nothing for a long time, but when she finally did talk, Valja was surprised by what the priestess said.

"I know not which I find harder to believe—that there is a hidden citadel where dangerous magic has been kept locked away from the world for a thousand years, or that you are being directly guided by the hand of Ishtar."

"Ishtar guided me only once," Valja said, defensive now, "and that was more of a general warning. But Ravenhold *is* real. Magic used to be much more common in the age before Atlantis—"

Naerys held up a hand to stop her. "Gods do not intervene directly in people's lives," the priestess said, as if she were an adult speaking to a misguided child.

Valja did her best to ignore Naerys' tone. "What about Set?"

Naerys sighed. "I should have said that the gods of *good* do not interfere, if they exist at all. And as for Set, who says he is real? He could be a story Stygian sorcerers use as a simple way to explain where their powers come from. Or if he *is* real, perhaps he is not a god but rather an extremely powerful Stygian sorcerer who prefers to remain behind the scenes and act as a puppet master. But let us say, for the sake of argument, that everything you have told me is fact. What do you want me to do about it?"

Valja was becoming exasperated now. "What else? Help me stop Uzzeran—again!"

"And how do you expect the two of us to stop a powerful sorcerer who has access to a treasure trove of deadly magic spells and artifacts?" Naerys pressed. "You with your throwing knives and me with my old flail..." She shook her head. "It would be suicide. If Ishtar truly is guiding you, she is sending you to your death." She paused, as if realizing what she had said. "To your *destruction*," she amended. "Look what happened to us last time, and there were four of us then."

"Nothing happened to Conan," Valja pointed out.

"He lost you," Naerys countered.

And then something occurred that Valja hadn't thought possible. Her face blazed with heat, her jaw clenched, her stomach muscles tightened, and she felt *all* of it. Anger raced through her like a wildfire, and she raised her hand to slap Naerys. But she looked into the woman's eyes then and saw someone who had been broken by failure and was unable to get past it.

She lowered her hand, her anger ebbing away.

"I do not know how long the effects of shadow-snake venom last," she said, "but I would think that after fifteen years, your body would be free of it. Whatever dark emotions you feel now come from *you*, not from Set. You have forged your own chains, Naerys, and it is your choice whether to keep wearing them or finally break free."

A single tear slid from one of Naerys' eyes, and she gave Valja a lopsided smile. "You know something? You would make a far better priest than I ever—"

The muffled sound of splintering wood interrupted Naerys, followed by angry shouts, the roar of a crowd, and a deep voice bellowing, "Crom's devils take you!"

The two women looked at each other in disbelief, and then sprang off the benches and ran for the temple door.

The fight began well enough. One of the Turanian men was the first to engage Conan, and he thrust his scimitar at the Cimmerian's midsection, going for a disemboweling strike, but Conan swept the curved blade aside with contemptuous ease and then, with a second swing, laid open the man's throat. Blood sprayed from the wound, but the man did not fall right away, glaring at Conan with eyes that were already glazing over.

"This is from the Sülale," he whispered, then spit blood at Conan's face, striking him beneath the left eye. Final message delivered, the man fell, dead before he hit the floor.

What in the nine hells did he mean by that?

Qiang traded sword strikes with one of the Zamorians, but while his foe's tulwar was a fine weapon, it could not compare to the exquisite craftsmanship of the Khitan's katana, nor could the Zamorian hope to match the warrior's skill level. The katana blurred and the razor-sharp blade struck the wrist of the man's sword hand, slicing through skin, tendon, and bone as if they were no more substantial than air. The hand—still gripping the tulwar—spun away, and the Zamorian howled in pain as blood fountained from his newly made stump. On the backstroke, Qiang sheared off the top of the man's head, and he dropped as silent and heavy as a stone.

The Aesir woman kicked a chair toward Conan's face to distract him as she attacked. He caught it with his left hand before it could hit him and slammed it against the skull of the Turanian foolish enough to attack from the side while the Aesir came at him from the front. Blood jetted from the man's nostrils and ears as the side of his head caved in and he went down. Dealing with the Turanian took only seconds, but that was more than enough time for the Aesir to hurl her hatchet at Conan as she ran. The weapon spun end over end as it flew toward his chest—she'd aimed for the largest part of his body to have the best chance of a strike—and if Conan had been anyone else, the hatchet would have cut through his chainmail vest and into his breastbone. But the Cimmerian fought as much from instinct as from training and experience, and his sword arm moved of its own accord with cat-like swiftness, striking the hatchet's metal head with a loud *clang* and swatting the weapon out of the air.

The Aesir was almost upon him now. Conan had spent time with her people when he was younger and he had great respect for their fighting skills and ferocity. He had also learned a number of their tricks, and so he was ready when she feinted with her sword to draw his blade away from her and punched at his throat. Aesir did this to crush their foe's windpipe, rendering them unable to breathe. The injured opponent would panic, which would give the Aesir warrior the opportunity to finish them off—if they were feeling merciful. Otherwise, they would move on to the next foe and leave their victim to suffocate.

Conan turned his head and tensed his thickly corded neck muscles, and when the Aesir's fist struck, she hissed in pain, for it was like hitting a rock. She recovered quickly and attempted to drive her sword point into the other side of his neck, but before she could do so Conan drove the point of his broadsword into the soft flesh on the underside of her jaw. He shoved hard, and the blade pierced her tongue and the roof of her mouth before finally burying itself in her brain. Blood poured over her lips and her body jerked as if she were having a seizure. Conan lifted the woman high, his sword sinking further into the meat of her brain until the tip scraped the top of her skull, and then, with a bestial roar, he swung her around and flung her still-jerking body at the second male Zamorian. The man gasped as the Aesir flew toward him and crashed into him, the impact driving him violently into a wall. The back of his head collided with the stone, and then the Zamorian and the Aesir slid to the floor, the man's broken skull painting a crimson trail on the wall as he went down.

The last Zamorian, the female, looked at Conan as if he were a monster risen from the darkest, deepest pit in Hell, and she dropped her saber and ran for the back of the tavern, the exit there likely leading to an outside privy. The barkeep and the few customers who hadn't been mercenaries had already fled that way and left the door wide open behind them, and the Zamorian flew through the doorway like a pack of starving wolves was at her heels.

Conan shot a glance at Qiang in time to see him withdraw his katana from the chest of the Hyperborean warrior. The sword had been the only thing keeping the man on his feet, and he fell to the floor where he lay dead and bloody next to the pieces of his shattered sword.

Only three mercenaries remained: the Shemite, the Kothian, and the last Turanian. The latter looked too scared to attack, but the other two had hung back so far, not out of fear but to watch and wait as their fellow mercenaries got slaughtered. Conan understood their strategy, and it was a smart one. Let the lesser fighters tire out the barbarian and the Khitan, and while they do, observe the newcomers' fighting styles, looking for any weaknesses.

"Y-you two should go first," the Turanian said. He was a young man, no older than twenty, if that.

The Shemite growled, swung his broadsword one-handed, like Conan, and decapitated the youth with a single blow. The two parts of his body fell, and more blood soaked the floor of the Worthless Dog.

The big Shemite locked eyes with Conan, and he did not look away as he spoke to the Kothian. "The barbarian is mine."

The other mercenary did not argue.

And then the Shemite did something that surprised Conan:

he tossed his sword onto a nearby table and stood, weaponless, and grinned, madness gleaming in his eyes.

Conan smiled. The Shemite wanted to fight him hand to hand. Qiang stepped to Conan's side and spoke in a low voice.

"Surely you're not going to accept the man's challenge? A wise man does not allow his enemy to choose the battlefield."

Conan turned to his companion. "I told you, I have never claimed to be wise."

He crouched, laid his broadsword on the floor, and stood.

Grinning like a lunatic, the Shemite came running toward the Cimmerian, large hands outstretched, booted feet pounding the floor like thunder. Conan bent his knees slightly and leaned forward to prepare himself to meet the man's charge. The Shemite slammed into him like a mountain made of flesh, wrapped rock-hard arms around his torso, and then lifted him off his feet as if he weighed no more than a child and bore him toward the tavern's entrance. The wooden door exploded outward beneath the impact of their two heavily muscled bodies, and Conan and the Shemite hit the ground hard.

People on the street hurried away from the combatants, some fleeing the scene entirely, most stopping after a short distance to watch the excitement. They cheered and hurled insults, but Conan paid no mind. All of his attention was focused on the man doing his damnedest to squeeze the life out of him.

The Shemite was on top of him, the man's great weight pinning him to the ground.

"Crom's devils take you!" Conan roared.

He balled his hands into fists and slammed them against the Shemite's ears.

17

Valja and Naerys joined the crowd that had gathered to watch Conan fight the giant Shemite. Valja should have been shocked to see the Cimmerian, but she found it seemed right somehow, as if they were both supposed to be at this exact place at this exact time.

"Is that... Conan?" Naerys asked. "He got even *bigger?*"

He had, indeed. He had already been tall and strong when Valja had known him, but the years had put even more muscle on the man, and yet somehow his movements were still as graceful and fluid as a jungle cat's. He had also added quite a few scars to his collection, and she did not doubt that every one of them represented a life—whether that of man, beast, or fiend—that the Cimmerian's sword had cut down.

"I like the cape," Naerys added.

Valja nodded. The scarlet suited him.

Conan and his foe stood in the street, slowly circling one another. The Shemite's ears were red and swollen, and it was clear that Conan had gotten in at least one good strike. Both men were without swords, but each had a dagger sheathed at his belt, and the fact that neither man had drawn his blade told

Valja that they had decided on a contest of sheer brute strength. She smiled—that was exactly what the Conan she remembered would have done, and she was glad to see some things never changed—but she was not certain that her former lover had made a wise choice in this regard. The Shemite he faced was even more massive than Conan was and looked like he could tear a man apart as easily as pulling pieces of meat off a roast pig. Blood-hunger burned bright and hot in his eyes.

Then the Shemite bellowed like a beast and ran at Conan, moving with surprising speed for one so large. Conan made no move to avoid the man's attack, and just as the Shemite was about to reach him the Cimmerian tore off his cape, sidestepped, wrapped the crimson cloth around the man's head as he passed, then turned, planted a booted foot against his rear, and shoved hard. The Shemite stumbled toward the tavern's wall and his head struck the stone with a loud *crack*. He stepped back, legs wobbly, and with a snarl yanked off the cape and hurled it aside. Blood flowed down the big man's forehead, past his nose, and over his lips. He wiped a hand across his mouth, then looked at the blood smeared on his fingers.

The Shemite glared at Conan, then shouted, "No fair!" He sounded like a petulant child.

There is no such thing as a fair fight, Conan had once told Valja. *All that matters is who walks away when it is over.*

Before Conan could make his next move, the sound of clanging steel came from within the tavern, and a red-robed Khitan wielding a katana backed out through the splintered remains of the front door—without tripping, which was an impressive feat in its own right. A Kothian armed with a broadaxe followed him into the street, swinging his weapon wildly, trying to get past the Khitan's defenses, but the eastern warrior fended off every strike with unerring precision. The Kothian was clearly stronger than he was, and the sheen of sweat on the Khitan's forehead showed that the strain of blocking the axe blows was beginning to wear on him, yet this did not appear to concern him. In fact, he was smiling.

The crowd continued growing as the fight went on, and now people packed the street in both directions, cutting off easy escape for the four warriors—not that any of them were the type to retreat from battle. The onlookers cheered and booed and wagered on who would be the first to die. *Humanity at its finest*, Valja thought sourly.

Naerys leaned her head closer to Valja's. "Do you have your throwing knives?" she asked softly.

She nodded, and if it looked like the Shemite was going to kill Conan, she would use them, but not before; Conan would never forgive her for interfering in the fight prematurely. She was not certain whether the Khitan was an ally of Conan's—the man could be a stranger who had happened to get swept up in whatever dispute had erupted in the tavern—but if she needed to intervene to save the man from the crazed Kothian, she knew she would do so. Instinct told her it would be the right thing to do. She slipped a pair of knives from her cloak pockets and held the blades at her side, ready to use them if necessary.

The Shemite's face was crimson with fury and he turned to look back at the wall where his head had struck. The stone was ancient, and the impact when the Shemite struck it had broken off a small piece, leaving a divot in the wall. He turned around, jammed his blood-slick fingers into the divot, and tore free a large chunk of stone, then spun around and hurled the rock at Conan with a grunt of effort.

The missile smacked against Conan's hand as he caught it, but rather than hurl it back, he tossed it aside, released an ear-splitting Cimmerian war cry, and charged at the Shemite. The big man swayed, eyes half closed and legs unsteady, his head injury finally starting to take its toll—at least, that was what the

Shemite *wanted* everyone to think, for when Conan came close enough, the man miraculously regained complete control of his body and swung his right fist into the side of the Cimmerian's head. The blow landed with a sound like two boulders colliding and Conan went down on one knee, blood trickling from his left ear. Before he could rise, the Shemite grabbed hold of his mail shirt and began raining blows on his face. The Cimmerian kept trying to rise, but the Shemite continued hitting him so hard and fast that he was unable to lift his knee so much as an inch before it was driven back down.

"Do it now!" Naerys said. "If you don't, the Shemite will surely kill him!"

Valja's hands tightened on the hilts of her blades, but she did not raise them.

Come on, Conan, you can do this...

More blows, and Conan went down on his other knee. Now it looked as if he was kneeling in supplication before the Shemite, who still continued punching Conan. The skin over the man's knuckles had split, and every time he struck Conan he left splashes of blood on the Cimmerian's face.

The Khitan still struggled against the Kothian axe-wielder, but he saw what was happening to Conan and an expression of alarm came over his face. The Kothian struck three blows against the warrior's katana in rapid succession, driving him back against the tavern wall, only a few feet from the hole created by the Shemite. The Khitan was breathing hard and his sword point dipped several inches, as if the weapon had become too heavy for him to hold. The Kothian grinned savagely and swung his axe in a downward arc designed to split the Khitan's head in two—but like the Shemite a moment ago, the Khitan warrior was only feigning weakness and lunged forward, slipped his blade between the Kothian's ribs, and pierced the man's heart.

The Kothian's strike went wide and his axe struck stone

without coming near the Khitan's head. The warrior withdrew his blade in a single swift motion and the Kothian took a step back, then two. The axe slipped from his hand and fell to the ground, and a second later its owner joined it there.

Blood dripped continuously from the Shemite's fist now, but evidently the pain meant nothing to him because the pace of his strikes did not slacken. Valja raised both of her knives and the Khitan warrior stepped forward, both intending to go to Conan's aid.

They need not have bothered.

With a roar like an enraged lion, Conan surged upward. He grabbed the Shemite by the hair, yanked his head backward, and sank his teeth into the man's throat. A river of blood poured down the front of the Shemite's studded leather armor and he pounded his fist against Conan's back in a desperate attempt to make him let go, but the Cimmerian ignored the blows and slowly brought his teeth together, then yanked backward, tearing out a large chunk of the Shemite's throat. Face ashen, the man slapped a hand to the wound in an attempt to stop the blood flow, but the injury was too severe and the man's blood-slick hand slipped away from his neck, the life drained from his eyes, and he fell to the ground.

Conan, his face a crimson mask, glared down at the Shemite, and then spit the bloody gobbet of meat onto the dead man's chest.

The crowd of onlookers, who until this moment had been whipped into a frenzy of bloodlust, fell suddenly silent. A second later, a gentle voice broke the silence.

"That man needs no weapon. He *is* one."

Everyone turned to see who had spoken, and Valja, Naerys, and Conan recognized the Kushite woman standing in the midst of the crowd. It was Anot, and she was smiling at the Cimmerian in approval.

"You should try to sleep, master. I am sure you will feel fully restored in the morning."

Shengis knew no such thing, of course, but it was what people said when a family member or close friend was ill, so he said it.

On their first night at Ravenhold, Uzzeran had selected one of the dead magisters' rooms as his. The council members' rooms on the first floor were larger and the beds more comfortable, but Uzzeran preferred to sleep near his workroom. He had a simple bed, a nightstand, a desk and chair, and bookshelves. *What more could a man want?* he had said at the time.

Uzzeran lay in his bed now wearing a sleeping robe, his blanket drawn up to his chest, green coldfire burning in a lamp on the nightstand, his left forearm slathered with healing ointment and wrapped in cloth bandages. The ointment gave off a sickly-sweet odor which reminded Shengis of the cloying scent of flowers at a burial ceremony.

In the library, Shengis and Rynthia had been able to get the knife away from Uzzeran before the sorcerer had cut himself too badly. He had become quiet and docile after that, and they had been able to lead him downstairs to the infirmary, where they treated his self-inflicted injury.

The door to the isolation area had been closed and locked, for which Shengis was grateful; he did not think he could stand looking into Taolin's eerie red eyes after coming so close to choking the boy to death. After this episode, he had asked Rynthia to take over caring for the patients in isolation, and she had agreed without asking why, though he wondered if she suspected the reason. She was extremely intelligent, albeit not on Uzzeran's level, and she was quite perceptive as well. Kekk had been the one using Shengis' hands to try to kill Taolin, but Shengis felt responsible for the incident because they *were* his hands. He should have been able to prevent Kekk from taking even temporary control of his body, but to his shame, his mind and will had been too weak.

Uzzeran scowled. “I can sleep after the solstice. Until then, there is work to be done.” He started to pull back the covers, but when he placed his left hand on the mattress to brace himself so he could sit up, he hissed in pain.

Shengis put his own hand on his master’s right shoulder and gently pushed him down onto the bed again. “If you do not get at least a little rest, there is a high chance you will make a mistake when you conduct the rite. We have waited fifteen years for this opportunity. Do you not think that is long enough?”

Uzzeran scowled. “I should flay you alive for having the temerity to speak to me like that.”

Shengis smiled. “Maybe after the solstice.”

In the end, Uzzeran promised to sleep if Shengis tended to a list of tasks for him. Shengis agreed—although, as the sorcerer’s servant, he could have hardly refused—and left his master’s room, closing the door gently behind him. As he started down the hall toward Uzzeran’s workroom, he wondered how long it would take for Uzzeran to get out of bed, walk over to the bookcase, select one of the volumes on transformation magic he had taken from the library, then return to bed and start reading. Less than five minutes, he decided.

Shengis could hardly fault his master. Most sorcerers sought great power solely to dominate others, but Uzzeran’s motivation was different. The Dread One herself had enlisted the sorcerer in his campaign to stop The Woeful Eye’s conquest of Earth. Shengis could not imagine the terrible pressure his master must feel to succeed, especially after his last attempt had failed so spectacularly. Shengis wished to serve Set too, but he wanted to help his master even more.

Blasphemer! Do you think you are helping him by ignoring what happened in the library?

Kekk had been silent in the hours since his attempt to kill Taolin, and Shengis had enjoyed the respite from the Serpent Man's thought-voice constantly haranguing him. Unfortunately, it seemed as if that respite was over.

"I am not ignoring it, and neither is Rynthia. We asked Uzzeran what he experienced during his last episode and why, when he came out of it, he harmed himself. But you know this. You were there. You are *always* there."

Uzzeran had returned to himself while Shengis and Rynthia were tending to his wounds, but when they questioned him, he claimed to have no memory of the episode. Shengis had served the sorcerer for most of his life, however, and knew when the sorcerer was lying, though he said nothing. It wasn't his place.

Your "place" is to protect your master, even from himself. If he has another of these episodes when conducting the rite, it could prove disastrous.

"I thought you did not want Uzzeran to succeed."

Shengis reached the workroom and entered. A coldfire brazier filled the room with eldritch light, revealing tables covered with vials and containers, crystals and gems, ancient books and scrolls… and a clay jar holding the scales Uzzeran had harvested from the dire wyrm. The second Eye of Set rested on a stone column between two tables outfitted with manacles and chains for immobilizing test subjects. The arrangement was much the same as what they'd had beneath the ruins of the Elephant Tower, as well as in the cave near their cabin. Like most sorcerers, Uzzeran was a methodical creature of habit.

You are correct. I do not wish your master to succeed in creating a race of Serpent Lords, Kekk said. *The concept is obscene, and I do not believe Set would ever countenance it, let alone originate such a plan. But I do believe that Uzzeran and the storehouse of mystic artifacts contained in this castle are our best hope for becoming two separate beings again. But if the sorcerer has another episode during the rite and loses control of the Eye, not only might he end up dying, he could conceivably destroy Ravenhold as well. And where would we be then?*

"Most likely dead ourselves," Shengis said.

That is another outcome I would like to avoid.

Shengis couldn't argue with that.

Uzzeran had tasked Shengis with tidying the materials on the tables and making sure everything was where it should be. His master rarely left anything out of place, so Shengis doubted there would be much work for him to do, but if his checking things allowed Uzzeran to relax and, hopefully, drift off to sleep, then Shengis was happy to do it. Kekk remained silent while he worked, which Shengis was grateful for, and half an hour later he was finished. As he had anticipated, he'd needed to move almost nothing.

His next task would be simple enough but was more hazardous. *The tools a sorcerer employs must always be kept in the highest state of cleanliness*, Uzzeran had told him. *Magic is incredibly difficult to perform, and even something so seemingly minor as a light coating of dust or a fingerprint smudge on an object like the Eye of Set can result in a spell's failure.*

Shengis needed no explanation. While no sorcerer himself, he knew much about the basics of magic after serving Uzzeran for so many years, and he regularly kept the master's tools clean. He did not, however, often work with objects as powerful—and dangerous—as the Eye.

It should need nothing more than a quick dusting and a light polish, Kekk said. *You kept the first Eye clean for your master, did you not? This one is no different. So get to it.*

The Serpent Man was right. He took a cloth from one of the tables and then went over to the Eye. One of the things that always surprised him when he stood this close to it was that, even though the artifact had a glossy surface, no reflection could be seen in it. It was as if the Eye pulled light in but refused to give any back. But what he really didn't like about being in the Eye's presence was how the fragment of its twin embedded in his brain reacted. It thrummed like a winged insect in flight, and with this sensation came a piercing pain, as if a sharp spearpoint had been thrust into his head.

It is nothing to be concerned about, Kekk said. *As you surmised, the fragment is merely responding to the second Eye in thaumaturgic resonance. When you finish your work and leave this chamber, the sensation will fade.*

Whatever *thaumaturgic resonance* was, Shengis liked it not, and would be glad when his task was over. He raised the cloth, moved it toward the Eye... and his hand froze. He frowned, willed his hand to obey him, but it remained motionless.

Kekk.

He tried to use his other hand, but it also refused to move.

"Release me!"

No. Being joined with you has been a living hell, and I am going to use the Eye's power to separate us. I intend to cast out your spirit and claim your body as mine, but if the opposite should happen—if my spirit is forced from your body—at least I shall be free of you.

His hand released its hold on the cloth, which fell to the floor. And then, as Shengis watched in horror, Kekk placed his hands on the surface of the Eye.

"Stop! You don't know what you're doing!"

Nonsense. My people were casting spells while yours were still learning to count their fingers and toes. Now be silent and let me concentrate.

Shengis had never directly touched the Eye before, and he was surprised at how ordinary it felt. It wasn't freezing cold or burning hot, and he didn't experience an overwhelming sense of vast, inhuman evil. The surface of the Eye felt smooth to his touch, but that was all. Perhaps Kekk knew less about magic than he had claimed, or perhaps Set herself would not allow the Serpent Man to access the Eye's power since he did not support the dark god's goal of creating a human–Serpent Man hybrid species. Whatever the reason, the Eye was not responding to Kekk, and this came as a great relief to Shengis.

"You might as well give up. The Eye isn't—"

Two black tendrils, thin as threads, shot forth from the Eye's surface and struck Shengis' own eyes. He felt the tendrils push through, penetrate his brain, and start feeling their way around as they explored, searching for—

They found the fragment of the first Eye and released Kekk's spirit. Shengis could feel the Serpent Man loose inside him and knew then that Kekk's spell had worked, that the Serpent Man was going to take over his body and he would either be a passenger as Kekk had been, able to communicate with the Serpent Man but nothing else, or his spirit would be forcibly ejected from his body and he would end up... what? Wandering the halls of Ravenwood as a restless ghost for all eternity? Being gripped by some unknown power and pulled toward whichever afterlife waited for him?

As it turned out, neither of these things happened.

He had felt Kekk's presence inside his head almost from the moment the fragment of the first Eye had become embedded in his brain, but there had always been a separation between them, a distance that had remained intact for fifteen years. But now the lines between Shengis' and Kekk's minds began to blur and the Stygian found himself having a new awareness of the Serpent Man's thoughts and emotions, almost as if they were his too.

No! This should not be happening! I… you… we are—

Kekk's thought was cut off before he could finish it, but that was because the Serpent Man ceased to exist, as did Shengis. There was a sensation of great pressure, as if they were being pressed on all sides by some powerful force…

And then they were one.

Not Kekk, not Shengis.

Someone else.

Some*thing* else.

And that something smiled, revealing its new fangs.

"Set be praised," it said.

Conan's face was as hard as the rest of him, and while his skin was cut and bruised, the only significant damage he had suffered from the Shemite's fist was a broken nose. He'd had experience with broken noses before, though, and had set it with as much ease as any healer by placing his fingers to either side and pushing hard. With a sickening crunch, it was over. It hurt like blazes, but he'd felt worse—much worse—in his time. As a child, he had burned himself once on the back of his hand while helping his father, Corin, at the forge. *Only the dead feel no pain*, Corin had said when his son had shown the injury to him.

Even as the fight had been happening, the merchants' circle had dispatched their guards to clear away the corpses. When it was over and Conan had finished tending to his nose, one of the guards approached the Cimmerian and asked who was going to pay for the removal of the dead.

"I care not," Conan said, "but unless you wish to be hauled off to a grave as well, you will leave me be."

The guard paled and scurried away.

Now that the excitement was over, the crowd began to

disperse. Conan, energized after the fight, turned to Qiang, eager to celebrate their victory with his new friend. But before he could say anything, he caught sight of three women who were not leaving with the rest of the onlookers. Naerys and Anot were older, but he had no difficulty recognizing them, and as for Valja, she looked exactly the same as she had the last time he had seen her, fifteen years ago. He had never given any thought to what her condition would mean for her as the years passed, but he supposed it made sense that she had not aged. The dead never grew any older.

Valja looked as uncomfortable as Conan felt, but when the other two woman started walking toward him, she joined them after a short hesitation. Qiang stepped to the Cimmerian's side, and when he saw the three women approaching, he said, "Who are they?"

"The reason Ishtar sent me to this town," Conan said.

The guards sent by the merchants' circle were still removing the dead from the Worthless Dog, so Naerys suggested they help themselves to several bottles of wine from the place and go to her temple to talk.

"I did not know priests in this land advocated theft," Qiang said.

Naerys smiled. "Consider it an unofficial donation to my temple."

"I shall join you soon," Conan said. "First, I need to clean up."

This was true enough, as he was covered with blood, most of which wasn't his. But the main reason he wanted to postpone this reunion was because he was conflicted about seeing Valja again. He felt no anger toward her for leaving him in Arenjun the way she had. He felt guilty, in fact, because he had been relieved that she had done so. Yes, he had looked for her, but had he truly searched as hard as he could have?

He found a tent where travelers could bathe for a nominal fee, but when the proprietor, an old Iranistani woman, saw the bruises on his face and his split lower lip, she said, "You are *not* getting into one of my tubs." She tossed him a threadbare rag and said, "Give me a copper piece and you can wash yourself at the well in back." She wrinkled her nose. "You can keep the rag."

Conan paid her, walked around to the back of the tent, and stripped off his bloodstained clothes. He then spent several minutes bringing up buckets of silty water from the small well, pouring the gritty liquid over himself, then scrubbing away the blood and grime as best he could. Eventually, he felt someone's eyes on him and he turned to see several holes in the rear of the tent. He had no idea who was watching him bathe—the proprietor, most likely, and perhaps some relatives who helped her with her business, daughters and granddaughters. Grandsons as well, for all he knew. His nakedness did not make him feel self-conscious, and another time he might have entered the tent after he was clean and dressed to see if any woman there caught his eye. But he was not in the mood for that sort of companionship today.

He finished washing, stood for several moments to let himself dry a bit, then dressed. He lamented the loss of his scarlet cape, but it had torn when he had yanked it off during the fight with the Shemite, and the guards had taken it with them when they had carted off the bodies. He took the towel with him when he left and tossed it onto the first trash pile he came to. Then, deciding he had put it off long enough, he headed for Naerys' temple

18

Conan arrived just as Qiang was finishing telling his story to the women.

"Two hundred years?" Valja said. "I cannot imagine living that long. But… I guess I will, won't I?"

"No matter how long we stay in this world, we all live one day at a time," Qiang said. "Our situations may have had different beginnings, Valja, but they are much the same. I have done my best to adapt to my circumstances, as have you. We shall both continue to do so, yes?"

Valja smiled. "Yes."

Whatever Valja was now—a ghost in flesh, a woman frozen in time—that smile was the same as the one Conan remembered, and seeing it tempered his instinctive revulsion to her unnatural nature.

The group had arranged benches to form a circle so they could face one another as they talked. Another bench had been placed in the middle to hold the wine bottles and mugs they had taken from the Worthless Dog, and everyone except Valja was drinking. The only open seat was next to her, and Conan considered pulling up a bench just for himself, but he decided against it. He had no wish to hurt Valja's feelings, and he had sat on many a war council in his time and knew the importance of establishing a feeling of camaraderie before heading into battle. He stepped into the circle, grabbed a bottle of wine, and sat beside Valja. He gave her a brief nod and she smiled in return.

He took a long pull of wine and wiped his cut and swollen lips with the back of his hand.

"Where do we begin?" he asked.

Valja spoke of how she had come to live at Ravenhold and of Uzzeran's assault on the castle.

"We had only recently acquired the second Eye of Set, and I believe Uzzeran came because the spring solstice occurs in three days. He plans to use the Eye to recreate the mystic rite he attempted in Arenjun fifteen years ago."

"And you have no idea what the actual purpose of this spell is?" Qiang asked.

"I believe I know," Valja said, and she told them that Uzzeran was attempting to create creatures that were half human, half Serpent Man, although why the sorcerer wished to do this, she had no idea.

"Uzzeran is a sorcerer, and all his kind are mad," Conan said. "They do things just to see if they can, consequences be damned. This is why they need to be slain, every damned one of them." He glanced at Anot. "Not shamans, though." He reconsidered. "Not *all* shamans," he amended.

"It is indeed auspicious that we have found ourselves here at this time," Qiang said. "I believe Yun, Ishtar, and Mitra have brought us together to counter Uzzeran's foul plan. And who knows? Perhaps the sorcerer will prove to be the evil greater than Guangzhi that I have sought for so long."

For the first time since Conan had met Qiang, he heard a note of hope in the warrior's voice. *I hope you find the redemption you seek, my friend*, the Cimmerian thought, then took another long drink of wine.

"I dislike being a plaything of the gods," he said. "If Mitra, Ishtar, and Yun wish to war with Set, they should fight her themselves and leave us mortals out of it."

"I believe they would if they could," Anot said, "but the gods are so unimaginably powerful that if they were to battle each other directly, they would risk destroying reality itself. The only way they can act within our world without damaging it is through their worshippers." She looked at Naerys. "Or those who used to worship them."

Naerys scowled at the shaman but did not reply.

Anot turned to Conan. "Perhaps the god of your people is involved in this struggle as well."

Conan snorted. "Crom has no interest in what happens in our world."

"No?" Anot said, a mischievous twinkle in her eye. "He gave you strength greater than other men, as well as a restless nature that keeps you roving about the world. Perhaps you are his instrument, a weapon he wields when necessary."

"Conan of Cimmeria, the Sword of Crom," Valja added with a teasing smile.

Conan looked at the two women for a moment, then said, "Bah!" and drank more wine.

"You are not the only one uncomfortable at the thought of being manipulated by gods," Naerys said. "I rejected Mitra and his teachings when I left Arenjun. Why would he call on someone who turned her back on him?"

"Perhaps because *he* has not rejected *you*," Qiang said.

Naerys looked startled, as if such a thought had never occurred to her. She took a deep breath, then spoke of what had happened to her and Anot after Conan and Valja became separated from them and how both women eventually ended up in Charhelm.

"But Anot didn't remain there long," Naerys finished.

Conan heard both anger and sorrow in the priestess' voice, and he could not say which was stronger.

Naerys fell silent then and Anot began to tell her story.

"I needed to find a way to reconnect with the Wild," said the shaman, "so one morning before sunrise, I wrote a note for Naerys, telling her of my intention to find what I had lost. I know I should have told her this to her face, but I feared I would not have had the courage to go if I had looked into her eyes that morning."

Naerys looked at her, and the two women shared a brief smile before Anot continued.

"I left Charhelm on foot and started walking east, with nothing but the clothes I was wearing and a full waterskin. I cannot adequately express how empty I felt after being bitten by the shadow snake. It was as if my soul had been ripped away, leaving me a hollowed-out thing that only appeared to be alive. All my life, I had been able to hear the wind, rain, and earth speak to me. I could communicate with animals, sense their thoughts and feelings. That was all gone, taken from me by one of Uzzeran's foul revenants.

"I had hoped that by immersing myself in the natural world once more, without the distractions of civilization surrounding me, I would be able to restore my connection to the Wild. I wandered alone for two weeks, but at the end of this time I was still as empty as when I had left Charhelm. I began to fear I would never find healing and peace, and I contemplated ending my life."

Naerys reached over to take Anot's hand, and the Kushite woman gripped it gratefully.

"By this point, I had reached the foothills of the Kezankian Mountains, and I decided to keep going for no other reason than I was not quite ready to die yet. I climbed slowly, taking my time, all my senses open and questing, searching desperately for any hint of the Wild. I had eaten very little during my trek from Charhelm, and I quickly grew weak. I believe I must have passed out, for when I woke next it was morning and I found myself lying upon a bed of green leaves and fresh grass next to a small fire. I did not remember making either and assumed I had an unknown benefactor. Whoever it was had also gathered some roots and nuts for me and refilled my waterskin. So I warmed myself by the fire as I ate and waited for my new friend—or friends—to appear.

"I examined my surroundings and saw I was in a small canyon with walls so steep they were nearly vertical. Partway up the cliffs was a series of caves with semicircular entrances, obviously carved by hand. Now that I knew where my new friends likely lived, and had a full belly for the first time in a while, I grew relaxed and drowsy, and before long I fell asleep again.

"I woke later that afternoon to find three figures squatting around me wearing brown robes the same color as the canyon rock. They seemed curious but not threatening; I knew that if they had wished me harm, they could have killed me while I was sleeping or simply not have rescued me in the first place. This was my introduction to the M'lima."

Conan had never heard of such a people, but the Kezankian Mountains covered hundreds of miles and he had explored only a small part of them. Who knew who—or *what*—else dwelled there?

"They allowed me to stay with them, and I learned their ways. Time passed as I slowly healed from the emotional effects of the shadow-snake venom, and while I came to love the M'lima and began to think of them as my people, I still could not reestablish my connection to the Wild, and I had started to fear I never would. But then, one day, I was sitting in the cave the M'lima had given me for my home and I felt a breeze on my face. I realized then that the wind had *not* left me, that it had always been there and had never stopped talking. *I* had stopped listening to it. In that moment, my connection to the Wild returned—or rather, my awareness of it did—stronger than ever before.

"In the note I had left for Naerys, I said I would return when I could feel the Wild again. But so many years had passed since I had left that I feared it was too late for me… for us." She turned to Naerys. "I am so sorry."

Naerys' only reply was a smile, but her eyes glistened with tears.

Anot returned to her story.

"A month ago, I climbed to the top of a large mountain near the M'lima settlement. The view was wonderful—I felt as if I could see to the edge of the world. I could not, of course, but what I *did* see was a mountain some miles away which had a strange rock formation on it, one that looked almost like—"

"A castle," Valja said.

"Yes. And it was at that precise moment that the mountain I stood on spoke to me in a voice loud as thunder. It said: *Uzzeran*. That was all, but it did not need to say anything else. I understood.

"It took me several days to climb back down the mountain, and when I returned to the M'lima, I told them I needed to travel to Charhelm. When they asked why, I told them about our encounter with the sorcerer in Arenjun. The M'lima live in complete harmony with nature in ways that humans forgot when they first climbed down from the trees. If a sorcerer threatened the Wild, they would stand with me against him. Three of the M'lima accompanied me on my journey to Charhelm to ensure my safety. This was not necessary, of course, for I can take care of myself, but the M'lima wanted to contribute to the effort against Uzzeran and I was not about to stop them."

Conan frowned. "Where are they? Didn't they come into town with you?"

"They... have no love of civilized places, and thus chose to camp half a mile away from the town. If I have need of them, I can ask the wind to summon them and they shall arrive within moments."

"They will definitely aid us against the sorcerer?" Conan asked.

Anot nodded.

Conan finished his wine and put the empty on the floor, but he did not get another bottle. It was time to make plans. He turned to Valja.

"Tell us more about Ravenhold," he said.

The companions spent the remaining daylight hours preparing for their journey, and at dawn the next morning they set out for Ravenhold. They had talked and drunk most of the night, and none of them had gotten much rest. Today, they were all tired and bleary-eyed, save for Valja, who had no need for slumber, and Conan, whose Cimmerian constitution compensated for his lack of sleep.

Conan and Valja rode in front of the group on his sturdy lakan, and Qiang, Naerys, and Anot followed a dozen yards behind, a pair of packhorses loaded with supplies tethered to the women's mounts. Qiang rode his haraghi while Naerys and Anot rode hardy Hyrkanian steppe ponies. When they had visited the stable the previous day to get mounts for the women, all the other horses had been terrified of Valja and refused to go anywhere near her, but Conan's lakan was more accepting of her presence so she now rode seated behind him, her arms around his waist. They kept their distance from the other mounts so as not to upset the animals but had lessened this distance every fifteen minutes or so, and hopefully, in a few hours, all the horses would have adjusted to Valja. The distance gave the former partners in thievery the opportunity to talk in private, too, although for a long time neither could think of anything to say.

The air was cool that morning, and it felt good on Conan's bruised face. He was lucky the Shemite had not dislodged any of his teeth yesterday. That bastard hit hard.

As they rode, Conan kept looking for the three M'lima Anot had said accompanied her to Charhelm, but they had not appeared when the group left the town, nor had they attempted to join them since. When he asked Anot about this, she said, "They like to keep to themselves. But do not worry. They are with us."

Conan was skeptical, but he decided to place his trust in Anot and thought no more of the matter.

During their council the previous day, Valja had said the journey to Ravenhold was a three-day ride from Charhelm. The solstice would occur in three days, so if they were to have any hope of stopping Uzzeran this time, they needed to reach the castle before then. Conan had suggested they alternate cantering the horses and walking them, with periodic breaks for the animals to rest, eat, and drink. This way, they could travel as swiftly as possible without killing their mounts.

I can help, too, Anot had said. *I'll ask the wind to speed us along, and I'll ask the earth to soften beneath us so the journey will be easier on the horse's legs.*

Conan had traveled to the Kezankian Mountains before and was familiar with the general terrain they had to traverse—flat grassland and shrubland, sparse trees, ground becoming hilly closer to the mountains. The grassland attracted deer, gazelle, and bison—camels sometimes too, though they tended to stay closer to the mountains. The plant-eaters naturally attracted predators—wolves, lions, hyenas, and jackals—and although the beasts usually left travelers alone, *usually* did not mean *always*, and Conan told everyone to keep close watch on their surroundings as they rode.

From time to time, he heard laughter coming from Qiang, Anot, and Naerys. The Khitan warrior got along well with the priestess and the shaman, and he was likely regaling them with more tales of his adventures over the last century or two. Conan had noticed the previous night that Qiang was careful about which stories he shared with others, offering lighthearted tales rather than dark ones. The Cimmerian thought he did this out of the Khitan sense of propriety. His people valued politeness above almost everything else, something Conan thought he would never understand.

After a time, Valja spoke. "What does it feel like to have me holding on to you while we ride?"

Conan thought for a moment. "It brings good memories of our time together," he said.

"Does it feel strange?"

Conan frowned. "What do you mean?"

"I have neither held nor been held by anyone since the last time we saw each other. Do I still feel… human?"

He was unsure how to answer this. "Your touch is cold, and since you do not breathe, except to speak, your body is motionless much of the time. You have not aged—you are like a memory come to life. These things do feel strange to me, but you are still Valja, and that is what is important. I am like the horses. I just need some time to get used to your… differences."

He wasn't certain he had said the right thing, but after a second she hugged him tighter and he was relieved.

"What *is* strange to me is that you have chosen to live in a castle filled with magic these last fifteen years," he said. "If it were not necessary that we go there now, I would never set foot in such a place."

"It was an adjustment, for sure," she replied. "I came to love it after a time—the people as well as the place—and I was proud of the work I did as a seeker and scholar." She paused for a moment, and when she resumed, her voice was barely above a whisper. "Everyone I knew at Ravenhold is dead now. My friends, my colleagues..."

"We will avenge them," Conan said.

Valja's voice grew cold. "Yes, we will."

About an hour before sunset, they came to a small group of oak trees next to a stream and decided to make camp there. If Conan had been traveling alone to Ravenhold, he might well have continued on. Yes, he would risk his mount taking a bad step in the dark and becoming injured, but he had ridden at night many times before when his need was great. His Cimmerian-bred instincts, combined with his long years on horseback, gave him almost preternatural skill when it came to guiding a horse across a landscape in darkness. But except for Qiang, whose long lifetime in the saddle made him almost as good a horseman as a Hyrkanian, the others in the group, while competent riders, did not have the skill or experience needed to travel at night on horseback. Conan and Qiang could have ridden on while the others rested, setting a pace that would allow the two men to reach Ravenhold a day before the others, maybe more, but they needed Valja's knowledge of the castle, Anot's shamanic magic, and Naerys'... Actually, Conan and Qiang would likely do fine without the priestess. The woman he had known fifteen years ago had been a smart and driven holy warrior, but unlike

Anot she had not recovered from her shadow-snake bite and was also cynical, uncertain, and indecisive. Perhaps now that she had been reunited with Anot, her warrior self would emerge. Otherwise, she might prove to be a liability when they went up against Uzzeran.

One advantage the small group had was that the solstice was still two days away, which meant they should have enough time to reach Ravenhold before Uzzeran used the second Eye of Set for whatever his dark purpose was—assuming they encountered no ill fortune on the way to the castle. Conan hoped that, if the gods were truly aiding them, they would ensure their path was free of trouble—although why the gods could not have managed to get all of them together in Charhelm a week or two earlier, so that they had plenty of time to reach Ravenhold, he did not know. Qiang would probably say the gods' ways were ultimately unknowable, and Anot might say that, if the gods had acted sooner, it would have given Set more time to react to their plan, potentially causing its failure. Conan, however, ascribed it to the gods' endless self-absorption. They were always so caught up in their own affairs that they could never be bothered to pay attention to such petty mortal concerns as time and distance.

The nights in Zamora could be chilly this time of year, and they decided it was safe enough to make a fire. They had no enemies pursuing them, and bandits rarely strayed from the caravan routes. As for predators, the fire would keep them at bay, and of course the group would set a watch. Valja did not sleep, so she volunteered to keep watch alone throughout the night so that everyone else could rest, but the others would not hear of it. They would take their turns at watch as well because two sets of eyes, living or undead, were better than one.

They unsaddled the horses, watered them, and then tethered them to trees, allowing them enough rope to walk as they grazed. They were content.

The group talked as they ate a simple meal of cheese and flatbread.

"Where are your M'lima friends?" Conan asked Anot.

"They have almost no contact with the outside world," Anot said, "and they are hesitant to interact with anyone they do not already know. It took them a while to warm to me. Rest assured, they traveled all day, just as we did, but they kept their distance from us. They have made their own camp for the night, but I am sure it is not far. When we resume riding in the morning, so will they."

Qiang gave the shaman a quizzical look. "Do they intend to help us when we reach Ravenhold? If so, will they not be forced to reveal themselves to us then?"

A small smile played about Anot's lips, as if she was enjoying a private joke. "You will see them when the time comes," she said. "*All* of them."

Conan liked Anot better than any other wizard he had ever met, and more than that, he trusted her. But like all wizards, she delighted in keeping secrets at times, and that he most assuredly did *not* like. Sorcerers, wizards, witches—they all shared a common trait: they loved knowing things that no one else did. Sometimes he thought it was that, rather than the acquisition of power, which truly motivated them.

Conan decided to put the matter out of his mind. During his travels, he had encountered many different groups of people, some with far stranger customs than the M'lima. If Anot's shy friends wished to keep to themselves, so be it.

Everyone put out their bedrolls—except Valja, who didn't need one, and Conan, who needed only a blanket—and tried to get some sleep. Qiang chose to take the first watch with Valja, and after two hours Anot would relieve him, after which it would be Naerys' turn and then, finally, Conan's. The Cimmerian wasn't particularly tired, but he had long ago learned to take rest when he could. And when he slept out in the open like this, he always kept his clothes on, including his boots and armor. He did unbuckle his sword belt, but he placed the scabbard on the ground next to his blanket, within easy reach should he need it during the night. He lay down there and moments after closing his eyes, he was asleep.

He always slept lightly, though, for even in slumber, a part of his mind remained alert for danger. And thus, an hour later, he was on his feet, broadsword in hand, fully awake and ready for battle. He looked around quickly, unsure what had woken him, but then he heard it again—an unearthly sound, part scream and part howl, unlike anything he had ever heard before. Valja and Qiang were on their feet, eyes scanning the darkness beyond the firelight, searching for the demon-thing that had produced such an awful cry. Anot and Naerys were awake now, too, and they rose and joined the others.

"I am sure that sound is nothing to be concerned about," Anot said. "Most likely some she-beast in heat, uncomfortable and in search of a mate. Hopefully, she'll soon—"

The sound came again, louder this time, closer.

Conan, acting entirely on instinct, dashed out into the night and ran in the direction from which he judged the sound had originated, his tread far lighter than should have been possible for a man of his size, but he was Cimmerian and could move with the stealth of a wild animal when he needed to. He was concerned about Anot's friends. He had never heard of the M'lima until earlier that day, and he had no idea what sort of fighters they were, but even seasoned warriors might have difficulty defending themselves against a creature that could make such a spine-chilling sound. The M'lima might have dire need of his sword right now.

He heard Anot calling for him to return to camp, but he ignored her. His mind was focused entirely on reaching the

M'lima as fast as he could and killing whatever foul thing threatened them. The moon was a thin silver crescent, but with Conan's strong night vision it provided enough light for him to make out his general surroundings. He saw no movement ahead, heard no sounds of a struggle, and was beginning to wonder if he had run in the wrong direction when the scent of blood hit him. He halted, half crouched, sword gripped tight, ready for something to come rushing at him out of the darkness. But nothing did.

He inhaled, and this time he detected another scent mingled with the blood-smell: the odor of reptile.

He proceeded slowly forward, eyes scanning the ground as he went, and he soon came across the long, thick form of what could only be an extremely large snake. The creature was motionless, but Conan thrust his sword into its body to make sure it was dead, though the serpent didn't so much as flinch. Sure now that the reptile was no longer a threat, Conan walked up and down its the length. While it wasn't stretched out in a straight line, he judged that it measured thirty feet, but it was difficult to tell because the animal had been torn into three sections and the pieces were strewn about. He was surprised to find the thing here. As far as he knew, serpents this large lived only in the jungles of the Black Kingdoms, far to the south, but then he supposed Set could send her servants wherever she wanted.

The head was separate from the rest of the body, and Conan speared it with his sword and carried it with him back to camp, where everyone was standing together, waiting for him, Qiang holding his katana at the ready. Conan did not need to ask the warrior why he had chosen not to follow him into the darkness; he knew the Khitan had remained behind to protect the rest of the group in case of attack. Not that their companions were helpless—Valja held a pair of throwing knives, Anot gripped a dagger and of course had her magic to rely on, and Naerys held both a dagger and her flail. Conan was glad to see the priestess had been ready to fight. Perhaps she would be more her old self by the time they reached Ravenhold.

When Conan reached the edge of the fire, he used his boot to dislodge the snake's head from his blade and let it fall to the ground for the others to see.

"It was already dead by the time I got there," he said. "Something had torn it apart. Or some*one*." He looked at Anot, but she had crouched down to examine the head, holding it steady against the ground with one hand while she prodded its mouth with her dagger.

"This is not a natural creature," she said. "There are serpents this large in my homeland, but they are constrictors, the kind that squeeze their prey to death before swallowing them whole. But this one has fangs and venom glands. It is poisonous." She stabbed her dagger into the head and, with a flick of her wrist, tossed it into the fire, where it immediately began to burn, releasing a rank odor like spoiled meat into the air.

"We don't need to worry about the rest of the body drawing predators," Anot went on as she wiped her dagger clean on the grass. "No natural creature will touch the carcass."

The shaman stood, but despite her reassurance to the others, she continued to hold on to her blade, gazing warily out into the night.

"The thing was sent to kill us as we slept," Naerys said. "Set knows we are coming."

"Snakes, no matter their size, do not make sounds like what we heard," Conan said.

"Maybe whatever made that sound was what killed the serpent," Valja said.

"I've encountered many strange and wondrous creatures in my time," Qiang said. "Perhaps this serpent is one who *can* make sounds."

Conan looked at Anot. "Or maybe what we heard was the war cry of the M'lima as they fought with the beast."

"Surely not," Naerys said. "No human could have made that sound."

Conan did not take his gaze off Anot.

"I did not say they were human," she said, then gave the Cimmerian an enigmatic smile.

What bothered Conan the most was a nagging feeling that he had heard such a cry or something like it before, but he could not place it. He remained awake for the rest of the night, looking up at the stars, trying to remember and failing.

19

Uzzeran sat in a leather chair in the lesser library, sipping a mug of hot tea beneath the green light of a coldfire brazier, a book open on his lap. This chamber was nowhere near as large as the main library, but it had a much cozier atmosphere, due in no small part to the fireplace, which currently had a cheery blaze of actual flame going. The sorcerer had lived an ascetic lifestyle for most of his years, dedicating himself completely to developing his craft and serving his god. Now, on the verge of his greatest triumph, it was nice to indulge himself a little with the tea, the fire, the chair, but most of all, the book. The lesser library had been created solely for pleasure reading, and it contained no books on magic. There were stories, biographies, science, economics, architecture, religion, myths and legends, and more, but not a single word devoted to the thaumaturgic arts. At the moment, he was perusing a volume on horticulture, and he felt absolutely decadent. The residents of Ravenhold had been wise to give themselves recreational outlets for their minds. If he could, he would have spent the rest of his life in this room, reading one book after another, never thinking about magic again.

And he would never have to think about the horrible realm

of endless darkness he had visited in that dream or vision or whatever it had been. He had told Shengis and Rynthia that he had no memory of the experience, but that had been a lie. Not only did he remember but he had difficulty thinking of anything else. A huge reason why so many men and women studied sorcery was so they could gain a deeper understanding of reality, see into other worlds, catch glimpses of the past and future, but what he had seen in his vision had shaken him to his very core. What if that darkness, that *nothingness*, was what truly lay behind the illusion of what mortals considered the real world? And if that was so, what did it matter if Set became more powerful than all the other gods combined? What could she *do* with all that power when nothing truly existed, perhaps not even herself? Uzzeran had no answers to these questions, and he doubted he ever would. He would continue as he had for so many years, heeding the commands of his god and hoping his efforts would have an impact in the end. What else was there for him?

He tried to return to reading about flowers, but he could no longer concentrate on the words, so it was a relief when Rynthia entered the library a few moments later. He closed the book and waited for her to approach.

When she stood before him, he asked, "How are the preparations coming along?"

"They are nearly finished," she replied. "The revenants cleared a space in the repository and set up tables, and Shengis brought the Eye down from your workroom and set it up per your instructions. The serpent scales are in place and ready as well. The only thing left is to bring the test subjects to the repository and sedate them, and we will not do that until a few hours before the ceremony. I have gone over a dozen different astronomical charts and am confident I have identified the best moment you should activate the Eye. And if for some reason the spell cannot be cast at that time, I have selected several later moments that, while less than perfect, should still work."

"Very good," Uzzeran said. "Come get me an hour before the best time arrives. Until then, I shall be in my room fasting and meditating."

He lifted the mug of tea from the side table next to his chair and quickly downed the rest of it. It was cold now, and he made a face as he swallowed. Then he handed the empty mug to Rynthia, rose from the chair, and laid the book down on the seat. He knew not what would happen to him after the ceremony's completion, but if he still lived, he planned to return here and finish the book.

Rynthia made no move to leave, however, and he sensed the woman had something on her mind.

"Is something troubling you?" he asked.

"It's Shengis. He's… different."

Uzzeran frowned. "How so?"

"He's colder, more distant, and he approaches everything with an attitude of mocking amusement."

Uzzeran had noticed none of these things, but then he had seen little of Shengis over the last several days. "Perhaps Kekk's personality is coming through more strongly now that we are so close to achieving our goal."

"I suppose that *could* be it," Rynthia allowed.

"I am sure it is," he said, smiling. "Nothing to worry about."

Rynthia left Uzzeran in the lesser library and carried his empty mug to the dining hall. Normally, she might have resented the sorcerer treating her like a servant. She had been a seeker for Ravenhold, after all, and had traveled alone through some of the most dangerous places in the known world in search of deadly mystic artifacts. She had dealt with bandits, thieves, slavers, and killers, walked on cursed land, contended with vengeful spirits, fought things that refused to stay in the grave, and made bargains with demons—all without the aid of any magic of her own—and she had always, *always* returned alive and whole, her sanity intact, her soul unstained, bearing whatever object she'd gone in search of.

Until, that was, she had found the Eye of Set and everything had changed. The Great Serpent had owned her body and soul after that. She had taken the Eye to Uzzeran in Arenjun, just as Set had commanded, but the sorcerer had run afoul of a couple of thieves who had destroyed the Eye. Rynthia had continued working as a seeker, maintaining the pretense that her allegiance remained with Ravenhold, but for the next fifteen years she had sought the second Eye. She wished the dark god had guided her, but she had only ever felt her majestically malign presence when she had been in physical contact with the first Eye.

But it had not been her who had found the second Eye; it had been brought back to Ravenhold by another seeker, a pleasant middle-aged Aquilonian man named Numedactus. Unlike her, he had taken the precaution of never touching the second Eye without wearing gloves, and so he was never claimed by Set. She had been ecstatic that the other Eye had been unearthed, of course, but she had been furious that Numedactus had found it instead of her. So, a month after he had brought the Eye to Ravenhold and it was safely stored in the repository, the poor man had taken his own life by leaping out of a tower window—with a little assistance from her, of course.

She entered the dining hall. The two hundred revenants that had once been her friends and colleagues stood motionless, organized in rows, shadow snakes nestled inside their dead bodies, waiting for the call to action. They would be deployed throughout the castle before Uzzeran began the spell to create the human–Serpent Man hybrids. He had been interrupted once before by intruders, as the shard jutting from his eye socket testified, and he was determined that it would not happen again. She thought the odds of that happening here, atop Skycrest Mountain, were infinitesimal, but she supposed it hurt not to take precautions.

She took the mug into the kitchen and placed it in a bucket of water to be tended to later, then left the dining hall without giving the revenants another look.

She *was* a servant, but not Uzzeran's; she was a devotee of Set and would do whatever it took to fulfill the wishes of her god. Despite the sorcerer's assurances to the contrary, she was certain that something was wrong with Shengis and could not escape the feeling that, whatever it was, it threatened the successful culmination of Set's plan. She could not allow that to happen.

Poor Numedactus had met with an unfortunate accident. Before this was all over, perhaps Shengis would, too.

The entity that now inhabited Shengis' body had spent a good part of the last few days trying to decide on a new name for itself. It had considered and rejected dozens before finally settling on Akh, which in Stygian meant "glorified spirit."

Akh had gone down to the repository to inspect Rynthia's setup for the upcoming ceremony. She was a highly intelligent person and there was no reason for Akh to think her work might be lacking, but in the end she *was* only human and Akh was so much more.

He was the first of the Serpent Lords.

Uzzeran had finally succeeded in creating the ultimate race, and he wasn't aware of it. Of course, right now Akh was a race of one, but there would be other Serpent Lords, even if he had to create them himself.

Ten tables were arranged in a circle around the second Eye of Set, which rested atop its stone pillar in the middle. Each table had iron hand and foot restraints attached to its surface to hold the test subjects steady while Uzzeran cast the spell, drawing on the combined power of all the magical objects in the chamber to fuel it. Small woven baskets filled with fist-sized scales had been placed on the floor next to each table, the final element in Uzzeran's "recipe." Akh did not know for certain if this new version of the spell would succeed where the previous one had failed, but he thought there was a good chance it would.

If it did work, Uzzeran would have only a few seconds to appreciate his victory, for in that moment, when the sorcerer's defenses were at their lowest, Akh would strike. He would kill Uzzeran and claim the Eye of Set as his own, along with all the artifacts in this chamber. Then, after killing Rynthia and any other surviving humans left in Ravenhold, he would make the castle his fortress and start creating more of his kind, until eventually he had built an army of thousands, *tens* of thousands. Then he would send them out into the world to conquer humanity in Set's name.

He could hardly wait to get started.

In the mountains surrounding Ravenhold, the Brood of Zath had gathered. They clung to sheer walls, hid in the shadows beneath outcroppings of rock, lay curled up and motionless in narrow crevasses, and there they waited.

And at the base of Skycrest Mountain, upon whose pinnacle Ravenhold had been raised many centuries ago, mysterious beings garbed in robes the color of stone, robes that allowed them to blend in and become nearly invisible in the Kezankians, also gathered.

The M'lima had arrived.

And they began to climb.

20

Conan and the others reached Skycrest Mountain at mid-afternoon on their third day of travel—the day of the solstice. When they drew close, they dismounted and walked their horses the rest of the way.

Skycrest's name was appropriate. It was the largest mountain in this part of the Kezankians, and it did indeed seem to touch the heavens. Near the peak was an odd formation of rock that resembled a quartet of towers, but if Conan had not known that those towers were part of Ravenhold, he would never have guessed there was a castle up there. The Khitan sorceress who had created Ravenhold had done an excellent job of camouflaging it. Conan thought it might well be the most impressive—and practical—use of magic he had ever seen.

They still had seen no sign of Anot's friends, and Conan was beginning to think that the M'lima existed only in her mind. But on the second night they made camp, they had once again heard those terrible screams out in the darkness. Both Conan and Qiang investigated, and this time they discovered three mutilated serpents, all as large as the one Conan had found the night before, all the same constrictor–viper hybrid species.

There was another thing different about the scene: Conan found several tufts of brownish-gray fur on the ground near the dead serpents. He did not recognize the fur as coming from any animal he knew, and yet he felt he should, as if he had seen it before, maybe only once, many years ago. If only he could remember…

Valja led the party around the base of Skycrest until they came to a large boulder pressed against the side of the mountain.

"This is it," she said.

Then she spoke a word in a language Conan did not recognize, and the sound of the strange syllables caused the hairs on the back of his neck to stand up. The boulder shook as if caught in an earthquake tremor, and then with a mighty heave it rolled to the side to reveal an opening large enough for four riders to enter side by side. This was the entrance Ravenhold's residents used to bring in supplies, and it was how Valja had escaped from the castle when Uzzeran had taken it over.

The previous night, they had spent several hours around the campfire discussing strategy for their assault on the castle, and a good portion of that time was taken up by debate on what would be the best way to enter Ravenhold. The supply entrance seemed to be the best and, in truth, only choice. There was a straight, steep path carved into the mountainside that led to Ravenhold's main entrance, but they would surely be detected long before they reached the castle if they chose that route, and climbing Skycrest was out of the question. Conan had spent much of his youth climbing the mountains near his home in Cimmeria, and he could scale Skycrest with the ease of a fly crawling up a wall, but no one else in their group had any experience climbing, not even Qiang. *I was raised in a city,* he had said, almost apologetically.

But even had they all been expert climbers, they decided that route was too risky. Uzzeran could use his magic in a thousand different ways to attack them while they clung to the side of Skycrest, helpless and unable to defend themselves. Or he might have caused the supply tunnel to collapse, blocking that route. Or he might have conjured a supernatural beast to patrol the tunnel and devour any intruders it caught. Or he might have filled the tunnel with his revenants, the undead things shuffling around, shadow snakes extruding from their mouths and eye sockets, swaying back and forth, ebon forked tongues flicking the air.

I know a way to make certain we can enter safely through the supply entrance, Anot had said. But when they had asked her for details, she had only said, *I will show you when we get there.*

Conan looked at the shaman now. "We are here. Now will you tell us how you will determine if it is safe for us to enter?" Conan had little patience with magic-users, even friendly ones, at the best of times, and he had almost none left now.

"I will not," Anot said with a smile. "But *they* will."

She nodded toward a section of the mountain wall to the left of the tunnel entrance, and an instant later two figures seemed to emerge from the very stone itself. Thinking this was an attack by some creatures of Uzzeran, Conan drew his sword and stepped forward to engage the things, but Anot quickly put a hand on his chest to stop him.

"These are my friends," she said. "I swear to you, they mean us no harm."

Conan remained where he was, but he did not take his eyes off the figures, nor did he lower his sword. On closer inspection, he saw that the pair wore robes the same color as the mountain stone, giving them camouflage when pressed against it. Clever. But there was something else about them that was strange: they had thick, stooped bodies with wide shoulders, and they walked with an odd gait, their lower halves swinging back and forth while their upper halves remained virtually motionless. A smell hit him then, a strong musky odor that he recognized as being more animal than human. They reached up with large hands covered with black, fur-like hair and lowered their hoods to reveal red-eyed faces with simian features. He knew them then at once, or at least knew their kind, and he would have leaped forward and slashed at them with his broadsword if Anot's hand had not still been on his chest, holding him back with surprising strength. He was about to shove her aside and attack the creatures anyway, but then a calming breeze played over the skin on his face and the fires of his fury dimmed, though they did not go out.

Conan continued to hold his sword at the ready and did not take his eyes off the ape-like creatures as he spoke to Anot. "That breeze was your doing, was it not?"

"You needed to cool off," Anot said. "Qiang too."

Conan risked a quick look at his Khitani friend and saw the man had drawn his katana and assumed a battle stance. Valja held a pair of her throwing knives, her expression a blend of fear and confusion. Naerys was the only one besides Anot who did not seem alarmed by the sudden appearance of these beast people. The priestess stepped closer to the shaman and laid a hand on her shoulder.

"I told you it would be a mistake to have them wait so long to reveal themselves," Naerys said.

Anot sighed. "You were right. Conan, Valja, Qiang, these are Krot and Gneb of the M'lima."

The two bowed their heads in greeting, the gesture making them seem more human than ape. Gneb, who Conan thought might be female, made a series of quick gestures with her hands.

"She says it is nice to finally meet you after only seeing you from afar for three days," Anot said.

"Were those her exact words?" Qiang asked.

Anot shrugged. "Close enough."

"I have met one of their kind before," Conan said. He looked at Valja. "It was soon after we parted. I encountered some trouble in Corinthia and was thrown in jail to await my execution. A man named Murilo came to my cell and said he would have me released and give me a bag of gold along with a way out of the city if I did just one small favor for him: assassinate a sorcerer named Nabonidus. After our encounter with Uzzeran and what happened to you, Valja, I would have killed the man for free.

"I eventually learned that Nabonidus had acquired an ape-man child whom he had captured, raised, and trained to be his bodyguard. He called the creature Thak, but I believe that was a name Nabonidus bestowed upon him, not the name he was born with. The sorcerer claimed he found Thak here, in the Kezankian Mountains, and that this was where the ape-man's tribe was located. It seems he told the truth.

"Thak and I eventually fought, and I was forced to kill him, though I took no pleasure in it. Thak may have looked different to me, but he was a man all the same, one who had been taken from his people and had his mind and soul twisted by an evil sorcerer for his own selfish ends."

"Please tell me you killed the bastard," Valja said.

"Yes. And that I took great pleasure in doing it." Conan turned to Anot. "So Thak's tribe was the M'lima?"

"I assume so. There are other groups of them in the Kezankians, though, so who can say for certain? They call themselves the Mountain People, but since they do not speak but only sign, I call them M'lima, which is their name rendered in my native language."

"I can see why they would be so cautious about revealing themselves," Qiang said. "Most humans would think them beasts without bothering to truly look and see what lies beneath their exterior."

"And they would respond with violence," Anot said. "The

M'lima can defend themselves, of course, but they have no wish to hurt others unless there is no other choice."

"How many of the M'lima have come?" Valja asked.

"All the adults," Anot said. "The very young and the very old remain at their mountain home, many miles from here. The adults are already on the mountain, in position near the castle, and will await our arrival before they attack."

Conan was impressed by the M'lima's courage and selflessness. They had no reason to love humans, yet every one of them who could fight had come to join the battle at Ravenhold. Yet one thought nagged at him.

"I am confused about something, Anot," he said. "You told us three friends accompanied you on your journey to Charhelm. Where is the third?"

The shaman frowned. "I assumed Yalet had already joined the others."

Anot spent a few moments signing to the M'lima, and Gneb replied, an almost human expression of sadness on her simian face.

"Yalet was killed on the second night out of Charhelm," Anot said, fighting back tears. "The three of them patrolled the area while we slept to keep us safe. It was their screams we heard at night—part battle cry, part warning of danger to others in the area. They killed the serpents Set sent to slay us, but Yalet was bitten by one, the venom killing him almost instantly. Gneb was his mate and Krolot one of their sons."

Anot walked over to them and the three leaned forward until their heads touched. They remained like that for several moments, all three crying. Eventually, they pulled away from each other and Gneb signed some more to Anot.

"Really?" the shaman replied, sounding quite surprised. She looked upward, shielding her eyes with her hand to block out the sunlight, then lowered her hand and spoke while she signed. "They are too well hidden for me to see, but I believe you."

"They?" Conan said.

Anot smiled. "It seems we have more allies than the M'lima. The Brood of Zath has come to our aid as well."

Conan looked upward and scanned the nearby mountains. His vision was sharp and he saw several large shapes that he thought were spiders concealed among the crags and folds of the mountains' rocky surface, though they would have been undetectable to most people. Still looking up, he said, "I was twenty-two when I first came to the Kezankians, but right before that I visited Yezud. There was a price on my head and—"

He felt eyes on him, and when he looked down, he saw that everyone, including the M'lima, was staring at him.

"You were going to tell us a story about you fighting the Cult of Zath, weren't you?" Valja said in a teasing voice.

Conan could not help but laugh. "Perhaps I have too many stories," he said.

"Nonsense," Anot said. "There is no such thing. Stories are what make us who we are, both those we tell and those we hear."

Gneb signed to the shaman again, and then she and Krolot pulled up their hoods, ran into the tunnel, and were swallowed by darkness.

"They will scout for us," Anot said. "They are swift and silent, and their robes will allow them to hide in plain sight if need be."

Conan detected movement on the mountainside and looked up in time to see a pair of spiders the size of large wolves, one of them a strange white color, scuttle downward, quickly crawl through the cave entrance, and disappear.

"It appears the spider god wishes to send some scouts of his own," Naerys said.

The supply tunnel had been designed for horses bearing riders and oxen drawing wagons to and from the castle. It wound upward in a gentle incline and took three hours to travel on horseback, five if you were driving an oxen-pulled wagon loaded with supplies. At both ends of the tunnel, lanterns created by the magisters containing light crystals were stored for everyone's use. All one needed to do was remove the crystal from a lantern, rub it vigorously between one's hands for a short time, and it would activate and provide light for thirty minutes, after which one simply repeated the procedure.

"The crystals cease working completely after a few months," Valja said, "and the magisters then make more." She paused for a second, then added, "I suppose the current crystals will be the last."

They took a lantern for each mount, and once they had activated their crystals Valja spoke the same word she had earlier, and the boulder that had hidden the tunnel entrance rolled back into place. Naerys walked to one of the pack horses and removed a cloth-wrapped object from a bag, then returned to the group and sheepishly unwrapped it. It was her flail. No one teased her, but both Anot and Valja smiled.

Once Naerys had mounted her horse, the five companions began the long ride upward. The mounts surely sensed the presence of the unnatural forces that pervaded the mountain, but while they were a little nervous, they tolerated being here well enough. Ravenhold's horses were trained to be accustomed to the presence of magic, but the group's mounts were not, so Valja had asked Anot to use her nature-based powers around their horses for a time every night—summoning fireflies, causing gentle breezes—when they made camp to help them get used to sorcerous energies. It had worked well.

Conan, however, was deeply uncomfortable being here. He had done his best not to show it, and while he suspected Valja knew, the others seemed unaware—at least, he hoped that was the case. He wasn't ashamed—to him, it seemed only common sense to distrust magic—but no one wanted to go into battle with a comrade who displayed a potential weakness. It could cause not only a lack of confidence among individuals but also a lack of cohesion in the group. He smiled to himself. Perhaps he had been in a command position too long and it was a good thing that the Red Brotherhood had stranded him in the Colchian Mountains.

But Ravenhold's magic was unlike any Conan had faced before. This was not the lair of a lone witch or the tomb of some restless ancient spirit; this was a centuries-old citadel containing a multitude of collected magical artifacts. It was like going from the well behind the wash tent in Charhelm to the bottom of the Vilayet Sea. His instincts screamed at him to leave this place and never return, but while he usually heeded such urges, this time he would not. Uzzeran had to be prevented from using the second Eye of Set, and he had to pay for what had happened to Valja. Yes, Conan had been the one to destroy the first Eye, and in the resulting explosion Valja had been struck by the shard that had turned her into something that was neither dead nor alive, but Uzzeran had been the one to summon that power and attempt to use it for evil ends. The sorcerer needed to die so that Valja would be avenged, and so that Conan could atone for his part in what had happened to his former lover. *Cimmerians always pay their debts*, he said to himself.

Naerys spoke then. "I must apologize to you, Valja."

Valja, sitting behind Conan on the sturdy lakan horse, turned to look at the priestess. "What for?"

"You have spoken of how you see the gods' hands at work in what is happening to us, and I doubted you. What's more, I thought you naive. How could you have faith in any god after what happened to you when we first went after Uzzeran? What god has reached down from the heavens to restore you to full life once more? But now that the five of us are here, along with M'lima and the Brood of Zath, I can see now how the gods are weaving a tapestry from our different threads—Ishtar, Anot's nature spirits, Yun, Zath, and yes, even Mitra. And who knows? Perhaps Crom as well."

Conan snorted at that but made no other comment.

"You have helped me find my faith again, Valja. And for that, you shall always have my everlasting gratitude."

Silence fell over the group after that, and each of them held counsel with their own thoughts as they rode toward Ravenhold and whatever destiny awaited them there.

Uzzeran sat cross-legged on the stone floor of his room, his eyes closed, his breathing slow and regular. He was deep in meditation, preparing mind and spirit for the great task that lay ahead of him. The practice of sorcery was about far more than memorizing spells from ancient texts and making bargains with dark powers. Even when a sorcerer had other sources of power to draw on, such as human sacrifices, the working of magic still required a mage to put forward a great deal of their own life force. Meditation helped to prepare them for this ordeal, but even then there was always the chance of a spell going wrong and harming the caster. Take the shard in his eye socket, for example.

However, the shard could well turn out to be a blessing in disguise, for through it he might be able to establish a stronger connection to the second Eye, allowing him to wield the artifact's power with far more precision than he had achieved with its predecessor.

The shard began to grow colder than normal, as if it was reacting to Uzzeran's thoughts. Ebon energy crackled forth from it, and Uzzeran heard a great sibilant voice speak in his mind.

They are coming.

Images accompanied the words: huge spiders beginning to mass on Ravenhold's roof and towers, figures garbed in robes the color of stone scaling the castle walls with inhuman ease, and in one of the tunnels a group of riders on horseback—two men and three women. He recognized the pair of thieves who had interfered with his work in the ruins of the Tower of the Elephant, though they were of course older now—or at least the male thief was; the female appeared not to have aged a day in fifteen years. He did not recognize the Kushite woman or the Khitan warrior, but the Ophirian garbed in the robe of a priestess of Mitra seemed familiar...

Then it came to him—*Naerys!* The orphan girl he had found on the street in Khemi, one of the first humans he had experimented on in his quest to create Serpent Lords. She had escaped his home one night, and although he had searched for her, he had never found her and had assumed she had been swallowed by one of the temple serpents that roamed the city, or perhaps captured by slavers. He had put her out of his mind and had not spared a single thought for her in over twenty-five years. He wondered why she had pledged her life to such a weak and pathetic god as Mitra, and what had led her to Ravenhold at this critical juncture in his plans. Perhaps he would ask her before he killed her.

A knock at the door brought him instantly back to full awareness. His eyes snapped open, and he bounded to his feet as Rynthia opened the door and poked her head in.

"It is time, master."

"Rouse the rest of the revenants and instruct them to guard the windows," he instructed. "If any remain, take them to the supply tunnel entrance and protect it." When Rynthia looked at him in puzzlement, he shouted, "Go!"

She went.

Uzzeran hurried out of his room and down the corridor, heading in the opposite direction Rynthia had taken. He needed to begin the hybridization spell and finish it before the attackers could stop him. He knew that the revenants, even two hundred of them, would not prove sufficient to defend the castle by themselves. They would need help, and he knew just where to get it.

He found a staircase heading downward and he took the steps two at a time until he reached the level where the menagerie was located. He twitched an index finger and a small globe of green coldfire appeared in the air above him. The verdant light illuminated dozens of strange and exotic beasts, some that lived now only in myth, others that dwelled solely in humanity's nightmares.

He recalled what Rynthia had told him and Shengis about these creatures when she had brought them through here: *The magisters have placed stasis spells upon them, rendering them immobile and unaware of their surroundings. Only a magister or a powerful sorcerer can lift the enchantments and restore them to full life.*

Was Uzzeran powerful enough? He was about to find out.

He raised his arms high and began chanting words of power, his voice echoing from the walls of the chamber. Sparks of ebon energy shot from the shard in his eye socket and flew toward the individual creatures, and wherever a spark landed, the creature it touched began to move.

Uzzeran smiled in grim satisfaction, and when the last creature shrugged off its stasis spell and became animate again, the sorcerer gave them all a command:

"Go forth and kill!"

He sent a bolt of black energy from the shard toward the staircase that led to the castle's upper levels. It was too narrow for the largest creatures to pass through, so Uzzeran widened it. Dark energy filled the stairwell, expanded, and wherever it touched, stone faded away, like smoke being dissipated by a strong wind. When Uzzeran judged the stairwell wide enough, he ended the spell and watched with satisfaction as the menagerie's inhabitants, some of which had not walked upon the face of the planet in untold millennia, raced for the newly made tunnel, shrieking, howling, and roaring for blood.

21

The intruders were almost at the castle entrance when Conan saw the two wolf-sized spiders—one black, one white—scuttling across the ceiling toward them. He believed that Zath's children had come to betray them and drew his broadsword, prepared to fight, but Anot told him to stay his hand.

Conan had no intention of heeding her, but when the spiders drew close enough, they stopped and clung to the ceiling without attacking. Their bodies quivered strangely, and Anot focused her gaze on them for several moments.

"They have come to warn us," she said. "There were several revenants guarding the entrance into the castle, but Gneb and Krolot slew them."

"So the way in is now clear for us to proceed," Qiang said.

"Not quite," Anot said. "More of the damned things have started to arrive. I fear Uzzeran has become aware of us."

"Then we have no more time to waste!"

Conan gripped the reins of his mount with his left hand, raised his broadsword in his right, kicked his heels into the horse's side, and roared a Cimmerian battle cry. The lakan may have been bred for strength rather than speed, but it surged forward as if born for battle. Valja wrapped her arms around Conan as the barbarian rode forth to meet the enemy, as he had done so many times before. After a second's hesitation, the others followed as fast as their steeds could carry them, the two spiders racing along on the ceiling above as if determined not to be left behind.

It took Conan and Valja only moments to reach the entrance at a gallop. The light crystal in their lantern illuminated the nightmarish scene that waited for them there. A dozen revenants filled the tunnel ahead, and Gneb and Krolot, their robes discarded, fought their undead opponents with all the savagery of the wild beasts they appeared to be. Conan could see the raging fury in their eyes, but he also saw intelligence there that belied their physical forms. The two M'lima leaped around the tunnel like black-furred blurs, tearing off revenants' arms, legs, and heads while avoiding the strikes of the shadow serpents inhabiting their undead foes.

"Sweet Ishtar," Valja said, horrified. "Those are people from Ravenhold! Scholars, magisters, seekers, librarians, members of the cooking and cleaning staff… I know—*knew*—them all!"

"Those you knew are gone," Conan said gruffly. "All we can do now is destroy their bodies and grant their spirits release." He raised his voice so everyone could hear. "To destroy them, you must cut off their heads, stab them in the heart, or slice their shadow serpents in two."

He reined the lakan to a halt, leaped out of the saddle, dropped the light-crystal lantern to the floor, then ran toward the revenants without waiting for Valja, broadsword gripped tightly in his right hand. Krolot and Gneb were fighting valiantly with teeth and claws, but they were outnumbered by the revenants and Conan was determined to even the odds. He waded into the fray, swinging his sword in vicious arcs, each strike severing a head or an arm. Whenever shadow serpents attempted to bite him, he jumped back, sliced them in two, and watched with satisfaction as both parts faded. When all three of a revenant's serpents had been dispatched, the body ceased moving and fell limply to the floor.

That was one good thing about slaying revenants, Conan thought. They did not bleed, so you did not have to watch your footing after you had killed them.

Valja joined the battle, knives in hands, moving among the revenants and slicing shadow serpents in two with deadly speed and precision and the tirelessness of the undead. The others arrived then, and the two spiders were the first of their group to attack, dropping onto revenants, covering their faces, and using their fangs to tear at the shadow serpents that emerged from the dead creatures' mouths and eye sockets. When one revenant went down, they leaped onto another and started the process over again. They seemed to be immune to the shadow serpents' venom, and Conan assumed this was because their sire was a god. Demi-divinity evidently had its advantages.

Qiang was next to hurl himself into battle, and he moved among the revenants like an avenging spirit, decapitating them so quickly his katana was a metallic blur. Naerys and Anot came last, the priestess using her flail to destroy shadow serpents, while Anot summoned beetles from within the tunnel walls to flood forth from their holes, swarm over the revenants, and devour their dead flesh.

The battle finished sooner than any of them expected. Soon the tunnel floor was covered with lifeless revenants—some intact, most cut into pieces—and the only casualty they had suffered was one of the spiders, the black one, which lay dead on its back, legs curled inward. The white spider appeared uninjured.

Their mounts had bolted sometime during the fighting. While the animals might have grown used to Valja's unnatural presence during the journey here, a dozen revenants, a pair of giant spiders, and a couple M'lima had been too much for them to take.

At the end of the tunnel was a set of stone steps that led to a pair of large wooden doors. Conan retrieved his light-crystal lantern, then ran up the stairs and attempted to push the doors open, but he found them locked. He was going to try kicking them open, but the two M'lima ran past him on either side and hurled themselves against the doors. Wood cracked and the doors bowed inward, but they did not open. One kick from Conan finished the job the M'lima started, and the doors flew wide.

Conan led the way, his lantern illuminating a large storeroom filled with large amounts of dried wheat and barley, salted meats, cheeses, dried fruits and vegetables, honey, ale, wine, and clay jars containing various seasonings. Conan eyed the wine covetously—slaying was thirsty work—but he continued on, leading the humans, the M'lima, and one wolf-sized, snow-colored spider out of the storeroom and into Ravenhold's kitchen. It was deserted, so they kept going, entering a dining hall with many long tables and chairs. It too was empty. It was not, however, quiet.

The double doors that led out of the dining hall were closed, but it sounded as if Hell itself lay on the other side of them. Inhuman screams and roars cut through the air, along with the scraping of claws on stone, the thud of heavy bodies slamming into walls, the fast scritch-scratching of arachnid legs.

Conan sheathed his sword and tried the doors. They were unlocked and swung open easily.

The hallway outside the dining hall was a scene from a lunatic's fever dream. M'lima and giant spiders of varying sizes fought revenants and an assortment of monsters the like of which Conan had never before seen: two-legged things covered in scales, with huge bulging eyes, mouthfuls of dagger-like teeth, and serrated fins running along their spines; sleek black panthers with large dragon wings sprouting from their backs; and more, each thing more hideous than the last.

“Mitra preserve us,” Naerys said, her voice nearly lost in the din.

“Uzzeran released these creatures from the menagerie!” Valja said.

Conan knew not what the menagerie was, and neither did he care. He quickly pulled the doors closed again, then turned to Valja.

“Where will the sorcerer cast his spell?” he asked her.

“The repository, I think. He will be able to tap into the magic of the artifacts stored there for additional power, the same way he used the ruins of the Tower of the Elephant in Arenjun.”

“Where is this place?” Conan asked.

“On the lowest level,” Valja said. She paused, then added, “And the stairs that lead down to it are on the other side of the castle.”

Conan looked at the closed door and sighed. Then he gripped the metal handles once more and looked over his shoulder at his companions. “Ready?”

The humans gripped their weapons tighter, the M’lima bared their sharp teeth, and the white spider, still clinging to the ceiling, tapped a foreleg three times. Conan assumed that meant yes.

He threw open the doors, drew his sword, and ran into the hall, the others right behind him.

Akh stood next to Rynthia in the repository. All was ready for Uzzeran to perform the great spell that would finally give birth to the Serpent Lords he had dreamed of creating for so long. Not that Akh, the *true* Serpent Lord, had any intention of allowing that to happen or of letting Uzzeran live long enough to see the next sunrise. All he needed to do was remain patient. It would not be much longer now.

Akh and Rynthia had cleared a space in the repository large enough to fit eleven tables. Ten were arranged in a circle, and upon them lay naked men and women, their wrists and ankles locked in manacles whose chains were bolted to the wood. Their bodies were covered with blood-slick runes carved into their flesh, and although they were all in great pain, they lay motionless, features as still and impassive as any statue's, thanks to the diluted serpent venom coursing through their veins.

The eleventh table had been placed inside the circle, and the boy Taolin lay shackled upon it. He was also naked, but his skin was unmarked. The serpent venom had only a minimal effect on him, likely due to the intense pain he constantly experienced, so he was drowsy but still awake. Sluggish tears flowed from his eyes like slow rain, and the sight might have stirred Akh's pity had he possessed any.

The scales that Uzzeran had collected from the preserved body of the dire wyrm in the library had been worked into the runes that the sorcerer had carved into the subjects of his experiment. Not Taolin, though—the boy was here solely so Uzzeran could tap into the power of the curse that held him in thrall.

Behind Taolin's table was the stone column atop which the second Eye of Set rested, and behind this stood Uzzeran. He wore his usual dark gray robe, and a skein of miniature black lightning crackled over the shard protruding from his left eye socket. Akh pitied the Stygian sorcerer for not recognizing the grandeur of this moment. Would it have killed the man to don a robe fashioned from spun gold and perhaps a helmet adorned with blood-red rubies with huge ram's horns attached to the sides? When all this was over and Akh no longer had to masquerade as human, one of the first things he intended to do was get himself clothing that befitted his exalted station, perhaps something fashioned from Uzzeran's skin—provided, of course, any of it remained after today.

There had been one wrinkle in Akh's plan. He had intended to stand behind Uzzeran as the sorcerer cast his spell so that he could attack the man unawares, but the sorcerer had displayed uncharacteristic concern for his servants and told "Shengis" and Rynthia to stand well off to the side so they would be at less risk while he worked his magic. Akh had been unable to come up with a believable reason why Uzzeran should allow "Shengis" to stand behind him, and so Akh now stood with Rynthia, too far away to dispatch Uzzeran easily and certainly not without the woman realizing what he was doing.

Had Uzzeran begun to suspect that something was wrong with "Shengis"? Was that why he had directed Rynthia and him to stand here? Akh supposed it was possible, but it seemed unlikely. Ever since arriving at Ravenhold, Uzzeran had been far too preoccupied with preparing for the spell, and the sorcerer had been experiencing those episodes of non-awareness as well. Akh seriously doubted Uzzeran suspected anything, which was good, but he needed to find a way to deal with Rynthia. He still carried Shengis' poison-coated dagger, and he had also continued to wear the medallion Uzzeran had created for ensnaring Serpent Men, but he did not see how either would be of any help to him right now.

He felt something pinch at the base of his spine then, and frowned in puzzlement. The sensation had been so mild he had barely felt it, and had he been human he might have thought he had pulled a muscle from all the lifting and carrying Uzzeran had been making him do. But Akh's body, while currently appearing human, was far stronger, and it could heal even severe injuries rapidly. It should not be possible for him to pull a muscle, and yet...

All of a sudden, he felt overwhelmingly sleepy, but that made no sense. Akh needed very little sleep—an hour a day was more than enough for him, and he could do without that if necessary—so what...

Rynthia.

He tried to turn and look at her, but he could barely move his head. As if she knew this, she stepped in front of him.

At that moment, Uzzeran began the spell. The sorcerer looked toward the ceiling, spread his arms wide, and began chanting in a loud, sonorous voice, completely unaware of what was transpiring between his two servants.

Akh tried to speak, but his tongue refused to move. He found it hard to breathe now, too, and his heart beat more slowly.

Rynthia leaned close to his face and whispered so Uzzeran would not hear her. "I have been watching you, Shengis. Or am I speaking to Kekk? I know not what sort of scheme you have cooked up, but I know you are planning something. Maybe you dislike sharing your master with another servant and you thought you would slip your poison dagger between my ribs while Uzzeran was distracted. Or maybe you planned to betray Uzzeran in some manner. The details matter not. You are a terrible servant, Shengis, and the master deserves so much better. He deserves *me.* In a few moments, you will be dead, or as good as, and I shall tell Uzzeran what happened to you must have been a side effect of the energies released during the spell. I doubt he will care enough to check, though. And Kekk, if I *am* speaking to you, you will be dead too."

Akh tried to speak again, but all he was able to do was make his lips twitch.

"Let me guess: you want to know what I did." She held up her right hand, and he saw she wore a silver ring on her middle finger, and upon it was etched the image of a serpent with its tail in its mouth—the symbol of Set. "I took this from the repository. It belonged to a powerful Stygian sorcerer who lived over a hundred thousand years ago. He created a breed of viper whose venom turned living tissue into stone, and then he employed the darkest of magics to strengthen that venom so that no power, not even that of the gods, could neutralize it. The ring has a hidden compartment containing a small needle which, when released, injects venom into the victim. The ring held no more than a few drops, but that is more than enough to slay you, Shengis… and Kekk. Farewell to you both."

She gave him an extremely self-satisfied smile and then turned away to watch Uzzeran as he continued casting the spell.

Akh could not move, could barely breathe, and his heart thudded heavily in his chest as it struggled to pump blood that was now the consistency of river mud. Inwardly, he burned with white-hot fury at Rynthia's betrayal, but he also held a measure of respect for what she had done. His murder had been well planned and masterfully executed. He knew he had only moments left before he was fully transformed into stone. If he had been human, he would already have been dead. His thoughts were slowing down, too, but he tried to hold the paralysis back so he could think.

Rynthia had said the venom had been enchanted so that no power could counter it, and while that may have been true once, after a hundred thousand years the magic had to have lost some potency. Even the gods could exist for only so long before their time passed and new gods arose to take their place. As an amalgamation of human and Serpent Man, Akh had great potential for magic but had had no time to develop it, as he had only recently been "born." And now he would never get the chance to—

Then he remembered: the Snare. If he could tap into its power, adapt it for a different purpose…

He knew no magic words, and he could not have spoken them if he had. And he had no formal knowledge of the complex interplay of thaumaturgic energy that comprised spells, especially powerful ones like the stone venom. All he had was the desire to live—and to make Rynthia suffer for what she had done to him—so he focused the entire force of his considerable will on a single thought:

Move.

Then he reached out to the Snare, mentally took hold of its magic, and pushed.

Nothing happened, and as his desperation grew, he tried once more, putting his entire self into the effort, and pushed *hard*.

He felt a tearing sensation then, his vision blurred, and when it cleared, he found himself looking down at his own body, his flesh now transformed completely into hard, gray stone. He watched as Rynthia reached over and poked his cheek with an index finger, grinned, and then turned her attention back to Uzzeran. Akh realized the tearing he'd felt was his soul detaching from his body. He had wanted mobility to return to his flesh, but the stone-venom prevented that, so the magic he had drawn from the Snare had done the next best thing: it had allowed him to escape his body. Kekk had been a disembodied spirit when he had entered Shengis, and now Akh had returned to that state. But what could he do as a spirit? To interact with the material world, he needed a body. But where—

Then he had another idea—an absolutely *delicious* one.

He willed himself to move, and his spirit began to drift toward the repository's door, slowly at first but then faster, and then he passed through the substance of the door as if it were no more substantial than air, and continued on, faster yet, moving upward through the ceiling as if it were mist.

Heading toward the library.

22

In his later years, when Conan thought back to the battle to get from the dining hall to the repository, what he remembered most about it was the assault on his ears. As a youth in Cimmeria, he had once climbed alone to the top of a mountain during a raging thunderstorm, and there he had experienced the full fury of nature in a way he never had before and never would again. Cold rain lashed him like whips of ice, strong winds battered him like hammer blows, and lightning flashed across the sky so bright its glare struck his eyes with almost physical force. But the sounds were what had the greatest impact on him—the shriek of the wind stabbing into his ears, the angry sizzle of lightning when it came too close, the crack and boom of thunder so strong he felt the vibrations deep in his bones.

Sometimes he thought those vibrations had never stopped.

As his broadsword cut through flesh both natural and unnatural, as the blood he shed flowed in great crimson torrents, as he fought like a frenzied beast for every inch of ground he gained, it was the hoots and roars of the M'lima, the hiss and click of Zath's children, the high-pitched shrieks, ululating cries, and nightmare-inducing screams of the strange beasts released from the menagerie that formed the greater part of his awareness.

Qiang fought at his side, the warrior moving with almost supernatural speed, his katana dealing death with every controlled and precise strike. Conan had cuts and scratches on his face, neck, hands, and arms, and his chainmail vest had been riven in several places, front and back, though he had received no serious wounds yet. Qiang's crimson robe hung from his lean, strong frame in tatters, and Conan could see that he was bleeding in dozens of places and that several of the wounds looked severe, but the enchantment placed upon him by his god would not allow him to die and thus his injuries, numerous though they were, healed swiftly. Conan had wondered why the Khitan chose not to wear armor of any sort, originally thinking it was because he did not want the weight of it to slow him down—he himself sometimes eschewed armor, and most clothing, for this very reason—but he realized then that Qiang had no need of armor with the power of Yun protecting him.

When he had the opportunity, Conan risked a quick glance behind him to see how the others were faring. Valja's condition might have had a much different cause than Qiang's, but she too could not die, and while her cuts—which did not bleed—healed far more slowly than the Khitan's, heal they would—or perhaps a better way to put it was that the damage to her would be undone.

Valja moved swiftly, if more slowly than Qiang, but because she did not tire or need rest, she continued to fight at the same relentless pace, employing her blades with surgical precision and a focus that only someone who felt no pain could achieve.

Naerys fought with her flail and her dagger, and for an instant Conan thought he saw a glimmer of orange-yellow light flash along her blade, but then it was gone and he decided he had been mistaken.

Anot fought far differently than the others. She avoided the revenants, but whenever one of the strange creatures came at her, she reached out and touched it. Whatever the thing was—a wolf with two heads, a bear with a mass of tentacles growing from its back, a great clump of what looked like moving moss—her touch would immediately cause it to break off its attack, look confused for a moment, and then calmly wander off, no longer interested in fighting. Conan thought it an odd way of doing battle, and to his mind not particularly satisfying, but he could see where it might have its uses, such as now.

But as hard as the five humans fought, Conan knew that if it had not been for the M'lima and Zath's giant spiders, they would all be dead by now, him included. He had given little credit to Naerys' assertion that the gods—a few of them, at least—were aiding them in their quest to stop Uzzeran from implementing Set's plan, but it was difficult to deny now. Maybe for once the bastards were good for something other than manipulating mortals and ruining their lives.

Their nonhuman allies were paying a heavy price, though. The bodies of dead and dying spiders and M'lima filled the corridor behind them, mixed in with the mutilated corpses of menagerie creatures and revenants, and the floor, walls, and ceiling were drenched in blood.

Conan did not know how long it took the companions to reach the stairwell that led down to the repository—it could have been minutes or hours—but when they got there, he saw the stairwell was empty. No revenants, no monsters. As they all hurried downward, a huge gray spider skittered over to block the entrance behind them, making sure they were not followed. The battle continued to rage on in the corridor, but the sounds of combat grew fainter the farther down they went until they became a dull, distant roar, like a storm somewhere off in the distance.

The stairwell ended at the castle's lowest level, and they entered a hallway illuminated by the eerie green light of coldfire braziers, at the end of which lay the door to the repository. It was fifteen feet high, ten feet wide, and made of thick, strong oak. There was no obvious way to open it—no handle or knob.

The damned thing probably only opens by magic, Conan thought. *Like the boulder in front of the supply-tunnel entrance.*

"Uzzeran has started the spell," Anot said. "I can feel it." Blood stippled the shaman's scratched face and stained her torn clothes. The rest of them didn't look any better.

"I have had a bellyful of magic this day," Conan growled. "Now is the time for steel."

He stalked toward the door, blood from the battle above still dripping from his sword. He put his left ear to the wood and heard the faint sound of a voice chanting on the other side. He couldn't make out the words or identify the speaker, but he had no doubt it was Uzzeran.

Sorcerer, Conan thought, *I hope you are prepared to meet your foul snake god, for I will be sending you to her shortly.*

He turned to Valja. "Can you open this?"

"I fear not. Only the three magisters are—were—permitted to enter the repository, and only they knew how open it."

"Uzzeran got inside," Valja pointed out.

"He may have discovered the secret on his own," Naerys said. "He *is* highly intelligent."

"Does the door remain unlocked when someone is inside?" Conan asked. He handed his sword to Qiang, placed his palms on the door's wooden surface, and pushed, gently at first but then with increasing pressure, until his arm and leg muscles trembled from the effort. But the door didn't budge. He let out a snarl of frustration and turned to Anot.

"Shaman, can you open it?" he asked.

Anot walked up to the door, touched her fingertips to the

surface, then pressed her face close, eyes narrowing as if she was trying to see into the wood. When she pulled back, she looked at Conan.

"I can try. Everyone move back."

They did, and the shaman went to work.

Like Conan, Anot pressed her palms flat against the door, but she also touched her forehead to it. She closed her eyes and began to hum a rising and falling rhythm:

hhhmmmHHHMMMhhhmmm…

She continued repeating this, her voice becoming louder each time. Conan wasn't certain, but for an instant he thought he saw the wood ripple, like water on the surface of a pond. Then Anot drew back from the door and turned to her companions.

"The wood has done what it can to combat the spell the magisters put on it. The substance of the door is weaker now, but we must do the rest."

Without a word, Conan walked to the door, took a two-handed grip on his sword, and swung the blade with all his might. Steel bit into the door and sheared off a chunk of wood as easily as if it were pine or beech instead of oak. The Cimmerian smiled. Now *this* was a kind of magic he could appreciate!

Qiang joined him, and working together the two warriors swiftly hacked away at the door. Conan was stronger than Qiang, but the Khitan had worked as a woodcutter for a time and was more skilled at the task. In a short time, they had cut through to the other side and the sound of chanting flowed out into the hallway, much louder than a human throat should be able to produce—part of the magic, Conan assumed. He hoped it was loud enough to cover the sound of their chopping at the door; they needed every advantage they could get. He could tell the voice was Uzzeran's, and judging by Valja's expression, so could she. Fifteen years ago, neither Naerys nor Anot had made it to confront Uzzeran, but they were here now, as was Qiang, all of them ready to bring the fight to the sorcerer.

Encouraged by their progress, the two warriors cut faster, and soon they had carved an opening wide enough for everyone to go through—except Conan.

"Go," he said. "I will follow soon."

Qiang went first, lying on his stomach and crawling through using his elbows. After him came Valja, then Naerys, and then Anot. Once the shaman was through, Conan continued swinging his sword until the opening was wide enough for him to pass through. Then he quickly joined the others and surveyed the scene.

The repository was well named, for magic artifacts of all shapes and sizes were stored here, some on shelves, others on pedestals, still others in wooden boxes with elaborately carved surfaces or in iron-barred cages, as if they were alive—and, in a way, maybe they were. There was jewelry there, amulets, and gems, along with wands, bones—human, animal, monster, demon—items of clothing, crystal orbs, chalices, staves, chains, swords, axes, spears, daggers, helms, and gauntlets. The sheer amount of magic power contained in the chamber stunned Conan, and he felt as if he had jumped into an active volcano that might erupt at any moment.

Otherwise, the scene matched the vision Valja had told them about. Ten tables in a circle holding shackled men and women, runes carved into their skin, drugged and motionless. An eleventh table for the boy Taolin—also shackled, but flesh unmarked, partially awake, and crying softly.

The sight made Valja gasp in horror. She tried to run to him, but Conan grabbed her arm.

Not yet, he mouthed.

She scowled at him but nodded.

Behind the boy was a stone column on which the second

Eye of Set had been placed. Uzzeran stood behind it, arms outstretched, face turned toward the ceiling, his inhumanly loud voice chanting words in an ancient language no one but sorcerers had spoken for millennia.

There was one difference, though. Off to the side stood two people: a Zamorian woman wearing a tunic, breeches, and boots, and a Stygian man in a brown tunic—except it wasn't a man but a *statue* of a man, carved from gray stone. The tunic was actual cloth, though, and real sandals were strapped to the statue's feet, which Conan thought strange. It was possible that the figure resembled Uzzeran's servant, but the Cimmerian had seen the man only once, briefly, fifteen years ago, and he could not be sure it was him.

Neither Uzzeran nor the Zamorian seemed aware of their presence. Not only was Uzzeran's voice loud but he was focused entirely on the mystic rite he was performing, and the servant was focused on her master. Conan hoped they remained oblivious for the few seconds it would take him to run across the chamber and decapitate the bastard sorcerer. But before the barbarian could take a step toward Uzzeran, the man shouted a word and clapped his hands together with a sound like thunder. Throughout the repository, tendrils of bluish-white energy leaped forth from artifacts and streaked toward the sorcerer, striking him like thin bolts of lightning. His mad laughter filled the chamber as an aura of blue-white energy appeared around him and began to grow.

"He is absorbing the artifacts' power!" Anot cried.

Conan's blood was still up and he started forward, not giving a damn that the sorcerer was gorging himself on magic. This time, it was Valja who grabbed hold of his arm, and he stopped and turned to her, an angry scowl on his face.

"It is too dangerous to attack him directly," she said. "All that power..."

The wildness that lay at the center of every Cimmerian soul roared at him to ignore Valja and *kill.* But he had learned much since leaving his homeland, and one of the most important lessons was that strategy can often be a warrior's best weapon. He gave her a quick nod and she let go of his arm.

"How can we stop a man so powerful?" Qiang asked. The Khitan, usually cool as Nordheim snow under pressure, looked worried.

"I am not sure," Anot said. The shaman sounded confused and tired, and Conan knew what was happening to her. She had fought before, but she had never experienced anything like the sort of battle she had seen this day, and the stress of it was starting to take its toll on her.

Naerys stepped to Anot's side and put an arm around her shoulder, but judging by the priestess' frightened expression as she watched Uzzeran's aura continue to expand, she was coping no better than the shaman was.

Unlike the others, Valja's gaze was fixed not on the sorcerer but on Taolin. "We have to find a way to end this, Conan, before—"

She did not get to complete her thought, however, because just then a bolt of energy—as crimson as the boy's skin and brighter and wider than any of the other bolts—shot out of Taolin's chest, streaked toward Uzzeran, and joined in feeding the sorcerer's expanding aura of magical power.

Taolin's body spasmed and shook as the red energy poured out of him and into Uzzeran. Conan understand not what was happening. Was the sorcerer draining the power of the boy's curse? Yes, that had to be it. He turned to Valja, but before he could speak her eyes flew wide, her mouth opened in a silent scream, and a bolt of black energy burst from her chest to join all the others fueling Uzzeran. Then, all at once, the beams of energy emanating from the magic artifacts winked out, including those connecting Valja and Taolin to the sorcerer. The boy fell back against his table, eyes closed, body unmoving, and Conan could not tell whether he was alive or dead.

Valja's eyes rolled up to reveal their whites and she started to collapse, but Conan caught her and lowered her gently to the floor. She was limp as a ragdoll, and when he knelt and patted her cheek, she did not respond. A terrible red mist of fury filled his vision then, and he stood and began striding toward the sorcerer, broadsword held in a white-knuckled grip. To hell with strategy! Conan was going to slay this man *now*, even if it cost the Cimmerian his life.

Uzzeran's blue-white aura was so large and bright that the sorcerer could not be seen within it and Conan was forced to squint to look at him. But then Uzzeran began to draw the energy he had stolen into his body and the aura swiftly receded. A small amount of blue-white energy remained, crackling and sparking across the ebon shard jutting from his eye socket, and he began to laugh like a lunatic.

Seeing his chance, Conan started to run, but he was still several yards from the sorcerer when Uzzeran slapped his hands against the ebon orb that was the second Eye of Set. Tendrils of night-black power burst from the ancient artifact, lanced toward the ten men and women on the tables circling Uzzeran, and plunged through their foreheads and into their brains. Another tendril did the same to Taolin, and Conan saw that the red color had faded from the boy's skin.

Now that Uzzeran had laid hands on the Eye of Set, Conan stopped running. With all the magic energy he'd absorbed *and* control of the Eye, Uzzeran might well be the most powerful sorcerer the world had ever seen.

The eyes of all eleven of Uzzeran's test subjects flew open and they screamed in agony as they began to change. Their skins took on a greenish hue and thick patches of scales formed over their chests and backs like armor. Their bodies became thicker and more muscular, and their fingernails lengthened into sharp black talons. Their hair fell out and was replaced by scales—a helmet to go with their armor. Their eyes grew larger and the whites turned amber, and they opened their mouths to display pairs of long, curving fangs.

The woman standing next to the odd statue had watched silently as Uzzeran had cast his spell, but now she shouted, "All praise the Queen of Dread, the Mistress of Oblivion, the Mother of All Misery—Set!"

The tendrils of dark energy winked out of existence, and the half-human, half-reptilian things the test subjects had become snarled and thrashed, fighting to break free from their shackles. Uzzeran gazed upon them, a father's love shining in his one good eye.

"Behold the Serpent Lords!" he proclaimed.

As Conan struggled to wrap his mind around what had happened, a massive body slammed into the door of the repository from the other side, the impact so strong it sent vibrations shuddering through the stone floor of the chamber. Whatever it was, Conan knew it had to be too large to fit through the opening he and Qiang had made, or why would it be trying to batter the door down? The thing struck a second time, then a third, and when it hit the door for the fourth time, the wood exploded inward and a giant green snake with yellow eyes slithered in. Conan estimated the serpent would measure a hundred feet from nose to tail if it were stretched straight, perhaps longer. Crom, what a monster it was! Long scratches and deep cuts crisscrossed its body, and Conan knew the thing had fought its way through the M'lima and giant spiders to reach the repository.

Uzzeran looked upon the giant snake, furious at having the moment of his greatest triumph spoiled. If he thought it strange that the spoiling had been done by a behemoth of a reptile, he gave no sign. He waved a hand, the blue-white energy around his shard flared bright, and the shackles restraining the newly created Serpent Lords fell away to dust. The hybrid creatures—one of whom was shorter than the rest—jumped up from their tables and immediately attacked, snarling and gibbering, amber eyes blazing with madness, and Conan realized that not only were these inhuman abominations savage killers but they were also completely insane.

Seven of the Serpent Lords, including the one that had been Taolin, ran toward the Cimmerian and his companions, while the other four headed for the giant serpent. Valja was still unconscious—Conan refused to accept she was dead; Taolin had survived, so why could she not?—and the Cimmerian ran back to stand over her, ready to protect her from the Serpent Lords.

"Come on, then!" he roared.

And the Serpent Lords obliged.

But before the green-scaled devils reached the Cimmerian, Qiang stepped to Conan's side and raised his katana. The two men shared a brief nod, then turned their attention to their oncoming foes.

Rynthia could not have imagined that things could go so wrong so fast.

Yes, she had killed Shengis/Kekk, and Uzzeran had succeeded in draining the repository's mystic artifacts of their magic and channeling that power through the Eye of Set to create the Serpent Lords, but a group of intruders had burst into the chamber, nearly ruining the sorcerer's spell. And one of them was former seeker Valja! Rynthia had not known the woman well, preferring to avoid the walking corpse, and had assumed she had perished with the rest of Ravenhold's people, but she realized now that she had not seen the woman's body and that Valja had not been among those who had been transformed into revenants. Obviously, she had escaped Ravenhold during Uzzeran's takeover of the castle and had recruited others to help her combat the sorcerer. Rynthia could not help but feel a grudging respect for the woman's courage.

And then, somehow, the preserved body of the dire wyrm, which had been on display in the library for centuries, had been restored to life and burst into the repository. Since Uzzeran had used some of the monster's scales to create the Serpent Lords, had some of the spell's power been transferred back to the beast, resurrecting it? Perhaps. And that connection could have been what led the dire wyrm to seek out the origin of the magic animating it, which was why it was now here.

Perhaps.

But as bad as those two developments were, far worse was the fact that Uzzeran had made a grave mistake in selecting people from the confinement level to be the raw material for the creation of the Serpent Lords. He had done so because he had hoped that the amount of mystic energy affecting them would aid in the transformation process, and it clearly had, but those held in confinement had been there because the enchantments they had suffered from had driven them mad—and that madness now belonged to the Serpent Lords. Instead of creating a new race of superior beings, Uzzeran had succeeded only in bringing a new breed of monster into the world.

Rynthia silently prayed as she made a hasty exit. *Forgive me, Great Set.*

Uzzeran had released the Serpent Lords from their shackles, and some now attacked the intruders while others targeted the dire wyrm. As Serpent Lords drew near the giant snake, the reptile lashed out with its tail and, with the ease with which men swat flies, swept the Serpent Lords off their feet and sent them flying through the air. Then the dire wyrm swung its massive head to look at Rynthia, and she saw unexpected intelligence in its large, amber eyes. A voice came into her mind then, one she recognized. It was Shengis, but… not. Partially him, but also partially something else.

Hello, Rynthia.

The giant tail lashed out again, this time to strike the statue that had been Shengis, or at least his body. The impact shattered the stone into fragments, which scattered across the floor.

Since you gifted me with venom, I thought I should return the favor.

The dire wyrm's head jerked forward and a spray of black liquid jetted from glands in its mouth. Rynthia had no time to evade the blast, and the venom splashed her face. She screamed as the toxic substance began to eat away at her flesh and bones like acid, and she clawed at her face, trying to clear away the venom, but succeeded only in tearing off handfuls of liquefying skin and muscle. She had time for one final thought before the venom reached her brain:

Perhaps I should have tried to ally with Shengis after all.

And then she fell to the floor, face gone, skull an empty hollow.

Naerys knew not what to do. A dagger and a flail were not enough to stop the serpent people, let alone a gigantic snake *and* a powerful sorcerer. Conan and Qiang swung their swords like men possessed, dealing devastating strikes that would have killed a human combatant instantly, but the Serpent Lords' wounds healed so swiftly they barely bled. How could two mortal men hope to stand long against such creatures?

Already, some of the Serpent Lords had managed to slash the two warriors with their claws, their talons so sharp they had cut through Conan's chainmail as if it were parchment. Qiang wore no armor, and while the wounds the Serpent Lords visited upon his flesh healed, they did so more slowly than those of the reptile people and he lost a good amount of blood with every strike. How many wounds could he sustain, how much blood could he lose, before his system was overwhelmed and he died?

Anot stood at Naerys' side, rapidly speaking to her nature spirits, attempting to summon wind or call out to the earth, but sweat beaded on her brow, and from the desperate look in her eyes, Naerys knew her entreaties would go unanswered. There was nothing natural about this place, and her spirits were not welcome here. There was nothing she could do, nothing any of them could do, to prevent their deaths. All they could do was delay them a little longer.

A thought came to her then, seemingly out of nowhere. There *was* one thing she could do. She could have faith.

She dropped her dagger and flail and stepped forward. She heard Anot call her name, but she did not respond, just kept walking as if she were in a trance, until she reached Conan and Qiang. One of the Serpent Lords saw her, broke off its attack on the men, and came at her, no doubt sensing she would be easier prey; but when the hybrid monster reached her, Naerys put out her right hand and pressed it to the creature's hard-scaled chest and the Serpent Lord stopped, as if puzzled by its prey's strange behavior.

A deep peace settled on Naerys then, and she smiled.

"May the blessing of Mitra be upon you, my child," she said.

Sudden warmth suffused her hand, intensifying rapidly until her flesh grew hot as furnace flame. It did not hurt, though; it felt good. No, more—it felt *right*.

Fire blossomed to life over every inch of the Serpent Lord's body, and within seconds the creature was engulfed in an inferno. It staggered back, letting out an agonized shriek, but then it inhaled flame, searing its throat and lungs, and its voice died. The human–reptile hybrid threw itself to the floor and rolled frantically back and forth in a desperate attempt to extinguish the flames ravaging its body, but these were no ordinary flames and, once started, they could not be extinguished by any means until their job was done. They burned so fast, so hot, so *deep*, that the Serpent Lord's extraordinary healing ability could not overcome the damage, and within seconds the creature had stopped moving. The flames died away then, leaving the creature a smoking, blackened husk.

Naerys smiled and looked around for another Serpent Lord to bless.

Conan and Qiang managed to hold the attacking Serpent Lords at bay, but that was all they could do. The blasted things healed their wounds as fast as the warriors could deal them, and Conan knew this was a fight he and his friend would inevitably lose. The Cimmerian had no fear of death, for it came to all in its own time, but he would be damned if he allowed that bastard sorcerer to claim victory in this battle! Uzzeran's aura of magic was gone, drained into the Eye of Set to create the Serpent Lords, and while the man was still powerful, this might be Conan's last opportunity to end him.

"I must get to Uzzeran," he said to Qiang as they fought. "If I slay him, perhaps these snake things will die as well, or will at least be weakened."

"Go, then."

"If I am wrong," Conan said, "you will die."

The Khitan flashed him a quick grin. "I certainly hope so!"

In that moment, Conan understood he had been wrong about the reason why Qiang wore no armor—not because he healed so swiftly, but because he hoped to encounter a foe that could do enough damage to his body to allow him finally to be free of Yun's curse.

"Die well, my friend."

Conan swept his broadsword in a wide horizontal arc to push back the Serpent Lords and then dashed past them and ran toward Uzzeran. Behind him, he heard Qiang's katana striking scaled flesh and the warrior laughing with joy.

23

With his good eye, Uzzeran saw the fighting taking place in the repository, but his other eye—the one that had once been part of the first Eye of Set—showed him something very different.

Once again, he saw the starless black void, saw the crimson suns that looked so much like the eyes of a great serpent as large as the universe itself yet at the same time so much smaller than it seemed.

You have done well, sorcerer.

"But a battle rages within the castle and I cannot foresee the outcome. You must intervene and grant me victory!"

There is no need. Victory has already been achieved.

"But the Serpent Lords… I made a mistake. They are not the superior beings you wanted. They are nothing more than ravening beasts!"

Yes, but your efforts were only one possible path to my goal. There are others. And there may yet be some benefit to be salvaged from your failure.

The sorcerer was stunned by his god's revelation. "But Dread

Mistress, I spent my life trying to create the perfect hybrid race for you!"

A waste of mortal lifespan, but it was amusing watching you fail again and again.

The sorcerer was gripped by a despair greater than any he'd ever known in his mockery of an existence. He had been nothing but a tool for Set's use, and not even a cherished one, prized and well maintained. He was disposable, and when he was gone, Set would not give him a second thought.

True, but you have played the role I assigned you well. Take what comfort you can from that, sorcerer. Now go. It is time to end this.

Uzzeran's vision blurred and he once again stood within the repository. For an instant, he saw everything as if time were frozen. The dire wyrm—and how by Set's black coils had *that* thing obtained life?—fought several Serpent Lords, the hybrids' limbs twisted and bent as if they had been severely injured and were having trouble healing properly.

Shengis' body had been turned to stone and shattered by the wyrm, though Uzzeran had no idea how his servant's transformation had taken place.

Rynthia's headless corpse lay not far from Shengis' remains, the floor beneath where her head should have been now partially dissolved, as if by acid.

The remaining Serpent Lords fought the Khitan warrior, who was moving with almost preternatural skill and speed. The warrior and hybrids were blood-coated ruins of flesh from all the injuries they had sustained, and their overtaxed bodies struggled to heal the damage.

Naerys was aiding the Khitan, placing her hands on wounded Serpent Lords and... setting them aflame? He supposed it was only appropriate since the phoenix *was* the symbol of her god.

The Kushite woman knelt next to a Zamorian female who

was in the process of returning to consciousness. Uzzeran could have sworn the woman's skin had been chalk-white before, but now it was the normal deeply tanned hue of her people.

And as for the barbarian...

Time sped up again for the sorcerer and he saw the Cimmerian jump onto the table where Taolin had been shackled, then bound off it toward him, broadsword held high in a two-handed grip, features twisted with rage, eyes burning with a lust for blood—*his* blood.

Uzzeran had no reason to go on living after that last conversation with his god, but old habits died hard and he raised his hands, his fingers shaping an arcane configuration in preparation to hurl a death spell at the savage. But the sorcerer was too late—an instant before the barbarian's blade came down upon his head, he saw Naerys looking at him, an expression of grim satisfaction on her face. And then the sword bit into his skull and he knew no more.

Conan brought his full weight to bear on the strike as he came down on the sorcerer, but the instant his blade struck him, there was a silent explosion of shadow and the Cimmerian was hurled backward as if blasted by a gale-force wind. He fell onto the same table from which he had just launched himself, and it collapsed beneath him. He instantly rolled back onto his feet and fell into a crouch, broadsword still gripped in his right hand, ready to attack again, but where Uzzeran had stood a human-shaped outline now hung in space, and through it Conan could see a night-black void. The Cimmerian instinctively understood that he was looking into another realm, one not of this world, and his hackles rose at the unnatural sight. Far off in the distance, he saw a pair of crimson orbs that resembled snake eyes, and as he watched they drew closer, seeming to expand in size as they came.

"Set is coming!" Naerys shouted.

Conan had slain Uzzeran, but at the instant of his death Set had transformed the man—who had been infused with vast magic power and connected to the Eye—into a gate that would allow the Dark Serpent to enter this world.

Conan looked in Naerys' direction and was surprised to see Valja awake and standing next to the priestess and Anot. The shaman had an arm around her waist to support her, but Valja's skin had returned to its natural color. Was she alive again? Had she finally escaped the curse that had held her in its grip for the last fifteen years? He knew not, but he was not about to allow a great evil like Set to enter their world and slay her along with the rest of them.

When the Cimmerian had fought Uzzeran in Arenjun, he had destroyed the first Eye of Set to break the sorcerer's connection to his source of power. This time, he had opted to attack Uzzeran directly and the man had become an interdimensional doorway for his dark god. But Conan had learned much about dealing with magic in the years since that night in the ruins of the tower. Just as fire needed wood to burn, magic of any kind required power to fuel it. Uzzeran had absorbed a great deal of magic from the artifacts in the repository, but now that he was gone, that magic was too, most likely devoured by Set. The Old Serpent was likely keeping the gateway open on her side, so something else had to be sustaining it from *this* side, and it could only be the second Eye. If Conan destroyed it, the doorway would slam shut, leaving Set stuck on the other side. He hoped.

"Conan!"

It was Valja, shouting a warning to him. He spun around and saw the giant serpent slithering swiftly toward him across the stone floor, yellow eyes flashing with hate, mouth opened wide to display fangs as long and deadly as the sharpest of swords.

The Cimmerian gripped his own blade and prepared to meet this new attack.

Akh finished crushing the so-called Serpent Lords that had attacked him and relaxed his coils, letting the bloody mess that had been their bodies fall to the floor. *Let us see you try to regenerate now*, he thought.

He looked around and saw the remaining hybrids were dead, burned to a crisp by the priestess of Mitra. But what caught his attention was the barbarian standing behind the Eye of Set—or more accurately, the portal he stood in front of. Its outline was roughly that of a human form, and since Uzzeran was nowhere to be found, he assumed he had become the portal. The sorcerer had likely absorbed too much power and been unable to control it. *Fool.*

Akh then noticed the glowing red orbs in the void on the other side of the portal and heard a sly, sinister voice in his head.

Kill the Cimmerian for me and I shall give you a new body. You will become my most favored servant.

It was Set. And all Akh needed to do to gain the god's favor was kill one man?

Done.

Akh lunged forward and started slithering toward the barbarian as fast as he could.

Valja was awake but weak, able to stand only with the aid of Anot and overwhelmed with tidal waves of physical sensation.

When Uzzeran had drained all the artifacts of their magic, he had done the same to the shard embedded in her chest. She had lost consciousness when it had happened but had since returned to awareness, and a quick touch of her hand to her chest told her that the shard was gone, replaced by smooth, unmarked flesh. After not being able to feel her own body for fifteen years, the sudden influx of sensory input was nearly maddening. But there was a battle taking place and she forced herself to ignore her body and focus.

A few developments had taken place while she had been unconscious.

Uzzeran had succeeded in creating Serpent Lords, but they all appeared to be dead now, the majority of them incinerated, their smoking husks lying on the floor. The other hybrids were being crushed in the coils of what appeared to be the dire wyrm from the library, somehow alive and come down to the repository. Naerys knelt next to Qiang, who lay upon the floor, dead. The warrior's robe had been reduced to tattered strips of red cloth and his body had been so ravaged by claws that his chest and abdomen were nothing but a single red mass of torn meat and viscera. He lay in a slowly widening pool of blood, his katana on the floor next to him, as if he had finally been able to lay it down for good. The warrior's eyes were closed, but she was at a loss to explain why he had died with a smile on his face.

She realized then that one of the charred bodies was smaller than the others, and she instantly knew why: Taolin had become a Serpent Lord too, and now he was dead. Grief crashed into her with almost physical force, and for the first time in fifteen years tears ran down her face.

Uzzeran was gone, and in his place was some kind of interdimensional portal through which she saw two crimson objects hanging in a dark, empty void. These were the true eyes of Set, and she realized with horror that they were rapidly approaching the portal. She saw that the dire wyrm had finished crushing the last of the Serpent Lords, the giant snake reducing them to a slurry of bloody paste and splintered bone, and it now whipped its head back and forth as if searching for something to attack next. When it saw Conan standing in front of the portal, watching Set's swift approach, it lunged forward and slid across the stone floor toward the Cimmerian.

She shouted his name to warn him and he spun around to face the dire wyrm's attack.

She felt a gentle tapping on her leg and was startled to feel the sensation, but when she looked down, she was even more surprised. The wolf-sized white spider that had entered the castle with them—which they had all lost track of in the confusion of battle—crouched on the floor near her feet. It had brought her something, an object it had fetched from her room and carried down to the repository on its back.

It was the statuette of Ishtar in her warrior aspect.

No longer feeling quite so weak, Valja stepped away from Anot, reached down, and took the statue from the spider's back.

The barbarian saw the giant snake coming at him, but he also saw Valja waving to get his attention. In her other hand she held, of all things, the statuette of Ishtar that the two of them had stolen from the goddess' temple so long ago. One of Zath's smaller children, the wolf-sized white spider, crouched at her feet, and Conan thought he knew how the statuette had reached the repository.

"Conan! The mouth!" Valja cried and threw the statuette toward him, but even at her full strength she could not have made that distance. But then Anot puffed her cheeks and blew out a gust of air, which became a blast of wind that gave the statuette the extra push it needed, and it smacked into Conan's waiting hand. He clasped his fingers around it tightly as if it were another weapon.

He glared at the oncoming serpent as it crashed through the ring of tables toward him, mouth yawning wide and sharp fangs bared, and he knew he would have only one chance to get the statuette of Ishtar into the creature. While he was confident of his aim, he needed to make certain the serpent could not simply spit out the statuette, so as the dire wyrm lunged for him, he sidestepped and slashed the side of the creature's neck with his broadsword. It was not meant to be a fatal blow, but the strike opened a gash two feet wide and a gout of dark blood gushed out. The serpent tried to pull its head away from the barbarian to avoid a second strike, but as tempting as it was for Conan to continue hacking at the great beast until it was dead, he trusted Valja's words. If she said the statuette needed to go inside the thing, then that was where he would put it.

He leaped onto the dire wyrm's neck, gripped it with his legs, and thrust his blade into the scaly flesh behind its head, not to injure the creature—although he was gratified to see blood rise from this second wound—but to give him something to hold on to. The serpent writhed and thrashed, attempting to dislodge the Cimmerian, but Conan clutched the broadsword's handle with a death grip, held on to the beast with his legs, and rode the monster as if it were a bucking stallion. He leaned to the left as far as he could, and with a swift, violent thrust, plunged the statuette deep into the bleeding wound on the side of the dire wyrm's neck, then pulled his blood-slick hand free. The creature whipped its head back and forth, clearly in pain, and almost managed to throw Conan off, but the barbarian covered his right hand with his left to strengthen his grip on the sword and he managed to remain seated on the beast's neck.

The dire wyrm then tried another tactic. It reared its head

up and flung itself backward, hoping to crush Conan beneath its weight. But the Cimmerian had anticipated this and pulled his sword free, kicked off, and launched himself into the air. The dire wyrm's head slammed onto the stone floor as Conan executed a backflip and landed in a crouch, agile as a jungle cat, still holding on to his sword. He watched the giant serpent turn and smack the left side of its head on the floor several times in a futile attempt to dislodge the statuette. Conan smiled grimly.

Too bad you do not have hands, he thought.

He waited for the statuette to do whatever it was supposed to do, but nothing happened. Something else still needed to be done, but what?

"The portal!" Naerys shouted.

Conan turned toward the wound in space, which had increased a great deal in size, and saw that the dark shape of Set had nearly reached the opening. They had only seconds before the dark god emerged into their world, when all would be lost.

Then Conan had an idea. He ran to the portal, turned his back to it, planted his feet wide, and held his broadsword in front of him in a two-handed grip.

"What's wrong, you yellow-eyed bastard?" he bellowed at the dire wyrm. "That little cut I gave you stinging a bit? I would have thought you could handle far worse than that! You must be even weaker than I thought!"

The monster's head jerked up and it fixed its reptilian eyes on him. It might have been a gigantic snake, but at that moment the hatred that burned in its amber gaze was all too human. It slithered toward Conan at blinding speed, but the barbarian held his ground and waited for the creature to get closer… closer… At the last instant before the dire wyrm reached him, Conan threw himself to the side and the massive snake, unable to stop in time, passed into the portal.

Conan rushed to the Eye of Set, raised his sword above the

ebon orb, and kept an eye on the giant snake's tail. When the tip of it had disappeared into the void on the other side, Conan brought his sword down on the second Eye, just as he had on the first back in Arenjun.

Just before his steel struck the orb's glossy surface, Conan saw a bright flash of light far off in the void, and while it was hard to judge distance there from within the mortal realm, it looked as if the explosion had occurred directly between Set's glowing red eyes. It seemed Ishtar had gifted the Great Dark One a nasty surprise. Conan hoped the scaly bastard enjoyed it.

Then his sword struck the second Eye of Set and he was forced to raise his left arm to shield his face as the orb burst into a thousand fragments. The portal to Set's dimension vanished.

As it often did after a battle had been won, weariness hit Conan and he felt as if he could sleep for a week, maybe two. Bleeding and battered, his chainmail vest in shreds, but still alive, he trudged over to the others, his sword resting on his shoulder. He wasn't about to sheathe the damned thing until he had been able to clean it properly.

Conan walked to Qiang, knelt next to the man's body, and gently placed a hand on his shoulder. At last the warrior had found an evil greater than Guangzhi, and Yun had finally allowed the warrior to rest. Conan hoped that the spirit of Qiang's love had come at the end to escort him to whatever came next. Based on the man's smile, he thought that was exactly what had happened.

"You fought with honor and bravery, my friend, but your long battle is finally over," he told the warrior. "Fare you well, and tell your love that Conan sends his regards."

He stood and looked around. There was no sign of the white

spider that had brought the statuette to Valja. He assumed it had scurried off after its work was done.

Valja knelt next to the blackened husk that had been Taolin, tears streaming down her face to land on the boy's charred chest. Conan was glad she could cry again, but he wished there was a different reason for her tears. Naerys and Anot stood close by, an arm around each other's waist, heads bowed, mourning their friend's loss. It was true that death came for everyone, Conan thought, but for some it came far too soon.

But then he saw one of the boy's fingers twitch. He put it down to his imagination, but then he saw it again.

"What in Mitra's name?" Naerys exclaimed.

And then Taolin sat up.

Conan swung his broadsword off his shoulder. "Get back!" he shouted. "The boy is a Serpent Lord now, and—"

But the Cimmerian grew silent when Taolin shook his head vigorously and ashes fell away from his face—his *human* face.

The boy looked around, confused, but when he saw Valja, he relaxed, relieved to see a friend.

"What happened?" he said, then frowned. "I don't hurt." He grinned. "Not anywhere!"

Valja laughed and hugged him, dislodging more ashes from his human body.

Naerys looked at Conan. "A parting gift from the gods?" she ventured.

"Why not?" Conan replied, knowing that Crom had not lifted a single damn finger to help him. Then he smiled.

If only all the gods could keep to themselves like Crom.

Conan remained at Ravenhold for two more weeks.

They built a cairn for Qiang on a plateau near the castle. The view from there was a good one and Conan was sure their friend would have approved of their chosen resting place for him.

There was less cleaning up to do in the castle than Conan had expected. Zath's spiders and the M'lima removed their own dead from the castle—a task which took but a single day—which left only the bodies of the dead menagerie creatures for the humans to attend to. Anot summoned back some of the creatures she had freed to help, but it was still a big job. And there were two hundred or more revenants, so dealing with those bodies took some time as well. Conan thought they should just throw the revenants' bodies out a window and let them tumble down the mountain for the vultures to feast on, but Valja would not hear of it. Most of them had been her colleagues at Ravenhold, after all, the only true family she had ever known.

In the end, Conan had relented. Besides, he thought that even the vultures would avoid the revenants' diseased corpses.

Anot informed the others that the M'lima Krolot had survived the battle, though he had suffered an injury to his leg that would likely leave him at least partially lame for the remainder of his life. Krolot had also told the shaman that his mother, Gneb, had died, though he assured Anot that she would be buried with honor when he took her body home, and that her family line would sing songs of her bravery for as long as the M'lima endured.

Conan asked Anot why the M'lima had helped them at such a high cost to their people.

"They live in harmony with nature," she answered. "They understand that all things in this world are connected. Set threatened us all, and that included them."

"And Zath?"

"The spider god had his own reasons for aiding us," the shaman said. "But make no mistake, he is no friend to humanity, and the next time you encounter a giant spider, you should slay it on sight."

"Sharp steel and the will to use it solve most problems," Conan said, "even those caused by gods."

Naerys' powers had not manifested again since the battle in the repository.

"Perhaps I somehow tapped into a residue of the magic energy that had been released in the chamber," the priestess said. "Or perhaps all I did was serve as a channel for Mitra's power, and he will work through me again if there is a need in the future. Time will tell—or it will not." She smiled. "But I don't need answers. I need only to have faith."

Conan apologized to Valja for how he had reacted to her transformation when they had been younger, and she apologized for leaving him the way she had.

"We were little more than children," she said, as if that excused their behavior—and perhaps it did. Then she gave Conan a sly smile. "But we are not children anymore, are we? And I am eager to learn if my body is back to normal. *All* the way back."

Conan returned her smile. "I can help you with that."

It was a bit strange at first, given Valja's apparent age, but she reminded Conan that she was still a year older than him, chronologically, and he soon adjusted.

One day, when they were lying in bed, he asked her, "Do you think Ishtar guided you to choose that particular statuette that night in her temple?"

"Perhaps. Or perhaps she decided to make use of it after we stole it. We imagine the gods as being all knowing and all seeing, but I think they are just like us—making up their lives as they go along."

Taolin's curse had been lifted completely when Uzzeran had drained the magic from his body, and the boy enjoyed doing everything he had been unable to while in the grip of constant pain. He spent much time in the gaming hall, and he ate as if there was a bottomless pit where his stomach should have been. Conan learned that the boy knew nothing about fighting, and the Cimmerian spent some time tutoring him in the basics of self-defense and swordplay. Valja, Naerys, and Anot doted on the boy, and he enjoyed the attention of his three "aunts." Taolin had been through much in his young life, but Conan thought he would do well from here on out.

The women decided they would remain in Ravenhold and continue its mission. There were still people in isolation and confinement to tend to, if not as many as before, thanks to Uzzeran. And while all the artifacts in the repository had been drained of their magic, and no more creatures were kept locked away in the menagerie, they still needed to safeguard the contents of the library.

"You should burn every book and scroll in the place," Conan told Valja one day. "The world would be better off without all the misery that knowledge could bring."

They argued about the issue for a time, but in the end they realized they would never see eye to eye on the matter and agreed to let it drop.

Eventually, the day came for Conan to leave.

"I've drunk most of the wine and ale in the storeroom," he told them. "Besides, I have business in Charhelm."

They were sad to see him go, but they understood. Wanderlust was as much a part of him as his love of battle, and to stay in one place too long would mean the death of his spirit.

They assembled outside the castle's main gate, for this time Conan would leave by the most direct route down the mountain.

They had long ago recovered the horses they'd left in the supply tunnel, and Conan's sturdy lakan was saddled and ready to go. The Cimmerian had enough food and water to get him to Charhelm, he had a new tunic, he had repaired his chainmail vest, he had a new cape—purple instead of scarlet, but he liked the color well enough—and, most importantly, he had a newly sharpened and polished sword sheathed at his side.

As he climbed into the saddle, Valja said, "Do not be surprised if we call on you for help again someday."

"I hope you never have need."

Then, with a wave, he turned his mount away from his friends and began the next leg of the long journey that was his life.

24

Urak was giving serious consideration to leaving Charhelm and returning to Hyrkania. The Sülale were still angry with him over what had happened at the Worthless Dog. Three of their finest mercenaries had been slain by the Cimmerian jackal they had been supposed to kill, and while Urak had tried to explain that all he had done was what he had always done—pass along the message—the Sülale cared not. He had been given a task, and that task had not been carried out. More, it had cost the Sülale three lives. Yes, the mercenaries had been the ones charged with killing the barbarian, but they were dead, and Urak was alive, and so the blame fell upon him.

Urak had been part of the Sülale ever since marrying into it decades ago, but he would never understand their obsession with vendettas. Would they send an assassin to kill him for what they perceived as his failure? Perhaps. When he had been the only one who trained the family's messenger pigeons, he had been too valuable to lose, but he had trained many apprentices over the years, and they had trained many more, and so on, and he was no longer vital to the Sülale's operation.

To be on the safe side, he had been working on reducing his

stock for the last several days, selling his songbirds at a discount, though not too large—he was no idiot. Yes, he could always simply release his birds if he needed to leave town right away, but the idea of losing the money the birds would bring him was galling—he was a businessman, after all—so he stood in front of his tent, songbirds tethered to their display perches, and called out to every passerby.

"Songbirds! Songbirds for sale! Give yourself or a loved one the gift of music! Your soul will take flight when you hear these beautiful creatures sing!"

"So the Worthless Dog sells the best wine in town, eh?"

The sound of that deep rumble of a voice—one he recognized—sent a chill rippling down Urak's spine. He fixed a smile firmly on his face before turning to face its owner.

"A fine day to you, sir! Can I interest you in a songbird? It will make a wonderful gift for a lovely lady—or gentleman, if you prefer. It will be as if you are always there to serenade them! They will never stop thinking about you!" Urak let his mouth run without paying attention to the words that tumbled out. He was desperately trying to think of an excuse he could use to get away from the Cimmerian. Once he had achieved that, he would leave Charhelm immediately, and to hell with his birds.

"I have not come to buy a gift," the Cimmerian said. "I have come to give one."

This surprised Urak. "Oh?"

"Yes." The barbarian's smile was cold as ice. "I've come to help your soul take flight."

And the Cimmerian slowly began to draw his sword.

25

Akh lay on a warm rock at the base of Skycrest Mountain, basking drowsily in the early-morning sunshine. His blood was cold and sluggish after the long night, and he needed the heat to help him wake so he could begin searching for food. It had been some time since he had last eaten, and he hoped he might find a lizard this day or, if he was very lucky, a fat, juicy mouse. The mating time was fast approaching, and he needed energy if he was to—

This is wrong.

The last thing he remembered was racing across the repository floor toward the Cimmerian, the bastard stuffing some object into a wound in his neck, then jumping aside. Unable to stop, Akh—in the body of the dire wyrm—continued into the portal and found himself in a vast expanse of nothingness, but was then relieved to see Set's burning crimson eyes. His god would surely rescue him and send him back so he could slay the barbarian—but then whatever was lodged in his neck exploded with a force beyond comprehension and he knew nothing after that until now.

Now, he found himself in the body of an ordinary snake, and a small one at that, but he had no idea how he'd gotten here.

It was my doing. I should have allowed your miserable excuse for a soul to remain in Oblivion after what you did to me. All the power I had gained from Uzzeran and the repository, taken from me in a single blast of magic-negating energy, thanks to that syphilitic cow Ishtar! But you intrigue me, Akh. Perhaps you are the Serpent Lord I have been searching for. So, I have decided to give you a second chance. Do not waste it, for you shall not receive a third.

The voice faded and Akh contemplated Set's words. Slowly, a plan began to form in his mind, and he intended to get started on it right away…

…after he lay here in the warm sunlight a bit longer.

ACKNOWLEDGMENTS

Thanks to Daquan Cadogan for inviting me to play in the Hyborian Age and serving as a guide along the way, and thanks to Chris Butera for helping to make the book the best it could be. Thanks also to Titan and Heroic Signatures for letting me participate in the Scourge of the Serpent comic event.

With deep appreciation, this is for everyone who followed in REH's footsteps with their own take on the Cimmerian, but especially to Roy Thomas, who wrote issue #1 of Marvel Comics' *Conan the Barbarian* in 1970. I read that issue so often when I was a kid that the cover eventually fell off. And, of course, with deep respect and awe, thanks to Robert E. Howard, who, in his all-too-short life, gifted the world with so much. It is an honor to be a small part of his grand legacy.

ABOUT THE AUTHOR

Tim Waggoner's first novel came out in 2001, and since then he's published over sixty novels and eight collections of short stories. He writes original dark fantasy and horror, as well as media tie-ins. He's written tie-in fiction based on *Supernatural*, *Conan the Barbarian*, *Grimm*, *The X-Files*, *Alien*, *Doctor Who*, *A Nightmare on Elm Street*, and *Transformers*, among others, and he's written novelizations for films such as Ti West's X trilogy, *Halloween Kills*, *Terrifier 2* and *3*, and *Resident Evil: The Final Chapter*.

His articles on writing have appeared in *Writer's Digest*, *The Writer*, *The Writer's Chronicle*. He's the author of the acclaimed horror-writing guide *Writing in the Dark*, which won the Bram Stoker Award® in 2021. The follow-up, *Writing in the Dark: The Workbook*, also won a Stoker in the same category in 2023. He won another Stoker in 2021 in the category of Short Nonfiction for his article "Speaking of Horror," and in 2017 he received the Stoker for Long Fiction for his novella *The Winter Box*. In addition, he's won the Scribe Award, given by the International Association of Media Tie-in Writers, and he's been a two-time finalist for the Shirley Jackson Awards and a one-time finalist for the Splatterpunk Awards. He's served as a mentor for HWA for many years, and in 2015, he was given the organization's Mentor of the Year Award. He's also served on HWA's Lifetime Achievement Award committee several times. His fiction has received numerous Honorable Mentions in volumes of *Best Horror of the Year*, and he's had several stories selected for inclusion in volumes of *Year's Best Hardcore Horror.*

His work has been translated into Russian, Portuguese, Japanese, Spanish, French, Italian, German, Hungarian, and Turkish. He's also a full-time tenured professor who teaches creative writing and composition at Sinclair College in Dayton, Ohio. His papers are collected by the University of Pittsburgh's Horror Studies Program.

CONAN: CITY OF THE DEAD

John C. Hocking

Two epics in one book!

The long-awaited follow-up to Conan and the Emerald Lotus brings John C. Hocking back to the sagas of the Cimmerian.

In *Conan and the Emerald Lotus*, the seeds of a deadly, addictive plant grant sorcerers immense power, but turn its users into inhuman killers.

In the exclusive, long-awaited sequel *Conan and the Living Plague*, a Shemite wizard seeks to create a serum to use as a lethal weapon. Instead he unleashes a hideous monster on the city of Dulcine. Hired to loot the city of its treasures, Conan and his fellows in the mercenary troop find themselves trapped in the depths of the city's keep. To escape, they must defeat the creature, its plague-wracked undead followers, then face Lovecraftian horrors beyond mortal comprehension.

CONAN: CULT OF THE OBSIDIAN MOON

James Lovegrove

A NEW CHAPTER OF THE TITAN COMICS & HEROIC SIGNATURES MASSIVE NARRATIVE EVENT: THE BATTLE OF THE BLACK STONE.

Still mourning Bêlit, Conan attempts to drink away his sorrows. In his tavern-hopping journey he meets and befriends married couple Hunwulf and Gudrun and their son, Bjørn. A decade ago, Hunwulf eloped with Gudrun after killing her betrothed, they live on the run from her tribe, who are desperate for revenge.

Bjørn has the makings of a shaman, while Hunwulf is prone to having strange fits which bring him visions of past and future lives. When a descendant warns Hunwulf of imminent danger, he and his wife ride out to ambush the tribe, leaving Bjørn with Conan, who vows to protect the boy with his life.

Unfortunately, Conan is betrayed by a former accomplice, and Bjørn is kidnapped by the tribe. Conan and Bjørn's vengeful parents search for the lad. They catch up to the tribe, only to find Bjørn has been taken by murderous bat-winged figures, who fought with talon and sword. The boy, and other "gifted" children have been taken to the Rotlands, a place plagued by a contaminating supernatural force that warps all who go there. To save Bjørn, the trio must go to the heart of the Rotlands, where strange, horrifying fates await at every turn.

CONAN: SONGS OF THE SLAIN

Tim Lebbon

KING CONAN

When Conan of Cimmeria was a prisoner of war on the verge of death, he made a promise to a fellow prisoner, Baht Tann. Conan would grant a favor, wherever and whenever Tann called it in, in return for Tann's meagre water ration. The men escaped, parted ways, and the rest is history. After a life filled with violence and tumult, Conan met his destiny and became King of Aquilonia.

Married with a child and presiding over a period of peace and stability, the legendary barbarian's sword has been sheathed for too long. When Baht Tann arrives in Aquilonia, he is wounded, his wife has been murdered, and his two children kidnapped. He asks Conan to save his children and avenge his wife. It will be a perilous journey, chasing men with no honor. Conan leaves without hesitation.

Disguised as a scruffy wanderer and armed with a broadsword, Conan ventures into hostile lands in pursuit of Tann's assailants. He is soon beset by assassins and learns there is a price on his head. Unknown to Conan, for reasons of honor, revenge and glory, powerful warriors want him dead. Violence and vengeance ensue as Conan takes on his mysterious foes and attempts to fulfil his promise.

For more fantastic fiction, author events,
exclusive excerpts, competitions, limited editions and more

VISIT OUR WEBSITE
titanbooks.com

LIKE US ON FACEBOOK
facebook.com/titanbooks

FOLLOW US ON TWITTER AND INSTAGRAM
@TitanBooks

EMAIL US
readerfeedback@titanemail.com

FOR EVERYTHING CONAN RELATED
CONAN.COM